∽ IN THE ∽
TUDOR C...

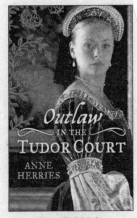

April 2014

May 2014

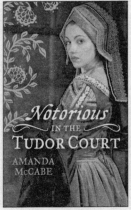

June 2014

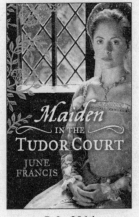

July 2014

Maiden
IN THE
TUDOR COURT

JUNE
FRANCIS

Published in Great Britain 2014
by Mills & Boon, an imprint of Harlequin (UK) Limited,
Eton House, 18-24 Paradise Road, Richmond, Surrey, TW9 1SR

MAIDEN IN THE TUDOR COURT © 2014 Harlequin Books S.A.

His Runaway Maiden © 2009 June Francis
Pirate's Daughter, Rebel Wife © 2010 June Francis

ISBN: 978 0 263 24629 2

052-0714

Harlequin (UK) Limited's policy is to use papers that are natural, renewable and recyclable products and made from wood grown in sustainable forests. The logging and manufacturing processes conform to the legal environmental regulations of the country of origin.

Printed and bound by
CPI Group (UK) Ltd, Croydon, CR0 4YY

June Francis's interest in old wives' tales and folk customs led her into a writing career. History has always fascinated her and her first five novels were set in medieval times. She has also written sagas based in Liverpool and Chester. Married with three grown-up sons, she lives on Merseyside. On a clear day she can see the sea and the distant Welsh hills from her house. She enjoys swimming, fell-walking, music, lunching with friends and smoochie dancing with her husband. More information about June can be found at her website: www.junefrancis.co.uk.

His Runaway Maiden

JUNE FRANCIS

Prologue

January 1502

Alex steadied his restless horse with a firm hand but, just like his steed, he was impatient to be on his way.

'You understand what I want you to do?' growled the Earl of Douglas.

'Aye,' said Alex, meeting the Scotsman's gaze. 'You want me to act as your spy.'

'I'm led to believe that you have a particular talent for gathering information and you will be well rewarded for your troubles. I had a particular fondness for your mother and propose to give you the house and land that she loved in recognition of you as my son.'

Alex thanked him in a dry voice, thinking that a house on the east coast of Scotland, close to the border with England, could prove useful, but such 'recognition' from his natural father was a little late in arriving. But the journey had not been a waste of time—the earl had provided him with information about the McDonalds that had shed a light on a matter that had vexed him during his investigations in London six months ago.

'You have memorised the password?' asked the earl.

'Aye. I'm not a fool.'

'Nay, you just showed a bad lack of judgement in the woman you chose to lavish your attentions on,' growled the earl. 'You're not the first man to do so, and neither will you be the last.'

Alex's jaw clenched and he wished his beloved grandmother had not been so frank in her missive to the earl about Ingrid. His romantic attachments were certainly none of his father's business and, looking at the man before him, he wondered what it was that had attracted his own mother to him. However, it had been his grandmother's dying wish that he make himself known to his father. Perhaps to make amends for the falsehood she had told him as a small boy, something that he had believed to be true until the day she died.

'Well?' demanded the earl.

'I am to make myself known to the elderly Lady Elizabeth Stanley and she will see to it that I am enlisted in her troupe of performers for the proxy wedding of the Princess Margaret to your King James of Scotland at Richmond Palace. You trust this woman?' There was a touch of irony in Alex's voice.

The earl frowned. 'She is kin by marriage to the wife of one of my allies, and both are related to King Henry's stepfather, the Earl of Derby.'

'Aye, so you have already said, but even those closest to us can prove false,' said Alex.

'According to your grandmother, she was also a highly regarded customer of your grandfather for several years.'

A vague memory stirred in Alex's mind. 'Where will I find her? If she is the person I remember, she was fond of travel.'

'She is spending the twelve days of Christmas at Lathom House in the Palatine of Lancaster.' Alex stiffened, but remained silent as his father continued. 'If the weather worsens or you lose your way and find that she has already left by the time you arrive there, then make all speed to her mansion in London.' The earl gazed at the shadowy, powerfully built figure beneath the dark, leafless branches of the trees. 'If my enemies were to learn of your relationship to me, then your life could be in danger, so take care. We must stop the piracy in the northern seas so the peace pact can go ahead.'

Alex agreed, but his expression remained impassive. He had lived with danger for years, risking his life on several occasions during his travels gathering information for his Swedish grandfather and his country; but it was in London that Alex had come closest to losing his life.

'Hopefully, I'll find that all is as you say,' he murmured.

'Aye. Fare thee well, then, laddie.' The earl clapped him on the shoulder. 'Trust no one. A man can so easily be persuaded to reveal secrets when between the sheets.'

Alex ignored this sally and bid his father '*Adjö*!'

As he set off on the road south, his thoughts were not of his mission, but of the beautiful Ingrid and Harry, whom he had cared for like a younger brother, but whom he suspected had betrayed him for love and money.

His grandmother had told Alex not to pursue revenge. She had called Harry that *crazy English boy*, but did not believe him duplicitous. *You must seek the truth*, she had said with her dying breath. Part of him had wanted to yell at her, *But you deceived me, just as they did, and this day you have taken something precious from me that was lodged in my heart and helped to make me the man I am.* But instead, he had quashed his hurt and anger and gathered her emaciated body in his arms and wept, for she had cared for him since he was a babe and had loved him unconditionally.

Despite her words, the desire for revenge still burned in Alex's heart and he decided to seek out Sir James Appleby, who had a manor in the Palatine of Lancaster, and see if he could help him find the treacherous couple.

Chapter One

They were coming!

With a rising panic, Rosamund Appleby gazed about her, searching for a place to hide. Her eyes alighted on the oak chest, carved with field mice and conies and curling tendrils of woodbine, and she hurried over to it. Bundling her faded brown homespun skirts about her thighs, she climbed inside the chest and hastily closed the lid. The slap, slap, slap of their leather-soled shoes on stone came nearer and nearer. Their voices grew louder. She buried herself amongst the garments in the chest and, scarcely breathing, prayed they would not find her.

'Where in the devil's name has she gone now?' demanded Rosamund's stepmother, Lady Monica Appleby. 'I checked her bedchamber and she was not there.'

'You frightened her, Mama. She fled like a rabbit with a ferret on its heels and has probably left the house.' William giggled. 'Edward said six months ago that she should be locked away. I know you agreed with him, so why did you wait until today?'

'Because her death, so close to her father's, could have roused suspicion. Whilst Sir James lived, I had to pretend to care about her well-being.'

Rosamund's eyes filled with tears when she thought of her father and her fists clenched at the memory of her step-mother's cruel duplicity. She wished she could spring out of the chest and tell her exactly what she thought of her— but that would be foolish.

'Now time has passed since his *very timely* death, I must deal with her,' muttered Lady Monica. 'Especially since *that woman*'s servant called here yesterday. I cannot risk Rosamund voicing her suspicions to her.'

'Who is this woman?' asked William.

'Lady Elizabeth Stanley. I knew her when I was a girl and I hated her even then. She's been staying at Lathom House after spending years going backwards and forwards between England and Europe, but hopefully she should be leaving for London soon. I told her messenger that her goddaughter was sick abed and could see no one. Her taking notice of Rosamund right now is extremely incon-venient. I can see her proving a nuisance.'

Rosamund stuffed a handful of linen into her mouth to stifle a gasp. She had been a child last time she had seen Lady Elizabeth and her memories of that period in her life were hazy. She had believed that her godmother had died of the same disease that had killed Rosamund's mother. If only she could speak to Lady Elizabeth, perhaps she could help her out of the terrible situation she was in.

'You should have sent her a message asking her to call and given her one of your potions,' said William with another of his irritating giggles.

Rosamund heard the sound of a slap and memories of past punishments caused her to shudder.

'That would not have served us, dolt,' snapped Lady Monica, sitting on the lid of the chest, so causing the wood to creak with the force of her weight. 'I'd have the whole of the Stanley family down on my head. Oh, why couldn't you have been born with your brother's wits?'

'That hurt!' wailed William.

'Well, think before you speak. At least I'll be able to mould the wife I have chosen for you into shape.'

'A wife for me!' babbled William. 'What's her name?'

'Bridget,' replied his mother. 'She is sixteen and the niece of a close kinsman of mine. You'll be meeting them soon.'

'You won't leave me alone with her, Mama?' William's voice was sharp with anxiety.

'Of course not,' she said in a soothing voice. 'There are questions her uncle and I need answers to from her. She'll need a close watch kept on her, but first we need to find Rosamund. If only Edward was here instead of in London. He would have been able to deal with this troublesome girl. As it is, he is obsessed with his campaign to be the next Lord Mayor of London and that will need a fortune to fund it. But enough of this talk—we must get on with our search.'

William said, 'Perhaps Rosamund has gone to the woodcutter's hut. You know how friendly she was with Joshua Wood.'

'If she has fled there in the hope of gaining his help, then she will be disappointed. He has gone, never to return. But you could be right about her visiting that hovel. We'll hasten in that direction. If we find her, then...' Lady Monica made a sound that sent a chill through her stepdaughter.

Rosamund waited until their footsteps had died away before pushing up the lid and casting aside the garments in the chest and climbing out. She felt heartsick, knowing that, with Joshua gone, she was utterly friendless. Tears trickled down her cheeks as she remembered two boys at swordplay. One of them was Joshua and the other her brother, Harry, who had drowned round about the same time as their mother's death. His clothes had been found by a river where he used to swim. Sometimes in her sleep, she had dark dreams of her mother crying out to save her and of Harry, warning her to run for her life as he was carried away before he was silenced. She would wake up, filled with fear and drenched in perspiration. Perhaps, once she was away from this place, the dreams would fade.

She dried her eyes on her sleeve and considered her situation. If she were to make her escape in her present guise, she would be too easily recognised. She picked up the white shirt that she had thrown to one side and remembered the time when she had dressed as a boy. Delving into the chest, she found a pair of hose, a russet doublet and a boy's hat with a feather in it. She gnawed on her nether lip. Did she dare? Last time she had donned these garments her stepmother had whipped her until she could scarcely stand. Rosamund's father had been away at the time and Lady Monica had warned her that if she dared to speak of it to her father then she would be punished more severely. She needed the devil beaten out of her for such sinful behaviour.

Rosamund wished she'd had the courage to talk to her father about wanting to have been born a boy, then he might have cared for her as much as he had for Harry. Instead, fear had guaranteed her silence. But what was she thinking of standing here, wasting time? She had to escape. She must change her clothes. There was naught so comfortable as a youth's nether garments for sitting astride a horse and riding hell for leather. Not that she'd had the opportunity to ride out alone since her father's death. There was only one problem about pretending to be a youth now. She gazed down at her breasts and attempted to flatten them with both hands and knew she would need binding.

Fortunately there was no one in sight as she passed, like a shadow, to the turret where her bedchamber was situated. It was the work of moments to find the binding she used for her monthly courses. She removed her clothes and bound her breasts before donning the shirt, padded brown hose and a green woollen doublet. Slipping off her shoes, she shoved her feet into a pair of stout boots before pulling on the feathered hat over the linen cap that confined her dark hair. Removing her winter cloak from a hook on the back of the door, she swung it round her shoulders and fastened its strings. Her heart was beating fast and, in her haste, she almost forgot Harry's short-sword that she had found hidden away in a chest several years ago. Although England was more settled and peaceful than in those early years after Henry VII had defeated Richard III at Bosworth Field, it still did not do to go out unarmed.

She picked up her gloves and hurried downstairs, relieved that she could hear no sounds of activity coming from the kitchen. She left by the door that led into the yard and made her way to the stables. Her lips moved in silent prayer, hoping that the groom and stable boys were busy elsewhere.

To her relief the building was empty, but there was only one horse in the stalls and that was the oldest nag on the manor. Her spirits sank at the sight of Betsy, but she knew that she had no option but to saddle her up. She did so with hands that trembled.

Away from the house she found pleasure in the bite of the wind that whipped colour into her cheeks as she set out across the fields in the direction of Lathom House. Twenty-two years old and penniless, she could only pray that her godmother would help her. Fear and apprehension was a cold knot in her belly. Yet surely when she explained her situation, her godmother would understand her need for such a disguise?

Rosamund was still fretting about whether she would be turned away from Lathom's gates when a hedge loomed up. She groaned and had to back up Betsy. Taking a deep breath, she urged the horse towards the jump. They barely cleared the thicket of hazel. As they landed Rosamund sensed that the nag had caught a hoof on something. The beast landed awkwardly and one of Rosamund's feet came loose from the stirrup. The force of the jolt caused her to slip sideways. For several moments she dangled with her hands brushing the ground and then she managed to free her other foot. She fell into a patch of half-frozen muddy turf.

Pushing herself up, she spat out dirt before wiping her face with the back of her glove. Then she glanced back towards the hedge and saw a man stretched out on the ground. Her heart jerked inside her breast and, with knees that shook, she walked towards him.

His hat lay a few feet away and Rosamund picked it up before hunkering down beside him. She stared into the stranger's handsomely rugged face and with a sinking heart observed a swelling and an abrasion on his jaw where

Betsy's hoof must have caught him a blow. To her relief his golden lashes lifted and a pair of penetrating tawny-brown eyes gazed into hers. She experienced the oddest sensation. Then his arm shot up and seized her by the throat and in one swift movement he rose to his feet, carrying her with him.

'Who are you?' he growled.

The hat fell from her fingers and, terrified, she clawed at that hand that threatened to cut off her breathing. She wanted to say, *Are you mad? I can scarcely breathe, never mind speak.*

As if he had read her thoughts, his fingers slackened a fraction. 'Answer my question!' he demanded.

But Rosamund could not get a word out, for fear still held her in its grip. She felt him fumble beneath her homespun cloak and a strangled gasp escaped her lips. Instinctively she kicked out at him. He swore in an unfamiliar tongue as he disarmed her. Her short-sword was thrust in his belt before he seized her dainty booted foot.

'I would not try that again if I were you,' he warned.

Alex was not in the best of moods. Not only had he failed to meet Lady Elizabeth at Lathom House, but he had also lost himself in the back lanes in his search for Appleby Manor. He had asked for directions from one of the guards, but obviously they had not been clear enough.

'Come, lad, speak!' he ordered, loosening his grip a fraction more.

Rosamund was not about to admit to being a woman to this barbaric stranger, whose voice held an inflection that, despite her fear of him, she found attractive. He was obviously a foreigner and perhaps that was the reason for his aggression. She blurted out the first name that came to mind. 'Joshua Wood!'

Alex flicked back a lock of flaxen hair and brought the youth's filthy face closer to his and rasped, 'I deem you deliberately rode me down, Master Wood.'

'No! You were out of sight behind the hedge so I could not see you,' she croaked, struggling to free her foot. 'If I was as suspicious of folk as you are, then I would want to know if you were hiding there to waylay me.'

'You flatter yourself that I should consider you important enough to wish to pounce on you.' His hand moved disturbingly from her foot to her knee and he hoisted her higher against him.

'That is true,' she stammered. 'I—I am b-but a simple woodcutter.'

Alex scrutinised the frightened face with its uncommon blue-violet eyes and long black lashes and he had the strangest feeling of familiarity. Abruptly he released his captive. 'You lie!'

'You brute,' she gasped, slumping on the ground and rubbing her throat.

'You will come with me,' he said, going over to his horse.

'What!' She sat up straight. 'Why should you believe I would want to go anywhere with you?' she said hoarsely. 'Your intention might be to kill me.'

'Aye, you could be right. Keep that in mind, my fine lad, if you wish to see the end of this day. You deal honestly with me and I will free you when I have finished with you.' Alex took a coil of thin rope from his horse and strode over to her. 'I am looking for Appleby Manor. You will take me there.'

His words filled her with dismay. It would be disastrous

for her to do what he said. Yet if she didn't, perhaps he would slit her throat. A squeak of fear escaped her. What could he want at Appleby Manor? Did he have aught to do with her stepmother's schemes? Surely he could not be the close kinsman she was expecting? He did not speak like a Scotsman. What was she to do? Suddenly she realised that there was only one thing she could do and that was to lead him astray.

'Why do you hesitate? Is it that you are not frightened enough?' growled Alex. He had met some effeminate young men in his time, but there was something different about this one. Perhaps Master Wood felt a need to prove to himself that he was a real man and that was why he had lied about being a woodcutter. To wield an axe, to chop down trees and slice trunks into planks needed strength.

'I would be mad not to be frightened of you,' said Rosamund, trying to control the tremor in her voice. Slowly she rose to her feet. 'But return my weapon to me and I will prove my courage by fighting with you.'

Alex's smile was grim. 'You are a brave but foolish young man to challenge me. Who are you really? I reckon your weapon is too good to belong to a woodcutter. It would fetch a goodly sum if placed on the market. No doubt you stole it. You could be part of a gang of ruffians out to act as a decoy and lead me into a trap.'

'I am no thief,' she said indignantly. 'Nor do I belong to a gang.'

'I have only your word for that,' said Alex calmly, unwinding the cord. 'We will be roped together so you cannot gallop off and warn the others that there's rich pickings on the way.'

Rosamund was aghast and backed away from him, only

to slip in a patch of mud. He dragged her to her feet and, despite her struggles, he managed to tie one end of the cord to her wrist and the other he looped about his hand.

'You are quite mad,' she said in a shaken voice.

'If I am, then I have been driven mad.'

She had spoken those very words to her father once and he had sunk his head in his hands. She had stared in anguish, watching his shoulders shake before he had waved a hand at her in dismissal. She, too, had wept as she had left the room. She could not believe this stranger could have descended to the depths that she had and that caused her to spit out at him.

'You mock me! I do not like having my word doubted. It is you who are the thief. Return that short-sword to me at once. It belonged to my dead brother and it is all I have of him.'

The lad sounded so sincere that Alex almost believed him. But then he reminded himself that he had heard many a word spoken in so-called sincerity. 'I will return it at my convenience,' he said coldly.

Rosamund felt a familiar helplessness creep over her. She told herself that she must not give in to the lowness of spirits that had gripped her so often in the past. She remembered how she had managed to overcome those dark moods by riding out on her beautiful horse. The one that Edward, her elder stepbrother, had removed from the stable after her father's death. She had not been allowed beyond the gardens after that and there had been times when life was so utterly unbearable that she had given vent to her anger by smashing many a jar. Then they had locked her in her bedchamber and she had resorted to the submissive behaviour that had served her well in the past. But she was in no mood to act so at the moment. After all, she was supposed to be a brave youth, not a fearful girl.

'I should have left you lying on the ground and ridden over you,' she seethed. 'Instead, I behaved like a Christian, and what thanks do I receive? You treat me like a cur.' She glowered at him, thinking that she would have her revenge when they reached Lathom. She would call on the guards to take this foreigner prisoner.

'If you wish for better treatment, Master Wood, I suggest you only speak when spoken to,' said Alex.

He tugged on the rope and she went flying into him. He picked her up as if she weighed no more than a bundle of rags and threw her into the saddle. As Rosamund grappled for the reins, Old Betsy let out a deep sigh and seemed to sag in the middle. The next moment Rosamund was almost dragged off her horse as Alex swung up on to his own mount.

'This is intolerable!' Her voice shook. 'What is your reason for wishing to go to Appleby Manor, anyway?'

'That is none of your business, lad,' said Alex, giving her some slack. 'Take me there and I might even reward you.'

She wanted to give him a hot answer, but her sense of desolation was suddenly such that she knew if she spoke she would burst into tears and that would never do. She felt another jerk on the rope.

'You are supposed to be leading the way,' he said.

Rosamund darted him a poisonous look.

'Forgive me if I appear overly cautious, Master Wood, but one has difficulty these days even trusting one's friends,' said Alex. That slight inflection was evident in his voice and once again Rosamund was oddly affected by it. 'Now tell your horse to walk on,' he added.

Rosamund did so. Then she spent several seconds imagining the moment when he would get his comeuppance. Then the reality of her situation struck her and the corners of her mouth drooped. A mournful sigh escaped her.

Alex gave her a sidelong glance and felt a stir of pity at the sight of such abject misery. Then he hardened his heart. Pity could have no place in his armoury. The youth had lied to him. He could be all that he had accused him of being, but Alex was prepared to risk that to discover if Harry and Ingrid were at Appleby Manor.

They rode on in silence between high, bare hedgerows until they reached an open aspect. Suddenly Alex had a growing conviction that he had passed this way before. When he recognised the walls of Lathom ahead, he turned on his companion and pulled on the cord, causing Rosamund to almost tumble from the horse.

'Do you take me for a fool, Master Wood?' roared Alex. 'This is not Appleby Manor, but Lathom House!'

Rosamund managed to grab the pommel and heave herself back into the saddle. 'You could have killed me!' she cried.

'But I didn't,' snapped Alex. 'What jape is this you play? I left this place only a couple of hours ago.'

His words took Rosamund utterly by surprise. 'What were you doing at the Earl of Derby's mansion?'

'That is none of your business.' His eyes flashed golden fire 'Answer my question or I'll cut your throat. Why have you brought me here?'

'I—I have no w-wish to return to A-Appleby Manor,' she stuttered. 'They would kill me.'

Alex gazed into the delicate features and his anger abated. 'Why? What wrong have you done?'

Rosamund felt her ire rising again. 'Why do you believe it is I who am in the wrong when I am fleeing for my life?'

Alex frowned. 'Because, Master Wood, I deem you are no woodcutter, which means you lied to me.'

She felt sick with fear. 'Wh-what evidence do you have to make such an accusation?'

Alex smiled humourlessly. 'Your stature is enough. It takes strength to chop down trees, Master Wood—you look more suited to needlepoint. Tell me, who is it you fear at Appleby Manor?'

Rosamund had no intention of telling him. After all, he could be in the pay of her stepbrother, Edward Fustian, who had dealings in London with foreigners.

'Why should I answer your question when you will not answer mine?' she muttered.

'Because I am the stronger, little bantam.'

'You mean you would bully me like you have already done in order to have your own way,' she said sullenly.

He raised his tawny eyebrows. 'I beg pardon if I have hurt you,' he said in a mocking voice. 'But if you do not wish to take me to Appleby Manor, then answer my questions.'

'Will you let me go if I do?'

'If I judge you are telling me the truth. Who dwells there?'

Rosamund could see no harm in answering him. 'The family is small and consists of Lady Monica Appleby and her son William. She has another son who lives in London.'

This news was not what Alex had hoped to hear. 'What of Sir James?'

'Dead!'

The news came as something of a shock.

Rosamund saw that he paled beneath his tanned skin. 'You knew Sir James?' she asked.

Alex pulled himself together. 'I met him only the once.'

'You seem very shocked by the news, sir.'

'Indeed, I am. I had hoped to gain information from him. When did he die?'

'Six months ago.' Her expression was bleak.

That news was a further shock. 'I met him shortly before he died,' said Alex. 'He made no mention that he had two sons.'

'That is because they are *not* his sons, but belong to his second wife, Lady Monica.' Rosamund watched his expression alter and wondered what this information was that he had wanted from her father, but she did not see how she could be of help to him on that score. 'Did you meet him in London?'

'Aye, and that is where I must go now. I will risk showing you some trust. Are you able to guide me out of this palatine and set me on the road to that city? I will pay you to act as my guide.'

She shook her head. 'No! I can't come with you. I have business at Lathom House.'

Alex scowled. 'So that is why you brought me here. I don't care what your business is, you will guide me out of this backwater or you will be sorry.'

Alarmed, she said, 'I will do what you say if you answer me one question. Did you speak to Lady Elizabeth Stanley whilst you were at Lathom?'

Alex's suspicions were immediately roused. 'Why do you ask, lad? What business do you have with the lady?'

Rosamund knew if she told him the truth, then he would know for certain that she had deceived him. 'It is a private matter.'

'I wager it is,' said Alex silkily. 'Well, I will not keep secret from you that the lady and her entourage left yesterday afternoon for London.'

Rosamund's spirits plummeted. Her hope in coming here was all in vain. What was she to do now?

Watching the dismay cloud Master Wood's face, Alex had the strangest feeling that he was right to be suspicious of this slender youth and determined to discover more about him. 'If you still wish to speak to the lady, then I suggest you accompany me to London.'

Rosamund knew that she should not agree to his suggestion. Yet, he was giving her a second chance to gain the help of her godmother. Would it be a bigger mistake not to agree? On the other hand, was it crazy to even consider going with him? He was a foreigner who had almost choked the life out of her. This should have told her, if aught else didn't, that he was a dangerous man. No, it would be sheer folly to fall in with his plan.

She tilted her chin. 'I do not wish to go with you! In fact, I refuse to do so!' She dug her heels into Betsy's flanks. The horse jerked forward and then collapsed.

Chapter Two

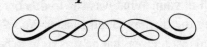

Rosamund's shock was intense. She barely had time to kick her feet free of the stirrups before she felt a tug on her wrist as Alex bent over and lifted her from the saddle. He lowered her to the ground before dismounting and hunkering down beside the horse. He placed his hand on the beast's neck and held it there for several moments before looking up at her.

'I'm sorry, Master Wood, but your horse is dead.'

Rosamund fell on her knees besides the horse and a sob burst from her. She stroked the horse's head before burying her face against its shaggy coat to hide her tears. 'Poor Betsy,' she whispered.

Alex gazed down at the bent head and the exposed slender neck. Had he imagined that sob? What conclusions could he draw from it? He could recall having difficulty holding back tears when his first pony had died. Grieving for a beloved horse was natural. Perhaps he was mistaken to have considered even for a moment that this uncommon youth was a thief.

'We are presented with a problem, Master Wood,' he said. 'I am short of time, but you are without a mount. What do you want to do?'

Rosamund turned a tearstained face towards him. 'You are giving me a choice?'

Alex wondered if he was being overly sympathetic, but told himself that it was important that he discovered what Master Wood's business was with her ladyship. 'I need to go to London. You wish to speak with Lady Elizabeth, who is on her way there. Someone is bound to pass this way and they will find your horse and do what is necessary.'

Rosamund wiped her face with the back of her hand and rose to her feet. 'I will walk to London,' she said in a small voice.

Alex frowned. His suspicions, his common sense and his sympathy for a fellow human being in such a situation were at war with each other. 'You will not catch up with the lady on the road, Master Wood. I doubt I will do so on horseback. Besides, it will take you a long time to walk to London. If your strength does not fail you and you are not attacked by robbers and you manage to reach your destination, it is even possible that you might find the lady not at home. What would you do then?'

'I had not thought so far ahead.' She heaved a deep sigh.

'You must make a decision.'

Rosamund lifted her head and saw a look in his eyes that surprised her. 'Are you suggesting that I share your horse?' she asked.

'I do not have all day, Master Wood,' said Alex, untying the cord at her wrist. 'If I were in your situation, I wouldn't accept my offer. But of course, it would depend on how desperate I was to speak to Lady Elizabeth.'

Rosamund was extremely desperate. If she stayed here, who was to say that her stepmother and her men would not find her as soon as he left? Of course, in London there was the risk of being seen by Edward.

'If you are going to decide to come with me, we must make a move now,' rasped Alex. 'The horse will not be able to travel swiftly carrying the two of us and I need to be in London by the twenty-second of this month.'

'Why are you so keen to help me?' asked Rosamund suspiciously.

He shrugged. 'You are a fellow traveller and did not our Lord say we should help one another?'

'You have not particularly behaved like a Christian so far,' Rosamund dared to say. 'But what choice do I have? I pray that you will prove to be the better of my options.'

'I am truly honoured by your confidence in me,' said Alex drily.

Rosamund flushed and could only hope that he did not guess her secret. So far he appeared not to have penetrated her disguise and God willing he would never do so.

'But any wrong moves, such as trying to remove your weapon from my belt, Master Wood, and you're in trouble. I'm not so naïve as to believe you might not try.'

The thought had not occurred to her. 'I give you my word!'

'The word of a liar!' His gold-brown eyes flashed fire. 'I will be on my guard. I have not forgotten waking up with such a headache that I could not remember where I was or who I was and had a knife wound in my shoulder that almost killed me.'

Rosamund's curiosity was roused. 'Who was the person that did this to you? Perhaps you gave them such a dislike of your boorish behaviour that they feared what you might do next.'

Alex growled, 'Watch your mouth, lad. Ingrid knew I trusted her and that was why she was able to betray me.' He pulled himself up short. What was he thinking of, speaking of a matter that had cut him to the heart to this— this—? He bent over her. His nose twitched as the feather in Master Wood's hat tickled his nostrils and he sneezed, then swore. 'I hope you are not going to make me regret my offer, but you will come to no harm, unless you give me real cause to slit your throat.'

Rosamund went as white as a sheet beneath her dirt. 'I will do exactly as you say,' she said in a trembling voice. 'I like my throat as it is.'

I must be mad, thought Alex. Gaining information from this one could cause me more trouble than it is worth. Yet he felt a monster for frightening this slender youth. Yet his brush with death six months ago had proved to him the dangers of allowing anyone to get too close to him.

Taking a blanket from a saddlebag, he formed it into a kind of cushion. Then he told Master Wood he would give him a leg up. Rosamund placed a foot in his laced hands and gripped his shoulder. She felt his muscles bunch and thought with a man as strong as him on her side, she would not need to fear her stepfamily again. Then she asked herself what was she thinking of even to consider he could be an ally?

As soon as she was up on the horse, Alex climbed into the saddle. 'Now which direction do we take to reach the

London road?' he asked, thinking he would not be in this situation now if he had asked for a guide before leaving Lathom House, instead of just directions.

'Take the left-hand turn,' replied Rosamund.

As he took the turning, she was jerked against him and needed to clutch his cloak if she was not to slide from the horse. Suddenly she felt far removed from her previous existence and excitement stirred inside her. Even so, after a while, she began to feel apprehensive and questioned whether she had made the right decision. They would be on the road for days and that meant spending nights with this man.

'I want information,' said Alex, aware of those small hands on his back and the soft breath on his neck. 'Tell me—how did Sir James die?'

'It happened when he was in London. Lady Monica told me that it was an apoplexy, but I did not believe her. Far—' Rosamund clamped her mouth shut on the word and recalled how often she had been told *to watch her tongue* or *keep silent* and *no one is going to believe what a mad girl has to say.*

'Why do you not believe her?'

'If I say what I think, you might accuse me of being mad,' she said in a toneless voice.

'Why should I believe you mad?' he asked.

She did not answer him immediately, remembering vividly Edward accusing her of being possessed by demons. In her loneliness, she had created an imaginary companion to whom she talked. He had overheard her and taunted her. She had screamed her denial and flew at him. He had knocked her to the ground and then dragged her by her hair to his mother. Lady Monica had locked Rosamund in her bedchamber for three days and nights and fed her solely on dry bread and water. Rosamund had threatened that she would tell her father what they had done to her when he returned home. But her stepmother had said that Sir James would agree with their actions because he knew his daughter was mad, but pretended not to notice her strange behaviour because he was ashamed of her. So again, she had kept her mouth shut, wanting her father to love her and hoping that the next time he went away they would remember her silence and she would suffer less at their hands.

'Answer me!' demanded Alex.

'If I told you that I believed he was murdered, then you might agree with them that it was a figment of my fevered imagination,' she said in a fierce voice.

'Murdered! By "them" I presume you mean those that live at Appleby Manor?'

'Perhaps, but I will say no more and you cannot make me do so. Even if you were to dismount and drag me from this horse and beat me.'

What a strange mixture was this youth, thought Alex. One moment he is frightened of me and prepared to do what I say, but the next he speaks out bravely and it is obvious that he can be stubborn. He seriously considered the possibility that the youth had been beaten before in an attempt to gain information from him or for punishment. Another thought struck him. A father might beat an effeminate son, or—even a daughter who dressed as a youth. But the thought that bothered him most was that his travelling companion suspected Sir James of having been murdered in London. Was it possible? And if so—why?

He thought of Harry and recalled how when he had rescued him that he had been unable to remember whether he had once had siblings. Harry's earliest memory was of the cupboard-like space on the ship, where he had woken with a sore head and a frightening loss of identity.

Alex's thoughts were interrupted by his sudden awareness that Master Wood must have dozed off. His head was going bump, bump, bump against his shoulder. Alex reached behind him and seized the front of the youth's doublet and bellowed at him to rouse himself.

Rosamund started awake and at first could not think where she was and then the motion of the horse and the scent of the man filled her nostrils. She realised that her face was squashed against his shoulder and she found herself breathing in the smell of sandalwood and his maleness with an unfamiliar pleasure. Then she realised he was holding on to the material at her chest. Feeling hot all over, she tugged herself free. What if he had felt her breast despite the binding? Her secret would be out.

'Stay awake, Master Wood,' ordered Alex. 'What good is a sleeping guide to me?'

Rosamund said gruffly, 'It will not happen again.'

'It had better not.'

After that incident Rosamund made certain that she stayed awake. It amazed her that she had managed to fall asleep in such a precarious position and in the company of this foreigner who had threatened her. She forced herself to concentrate on anything but him. She gazed at the frosty landscape and recalled the only time she had travelled to London.

It had been in the company of her father, stepmother and

William. Edward was getting married and Rosamund could not help but pity his future wife, Marion. She remembered how besotted the new Mistress Fustian had been with her husband. Such adoration had not survived. Last time Marion had visited Appleby Manor with their two daughters, Rosamund had noticed the bruising on her neck and wrists. Edward wanted a son and his wife suffered for what he called her lack of success.

It was that kind of behaviour that caused Rosamund to consider spinsterhood preferable to marrying a man such as her stepbrother, although her stepmother had once suggested such a possibility. A long-suppressed memory reared its dragon-like head and she quickly quashed it. There were some things it was better not to dwell upon and fortunately her father had been against such a match.

The temperature had dropped by the time they crossed the border into the Palatine of Chester and the sun had disappeared below the horizon. Soon it would be dark and Rosamund was worried. Surely they should have reached an inn by now, but the road stretched ahead of them with no sign of a building.

Alex's thoughts were running in a similar direction and he twisted in the saddle to speak to his travelling companion. He had difficulty in making out the slender features beneath the brim of the hat. 'Have you any idea where the nearest inn is, Master Wood?'

'It is some time since I passed this way,' answered Rosamund. 'I was certain we should have reached the one I had in mind by now, but I must be mistaken. Still, I am certain if we continue along this road then we will come to another sooner or later.'

'If this is the main London road, then that is likely,' said Alex, exacerbated. 'I would know how far we have to go.'

'I cannot help you with exact distances.' She felt irritated by the tone of his voice. 'We must just travel on.'

'So be it,' he growled. 'Let us hope we don't have to sleep in the open.'

The idea alarmed her, but she remained silent, not wishing to annoy him further by complaining. Visions of mulled wine, hot broth and a warm bed began to float before her eyes and she was tempted to snuggle into his back to keep warm. She resisted and somehow managed to remain upright.

They continued along the road, watching the silhouettes of trees and hedges merge into the darkness and stars prick the sky. To their dismay, when they finally reached the dark outline of a building Alex had spotted some distance away, it was to discover that it was just a burnt-out shell with charred beams criss-crossed against the sky.

Alex dismounted and wandered about the ruins before returning to his horse. 'There is nowhere to take shelter here. We must ride on,' he said brusquely.

He half-expected his companion to complain, but despite being near to tears with disappointment, hunger and weariness, Rosamund remained silent. She pulled her hood over her hat and huddled inside her cloak and prayed that they would soon come to another inn.

The wind rose and she was glad of the bulwark his body provided. Frantically, she tried to remember whether there were any other places where they could take shelter. For a while nothing occurred to her and no inns hovered into view. At least she could be thankful that the moon had risen. By its light she noticed an odd-shaped escarpment ahead. Suddenly she remembered her father mentioning to William that there were old mine workings in the sandstone that formed the roots of this area.

'Master…' She paused remembering that the stranger had still not introduced himself, and then added, 'No Name, I believe there are caves somewhere around here.' Her voice sounded loud in the eerie silence. 'If I remember rightly, copper used to be mined in this area hundreds of years ago.'

Alex, who had been keeping his eyes peeled for even a hovel, hoped his companion was right. His horse would be too exhausted to travel the following day if they persisted on riding through the night. 'Can you remember exactly where these caves are, Master Wood?'

Rosamund looked up at the hill in the moonlight. 'I did not see them myself, but I remember William being told to follow a stream and that there was a shelf of rock a little way up that hill.'

'We'll walk and give the horse a rest,' said Alex, dismounting and holding up a hand. 'Come, let's not delay.'

Rosamund placed her small hand in his and slid down from the horse and almost into his arms. Their bodies collided and she withdrew her hand hastily and stepped away from him. At least a walk would warm her up.

'Stay close,' murmured Alex, considering not for the first time the smallness of that hand. He seized his horse's bridle and suggested Master Wood hold on to his cloak so they would not lose each other. Following the sound of running water, he ended up finding the stream by walking into it. He swore in his own tongue and added in English, 'Step back if you do not want to get your feet wet.'

'Perhaps I should have kept my mouth shut about caves,' muttered Rosamund, certain he would be in a bad mood after getting his boot wet.

'Too late now,' growled Alex, shaking his foot. 'Let us not give up. At least there is some moonlight to help us see the way ahead, although perhaps it is best you stay here with the horse whilst I see what I can discover.'

Rosamund did not want to be left behind, but decided as he seemed to be trusting her with his horse, that she would do as he said.

It was not long before he called down to her. 'I have found a shelf of rock. Let us hope that it is the one you mentioned. Bring my horse and help me search for the caves.'

Rosamund did not need telling twice and was soon standing next to him. They began to search, dislodging small rocks and punctuating the air with the sound of snapping twigs as they looked for an opening. She realised that she was finding a peculiar enjoyment in sharing in the search with him. She wondered what country he came from and whether he had a family waiting for him at home, worrying about him. She recalled his mention of a woman called Ingrid and deduced that, from the way he had spoken about her, that he had once been in love with her, but something had gone wrong, so it was unlikely that he had married her. Perhaps he had married someone else. If so, what was he doing in England, far away from his own country?

* * *

It took some searching, but at last Alex found an opening and called her over. He soon discovered that he had to bend himself almost in half to get inside. The cave was pitch-black, but at least it was out of the wind; as his hands searched the rock face, he realised that the wall was gaining in height and soon he was able to stand upright. When he turned and looked towards the opening, he could see a faint light.

'Shall I come inside?' called Rosamund.

'No, wait there. I will need to come out.' His voice seemed to bounce off the walls, causing an echo.

He felt his way to the outside and stretched. 'We need a fire,' he said.

'You have flint and steel?'

'Aye. And tinder. But we will need more kindling and twigs,' he said.

'There are plenty of them around,' said Rosamund. 'I will gather some up.'

'Good man,' he said, squeezing her shoulder and thinking how slender were the bones. 'This cave will do us for the night.'

She was warmed by his praise—she'd had little of that in her life—and set about gathering twigs. In the meantime he unfastened his saddlebags before removing his saddle and throwing a blanket over his horse. He carried both saddle and saddlebags into the cave and dumped them there before going back outside and helping gather firewood.

When they had collected great armfuls, he told her to take her bundle inside. She obeyed him and was glad to be out of the wind despite the intense velvet blackness inside the cave. She looked towards the faint strip of light and waited for him to follow her. Feeling close to exhaustion, she sank to the ground.

Rosamund did not have long to wait before she heard the sound of flint against steel. She saw sparks and then a flicker of light in the cave close to the entrance. Tiny flames began to curl about the tinder and she could smell burning. Then the flames grew and eventually there came the crackling of wood. Not long after, it was light enough in the cave for her to see the rosy colour of the sandstone.

'You've done it,' she said, relieved.

He darted her a glance. 'Come closer to the fire. I have a pot here and a flagon of ale that I can heat up.'

'I don't suppose you have any nutmeg and honey?' she asked wistfully, pushing back her hood, the better to keep an eye on him. Now she could see more clearly his expression and the attractive planes and angles of his face by the light of the fire.

'Then you suppose wrong,' he said. 'I once worked for a spice merchant and he paid me in cinnamon and nutmeg. You can have no idea how that pleased my grandmother.' He took several items from one of the saddlebags.

So he had a grandmother. 'You say you once worked for a spice merchant—what do you do now to earn a living?' she asked.

'You could say that I am a jack of all trades. I enjoy travelling and turn my hand to any task to support myself,' said Alex smoothly. 'Are you hungry?'

'Extremely so. But I had resigned myself to go hungry and thirsty this night.'

'I have a little salted pork, a couple of apples and a hunk

of wheaten bread and cheese.' He smiled good humouredly. 'A meal fit for a king if one is hungry.'

His smile took her by surprise and she found herself returning his with one of her own and agreeing with him. He seemed less frightening, more approachable than he had done earlier. 'If I had some money, I would buy some food from you,' she said. 'As it is, I left home in some haste, as I told you.'

'I deem you have well earned a meal, so let us not talk of payment. We would still be out in that freezing wind if you had not remembered about this cave.'

Rosamund flushed with pleasure at this second dose of praise. 'We have both contributed to the comfortable place we now find ourselves in,' she said shyly.

The hand holding an apple in mid-air hovered there. 'You consider this comfortable?' He could not conceal his surprise.

'We are warm and dry, are we not?' Her tone was a little on the defensive now. 'You have built the fire so that hopefully most of the smoke will find its way outside.'

Alex said drily, 'You are easily pleased, but I doubt we will be able to keep the fire burning all night.'

'But the cave will hold some heat and we have our cloaks,' said Rosamund, flinging back her own now the heat from the fire was beginning to penetrate the woollen fabric. She wanted it to get to that part of her that still felt chilled.

Alex's growing conviction that this youth was a woman in disguise intensified due to the delightful music in the voice that echoed around the cave. He took the knife strapped to his leg and cut an apple and offered half to his companion.

Rosamund thanked him and bit into the fruit. Her imagination took wing and she thought about Adam and Eve in the Garden of Eden. She grimaced. What nonsense was this? She and this foreigner were not the only man and woman in the world. And probably even if he knew that she was a woman, he would not be tempted to lie with her. Her stepmother and stepbrothers had told her often enough that she was ugly and no man would want her without an enormous dowry—and that was not forthcoming because her father believed she was mad. Tears itched the back of her eyes and she blinked them away.

'What is it?' asked Alex.

She started. 'What do you mean?'

'Is some smoke getting in your eyes?'

She was amazed that he had noticed that tiny movement and realised that there was little that this man missed. 'Aye, it is,' she said gruffly.

'Obviously it is also affecting your throat.' His penetrating gaze met hers through the flames.

Rosamund lowered her eyes and was silent.

Having finished his half of the apple and aware that he had unnerved his companion, Alex set about preparing the spiced ale. After grating nutmeg into the liquid and adding half a stick of cinnamon, he stirred it with his knife. Then he poured the ale into a small iron pot before placing it on the fire. He then divided the bread and meat and gave some to her.

She thanked him and bit into the food as if half-starved. She was not only grateful for his provision, but surprised by his generosity and capacity for caring for his own needs. It was difficult to imagine her stepbrothers doing what he had done. They had never shared what was theirs with her, but had always expected to be waited on hand and foot. Edward, in particular, had found a perverse pleasure in forcing her to her knees and insisting she remove his boots. She had done so with loathing in her heart, dwelling on the thought that one day she would see him grovel at her feet. Thank God, she had managed to escape from being humiliated in such a way again.

No sooner had she finished eating than Alex offered her a leather cup of steaming ale. 'I have but the one cup, so we will have to share,' he said.

'My thanks,' she said, adding awkwardly, 'I did not think that when we met you would willingly share what was yours with me.'

She felt a need to talk to someone of her suspicions, but although this foreigner might now be showing kindness to her, somehow the words stuck in her throat. She drew her cloak tightly about her and rested her back against a wall before closing her eyes.

Alex drained the cup and drew his own cloak about him and stretched out on the ground with his head against his saddle. Who was his companion? Possibly Sir James had bedded a serving wench who worked at the manor. Yet the attractive musical voice was not that of a servant, so it was possible that Sir James had been as fond of her mother as Alex's natural father claimed to have been of his mother and seen to it that he was treated like a son or daughter of the house. Unless—his companion was a legal offspring of Sir James! A daughter who resented her stepmother and had raised the lady's wrath by saying her father had been murdered. When threatened, the slightly crazed Mistress Appleby had fled and headed for Lathom House, only to encounter Alex on the way.

It was now that Alex's imagination stalled. His young

companion had not behaved as if crazed, although if she were seeking help to prove that her father had been murdered, it would have made more sense to speak to the Lord of Lathom House, the Earl of Derby, and not Lady Elizabeth, but that was women for you. Illogical. They were too often ruled by their emotions. He thought of Ingrid and how she had played him and Harry off against each other as the mood took her. No! He would not torture himself with painful memories.

He decided he would leave his musings there for the moment and catch up on some sleep. From beneath drooping eyelids, he watched his companion, aware of every movement as she sought the most comfortable position on the sandy floor of the cave. Eventually, she fell asleep. For one in fear of her life, who did not trust him, he reckoned she showed a foolish faith in her disguise. Alex made up his mind that, for now, he would play her game, but sooner or later he was going to have to inform her about what was needful to impersonate a man.

Rosamund woke the following morning to a cold and crisp sunny day. She ached all over, but had slept surprisingly well, considering the discomfort of sleeping on the ground. She glanced across to where Master No Name, as she was beginning to think of him, sat in the shaft of sunlight that flooded through the low opening. Their eyes met and an awareness of his maleness almost overwhelmed her. She wanted to shrink into a corner away from his muscular strength and that penetrating gaze. It made her feel small and vulnerable and intensely feminine. No doubt if he were to discover the truth about her, he would turn away in disgust and abandon her to her fate. Her safety lay in his never knowing what or who she was, so she must keep that constantly in her mind and strut like a youth.

'You have slept well, Master Wood,' said Alex, casting aside the folds of his cloak and getting to his feet. 'But the sun is up and it is time we were on our way.'

She remembered to deepen her voice when she opened her mouth to ask him a question. 'Do you think there is any chance of us catching up with Lady Elizabeth this day?'

He gave her an odd look and shrugged before lifting his saddle and asking her to carry out his saddlebags. She nodded, but did not immediately follow him, instead relieving herself in a distant corner of the cave. She determined that she would not be lured into telling him anything about herself. She still did not know in what circumstances he had met her father and what information he had wanted from him.

Chapter Three

Rosamund washed her face in the stream outside and then resumed her position on the horse with a determined tilt to her chin.

Alex soon realised that any hope he had of gaining information about Sir James and his stepson in London was firmly quashed. There was little he could do about it without bringing force to bear on his companion and he was reluctant to rekindle the fear in the blue-violet eyes. So he held his peace and prayed that his patience would eventually pay off. His conviction concerning his companion's femininity made it almost impossible for him to give his full attention to the passing landmarks. He had planned on committing them to memory, so that if he needed to travel to the north-west of England again, he would find his way without too much difficulty. The scent of the slender figure and the feel of that small hand against his back triggered his imagination.

He tried not to dwell on there being feminine curves beneath the male garb by forcing himself to concentrate on what part Lady Elizabeth would expect him to play in her troupe of performers. It would not be the first time he had donned the disguise of a player and part of him looked forward to doing so. Hopefully the disguise would serve its purpose in having him accepted by those attending the proxy wedding of Princess Margaret to James of Scotland at Richmond Palace and would not suspect his real aim in being there. He had committed to memory the names of those whom his father regarded as not only his personal enemies, but those of the proposed peace pact between England and Scotland. Peace between the two countries was essential if the piracy in the northern seas was to be brought to an end. Ships from his own country had discovered to their cost that the buccaneering Scots and English did not always differentiate between ally and enemy. But his task lay more than a sennight ahead and, right now, he would be glad when they came to a town. He was hungry and no doubt his travelling companion was, too.

They had travelled twelve leagues or more that day, stopping only once in Congleton to eat and drink and stretch their legs. As dusk fell they came to a village with but one inn. Alex dismounted and went inside, calling to Rosamund that he would see what were the sleeping arrangements.

Hastily, she slid from the horse and followed him inside and was just in time to hear the innkeeper say that there was only one sleeping chamber available. As they were his only guests, they would have it to themselves and sleeping pallets were included in the charge for the night. Alex had no choice but to accept what was on offer. On hearing the sounds of men roistering in the tap room and being told there was no private parlour available, he said they would eat their supper upstairs.

Rosamund assured herself that sharing a chamber with Master No Name was no different from sleeping in the cave, but she soon realised that she was deceiving herself. Conscious of several pairs of eyes upon them, she squirmed with embarrassment at having to be dependent on this man to see that she had a roof over her head and food in her stomach.

The innkeeper lit a lantern from a burning candle and handed it to Alex and gave him directions to the stables. He thanked him and went over to Rosamund. He gazed down into her sullen face, noticing the dark rings of weariness beneath the violet eyes. 'You're weary. Why don't you go upstairs and take your ease? I'll tend to the horse.'

Rosamund shook her head. 'I am no weakling. I will help you.' She did not want to be left alone in the inn. She went out into the freezing night and took hold of the horse's bridle and led it towards a huddle of outbuildings that showed up against the darkening sky.

Alex gazed after her, looking for those signs common to her sex. Was he right in believing her to be Sir James's daughter? He noted the swing of her hips and the way she held her head. He considered the possibility of training her as one of his accomplices if he could prove her trustworthy. She certainly seemed to possess some of the traits needed to be a spy by being prepared to set aside the mores of the day by disguising herself as a member of the opposite sex. Something Ingrid would never do; she much preferred donning a nun's outfit or the silken skirts of a lady. Mistress Appleby was obviously desperate and in need of money—and if she really turned out to be a little crazy after all, perhaps that was necessary when playing such dangerous games as spying. But he was running ahead of himself; she had not yet proved herself trustworthy and he must never forget that he had mistakenly trusted Ingrid to his cost.

Alex set the lantern down on a bench and glanced about the stable. His companion was struggling to unsaddle his horse, but it was obvious she was not accustomed to tending such a large animal, and was finding it difficult. Without a by your leave, he seized her by the elbows and lifted her out of the way. 'Leave this to me, Master Wood. You fetch some water,' he ordered.

Rosamund bit back a retort and looked about her for a bucket. She picked one up and went outside to where she had noticed a water trough. She scooped up as much water as she could, only to stagger beneath its weight when she lifted it up. She entered the stable, carrying the bucket with both hands.

Alex moved swiftly to relieve her of her burden. 'Allow me,' he said in a voice that brooked no argument.

Rosamund had no choice but to hand it over to him, though could not resist saying, 'I know you are the stronger man, but I could have managed it, you know.'

Alex realised his mistake in rushing to her aid and instantly tried to rectify it. 'Why must you be on the defensive, young Master Wood? We have both had a long day and are weary. Get inside and leave me to finish tending my own horse.'

Rosamund did not move, remembering the noise of the men drinking in the tap room. What if one were to come out and pick a fight with her? 'I would rather wait here,' she said.

Alex shrugged. 'Please yourself. I am not your keeper.'

Are you not? she almost said.

Alex decided to test her. 'Do you have a mother?'

'She is dead. Died when I was just a child. What about you?'

Alex decided that it should do no harm telling her a little about himself—it might encourage her to talk more. 'My mother died shortly after I was born.'

'So who looked after you?'

'A wet nurse and my grandparents.' Alex recalled his grandmother telling him that his mother, Maria Nilsson, had gone to Scotland in the train of Princess Margaret of Denmark on the occasion of her marriage to Scotland's then king. She was a widow and the Earl Douglas already married when they met. Apparently the affair had lasted several years. Maria had given birth to him in Scotland and he had been named Alexander Christian. His mother had died a week later.

'What about your father?'

The muscles of Alex's face stiffened, remembering as a boy asking his grandparents about his father. They had told him that Christian Nilsson had been a mighty soldier, killed in a battle with the Danes before Alex was born. He had grown up, believing himself to be the son of a Swedish soldier hero, and was proud of the fact. He had been devastated when he had discovered that he was Earl Douglas's bastard instead of the son of the Swedish hero.

'You don't have to tell me,' said Rosamund softly. She had been watching his expression and hazarded that his thoughts were not happy ones.

'My father had naught to do with my upbringing,' he said tersely. 'I was reared by my grandparents in Sweden.'

'So you are Swedish,' said Rosamund, satisfied that she now knew where he came from. 'I have heard that the sun scarcely rises there in the winter.'

Alex made no comment, only saying, 'You can go inside now. I'll only be a moment here. Perhaps you can carry the saddlebags.'

She was disappointed that he was not prepared to tell her more about his country. She hastened to pick up the saddlebags and managed to sling them over her shoulder in what she deemed a manly fashion.

Alex rolled his eyes and picked up the saddle. 'I don't know about you, but I'm famished, Master Wood.'

She agreed that she was hungry and followed him out and remained hard on his heels as they crossed the darkened stable yard. Alex had a word with the innkeeper before leading the way upstairs.

The sleeping chamber was not as large as she had imagined and the air was exceeding chilly. She soon discovered that the pallet and blanket were damp, but did not comment, unlike Alex. 'This will not do,' he muttered, bundling pallets and blankets beneath his arm and leaving her alone in the darkened bedchamber. She would have followed him, but the thought of facing the raucous crowd downstairs was enough for her to stay put. She perched on his saddle and hoped he would not be too long.

Rosamund had no idea how long she was there before she heard someone coming upstairs. Instantly, she rose to her feet and went to open the door. A buxom woman stood there, carrying a lantern in one hand and a pitcher in the other. 'Here you are, young master.'

'Thank you,' said Rosamund gruffly, taking both from her.

The woman entered the sleeping chamber. 'Your mate is making a right fuss downstairs. Yer'd think he owned the bloody place. A furriner, too. He wants to watch his step.'

'The pallets and blankets were damp,' said Rosamund, placing the lantern and pitcher on the floor. 'He paid good money for hiring this chamber.'

The woman sniggered and brushed against her. 'There's more than one way of keeping warm, young master.' She placed a hand on Rosamund's thigh.

Shocked, Rosamund reacted by pushing her away. 'Get out of here,' she said roughly.

'Oh, we've a haughty one here, have we? Or are yer one of them?' She placed a hand on her hip and swayed about the room.

Rosamund watched her uneasily. 'I don't know what you mean. Will you leave!'

The woman ignored her and went over to the saddlebags on the floor. 'What have we in here?'

Rosamund rushed over to her. 'Leave them alone! They're not your property.'

'What is going on here?' said Alex.

Rosamund felt a rush of relief as she whirled round to see him standing in the doorway. She noticed that he had slung the bedding over his shoulder and carried a tray. 'This woman is being offensive,' she said stiffly.

He thrust the tray at Rosamund, but before he could lay a hand on the woman she scuttled past him and out of the door. Alex slammed it behind her and locked it. He dropped the bedding on the floor and stared at Rosamund. 'What did she do?'

Her cheeks reddened. 'I'd rather not say.' She breathed

in the appetising smell of the broth and placed the tray on the floor. 'Now you're here, she'll not come back.'

Alex had some idea of what the serving wench might have said to her and thought that must have given *Master Wood* a fright. 'I had the innkeeper's wife air the bedding in front of her fire. She was willing to do so for an extra penny.'

'I am not surprised,' said Rosamund. 'One can buy a lot for a penny.'

Alex realised he had made a mistake by revealing he was not short of money. 'I deemed it worth it and we did not have to pay for our shelter last night. As for that wench, she was no one of importance, so you can forget aught that she said.' He took off his hat and his fair hair seemed to glow in the lantern light.

Her breath caught in her throat and for a moment she could only stare at that handsome leonine head. Then she pulled herself together and went over to the pallets and rolled them out several feet from each other on each side of the tray.

Alex picked up the lantern and pitcher and put them close by so they could see what they were eating and removed his gloves. 'The broth smells good,' he said.

She agreed and removed her own gloves, but decided against taking off her hat. She lowered herself on to the pallet and eased off her boots before reaching for one of the bowls. She placed it at her side on the wooden floor.

Alex glanced her way and noticed that the lantern cast light on her weary face with its delicate nose and generously curved lips. He considered how not a word of complaint had escaped her that day and could not help but admire her stamina. He reached for the jug of mulled wine and poured her a drink and decided to test her further.

'Have you ever paid court to a woman, Master Wood?' he asked casually.

Rosamund was in the act of tearing bread from the loaf and almost dropped it. She paused. 'No. I do not have the means to support a wife…and besides, I doubt a woman would find me to her taste.'

'Why? You've a handsome face,' said Alex, pushing the cup across the floor to her.

Rosamund looked at him in astonishment before picking up the cup and taking a thirsty gulp of the warm liquid. 'My stepbrothers told me I was ugly. I confess I am not in the habit of gazing at myself in a looking glass.'

'You are an extremely modest young man if you can resist preening in front of a mirror. Most youths of your age are obsessed by the growth on their faces.' He dipped his spoon into the bowl of barley broth and waited for her reaction.

Rosamund's stomach clenched. She had given no thought to the male need to shave. 'I am not most youths,' she muttered.

'I would agree,' said Alex smoothly. 'How old are you?'

She hesitated and decided it would serve her best to not give her proper age. 'I have seen eighteen summers.'

'Then you are young to know much about women or to have a beard.'

'I know enough about them to know what they want from a man,' she retorted without thinking.

Her reply amused him and he gave one of his rare smiles. 'Your confidence amazes me. I am twenty-eight years old and I reckon I will find women difficult to understand till the day I die.'

Rosamund realised her mistake in giving such a confident answer. She picked up her spoon with unsteady fingers. 'You don't have a wife?'

'No. I enjoy travelling too much to give much thought to marriage. Although, one day I will need to settle down, for I would like to have children. But not yet.'

'Tell me, do you consider women greatly inferior to men and good for nought but keeping house and bearing babies?'

Alex wondered who had said that to her. 'Is it not a woman's role to keep house and give her husband children? Even my grandmother believed that was only right. She was an intelligent woman who organised the family business when both my grandfather and I were away from home. She was wont to say that it was in her blood, for it was what the womenfolk of the Vikings of old had to do when their men were away for months—even years, sometimes. Unfortunately, except for my mother, all her children died in infancy.'

'How sad,' murmured Rosamund, dunking bread in her soup. 'I was told that the Vikings were bloodthirsty warriors who raided our coast.' She shot him a challenging look.

'Ach! The Danes and Norsemen might have been warriors, but according to my grandmother, who has Danish blood, they were also farmers, fishermen and traders. Their womenfolk had to be strong, not knowing if their husbands or sons would ever return. They had to be both mother and father to their children. Our folklore speaks of many a mythical heroine who bested the men.'

'The men must not have liked that,' said Rosamund, encouraged by hearing of such brave women.

'The men transformed some women into monsters when they told their tales round their fires in the great halls. I remember hearing of the Valkyries, or Odin's Maids as they are also named.' His eyes darkened as he remembered Ingrid referring to herself as one such maid—that was when she was not boasting of being a descendent of Lady Ingeborg Knutsdotter.

Rosamund smiled. 'I would hear more of them. I know of Odin. My brother used to tell me tales of the old gods when I was a child. Of Thor and his hammer and how he—' She stopped abruptly and looked confused. 'I had forgotten about that until you reminded me. How strange.'

'The mind has a habit of throwing up the unexpected,' he said softly. 'Do not let it disturb you. It has happened to me often since I received that blow on the head that rendered me unconscious. Do you remember aught else about your brother?'

'I was told that he had drowned.' She hesitated. 'For years I had dreams in which I saw him being carried away, but my stepmother said I was hallucinating and quite mad. There have been times when I wished that I had died like my mother and brother.'

Alex frowned. 'You should never wish death upon yourself. Life is for living, however painful it might be.'

She flushed. 'I know such thoughts are sinful, but my life was difficult after their deaths. I have long believed Lady Monica hated me because of my mother.'

Alex reflected on the selfishness of parents and the vulnerability of children. Had Sir James been aware of Lady Monica's treatment of his daughter? He remembered her mention of stepbrothers.

'What about Lady Monica's sons?' he asked.

Suddenly Rosamund realised that she had been talking

too much and wondered if the question was meant to trick her. She knew so little about this foreigner, not even his name. 'I have said enough,' she murmured, wondering what it was about this man that had so loosened her tongue—or perhaps it was the wine that had done that?

Alex would have liked to have continued the conversation, but decided that tomorrow would be soon enough to resume their conversation. So he ate his supper; when she had finished eating, he removed the tray. He returned to discover that she had fallen asleep curled up in her cloak, and seeing her so vulnerable, his instincts were to protect her. Then he told himself he must not allow his feelings to soften too much towards her. He already knew her to be a liar. Yet he found himself picking up the blanket folded at the foot of her pallet and covering her with it. Then he placed his saddlebags between them, settled himself on his own pallet and almost immediately fell asleep.

Rosamund woke, feeling snug and comfortable until she realised that she was using the Swedish man's saddlebags as a pillow. There was also a weight on her chest and a heaviness on her hip. She started up in fright and attempted to move her sleeping companion's hand without waking him.

Alex was having a nightmare and surfaced from fathoms deep, believing himself under attack. His hand curled on a slender hose-clad thigh and he struggled to free his other one that was being held. He dragged his hand free and the next moment had drawn his dagger and was astride his assailant with the blade against his throat.

Rosamund squealed and dug her fingernails into the back of his hand. 'I beg you don't kill me! I have no weapon!'

Alex paused, blinked and stared down into the panic-stricken face. Now he was aware of the curve of a very feminine hip against his thigh and felt a stirring in his loins. He watched the soft lips part and the tip of her tongue dart nervously along her upper lip and felt an overwhelming urge to plunder her mouth with lips and tongue. A long moment passed and he could feel the pulse in her neck racing against his fingers. The blue-violet eyes appeared larger than usual as they entreated him not to hurt her. He loosened his grip and backed away. Deeply disturbed by the feelings she had roused in him, he moved away from her over to the window.

A stupefied Rosamund could scarcely believe that from being convinced he might kill her, several heart-thudding moments later, she was persuaded that he had been about to kiss her. What madness was that? Surely if she had betrayed herself and he knew her to be a woman, then he would have turned away in disgust? She told herself that it might yet happen.

Warily, she gazed at his back and then her scrutiny lowered to his tapering waist and then even lower. She stared at the length of his long, muscular legs in the tightly fitting hose as he stood there, unmoving for several moments. Then he shook his head, yawned and stretched. Transfixed, she watched the hem of his shirt ride up over his thighs to reveal the swell of his buttocks beneath the hose. Blushing fiercely, she turned her back on him.

When face to face with him once more, it was to see that he had donned doublet and boots. 'We've slept too long,' he said, averting his eyes from her flushed face. 'Get yourself up, Master Wood.'

Rosamund wasted no time in doing so. 'Does the late hour and such haste mean that we do not have time to break our fast?' she asked gruffly.

'We'll eat in the saddle,' he replied. 'I'll speak to the inn-keeper about food and then fetch the horse.'

She nodded, wondering what it would have felt like to be kissed by him. Immediately she felt ashamed of herself for thinking such thoughts. He believed her to be a youth and she was wicked to even consider it. Besides, the only kisses she had experienced were those forced upon her by Edward and he had crushed her teeth against her inner lip so that it bled. Kissing was no fun and she still knew so little about this Swede.

Rosamund locked the door so she could tend to a desperate need in the chamber pot before hurrying downstairs, thinking how much easier attending certain bodily needs were for men. She was on her way to the stables when she saw her travelling companion coming towards her. He was leading his horse and carrying what appeared to be a pillion seat in the other hand. 'I have purchased this from the inn-keeper,' he said. 'I will fix it on to my horse and it will be more comfortable for you. We will stop to eat after we have a good few miles behind us.'

Her brow puckered, and reluctantly she said, 'We will not make much speed sharing the same horse. You'll reach London the swifter without me. Why do you not go on ahead without me?'

Alex was annoyed by her suggestion and thought he knew what had caused it. 'No,' he said tersely. 'You scarcely managed to cope with that woman last night. What if you were set upon by thieves? I reckon we will still arrive in the city in time for the business I have to tend to there. Besides, I deem you could be of use to me when we reach London.'

She was surprised. 'In what way can I be of use to you?'

'I will tell you when I know you better.'

'You know more about me than I do you,' she retorted. 'Do you not think it is time I have a name by which to call you?'

Alex studied her features. 'Why?'

'You address me as Master Wood as is polite, but you are Master No Name and that does not seem right to me.'

He hesitated. 'My name is Master Nilsson and my home is in Gotland, Sweden.'

Rosamund smiled. 'I recognise the name of the place. My father imported furs, amber and silver goods from your northern climes, although he complained about having trouble with Scottish pirates, as well as the Hanseatic League due to the latter's monopoly of trade in the Baltic.'

'Aye. I have experienced trouble with pirates myself,' he said drily.

'You have?' She would like to know more.

He looked thoughtful as he busied himself attaching the pillion seat to his horse. Then he seized her by the waist, causing her to squeal as he lifted her up on to the pillion seat.

She clung to the wooden arms. 'Why could you not have allowed me to climb into the seat myself?' she asked in a breathless voice, aware of a pleasurable tremor that she could only believe was the result of his actions.

'It was quicker my way,' said Alex. 'What of your stepbrother who lives in London?'

'Oh, he never complains of being troubled with pirates,' she said blandly.

'How fortunate.' And how suspicious, thought Alex.

Rosamund thought Master Nilsson's mouth tightened as he dragged himself into the saddle and guessed she was not going to discover any more about pirates from him. Which was vexatious—there were conversations she had overheard that could have interested him.

Chapter Four

Now Rosamund had the security of the pillion seat, she no longer needed to cling to Master Nilsson for safety and would be able to keep her distance from him.

Alex was also thinking that the pillion seat was money well spent. No longer would he be disturbed by thoughts of the wench's soft body brushing his back and those small hands holding on to him so she would not fall. Which meant he could concentrate on considering why her step-brother had no trouble with pirates. This caused him to consider with which countries he traded. It was possible that he had no interest in his stepfather's markets and instead did business with southern Europe and Africa, so his ships did not risk crossing the northern seas.

Having come to that conclusion, Alex let his mind drift to thoughts of the blonde and beautiful Ingrid Wrangel and the message she had brought him from Harry the morning after Sir James had asked about Harry, saying that the young man reminded him of someone he had known in the past. If Alex had not been distracted just then, he would have asked Sir James for more information. As it was, Alex had not seen him or Harry again that evening. Then had come the message and he had hastened to Cheapside, where the Royal Company of Mercers had their headquarters, in response to its summons. Apparently Harry had information concerning a stolen cargo belonging to Alex. There he was attacked in a cowardly fashion so that he did not even catch sight of his attacker. The only proof he had that his erstwhile friend had been there was a silver amulet of Thor's hammer reworked into the shape of a cross that he had bent down to pick up.

Fortunately a member of the Royal Company of Mercers had found the unconscious Alex with the amulet still clenched in his hand. He'd had him carried to the monastic hospital that was part of the building. There the monks had nursed him back to health until he was well enough to return to Sweden, having received a missive informing him that his grandmother was dying.

His thoughts were interrupted by a question from his companion. 'Do you visit London often, Master Nilsson?'

'Whenever it is necessary,' he replied, wondering what was behind her question.

'Have you ever met the Lord Mayor?'

'Why do you ask?'

'Because I am interested in your answer.'

'No, I have not.'

'A pity. I would have liked to have known your opinion on what kind of man makes a good Lord Mayor of London. Perhaps you have heard of Richard Whittington, who was a member of the Royal Company of Mercers and filled the position several times?'

'I can't say that I have.' Despite his denial, Alex was alert to any information to do with the Royal Company of Mercers. 'What is your interest?'

'It is my stepbrother's ambition to be Lord Mayor of London and he is a member of that exalted company. From what I have heard, it takes a plentiful supply of funds to become Lord Mayor,' said Rosamund.

'What are you suggesting?'

'I am not suggesting anything,' she answered in a colourless voice.

Alex guessed that she was doing exactly that, but showing caution. She wanted him to ponder on her words and come to a conclusion that might match her own. 'What is your stepbrother's name?'

'I would rather not say at this moment. If you have met Sir James, then perhaps you can work that out for yourself, too.'

'I suspect, Master Wood, you are playing games with me.'

'I would not dare, Master Nilsson,' she said, sounding horrified that he should consider such a thought. 'But there is always the possibility,' she could not resist adding mischievously.

'Do not push my patience too far, Master Wood,' warned Alex.

'I hear you and obey. I will not plague you any more,' said Rosamund meekly. 'I feel a megrim coming on so I will be silent.'

Alex was not sure if he believed in her megrim, but he hoped that she would keep her word and leave him to his thoughts that now concerned a stepbrother whose stepfather was Sir James Appleby and who was a member of the

Royal Company of Mercers and was in need of lots of money to fund his ambitions. He was not bothered by pirates, unlike his stepfather, and *Master Wood* suspected Sir James had been murdered. Was she saying that the prime suspect for his murder was her stepbrother? It seemed extremely likely. Well, it shouldn't be too difficult for him to discover the identity of Sir James's stepson once he reached London. But did any of this have aught to do with Harry and Sir James's words about a likeness to someone he had known in the past?

As the day wore on, the pain in Rosamund's head increased and her whole body ached. She worried in case Master Nilsson thought she was quite mad, playing games with him instead of giving him straight answers. She did not really believe that he was in the pay of her stepbrother, but how was she to know for certain?

The miles fell behind them until, just before dusk, they stopped at an inn a short distance south of Stafford. By then Rosamund's head was thumping and she had stomach cramps. As she dismounted, her knees buckled and she would have fallen if Alex had not been there to lift her upright. For a moment she rested her weary body against the strong line of his and was glad of his arm about her. Then with a start of fright, she realised she was behaving like a woman and drew away from him.

By means of clinging on to the horse's bridle, she managed to remain on her feet, but her gait was unsteady and she felt sick. Yet she insisted on leading the horse to the stable.

Once again Alex watched her with admiration. They had

spent hours on horseback and there had been no word of complaint from her. He was not surprised she was exhausted. He wasted no time going inside the inn. It was a finer one than that in which they had stayed last night and he was able to obtain a private bedchamber with a proper bed. He asked for a fire to be lit and supper prepared for them. Then, carrying a lantern, he headed for the stables where he found Rosamund resting against a stall with her eyes closed. He took one look at her face, which appeared to have lost all colour and was damp with perspiration, and told her to get to the inn and rest.

'But I have not…' she began.

'Never mind that. Tell the innkeeper to show you up to our bedchamber.' His tone was harsh.

'You're angry with me because you believe I am playing games with you. Perhaps you believe I am mad,' cried Rosamund in dismay.

'Not now,' said Alex sharply.

She made to continue, but he roared, 'Get yourself inside and to bed before you collapse!'

Rosamund shrank away from him and stumbled outside and threw up behind some bushes. She felt a little better after that and, despite being near to tears and aching all over, she managed to reach their bedchamber without falling. She peeled off her outer clothes and, with a sense of doom and horror, discovered blood on her nether male undergarment. She must have miscounted the days to when her next monthly courses were due. What was she going to do now? She had never been in such a dilemma before and, for a moment, was at a loss how to deal with the situation. Then common sense asserted itself and she locked the door.

Hastily she took off her shirt and began to remove the binding that constrained her breasts. Tearing a length of the material, she made it into a pad and placed it inside the nether garment. Then she put on her shirt and hose before ripping up more of the binding and placing them with her cloak and doublet before climbing into bed. She curled up on one side of it and fell into an exhausted sleep.

When Alex arrived outside the bedchamber it was to discover that the door was locked. He knocked at the wooden panel gently, but there came no sound from within. Had he frightened her so much by roaring at her earlier that she was scared he would hurt her? He tapped again and called, 'Master Wood, of your courtesy, open the door?'

But still there was no response and, due to the utter silence, he concluded that his travelling companion had fallen asleep. He went downstairs and told the innkeeper that he had changed his mind and would have supper in the parlour. As for Master Wood, he had fallen asleep and perhaps it was best not to disturb him.

Rosamund woke hours later. The candle had guttered out and the fire was but dead embers. She remembered locking the door and guessed that most likely Master Nilsson had remained downstairs to spend the night in discomfort. A groan escaped her. She had not intended keeping him from his bed. Had he decided that she had deliberately locked him out for losing his temper with her? But why had he not banged on the door to waken her?

Perhaps he had done so and she had not heard him. No doubt he was furious with her. Was it time she parted company with him? What had he thought of her suggestions? What interests did a so-called Swedish jack of all trades have in London after having visited Lathom House and seeking out her father? A man whom he had told her that he had only met once. And what was happening on the twenty-second of the month that he needed to be in London?

The cramps in her stomach had eased a little and she replaced the pad, anguishing over this evidence of her femininity. Despite the soreness beneath and her aching back, she managed to pull on her boots and buttoned up her doublet. She put on her hat and fastened her cloak and, picking up her pitifully few bindings, as well as the soiled one, she let herself out of the bedchamber and crept downstairs.

All was quiet as she drew back the bolts and peered outside. There was a pearly light in the sky towards the east, which meant it would soon be dawn. She went and dug a hole in the soil near the stable with a stick and buried the soiled cloth. Then she washed her hands in the horse trough before returning to the inn. She found her way to the kitchen and went over to the larder and took a hunk of bread and cut slices of ham from the joint there. Then she let herself outside again.

The freezing air seemed determined to take bites out of her face. Nevertheless, she pulled up her hood before hurrying across the yard to the stable.

She was in the act of trying to saddle up Alex's horse when a voice from behind said, 'And where are you going so early in the morning, Master Wood, and in such haste?' Her heart seemed to somersault as she turned to face the man silhouetted in the doorway.

'Have you no answer for me, little thief?' asked Alex coldly.

Rosamund took a deep breath in an attempt to calm herself. 'I am not a thief. I was just trying to have everything ready for when you came out. I thought you would be tired after my accidentally locking you out of the bedchamber. I beg pardon for doing so.' She swallowed nervously. 'I also knew that you would want to make an early start, knowing that my presence on your horse has lengthened the time of your journey.'

Alex was confounded. 'Are you being honest with me?'

'Why should I speak falsely?'

'Because you are scared,' he said bluntly. 'You ask much of me. I want to believe that you did not intend to steal my horse and escape, but give me a further reason why I should do so?'

'I will be honest with you and admit that I have deceived you.'

Alex's heart began to thud. Was she about to tell him that she was a woman? 'What is the manner of your deception?'

Rosamund's lips parted, but the words would not come and she despised herself for being a coward. Moments passed and Alex reached out and drew her towards him. 'What is wrong? Is the truth so terrible that you do not have the courage to reveal it?'

She nodded wordlessly, conscious that her breasts were crushed against his chest. Perhaps she would not need to speak because surely he could not be unaware of them and would guess her secret.

Alex was indeed aware that her breasts appeared to have sprouted overnight and to his astonishment his arousal was instant and he wanted to take her there and then in the straw. He imagined her expression if he should do so and instantly released her. He did not want such a complication in his life. 'I am disappointed that you still cannot be honest with me. I see you consider me no friend?'

She found her voice. 'How can I consider you a friend when I know so little about you?'

'I have given you a name and told you where I come from. You know that I like travelling and am a jack of all trades.'

'That is still not a lot of information when it comes to giving someone your trust,' said Rosamund.

Alex could not prevent a smile. 'You're not so crazed as your stepfamily seemed to want you to believe, Master Appleby.'

Rosamund started and a tiny laugh escaped her. 'How clever of you to guess my secret.'

Alex's smile deepened. Perhaps he should not blame her for wanting to continue to conceal her true identity from him. 'You gave yourself away on several occasions.'

'I would not make a very good conspirator, would I?'

'I disagree. You have deduced that it is not always safe to tell strangers your secrets and to answer a question with a question.'

Rosamund agreed.

'But of course, in providing me with the information that you have, I have come to the conclusion that you believe your stepbrother murdered your father.'

She hesitated. 'Would you say that is a sensible conclusion to draw?'

He nodded. 'But I would add that if you are Sir James's son, then surely you should be in charge of Appleby Manor and his business in London, not your stepfamily.'

Rosamund was silent.

Alex said abruptly, 'We will leave this for now. It is time we were on our way.'

Rosamund lifted her head and stared at him. 'I have some food I have taken from the kitchen as I missed supper—shall we eat it later?'

He nodded. 'Let us put some miles behind us.'

Whilst he was saddling up his horse, she went and fetched the pillion seat. They had travelled a few miles when Rosamund said, 'What was your opinion of my father?'

He glanced over his shoulder at her sombre face. 'As I told you, I met him but the once.'

'Where?'

'Down at the quayside,' answered Alex carefully. 'We were watching ships being unloaded. It was then he spotted the young captain of the *Thor's Hammer*. He said he reminded him of someone he had known in a past life.'

Rosamund said, 'What a strange comment to make. Did he say whom this captain reminded him of?'

'No. And I have not seen either of them since then.'

'Perhaps your young captain is dead.'

Her words gave him a shock. 'That I have not considered.'

'Why? If he is a seafarer, then it is a possibility, is it not?'

Alex could not deny it. 'I sense he is alive,' he said abruptly.

'Why, if you have not seen him? Would you have expected to have seen him during the time that has passed since you last did so?'

'In the circumstances, no.'

'What circumstances are these?'

He gave her an exasperated look. 'It is I who ask the questions.'

'I have already answered several of yours,' she said.

'Then answer me this one,' said Alex. 'Give me the name of your stepbrother in London.'

She sighed. 'I cannot understand your interest if you are but a travelling jack of all trades. I deem, Master Nilsson, that you are not being honest with me.'

'I admit it, but I still want an answer to my question,' he said in a steely voice.

'Can't it wait until we reach London?'

'No! I have much to do when I arrive there,' he said, hanging on to his patience.

'Then if I must, I must. I just pray to our Lady and all the saints that I can trust you, Master Nilsson. His name is Edward Fustian.'

Fustian! Alex had met the man and considered him a smarmy, arrogant, insular fellow. He had a certain attraction for the ladies, which irritated Alex exceedingly. He had heard it from Ingrid that he beat his wife and treated her like dirt beneath his feet. Yet he had not thought to include him in the names on the list of those he suspected might be guilty of passing on information about cargoes and times of departure of ships sailing from the port of London.

'I have met him, but do not know him well,' said Alex. 'I have heard he is not kind to his wife.'

Rosamund nodded and said in a seething voice, 'She had several bruises last time I saw her. She was a cowed little woman and so were her daughters. I felt so sorry for her because I understood what she was going through.'

'Could you not have helped her?'

'I would have liked to, but you have not met my stepmother, Master Nilsson, or grown up with Edward.'

'Tell me about it.'

Rosamund took a deep breath. 'I thought at first that Edward might prove to be another brother to me. He is some five years older and at first he showed me some kindness, but it was not long before he revealed his true colours.' Her voice quivered. 'Overbearing, arrogant and swift to lash out at me with his tongue and fist.' The memory she had buried burst forth and she remembered, when first she had shown signs of early womanhood, how Edward had whispered lewd suggestions in her ear and pulled up her skirts. She took a shuddering breath. 'I wish I'd had the courage to kill him.'

Aware that she was deeply disturbed, Alex said, 'You do not have to continue if you find speaking of it upsetting.'

'No. I deem there is a purpose in your questioning. If somehow you could bring Edward to his knees, then I would do anything to help you.'

'Is that a promise?'

'In as much as I will be able to keep it.'

'Was he never chided?' he rasped.

'He was always careful not to misbehave when my father was there. Fortunately there came a day when he was caught out and despatched to serve his apprenticeship in Father's business. I was never so glad of anything in my life. Although that was not the end of it. My stepmother was furious because she was in favour of a match between us, but she could not persuade Father into her way of thinking. That made her even angrier with me, but I pretended to be a fool and allowed her to treat me like one. I discovered a long time ago that, if I remained quietly in a corner, people would forget I was there and carry on all kinds of conversations with no thought to whom might be listening.'

Alex was impressed by her perception, even as he was aware that she had let two nuggets of information slip. She had touched on a match between herself and Edward and mentioned that she had thought he would be like another brother to her. Had she realised she had just revealed to him that she was a woman? Also, that was twice she had referred to a brother. How long was it since she had lost her brother? How and when had he died? Why should her stepmother wish for a match between her son and the step-daughter she believed crazy? Was it that she had persuaded her husband that he should not leave his property to his daughter and instead make her son his heir? Was it possible that she believed her son's position precarious and that was why she had suggested a match between the two? Obviously she had overplayed her hand. He wished that he could have met the lady so as to draw his own conclusions.

'What else have you learnt by your eavesdropping?' he asked.

She replied promptly, 'That the Hanseatic League's monopoly of trade in the Baltic infuriates Edward.'

That did not surprise Alex, for it angered most merchants who wanted to buy into such markets themselves. He asked her no more questions, deciding that a little silence would give them both time for reflection. He would like to know about her brother and how he had died, but that information could wait. They were still many leagues from London.

When they came to the next inn, Rosamund was too weary to attempt to converse with Master Nilsson. Indeed, she decided she had given him enough information about her stepfamily. Fortunately, he seemed in no mood to talk further; as it happened that night they were not alone in a sleeping chamber, but shared it with other travellers.

The next day she expected him to ask her more questions about Edward or Harry, but to her surprise he enquired instead about her other stepbrother.

The question startled her. 'William! You want to know about William?'

'Why not? Surely you have something to tell me about him?'

Rosamund's hands tightened on the pillion seat as she considered what he would make of her answer. She decided that it should be safe enough to speak honestly of William. 'He is a lack-wit, but one wonders if that is the fault of his mother. She is for ever hitting him across the head and comparing him to his elder brother. Yet he will do anything for her and his brother, which is a big mistake.'

'Why is that?'

'They are bad examples of how a decent man should behave. I feel sorry for the poor girl who is destined to marry him.'

'Who is this maiden?'

'I know only that her name is Bridget and that she is a niece to a close kinsman of my stepmother.'

'Your younger stepbrother takes no interest in your stepbrother's business?'

Rosamund shook her head. 'He does not have the wit.'

'Then who oversees Appleby Manor?'

'My stepmother,' she said bitterly. 'She persuaded my father I was incapable of doing so.'

'That must have infuriated you.'

'Indeed it did, but Father had no faith in my abilities. He believed my stepmother's estimation of my character.'

'Does your anger extend to him?'

Rosamund did not answer.

Alex did not press her. It was obvious that Mistress Appleby had been sorely treated by not only her step-family, but also her father. He recalled Sir James Appleby gazing up at Harry and the words he had spoken. Was the loss of his son reason enough for a father to treat his daughter so thoughtlessly? He set out to entertain her for the rest of the journey.

During the day he talked about the countries he had visited and told her about the ways he had kept body and soul together. He spoke of playing in a troupe of entertainers and made her laugh by telling her jests and describing some of the japes and dances they performed. He found himself enjoying sharing such tales with her. He spoke of Sweden and the beauty of its countryside and the splendour of its cities. Yet he never mentioned his title or wealth or the task his father had set him. He was only prepared to trust Mistress Appleby so far.

As for Rosamund, she was made only more wary by the change in him. Why was he trying to charm her? It was quite a struggle to resist him. Sometimes on wakening there was a moment when they turned over and their faces were but a foot away and they caught the other's eye. Then she thought she saw an expression in his face that melted her insides, but she fought against such feelings.

Chapter Five

By the time they arrived at St Albans, a town where two great battles had been fought between the Houses of Lancaster and York, she was feeling the strain of pretending that she was a man and she knew that she had to get away from Master Nilsson. This despite the promise she had voiced to bring Edward to his knees. For the last time on that journey, she went inside an inn and upstairs to the bedchamber that once again he arranged for them. The room was cold and she thought how often she would have liked to snuggle up to him and share his warmth and feel his strong arms holding her secure, but she told herself that this was confused thinking.

A sigh escaped her. Tomorrow they would arrive in London and she would need to find her godmother's house. The thought lifted her heart. She might be uncertain of its whereabouts, but she could ask for directions; surely if her godmother had sent a servant to enquire about her, then she should be pleased to see her. The trouble was that after being on the road for so many days, wearing the same garments, she was travel-stained and smelly. The worry of it all quite made her lose her appetite and imbibe more wine than usual.

'Ach! Master Appleby, you haven't eaten enough to keep a sparrow alive,' said Alex, staring across the table at the slender face made rosy by wind and wintry sun. 'You have proved your stamina equal to mine in the last few days, so what is it that has ruined your taste for food now we are nearing journey's end?'

'Would you say I have proved myself as good as many a man?' The words were slurred as she swirled the mulled wine in her cup.

Alex's eyes narrowed. 'There is no need for you to prove yourself to me. Although I suppose in the circumstances it is natural for you to do so.'

'What circumstances?' she muttered, staring at him from beneath drooping eyelids as she reached for the wine.

He did not answer her question, but moved the pitcher beyond her reach. 'You will want a clear head when you reach London,' he said.

'London,' she uttered drowsily. 'There all will change between us.' She yawned and closed her eyes and her head nodded.

Alex reached forward and cupped her chin before her face could land in the bowl of soup. He stood up, eased himself around the table and managed to place an arm beneath her knees. He lifted her and carried her over to the bed. There he drew back the bedcovers and laid her down before tucking them in round her. Then he went and sat in a chair and brooded on their situation and what to do when they arrived in London. Would she volunteer the truth at last?

He reached for his cloak and wrapped it round him and prepared himself for a long night.

At some point he must have dozed off, because he was roused by the sound of a woman sobbing. Forcing his eyelids open, he pushed himself out of the chair and went over to the bed.

'What is troubling you?' he asked gently.

She did not respond, but continued to weep. By the dying light of the fire he could see that her eyes were still closed. Suddenly, she ceased crying and, instead, started to speak. He lowered his head in an attempt to catch the words.

'Harry, where are you, Harry? Where are they taking you? Don't leave me alone with her!' Her voice dropped and he had to bring his head even closer to hers. 'Papa, listen to me. It was not my fault! I wanted to save Mama, but she would not let me near her. She would force that vile potion down my throat and Edward stood watching and laughing.' She fell silent a moment and then she spoke again. 'Edward, keep away from me! Do not touch me! It is wrong!' she cried. 'Papa, listen to me. I am telling the truth. I am not mad. Oh, why don't you believe me? Why can't you love me like you did Harry and Mama?' Suddenly she sat up and Alex had to draw away from her. Her hat fell off, along with her cap, and her dark hair tumbled about her shoulders. A small hand shot out and seized hold of Alex. 'You must find Harry!' she cried.

Alex was deeply disturbed by her distress. 'You need not fear. I will find him,' he assured her.

'Good,' she murmured, subsiding.

Only when he thought she had fallen asleep again did

Alex make a move to remove the hand that rested on his thigh. Her fingers tightened about his and she rolled over and rested her head against his leg. He could not resist stroking her hair or brushing her lips with his own. She let out a wine-scented breath against his mouth. He remained where he was for a long time, caressing the side of her face with a gentle hand until he was certain that this time she was truly asleep. Then he managed to free his hand and return to the chair. He wondered if, when she woke, she would remember what had taken place. He needed to discover how her brother had died—only then would he know whether he would be able to keep his word to her. As for Edward Fustian, the world would be a better place without him. He closed his eyes, but it was some time before he fell asleep.

Rosamund woke just as it was getting light and turned over on to her side. Stretching out a hand, she felt for the man she expected to find at her side. Empty! She sat up and the pain in her head thumped in rhythm with the in-creased beat of her heart. She was terribly thirsty and could not remember getting into bed or aught of their con-versation last evening. Where was Master Nilsson? Had he carried her to bed because she was drunk and, disgusted with her behaviour, left her to sleep alone? For this to happen now utterly depressed her spirits.

Her eyes pierced the dimness of the bedchamber and she was able to make out a figure in a chair. Now she became aware of his steady breathing and she slid soundlessly off the bed. She felt dizzy and her throat was tight with misery. This time there really was a need for a parting of the ways.

For him to choose a chair rather than remain in the bed spoke much of how he must feel towards her.

She searched for her outer garments and boots and, by some miracle, found them without waking him. She did not pause to put them on, but cautiously went over to the door and unlocked it. She opened it a fraction, managed to ease herself through the gap and closed the door behind her. She would travel the rest of the way to London on foot; if God forgave her and answered her prayer, then she would find her godmother's house before dark. If she and Master Nilsson were ever to meet again, she prayed that he would not recognise his erstwhile travelling companion in Mistress Rosamund Appleby.

Alex woke suddenly and wondered what it was that had disturbed him. It was morning and his gaze darted to the bed. He saw that the bedclothes had been flung back and the bed was empty. He found the door unlocked and hurried downstairs, hoping to find Mistress Appleby taking the fresh air to clear her head. There was no sign of her and he hurried to the stables. His horse was still there, but she was nowhere to be found. Why had she deserted him now? Had she not been fully asleep when he had kissed her? He could think of no other reason why she had taken fright and cursed himself for giving in to temptation. He saddled up his horse and knew he had to find her before she ended up in trouble.

Rosamund thanked the carter who had been kind enough to give her a lift on the last stage of her journey and limped along Aldersgate Street. She glanced up at the threatening sky and knew she had to find her godmother's house before nightfall. But first she needed a gown to wear. Perhaps she could exchange her cloak for a used gown. Surely there would be a used-clothes dealer somewhere in London? But where exactly? She passed St Paul's Cathedral and Paternoster Row where shops sold rosaries in their hundreds. She paused to gaze inside a workshop and marvelled to see books being produced on a printing press. She felt certain Master Nilsson would have been interested to see the printers at work because it had become obvious to her that he was an educated man. But she must not think of him, she had to hurry.

A short while later she had still not found a used-clothes dealer. She glanced up at the darkening sky and felt the cold sting of a snowflake touch her cheek; then a positive flurry of snowflakes threatened to blind her. She hurried, but soon realised that she was lost. Suddenly she heard a slithering sound and heavy breathing, then came a suppressed cough. 'Is there someone there?' she called. 'Can you help me?'

A figure loomed out of a doorway a few yards ahead. 'Depends on whether yer can make it worth me while,' said the man.

'What do you mean?' she asked with a tremor in her voice.

'What do yer think I mean?' he sneered.

A hand shot out and seized her arm. Her heart gave a frightening lurch and she managed to tear herself from his grasp. She made to run, but he caught hold of her cloak and dragged her back against him. Her hat went flying as he pinned her arms to her sides.

'What is it you want?' she cried.

'Coin to buy bread and a pallet for the night,' he replied.

'I have none. I'm just a poor lad who's come from the country to try to earn a crust.'

'Then I'll have to take yer cloak,' said that voice in her ear. His foul breath caused her to gag. 'And don't try any funny business or I'll choke the life out of yer.'

With shaking hands Rosamund attempted to unfasten the ties at her throat. But he grew impatient and dragged the garment from her, causing the ties to snap, before running off with it. Furious with herself for behaving like a frightened hen, she gave chase. After all, it was possible that he would lead her out of this maze of alleys. Instead, she ended up blundering into a wall. Her hands explored its surface and she discovered that it loomed high above her and carried on horizontally for what seemed an age.

Surely it must lead somewhere?

Rosamund jogged beside it, tripping over rubbish several times in the gathering gloom. At last she came to a gateway and was about to try to open the door when she heard footsteps on the other side. The door opened and a religious appeared. She gazed at Rosamund from beneath her wimple and suddenly her eyes widened.

'By the saints, Harry, where have you been these past six months?' she asked in a charmingly accented voice. 'Why did you have to go off the way you did? There was really no need. You won't know it, but Alex left London. Although perhaps you met with him on your travels?' she asked anxiously.

'I think you are mistaking me for someone else,' said Rosamund.

The nun looked uncertain and peered into Rosamund's

damp face. 'Aye, I see now that you are not Black Harry, but you are very like him.' She placed a hand on Rosamund's chest and smiled straight into her eyes. 'Is it possible that you are kin to him?'

'I don't know a Black Harry. I had a brother once called Harry, but he drowned.'

The nun's expression altered. 'You must come with me. I know someone who would be interested to meet you.'

Rosamund felt a prickly feeling in the nape of her neck and suddenly knew this religious was perhaps not what she seemed. At that moment there was the sound of a man's voice in the yard behind her. Instantly, Rosamund recognised her stepbrother's voice. She shoved the nun against the door and then she ran like the wind along the passageway.

To her relief there came a turning and the next moment she arrived at a tributary of the Thames. She paused to catch her breath, but she knew she could not delay. She might be completely mistaken about the nun, but she definitely was not about that voice. Lowering her head against the swirling snowflakes, Rosamund began to walk uphill. So it was she did not notice the tall, dark figure coming towards her and blundered into him. Caught off balance, he swayed. She clutched his cloak, but he slipped in the snow and they both fell to the ground with her on top of him. He arched his body in an attempt to throw her off, but she was entangled in his cloak so that proved impossible. He reached up and pushed. Rosamund gasped, thinking that he must not have realised where he had put his hands and dragged on one of his arms. 'Master, will you desist and release me!' she cried in a panic.

On hearing that muffled voice coming from somewhere beneath his cloak, Alex could scarcely believe his luck. 'Master Appleby! Or should I say *Mistress Appleby*?' he said in a velvety tone.

Rosamund collapsed on top of him and lay unmoving, listening to the heavy thud-thud-thud of his heart and the gallop of her own. He knew her secret, but she deemed him the lesser of two evils. 'Master Nilsson,' she gasped. 'I lost myself in the back alleys and was robbed of my cloak and then I saw a religious, who thought I was someone called Black Harry. I find that very strange in the light of my having had a brother called Harry. Then whose voice did I hear beyond the wall but that of my step-brother, Edward.'

'You mean Fustian was inside the Steel Yard?'

'Keep your voice down! So that's what that place is,' she murmured. 'I have heard of the headquarters of the Hanseatic League, but never set foot inside. What was Edward doing there? I knew I had to escape. If he catches me now, then it will be your fault. You're lying on part of your cloak and I can't tug it free.'

'Will you be quiet! Now, if you will release your hold on my cloak we can free ourselves.'

Relieved, she tried to do as he asked, but one of her hands was caught beneath his body and it required effort to free it. He hissed at her to stop.

'But you're lying on my hand,' she explained in an undertone.

He muttered indistinctly, lifting himself up and glancing about him as he did so. He tried not to think about what was going on in his loins. Mistress Appleby might have stopped wriggling, but the damage was already done and he could only hope she was unaware of his arousal. What was it about this woman that she could stir up a whole host of conflicting emotions inside him at such a dangerous time? If Fustian came upon them now, then they would be at a huge disadvantage.

'That's better,' gasped Rosamund, stretched her cramped fingers. She felt a bump against her belly and shifted to avoid it.

Alex groaned and, making an enormous effort, raised himself higher, taking him with her. With a final thrust he managed to throw her aside.

Rosamund scrambled to her feet and took several deep breaths. Despite the cold and damp, she had felt a heat between them that had her wanting to fan herself. But now was not the time to think of such things. They had to get away. She had only taken a couple of steps when a noise to her rear warned her that they were not alone. She called a warning to Alex before she was seized from behind.

'Let me go,' she cried, fearing that she had been caught by Edward.

'Youse shut yer mouth and keep yer orders to yerself,' snapped an unfamiliar voice.

Rosamund could scarcely believe that she had been captured by another ruffian. 'Not now,' she muttered, struggling to free herself.

'We wants to know what yer've got in yer pockets,' snarled the man, twisting her right arm up her back. She cried out in pain.

'Hold fast there,' said Alex, drawing not only his own

sword, but Rosamund's short-sword as well. 'Release her at once.'

'Another furriner giving his orders,' said a woman with a sniff.

'Just do as I say or I'll run you through,' said Alex.

The man who held Rosamund captive produced a dagger. 'Come one step nearer and I'll slit his throat.'

'You have too much to say for yourself,' growled Alex, and with one swift movement he knocked the dagger from the man's hand and then, with a twirl of the other sword, he caught him a blow beneath the chin with its hilt. The dagger flew off into the darkness and the man's hold on Rosamund's arm slackened as he slid to the ground.

'Hey, what have yer dun to him?' asked his accomplice.

Alex did not bother replying, but seized Rosamund's hand and dragged her away, hurrying her along the bank of the tributary until the woman's cries faded into the distance.

'Wh-where are we going?' asked Rosamund, needing to clench her teeth in an attempt to stop them from chattering. She could not see the way ahead.

Alex bit back an oath and removed his own cloak and wrapped it round her. His fingers brushed her throat as he tied the strings and she trembled.

'Keep still and be glad you're a woman,' he said brusquely. 'I wouldn't be so gallant if you were a man.'

'Why should y-you feel a n-need to be gallant when y-you must believe my behaviour w-w-wicked and unseemly?'

'I was taught by my grandmother to respect women. A habit I find difficult to break. Come, we must go carefully. I have friends who can provide us with a hot tub and dry clothing.'

'Where is your horse?' she asked.

'At their house. I stabled him whilst I visited a couple of places.'

'But I told you I had to see Lady Elizabeth Stanley. Did you not think of going to her home in search of me?'

'Aye. But not immediately. Anyway, we are some way from her mansion.'

'I was looking for a used-clothes dealer in the hope of exchanging my cloak for a gown.'

'Then you are in luck,' said Alex, stepping carefully. 'Tell me, how did you reach London so swiftly on foot?'

'A man took pity on me and let me ride in his cart. I was limping because my feet were sore.' Suddenly she slipped in the snow and was saved only by the strength in his wrist.

'You should not have run away from me.' His tone was vexed.

'I had to because I believed you had a disgust of me for getting drunk.' She gripped his hand tightly, still concerned about slipping in the snow. 'Tell me, how did I betray myself?'

'Your eyes, your lips and the way you swing your hips when you walk—the timbre of your voice and not even a hint of a whisker on your chin. Of course, there was also the slip about your stepmother wanting you to marry Edward.'

'How foolish of me!' She sighed heavily. 'But why did you not mention it at the time? I see I made lots of mistakes, but I swear on my mother's grave that everything I told you about myself and my stepfamily is true.'

'If I did not believe that, then I would not be taking you to my friends. How old are you, Mistress Appleby?'

'I have seen twenty-two summers, not eighteen,' she

said rapidly. 'Do you not think it strange that that religious mistook me for this Black Harry?'

'How did your brother die?'

'Lady Monica told me he drowned. His clothes were found close to a part of the river where he used to bathe.'

'Was his body ever found?'

'No, but she initiated a search.'

'It is still possible that he did not drown,' said Alex. 'I must tell you, Mistress Appleby, that you were crying in your sleep last night. You believed he was being carried away.'

Rosamund stopped in her tracks. 'You mean my dream of him being carried away was not a delusion, but real?' she asked in a strained voice.

'Aye. It can be the only answer to your not only being mistaken for this Black Harry, but also for your father seeing a likeness to someone in a past life in this same Black Harry.'

Rosamund's mouth fell open and then she clamped it shut and took a deep breath before saying in a rush, 'How do you know this about my father?'

'Because he spoke those words to me on the only occasion I met him.'

Rosamund experienced such a splurge of joy that it rocked her to her heels and she needed to clutch Alex all the tighter. 'I so want to believe it,' she said.

'Then you must because I deem it the truth.'

Tears welled in Rosamund's eyes. 'I remember my brother well. I loved him dearly,' she said softly. 'He was protective towards me and was brave and funny.'

'Do not expect him to be exactly the same as you remember,' warned Alex. 'That's if we ever find him. People change.'

'Not Harry,' she said firmly.

'How can you possibly know? I trusted him like you did. When I first knew him I believed he possessed all the qualities you mentioned. But he betrayed me for the love of Ingrid and a stolen cargo.'

'I don't believe my brother is a thief and you are saying that love changes people for the worst? I do not believe that either,' she said stoutly.

'I deem you have never been in love, Mistress Appleby,' he rasped. 'Passion, desire, lust can drive a man to do things that he would never normally do.'

'More fool the man,' she retorted. 'Oh, how I wish Father was here! This news would have made him so happy.'

Alex looked at her in astonishment. 'Your father treated you disgracefully. And he did not even say that that likeness was to his own son, but just someone in a past life.'

Some of her joy evaporated and Rosamund said, 'You would not know how badly my mother's death affected my father and then on top of those tidings came the news that Harry had drowned. I believe my stepmother—not that she was my stepmother then—told him that the grief had driven me mad. And it is true that I was bereft.'

'All the more reason for him to show you love instead of allowing that woman and her sons to try to sap your spirit utterly,' he said roundly. 'I am just amazed that they did not succeed.'

Rosamund was silent, touched by his championing her in such a way.

Alex smiled. 'I can see I have taken your breath away. Time to move on, I deem.'

To her further amazement, he swung her up into his arms. 'What are you doing?' she asked. 'You must let me down.'

'Be quiet, woman! You have caused me enough trouble already. Now relax and let me make haste.'

Rosamund said no more. She might be shivery and exhausted, happy and sad and utterly astounded by the fact that Harry was alive, not to mention being vexed with Master Nilsson for doubting Harry's loyalty, but at least he seemed willing to still help her.

'These friends of yours…?' she asked.

'As I said earlier, Mistress Appleby, you are in luck. They make a living from buying and selling used garments. My friend, Walther, is Swedish and married to Maud, who is a Londoner, born and bred. They have been of great help to me and I know that I can always count on finding a bed at their house when I stay in the city.'

'Will they have a separate bedchamber for me?' asked Rosamund.

His arms tightened about her. 'You worry needlessly, mistress. I will explain just enough to satisfy them why you are dressed as you are. Now, do you feel strong enough to stand?' he asked.

Despite still feeling shaky, Rosamund said, 'Of course. How can you ask after my surviving the journey we made together?'

He felt truly rebuked and set her down. After producing the key, he opened one of the doors and ushered her into a large yard. 'Beware of the washing lines.'

He stretched out a hand to her and she took it thankfully. He steered her between the lines towards a building at the far end of the yard, where light gleamed through the shutters. He knocked on a door and called out in the Swedish tongue. There came an excited voice and then bolts were drawn back. The door opened to reveal a man holding a lantern who addressed Alex in his own language. They spoke for several moments before Alex turned to Rosamund.

'This is my friend Walther. He welcomes you to his home.'

Rosamund thanked him in English and was relieved that he made no sign of disapproval of the way she was dressed. Even so she felt awkward and warm with embarrassment. Her awkwardness deepened when an older woman entered the room, but her primary attention was not for her, but Master Nilsson. Rosamund watched the woman smile at the sight of him.

'So, you have come back for your horse.'

'Aye, but I wish to ask more of you than stabling my horse.'

'Of course, anything you want.' She frowned suddenly. 'But you are soaking wet and…' She peered over his shoulder and whispered, 'Who is this you have brought us? One of your spies in need of a new disguise?'

Alex nodded. 'But do not speak of the work to her. Mistress Appleby is chilled to the bone and in need of a hot tub—as am I. You must also find for her several of your best gowns and the necessary accessories—we are to visit the Lady Elizabeth Stanley on the morrow. Can you provide us with bedchambers for this night? You will not lose by it.'

Maud nodded. 'Walther told me earlier that you have asked him to hire some men to keep a watch on Master William Fustian's house. We do not like the man. He would put us out of business if he could.'

Alex nodded. 'He has no liking for foreigners, which is

strange when he has to do business with them. Anyway, he is unaware that Mistress Appleby is in my company so he will not come here.'

She nodded. 'I will go now and speak to the maids and have them fill tubs for you both.'

Alex rejoined Rosamund. 'I have explained your needs to Maud, Mistress Appleby, and she is having a hot tub made ready for you.'

'You did not tell her everything?' asked Rosamund, mortified at the thought of the older woman knowing she had spent nights, never mind days, alone with this man.

'Of course not. She believes you are a spy in disguise and in need of a few changes of costume.'

Rosamund gasped and put a hand to her mouth and said in a muffled voice, 'You jest!'

He grinned.

Rosamund felt a tap on her shoulder and turned to see Maud smiling at her. 'It is a pleasure to have you here with us, Mistress Appleby. I have ordered a maid to fill a tub for you, but first you will follow me to the parlour.'

Her friendly manner made Rosamund feel at ease. 'I appreciate your kindness in coming to my aid.'

'It is always a pleasure to help one's friends. You will take a cup of mead? No doubt you are hungry, too. I've smoked eel and bread.'

Rosamund's face lit up. 'You are generous. I have not eaten all day.'

'Then follow me. You can warm yourself by the fire and I will have a maid bring food and mead whilst I see what I can find for you in the way of gowns for your latest assignment.'

Chapter Six

Rosamund nodded dumbly, glanced at Master Nilsson to see if he was coming as well, but he was in conversation with Walther. She followed Maud through an unlit chamber and into another room. There a fire glowed on the hearth and several candles provided extra light. She was shown to a cushioned settle and then left alone. She removed her wet gloves and placed them on the hearth to dry. Master Nilsson must be playing games with her. She was no spy!

A maid entered the room, carrying a tray upon which there was a platter of food and a drinking vessel. She slanted a curious glance at Rosamund as she set food and drink on the table and, then, with a whisk of skirts, she was gone.

By the time Rosamund had consumed the food and drunk the mead Maud had returned to the parlour. She bid Rosamund follow her and took her to a room containing a steaming wooden tub.

'This is where we wash the clothes that we buy. Some we just hang in the steam and clean any stains because washing would ruin the fabric,' she explained. 'You'll find all you need on the chair. I'll return in a short while.'

As soon as Rosamund was alone she stripped off her travel-stained garments. Then she tested the water with her elbow before lowering herself into its depths. For a moment she just sat there with her legs hunched up against her body, relishing the heat. Then she reached for the soap and gave herself a thorough cleansing, including her hair. As she did so, her thoughts were of Master Nilsson and how he had wrapped his cloak round her and lifted her off her feet. A picture suddenly flashed into her mind of a figure bending over her, crooning *'Little Rosie is crazy!'* A cold shiver ran down her spine and she was remembering someone holding her down whilst her stepmother forced her mouth open and spooned in the liquid. She could hear Edward asking his mother what effect the potion would have on Rosamund's mind. Loathing filled her and she so longed for them both to suffer for all they had put her family through that she vowed she would not rest until it came about. And she was convinced that Harry would feel the same.

She did not linger in the tub for long; by the time she had wrapped a drying cloth around her and was rubbing her hair dry, Maud returned with a woollen dressing robe. 'Goodness! How different you look already,' she said, holding out the robe to her guest.

Rosamund smiled shyly and slipped her hands through the sleeves and fastened the belt about her slender waist. Then she followed Maud from the room and up a flight of stairs.

'You will sleep here, Mistress Appleby,' said Maud, stopping outside a door.

Rosamund followed her inside, only to stop short when she saw Master Nilsson standing there. Alex's gaze washed over her and paused a fraction as his eyes rested on her cleavage. She had made a handsome young man, but she was even lovelier as a woman.

'I beg your pardon for invading your privacy. I saw a light in here and was curious. I stayed to approve Maud's choice of gowns,' he said.

With his eyes upon her in a way that made her aware of her femininity, Rosamund drew the opening of her robe closer together. She looked down at the garments spread out on the bed and her dark brows knit. 'I do not have any money to pay for them,' she said.

'I will do so,' said Alex firmly.

Rosamund shook her head. 'I know you paid for my food and lodgings on the journey, but that was different. I cannot allow you to do this for me.'

'Why?' He seemed amused. 'Perhaps you have me written off as a pauper.'

She hesitated. 'You cannot be rich if you need to wander hither and thither far from your own country, taking *spying* work where you can find it and performing in front of whoever will pay you. I know you have spoken of your grandfather's business, but—'

'You still know little about my life,' said Alex in a mild tone. 'But if it bothers you, I will simply loan you the money. You need to make a good impression on her ladyship if you wish to obtain her support in delving into the circumstances surrounding your father's death. These gowns will not cost a fortune, but should be suitable for that purpose.'

Rosamund moved over to the bed and fingered one of the gowns. Alex gazed over her shoulder and said, 'That is an excellent colour and will match your eyes.'

Rosamund felt her cheeks warm and was glad he could not see her face. 'Aye. It is the kind of dark blue I like,' she said casually.

She turned to speak to Maud about the blue gown, but realised she must have slipped out of the bedchamber whilst she and Master Nilsson were talking. 'Where has Maud gone? Now we are here in your friends' house, we must have a care for our reputations.'

He said seriously, 'You are right to be concerned about such matters, but Maud and Walther would not expect me to behave in any other way than honourably to a woman.'

'Tell me, when did you first realise I was a woman?' she asked curiously.

Alex leant against a bedpost where he could watch her expression. 'I suspected you were not all you seemed that first night back in the cave.'

She was taken aback. 'So soon!'

'Aye. But there is no need to feel that you must marry me. It is our secret that we spent several nights together.' The words were out before he could recall them and he wondered why he had mentioned marriage. It had not been in his thoughts at all.

Rosamund had not even considered the need for him to make a respectable woman of her, but she did now. The bedchamber appeared to tilt and then spin round so that she had need to clutch one of the other bedposts.

'I do not wish to be married right now. I have to find

Harry and make my stepmother suffer by bringing Edward to his knees.'

Alex felt a vague disappointment that she had no desire to marry him. 'I am glad that you are a woman of good sense,' he said brusquely. 'Marriage would be a complication in my life that I can well do without.'

'Then that is settled and we will not refer to it again,' said Rosamund, pushing aside the garments on the bed and sitting down. 'It is not that I do not enjoy your company,' she added, toying with her fingernails. 'But naught happened between us that either of us needs to feel guilty about.' Her cheeks burned as she remembered how she had wanted him to kiss her and hold her. 'I am still chaste,' she added, a quiver in her voice, 'so let us move on to talk of other matters.'

Alex went to a dressing table upon which were items for a woman's *toilette*. He picked up a comb and ran a fingernail along its teeth. 'As you are such a woman of good sense, I will broach a matter that is on my mind. Have you considered the likelihood of Lady Elizabeth refusing to help you and your stepbrother seeking you out and forcing you to go with him?'

Rosamund said, 'I do not believe that she will refuse me. I have not been completely honest with you concerning Lady Elizabeth. I kept from you that she is my godmother.'

Alex dropped the comb and whirled round to face her. 'Your godmother! Why did you keep this a secret from me?' he demanded.

'Because you would have questioned why the person I was pretending to be had a lady for a godmother,' said Rosamund. 'I am certain there is that in your life that you have not told me—and why should you when we scarcely know each other? Besides, I have not seen my godmother since before my mother died. Yet I have this hope that she will welcome me like a daughter. Then when Harry comes home I could keep house for him.' She paused. 'Which reminds me of something that religious said when she thought I was Harry.'

Alex fixed her with a stare. 'What did she say?'

Rosamund concentrated. 'Something like *"Why did you have to go off the way you did? There was really no need. You won't know it, but Alex left London. Although perhaps you met with him on your travels?"'*

Alex swore beneath his breath in his own tongue.

'Obviously it means something to you,' said Rosamund.

He nodded. 'It was Ingrid you spoke to.'

'Ingrid! But isn't she the woman who—?'

'Aye. And it seems I have misjudged her.'

'And my brother? How upsetting! She must have taken the veil because you both broke her heart.' She could not prevent a touch of sarcasm invading her voice.

'I do not think so,' said Alex drily. 'A nun's habit was one of her favourite disguises.'

Rosamund could not believe what she was hearing. 'You're not saying that Ingrid is a spy, too?'

'I really should not be discussing such information with you,' said Alex, feeling he needed to be alone for a while. He made for the door. 'I must go and bathe,' he said abruptly.

'No! Don't go just yet,' said Rosamund, holding out a hand to him. 'I would like to know how you met my brother.'

Alex flicked back a lock of damp, tawny hair and his expression was moody. 'All right. I will do so.'

Rosamund's heart was suddenly beating ten to the dozen.

'It was in the port of Visby in my own country twelve years ago. I found him hiding amongst some merchandise that had been carted to the port, ready to be shipped overseas for my grandfather,' said Alex. 'Harry looked half-starved and was covered in sores—his clothes were just rags. It was obvious that he needed help.'

'Poor Harry! Why was he in such a state?' she asked in distress.

'At that time we did not speak the other's language, but my grandfather knew enough English to discover that Harry had escaped from a pirate ship. I might have told you a little about pirate ships already. Anyway, one can encounter many a pirate ship in the northern seas—not that their captains would appreciate being called by that name. But you will find Scottish ships raiding English merchant vessels and English ones attacking their Scottish neighbours. It is not unknown for both to mistakenly attack vessels from my own country, as well as others from the Baltic.' He paused and held her gaze. 'It must be stopped, for it is disastrous for trade. That is why England and Scotland are signing a Pact of Perpetual Peace and Henry is marrying off his elder daughter to James of Scotland.' He frowned. 'But you will want to know what happened next to Harry.'

'Please.'

'We took Harry home with us and my grandmother fed him. That summer we spent getting to know each other. I taught Harry Swedish and he taught me English. We fished and sailed around the islands and were given work to do by my grandparents. Eventually Harry asked my grandfather if he could find him a position on one of his ships. This he did to their mutual satisfaction. Harry and I saw less of each other after that, but the friendship that was forged that summer remained and, when possible, we met up at various ports throughout Europe.' His voice trailed off and his expression was bleak. 'I've said enough. I will leave you. Sleep well.' He made for the door.

'No! Wait!' She hurried after him and seized his arm. 'You cannot leave the story there. Tell me—where does Ingrid come in all this? Where did you both meet her?'

Alex allowed himself to be persuaded to sit down again. 'I met her in Stockholm at a masque. She was young, lovely, charming and I believed her to be a lady.' He fell silent.

'And was she a lady?' prodded Rosamund, wondering what he had been doing at this masque. Spying?

A painful smile played about his mouth. 'That's what she believes, but I doubt it is true. The next time we met I was with Harry and we were unloading a cargo in Visby. She looked just as lovely, but was not so well dressed. She gazed right through me as if she did not recognise me, but she spoke to Harry, asking him about the cargo.' He frowned. 'I could see that he was just as bewitched by her as I was that night in Stockholm. The next time we met was in Bruges and then London. It was then I began to have my suspicions about her.'

'What suspicions? She certainly travels a lot,' said Rosamund, almost enviously.

'That is because sometimes she has to leave a country swiftly. She is not a real lady, but lives by her wits and has a definite gift for disguise and getting men to talk.' He rose and said firmly, 'I believe I've given you enough to mull over.'

'Aye. But I would hear more,' said Rosamund, wondering how much secret information Ingrid had managed to get out of him. 'You will tell me more tomorrow?'

He did not answer, and this time, there was no keeping him.

Rosamund returned to the bed and perched on it. She had no doubt that Master Nilsson had saved her brother's life that day in Visby. For that she would be eternally grateful. She longed to see Harry and get some answers from him about this woman, Ingrid. It seemed to her that Ingrid had truly woven a spell over both men. But for what purpose? And did she know Edward? After all, hadn't she heard his voice at the Steel Yard? Surely he was the person who Ingrid implied would like to meet her? And where was Harry if Ingrid did not know of his whereabouts?

Rosamund prayed that he was still alive. It would have been far better for her never to have known that Harry had not drowned all those years ago than to discover now, after having such hopes of being reunited with him, that he was dead after all. She felt a lump in her throat and tears pricked the back of her eyes. She needed to talk to Master Nilsson about this matter, but no doubt he was thinking of Ingrid. Perhaps he was full of hope that they could be lovers again, now he believed her innocent of betraying him with Harry.

If only Rosamund had know it was she that was much on Alex's mind, then she might have felt much more cheerful. As he immersed himself in hot water and rested a leg on the rim of the wooden tub, he had been shocked to realise that he no longer wanted Ingrid. He had spent too many months thinking of her with Harry and feeling hurt.

Of course, there were questions he needed to ask her, but somehow during the last week or more he had become accustomed to Mistress Appleby's company. He thought how enjoyable it would be sharing a large tub with her. But there was no way that he could have Harry's sister as his mistress. A pity, but there it was. He had promised to find Harry for her and he meant to keep his promise. There was still the matter of the message he had been sent and only Harry could explain that away.

Alex soaped an aching thigh muscle and imagined Mistress Appleby performing the task. He realised that he was obsessing over her now it was in the open that he knew her for a woman. They were going to have to be careful what they said when they reached Lady Elizabeth's mansion. If she was to suspect that they had spent nights together, unchaperoned, she would think the worst. They had to dissuade her from such thoughts. He found himself considering telling her ladyship that he had enlisted Mistress Appleby as one of his spies. She would be useful at court with her gift of self-effacement, whilst keeping her eyes and ears open. He could guess what she would make of that notion. In his mind's eye he could see her pretty mouth falling open and those blue-violet eyes of hers widening in astonishment. 'You jest, Master Nilsson,' she would blurt out.

He grinned, imagining himself silencing her protestations by kissing those luscious lips. He recalled the feel of her satiny skin beneath his fingers and the swell of her breasts against his chest as they lay in the snow. A definite stirring in his loins caused him to cut short such imaginings and reach for the cold-water jug.

* * *

That night when Alex fell asleep he dreamed that he and Mistress Appleby were making love. Afterwards he decked her out in silks and satins and velvet and the best amber jewellery from his country. He woke up with the words running in his head: *I give you a choice. You either marry me or be my lover spy.* It was then he realised just how desperate he was not to be parted from her and had to remind himself that he had once felt the same about Ingrid and that he no longer loved her.

Rosamund had also been dreaming, but hers were dark ones of her brother drowning and crying out to her to rescue him. She woke with tears on her cheeks and got out of bed and down on her knees and prayed that he was still alive and she would see him again.

She felt better after that and fell asleep once more. This time in her dream she was wearing a dark blue gown and on her raven hair she wore a silver circlet encrusted with gemstones of amber. Master Nilsson was facing her as he placed a ring on her finger. Strangely he was wearing a saffron-dyed tunic and a soft leather jerkin, but on his flaxen head he also wore a silver circlet. He was smiling tenderly down at her and then suddenly he vanished and in his place was her stepbrother's snarling face.

She woke in terror and this time she did not go back to sleep. She wondered what the dream could mean. No doubt her stepmother would have said it was a sign of her madness. On shaky legs, she went over to the window and drew back the curtain and peered outside. Daylight had come and the sun glistened on the snow in the yard. Her heart lifted and she told herself that she would believe that Harry was still alive. As she gazed down into the yard she saw Master Nilsson tending his horse.

The sight of him reassured her, but she could not help wondering if he had made time to go and take a look at her stepbrother's residence What had Edward and Ingrid been doing inside the Steel Yard? She must ask Master Nilsson what it was like on the other side of those high walls.

She moved away from the window and looked at the garments that she had placed on a chair before getting into bed, without having made the effort to try any of them on. She removed the robe that she had slept in and hastened to cover her nakedness with a cream, woollen under-gown. The feel of the soft, warm fabric gave her a *frisson* of pleasure. She pulled on the blue gown over it and the sensation when the skirts brushed her calves as she twirled round made her want to dance. The sleeves were puffed about her upper arms, but gathered tightly in a band just below the elbow, where they puffed out again to be gathered in embroidered bands at the wrists. She stretched forth her arms and did another twirl.

Then she frowned. What was she thinking of? She could only have this gown if Master Nilsson loaned her the money and loans had to be paid back. But she was going to have to wear a gown if she were to go with him to Lady Elizabeth's house, so she was going to have to accept being further in debt to him.

Having made that decision, she tried on several more gowns. She dithered over whether to take the dark blue one, but remembered what he had said about the colour matching her eyes. She selected another two gowns, one green and one saffron yellow, before also trying on stockings, garters, a couple of hats, shoes and boots.

She was combing her hair when there came a knock on the door.

'Mistress Appleby, are you awake? We must make haste.'

Her pulses raced. 'Aye. I am almost ready, Master Nilsson.'

'You have chosen some gowns to take with you?' he asked.

Rosamund hesitated and then opened the door. She caught a whiff of almond-and-honey soap and noticed he was clean shaven. His tawny hair curled about his ears and he had changed his garments and now wore a cream linen shirt beneath a russet doublet; his well-formed legs were clad in red hose. Her senses were roused; she realised that not only did she still want him to kiss her, but that she was desperate for his approval of her appearance.

Alex's breath caught in his throat at the anxiety in her eyes and he wanted to punch those who had given her such a low opinion of herself. 'Blue is a colour you should wear often,' he said, taking one of her hands and twirling her round. 'How lovely you look.' He felt some of the tension leave her and her obvious delight made him want to reassure her by taking her in his arms and kissing her. But he knew that he must keep a rein on his passions.

'You can have no notion of how different I feel wearing such a gown,' she said shyly.

'Your eyes are like sapphires. I scarcely recognise you as the same person who rode me down near Appleby Manor,' he teased.

'That seems so long ago now,' said Rosamund, blushing. 'But you must go downstairs, Master Nilsson.

There is no need for you to wait for me. I will be down as soon as I have tidied my hair.'

'I am content to wait for you.' He released her hand and went over to the dressing table and picked up a net of silken blue threads. 'What a pretty trifle this is. You will wear it?' Rosamund eyed the hairnet and agreed that it was indeed pretty. He handed it to her. 'Have you chosen other gowns to take with you?'

'I have picked another two,' she answered, 'that is, if you are willing to fund me to that extent? I need boots and shoes and other fripperies, as well.'

'Of course I am willing.' He picked up the cloaks hanging over the back of the chair. 'You will have these?'

Rosamund gave them a fleeting glance. 'I need only one.'

Alex placed a fur-lined blue velvet cloak about her shoulders. 'Now how does that feel?'

Rosamund had noticed the cloak earlier, but had deemed it too costly to try on. Now she could not resist stroking the blue pile. 'I have never worn velvet before.'

'You will need a brooch to fasten it as it has no ties,' said Alex.

'I do not have a brooch.' She made to remove the cloak, but he stayed her with a hand.

'I have a brooch you can use. Please accept this cloak as a gift. I know you do not wish to be beholden to me, but I would like to see you wearing it.'

She would have refused him, only he lifted a fold of the material and brushed it against her cheek. 'Imagine wearing such a cloak in your stepmother's presence. Picture her gnashing her teeth in envy and fury.'

A faint smile replaced Rosamund's serious expression.

'You tempt me, Master Nilsson. But I cannot wear it now—it is an evening cloak.'

'Then wear this brown woollen one for travelling and we will take the blue one with us. Now tidy your hair and let us be on our way.'

Rosamund submitted to his will. When Harry returned, she felt certain he would willingly pay her debts. She pinned up her hair beneath the blue silk net, whilst Alex neatly folded the garments she had chosen.

She followed him downstairs and into the parlour where Maud and Walther were eating breakfast in front of the fire. Walther said something in Swedish to Alex, but it was Maud who translated his words. 'My husband says how lovely you are and I agree with him. You will have some bread and honey and ale?'

Rosamund thanked her, and was shown to the table. Maud left her for a moment, but she was soon joined by Alex and Walther. Whilst their host poured ale into drinking vessels, Alex produced a silver brooch from a pouch. He handed it to Rosamund and she gazed at it with interest because its design was unusual.

'What does it symbolise?' she asked. 'It looks like Christ's cross, only…'

'It was once an amulet of Thor's hammer,' said Alex. 'As you can see, it has been made into a cross in the form of a brooch.'

'You must value it highly,' she said.

He hesitated. 'It belonged to Harry. I bent to pick it up and it was then that I was attacked from behind.'

She paled. 'You've kept this because you believe it is evidence against my brother?'

Alex shrugged. 'I kept it because I did not wish to be rid of it. You can keep it.'

She was greatly moved by the thought of having in her possession that which had belonged to her brother. 'Thank you. I will take care of it until I see him again.'

At that moment Maud returned, along with a serving maid, so no more was said about the brooch.

When the meal was over and Rosamund came to look for the bundle of clothes, there was no sign of it. She spoke to Alex about it.

'Maud has tied it up with cord and it awaits us in the next chamber. We will collect it on our way out.' He stood and helped her to her feet.

Rosamund thanked Walther and Maud for their hospitality.

'We hope all goes well with your plans and look forward to seeing you both soon,' they said.

Chapter Seven

Alex and Rosamund spoke little as they rode through the streets to Lady Elizabeth's mansion, which was situated near the Strand. Two watchmen stood on guard at the gates. Alex dismounted and spoke to them. The gates were thrown wide and a stable boy summoned to tend to the horse. Alex led Rosamund to the entrance of the house and the door was opened to them by the butler. Alex handed him a missive that he had written last night in his bedchamber. He exchanged a few words with him and, after a curious glance in Rosamund's direction, the man showed them into a large hall and told them to wait while he informed Lady Elizabeth of their arrival.

Rosamund's heart was beating fast, but she did her best not to reveal her nervousness to Alex and gazed about the hall. She hoped that her godmother would recognise her. But would Rosamund remember Lady Elizabeth? Suddenly her eyes alighted on a portrait on a far wall and she hurried over to take a closer look at it.

Alex followed her. 'Your godmother when she was

young,' he said. 'I recall that I once visited here with my grandfather. It had slipped my mind until I saw the house.'

'Godmother was beautiful! I wonder if she has changed much.'

'She is an old woman,' said Alex in a low voice. 'This was here when I visited as a boy.'

'Her skin looks as soft as rose petals,' she murmured.

Alex rubbed his chin with his knuckles. 'Aye, it is a pretty picture.'

Rosamund darted him a sidelong glance. 'How did your grandfather come to be invited here?'

'If I remember rightly, it was due to her having visited Visby a few months previously. She had been widowed the year before and had decided she wished to travel. She commissioned some amber-and-silver jewellery to her own design. Grandfather took on the role of her agent and she asked him to deliver the commission in person. He decided it would be useful for me to visit London and so brought me along.'

'I had no notion you were so long acquainted,' said Rosamund.

'The lady scarcely noticed me.' Alex paused. 'We need to decide what to tell Lady Elizabeth. We cannot tell her the whole truth.'

Rosamund went over to the fire and removed her gloves. 'If we did so, she wouldn't want to have aught to do with me.' She held her hands out to the flames. 'Besides, we don't know what else she might have been told about me during her sojourn in Lathom House except that I was ill and slightly crazed in the head.'

'I do not believe you were ever crazy. Anyway, hopefully she will be sympathetic to one in your situation,' said Alex, joining Rosamund by the fire.

'I pray so. Do we admit to having met up north?'

'Have you any other suggestions? I believe it is always best to stick as close to the truth as one can,' said Alex.

'I had believed my godmother dead until the day I met you,' said Rosamund. 'I think Father had mentioned that she was very ill some years ago. I believe he expected her to die.' She sat down and smoothed out the kid gloves on her knee.

Alex's gaze rested on Rosamund's bent head. 'I presume your plan that day was to tell your godmother of how you were being treated at home and of your suspicion concerning the death of your father?'

'Aye.' Rosamund sighed. 'When you told me that she had already departed for London, it placed me in somewhat of a dilemma, as you well know.'

'But if you were pretending to be Master Wood, how did you plan to gain entry to Lathom House and speak to Lady Elizabeth?'

She shrugged. 'Does that matter now? I am more concerned about what I am to say to her when I see her.'

He nodded. 'We will tell her that we met outside Lathom where you discovered that she had already left for London. I told you that I was acquainted with her ladyship and intended visiting her. You decided to travel to London, so I offered you my escort as we were travelling in the same direction.'

Rosamund shook her head. 'It will not do. She will suspect that we travelled alone.'

'Not if we can tell her that we had company on the road,' said Alex firmly. 'She is not to know otherwise.'

Rosamund plucked at her skirts. 'It sounds feasible, but you have not said what your reason was for calling at Lathom House?'

Before Alex could answer, there was a sound behind them. They both turned to see a woman standing there. She was dressed in a plum-coloured gown and her red frizzy hair resembled a bird's nest.

'I cannot believe that at last we are to meet, Rosamund,' she gasped with a hand to her chest.

Rosamund realised that this lady must be her godmother and could only hope she had not overheard their conversation. She rose to her feet and went to meet her. The lady seemed to glide across the floor towards her as if on wheels. Close up, Rosamund realised that the lady's face was painted white that gave her features a mask-like appearance. 'Lady Elizabeth?'

'Who else, my dear?' said the lady drily. 'I know I have altered somewhat, but it is still me beneath this paint.'

A flushed Rosamund apologised. 'I am delighted to see you again after all these years, Godmother.' She dipped a curtsy and then took the hand offered to help her rise.

'My appearance always gives people a shock, whether it be for the first time or after an age,' said Lady Elizabeth.

'You are very understanding and I thank you for your welcome. I would have visited you at Lathom House if I'd been able to do so. But it was not easy escaping my stepmother's domination. By the time I did so, you had already left for London,' said Rosamund.

'That woman!' snorted Lady Elizabeth, rolling her eyes expressively. 'I am still angry that your father put her in my dear Jane's place.' She looked at Alex and her eyes softened. 'Thank you for your missive, my dear Baron. You are so like your grandfather. If you will be so kind as to be patient whilst I talk with my goddaughter, I will give you my full attention in a moment.'

My dear Baron, thought Rosamund, puzzled by the title. She watched him remove his hat and incline his tawny head. 'Of course, Lady Elizabeth. I understand what a pleasure it must be for you both to meet again after all these years.'

'Charming,' she said, touching his cheek with a finger before resuming her conversation with her goddaughter. 'So that woman asserted her will over you.'

Rosamund pulled herself together. 'You sound as if you know the kind of woman my stepmother is,' she said.

Her godmother's eyes widened. 'My dear, your mother and I knew Monica McDonald when we were children. We all had kin living in the north.' Lady Elizabeth sat down and waved them to a settle. 'Jane refused to believe the rumours about Monica's wanton behaviour because she always believed the best of people. Anyway, Monica stayed on at Appleby Manor after Jane miscarried, supposedly to nurse her.' She sighed. 'Well, we know what happened after that! Monica's family was such a quarrelsome one and they were furious when she had an affair with her cousin's husband. No doubt it was that which made it impossible for her to return home.' She frowned. 'The whole lot of them were unstable and I knew Monica McDonald for what she was—a greedy, conniving madam.' She paused. 'I have heard that her lover is a widower now, so who is to say that she might not run off with him.' Lady Elizabeth grimaced and cracks appeared in the white paint and there was a peculiar smell.

Rosamund swallowed a cough and then hurried into speech. 'Thank you for telling me this story. My stepmother's background was always a mystery to me, for she seldom spoke of her family. Yet surely Father must have known something of my stepmother's past, so why did he marry her?'

'No doubt she tricked him into it. He was grief-stricken and lonely and most likely found it convenient to have a new *mother* for you close at hand.'

'She was no mother to me,' said Rosamund, her eyes smouldering. 'She told people I was mad and was going to have me locked up. She feared what I might tell them and that was why I had to escape.'

'I am sure she has plenty to hide and was, no doubt, jealous of you, my dear,' wheezed Lady Elizabeth. 'You have grown into a lovely woman, so like my dear Jane. I look a fright and know it. But when you reach my age, having survived the smallpox, then one must be forgiven for painting over wrinkles and pockmarks.'

Rosamund felt both pity and admiration for her. 'Father told me years ago that you were ill and expected to die. It was not until I heard my stepmother mention you that I realised you were still alive. I knew then that I had to see you.'

'Well, I am glad you made the effort, my dear. My intention in trying to get in touch with you was so we could become better acquainted before it is too late.' She patted Rosamund's hand and then turned to Alex. 'My dear Baron, I was so sorry to hear of the deaths of your grandparents. Your grandfather in particular was helpful to me on several occasions. I am delighted that we are to work together and you are to be part of my troupe. I do hope you will like the costumes for the dance. They are black and silver and there will be such carolling that it will surely gladden the hearts of the royal family and their Scottish guests.'

Rosamund wondered what they were talking about, but there was no mistake about him being a baron because her godmother had addressed him by that title again. Of course, it might be all of an act if he really was a spy. Whichever was the truth, it was obvious to her that here was an example of Master Nilsson's duplicity. He had not been honest with her.

'I presume there will be time for rehearsals?' he was asking.

'The members of my troupe will be here this afternoon,' informed Lady Elizabeth. 'If you are to take part, then I will partner you. But time enough to sort that out later and for you to learn…' she paused to catch her breath and patted her bosom '…your steps…and see what gossip you can rake through for information. We will leave for Richmond in the morning—' She broke off again, her chest heaving.

Rosamund gazed at her anxiously. 'Are you all right?'

'I am as well as can be expected in the circumstances' she gasped. 'I have decided that the troupe will wear masks to create an air of mystery. What is your opinion, my dears?'

'It sounds exciting,' said Rosamund.

Alex said politely, 'I am certain it will delight their Majesties and the Scottish lords and archbishops.'

'I am glad you deem it so.' Lady Elizabeth winced and rubbed her forehead with a trembling hand. 'I have such a megrim coming on. I will have to take my potion soon.'

Rosamund stared at her anxiously.

Lady Elizabeth forced a smile. 'You must not worry

about me, my dear. You know, when I heard your father had died, I could not help thinking it was a pity he did not go sooner in place of my dear Jane and your poor brother.' Her eyes were suddenly damp and she took a kerchief from the velvet pouch that hung at her waist and dabbed her eyes before flicking white flakes of paint from her gown.

'I must tell you some good news, Godmother,' said Rosamund, glancing across at the Baron. 'My brother, Harry, is not dead as we believed.'

Lady Elizabeth raised her head and fixed her with a hard stare. 'I don't understand. What sorcery is this? Your father told me fifteen years ago that he had drowned.'

Alex said, 'He was deceived. I met Harry twelve years ago in Visby. I will not go into all the details now, but he had escaped captivity aboard a pirate ship and was in need of a friend. After I missed seeing you at Lathom House, I met Mistress Appleby who was on her way to visit you. It came as quite a shock when we introduced ourselves because, just the same as yourself, she had believed Harry had died fifteen years ago. Now there was I informing her that I knew him and believed that Sir James had recognised him last time he was in London. Whether they met I do not know, because Harry disappeared and Sir James died unexpectedly.'

'I believe Father was murdered,' said Rosamund. 'And I believe my stepmother had Harry abducted.'

Lady Elizabeth drummed her fingers on the arm of her chair. 'This is all too much for me to make sense of right now. I do know that woman was ambitious for those sons of hers and gave the elder an exalted idea of himself. I remember thinking that they should be stopped. You know what this means?' she said breathlessly. 'Harry is the rightful heir and can evict that woman from Appleby Manor and get rid of the sons, as well. We have to find him.'

Alex smiled. 'Of course.' He glanced at Rosamund. 'My hope is that he is plying his trade in the ship my grandfather bequeathed him when he died.'

'You did not tell me that your grandfather willed my brother a ship,' said Rosamund, startled.

Lady Elizabeth let out a cackle. 'Good for Harry. The Baron must have thought well of him. Let us hope he will soon return. In the meantime I will mention this whole affair to my kinsman when we are at Richmond,' she wheezed, nodding her head vigorously and then groaning and holding it with both hands. 'You and I have matters to discuss, Baron. Rosamund, you must be weary after so much travelling. I will have a maid show you to a bedchamber. You must rest and will be summoned when the midday meal is ready.'

Rosamund felt she had been summarily dismissed, having noted that her godmother had called Master Nilsson Baron again. She supposed it was possible that at her age and in her state of health that she was confusing him with his grandfather, the baron. She wondered what the business was that they needed to discuss. The purchase of more amber jewellery, perhaps? She left them alone and went upstairs with the maid.

Lady Elizabeth leaned back in her chair and closed her eyes. 'So, Baron, your natural father wants my help,' she murmured.

'Aye.' Alex stared at her with a mixture of sympathy and exasperation, wondering what his father was thinking of when he suggested this interesting, but sick, old lady as a fellow conspirator. 'Have you ever met him? He said you are kin by marriage to the wife of one of his allies.'

'Cicely. She married Lord Mackillin. Like me, they are getting old,' she said mournfully.

'You are not too old to help ensure future peace between Scotland and England,' said Alex politely.

She opened her eyes and leaning forward, patted his knee. 'It was your grandfather who told me that Earl Douglas was your natural father. He was proud of you and often spoke of your sense of diplomacy and your courage.' Her voice was barely above a whisper. 'He is a loss to me, but I presume you will settle down soon and take the reins of the business into your own hands?'

'Eventually,' he said after a moment's hesitation. 'Right now it is my plan to prevent members of certain clans from destroying the proposed alliance between England and Scotland. I was interested to hear you say that your god-daughter's stepmother was a McDonald. We must keep our eyes and ears open and ensure that any plot they might conjure up will be thwarted. It is possible they will enlist those Englishmen who wish King Henry's rule to fail.'

'Sons whose fathers supported the Yorkist cause and whose lands were taken from them when Richard was defeated at Bosworth,' whispered Elizabeth. 'Young lords of noble birth who will have pledged their allegiance to Henry, not only to regain some part of their father's lands, but to be in a position where they know what is happening at court. I have one such lord amongst my troupe of dancers. I am not saying he will turn traitor, but it may serve you to have him watched.'

'His name?' asked Alex, his eyes narrowing.

'Lord Bude. He is fair-haired and handsome like you, but younger.'

'You will introduce us?'

'Of a certainty.' She smiled. 'I will introduce you to the troupe this afternoon. My health is not good, as you can see, but I will manage the steps as long as you follow my lead and do not rush me.'

Alex would have needed to be blind and deaf not to have noticed she had difficulty breathing and could not conceal his concern. 'You do not have to do this, Lady Elizabeth. I deem that your goddaughter could be of use to us.'

Her smile faded. 'I will not have her putting her life at risk. Do not stop me playing my part just because I am old and ill. I would gladly die in the service of my country. Now, I would appreciate your help in getting up from this chair and out of this hall.'

He did as she requested and she clung to his arm as they crossed the hall to the door. 'I suspect I do not have much longer to live,' she gasped, 'that is why I wanted to see Rosamund while I was staying at Lathom House.' Her expression was wistful. 'Unfortunately I caught a chill and could not leave the house. I would that I—I had made the effort sooner, but her father never approved of me.' She paused. 'I need to retire to my bedchamber for a while and take the potion that my physician prescribes. I must rest if I am to initiate you into the dance this afternoon.' They paused in the entrance. 'You will stay here, of course, Baron, until we leave for Richmond.'

'I will happily do so,' said Alex gravely. 'It has occurred to me that Mistress Appleby's stepmother might visit Lathom House and ask whether her stepdaughter left for

London in your company. She will receive a negative reply, but she still might decide that her stepdaughter has followed you to London. It is possible that she will travel south herself to inform her elder son that Rosamund has escaped. It is likely that he might reason that she will have come here.'

Lady Elizabeth gave him an exhausted look. 'You are suggesting that either or both of them might present themselves at my door. The nerve of that woman! What is her son's name? I have forgotten.'

'Edward Fustian. He is a member of the Royal Company of Mercers.'

'I will warn the servants not to allow either of them entry.'

'I would go further and have them deny that either of us have been here,' said Alex, grim-faced. 'I do not want him to know just yet that I am acquainted with either you or Mistress Appleby.'

'You will be our secret weapon,' she chuckled conspiratorially.

'Aye.'

Alex noticed a couple of servants approaching and was relieved to hand over their mistress to her maid. As he went upstairs with the male servant, he thought how he and Rosamund had managed to escape being questioned by her ladyship about how they had travelled to London and in whose company, although the sick woman might yet still do so. He and Rosamund should have discussed their answers further, but it was too late to do so now.

Rosamund wasted no time joining her godmother at the table in her parlour when the summons to the midday meal came. She felt rested and was eager to get to know Lady Elizabeth whilst the opportunity was available. No mention had been made about Rosamund travelling to Richmond with the other two, so she could only presume that she would stay here at her godmother's mansion in London.

'I hope you do not mind eating in here, my dear,' said Lady Elizabeth, 'but it is much warmer than the hall and easier for the servants.'

'I do not mind at all,' said Rosamund, smiling across the table. 'I hope you are feeling better.' It was hard to tell by looking at her painted face.

Lady Elizabeth's eyes smiled at her goddaughter. 'I feel better for seeing you, my dear. Tell me, what do you think of the Baron? An interesting, attractive man, is he not? He will make some fortunate woman an excellent husband.'

Rosamund's smile faded. *So Master Nilsson was definitely a baron like his grandfather before him.* 'I suppose he would. But why do you mention this to me?' she asked casually.

Lady Elizabeth did not immediately reply, but leaned forward and seized her goddaughter's arm with a claw-like hand. 'How old are you, Rosamund? I'm afraid I have forgotten what year you were born.'

'Two-and-twenty,' she answered.

Her godmother sighed. 'I thought as much. Of course, you are old enough to find a husband for yourself, but in the circumstances you could do with a little help.'

'Why do we talk of husbands?' asked Rosamund, her mind in a whirl. 'Has he spoken to you about my needing to get married?'

'Certainly not!' Her godmother looked at her keenly.

'Why didn't your father choose a husband for you years ago, when you were in the first bloom of womanhood?'

'I deem he believed my stepmother when she told him I was mad,' said Rosamund sadly. 'She wanted me to marry Edward, but thankfully, Father would not allow it. As for William, he said that no man would want to marry me. Not only was I ugly, but I was too much of a bad bargain for any man to take on.'

'What wicked things to say to you, my dear, and not true,' said Lady Elizabeth indignantly. 'Well, you've escaped them now and you will marry.'

'No. You must not concern yourself,' said Rosamund hastily. 'Besides, I have no dowry.'

'No dowry! Does the Baron know this?'

Rosamund stiffened. 'I do not remembering raising the matter with him. Why should I?'

'Because he is your best prospect. He does not need the money, but with a dowry you will not feel like a beggar maid when you accept him. I will send for my lawyer instantly and he will deal with this matter of a dowry before we leave for Richmond.'

Rosamund was stunned. 'No! You must not do this. I do not wish to marry and, even if I did, I have decided that I will wait until Harry's return before doing so,' she added rashly.

Lady Elizabeth gave her a shrewd look. 'Has the Baron compromised you, my dear?'

Rosamund gasped. 'Certainly not! How can you suggest such a thing? The Baron is an honourable man.'

Her godmother's eyes wore a satisfied expression. 'So he has proposed marriage to you?'

'I did not say that!'

'No, you did not, but I can imagine that he is determined that you will not suffer by your both succumbing to temptation. I do not blame you for being charmed by him. He is just like his grandfather, irresistible.'

'No! It was not like that at all,' cried Rosamund, jumping to her feet. 'I am chaste.'

A spasm twisted Lady Elizabeth's face and she removed her hairpiece and scratched her almost-bald pate. Rosamund could only stare at her. 'Close your mouth, dear. You look like a fish,' said her godmother, replacing her wig. 'So he asked you to marry him and you tell me you are chaste.' Her tone was thoughtful.

Rosamund was angry and embarrassed and attempted to change the direction of the conversation. 'It was extremely rude of me to stare at you in such an ill-bred manner.' Her voice was terse.

'No more than I was in removing my wig in your company, but it itches so at times and that makes my head ache even worse.' Lady Elizabeth paused. 'Don't be angry with me, my dear. I am only interested in your well-being. I did, after all, notice that neither of you arrived with servants, nor did you mention having company on the road. In the circumstances, you would be a fool to refuse him.'

Rosamund clenched her fists. 'He has not asked me to marry him and there is no need for him to marry me. I am chaste and I do not wish to marry him.'

'Why not? He is rich, handsome and charming.'

'Because…' Rosamund's voice trailed off. She could not tell her godmother that the Baron was in love with another woman. Most likely she would not believe her.

'I understand,' said Lady Elizabeth, shaking her head.

'Young women are always full of romantic notions. You wish to be wooed.'

Rosamund had not thought of that as a reason for refusing the Baron's proposal, but now she decided that it was as good a one as any other, so she acknowledged there was some truth in Lady Elizabeth's words.

Her godmother nodded. 'You must come with us to Richmond Palace for the celebrations. There should be time enough there for the Baron to woo you in the proper style.'

Chapter Eight

A thrill raced through Rosamund at the thought of being wooed by the Baron. 'You mean I can accompany you to the royal palace without prior permission?'

Lady Elizabeth gave a laugh that sounded like rustling dry leaves. 'I am related to the royal family and they are accustomed to my starts and fancies. In truth, they consider me a little mad at times and I would not deny that on occasions a certain mood takes me and—' Her expression changed. 'Here comes the Baron! He really is a fine figure of a man. I have not told you, but my troupe of players are all noble men and women. It is as the queen requested.' She hailed Alex. 'Come, sit with my goddaughter. I have decided that Rosamund will accompany us to Richmond.'

Rosamund watched his face to see if he was pleased or not, but he wore that bland expression that made his thoughts unreadable. What would he think if he knew about their earlier conversation?

'I already had it in mind that Mistress Appleby should accompany us,' said Alex, seating himself at the head of the table between the two women. 'She will be much safer at Richmond.'

'Good. I am glad we agree,' said Lady Elizabeth placidly. 'Here comes our meal.'

Rosamund knew that she should be relieved that her godmother and the Baron were in agreement. Yet now she felt oddly put out by the fact she appeared to have no say in what should happen to her with these two people for whom she had strong feelings. She watched as the servants began to serve boiled hare in a sauce that proved to be made from ale, pepper, bread and onions.

Lady Elizabeth began to separate the meat from the bones. 'My dears, I am thinking that God granted me ten extra years of life so that I could be of help to you both.' She broke off for several moments and Rosamund held her breath, thinking that her godmother might be about to reveal all to the Baron. Instead she continued with a change of subject. 'I hope you are both hungry. I asked for *toste rialle* to be made for pudding. No doubt you have tasted it, Baron. I first did so in Calais.' She signalled to the servant to pour the wine and drank off a draught all in one go.

'What is *toste rialle*?' asked Rosamund, thinking she could not help but be fascinated by all that her godmother did. How could she down her wine so swiftly when there were times when she seemed hardly able to breathe?

'It is a paste of sugar, spices and sweet wine,' said Alex, smiling at Rosamund as the lady paused to wipe her chin with her napkin.

'There is more to it than that,' said Lady Elizabeth, 'there is quince, raisins, nuts and flour spread hot over white bread and sprinkled with sugar.' She smacked her lips.

'It sounds delicious,' said Rosamund, quite affected by the Baron's smile.

Lady Elizabeth nodded. 'I want you to have some pleasure in life, Rosamund dear, because I fear you have been dreadfully unhappy. That is why you must marry a rich man.'

Alex almost choked on a morsel of meat and had to wait for the coughing to subside before saying, 'You have been discussing marriage with Mistress Appleby?'

'Aye. I have decided what she needs is a childless widower,' said the lady.

Rosamund stared at her in astonishment.

'I do not agree,' said Alex, putting down his knife. 'I wonder at your making such a pronouncement, Lady Elizabeth.'

'I shall tell you why,' wheezed the lady. 'I was younger than Rosamund when my parents chose a much older man for me. My head was full of nonsense. I was convinced I would be happier with a young, brave knight in shining armour. I wept on my wedding night. But when George died I inherited all his money and was still young enough to enjoy being rich.' She beamed at them both.

'It is vital that a man should be able to support his future wife, but there should be affection and respect and trust in a marriage,' said Alex, glancing at Rosamund before giving Lady Elizabeth his attention once more. 'You were obviously not happy living with your husband if you set about enjoying yourself once he was dead.'

'I agree with the Baron,' said Rosamund bravely.

'You feel like that because you are young, my dears,' mumbled Lady Elizabeth through a mouthful of food. 'Your blood gets heated and it is lust that drives you, not wisdom.'

Rosamund felt her cheeks burning and quickly lowered her gaze to her platter. What would her godmother say next? She hoped the Baron did not think that she had poured out all that had happened between them to Lady Elizabeth.

'You embarrass Mistress Appleby,' hissed Alex.

'If my goddaughter is to marry, Baron, then she needs to know what to expect when bedded by a young man driven by his animal passions. That is, if she does not know already.'

There was a whimpering sound from Rosamund.

'You will stop this,' said Alex in a furious whisper. 'Are you mad?'

'I do not mean to offend, Baron, but I suggest you remember your manners, too,' said the old lady, giving her attention to her dinner. 'You are a guest in my house and should not speak to me in such a way. I understand you are under a great strain and I will forgive you and say no more. Now, let us eat up this good food.'

Alex wondered what she meant by his being under a great strain, but at least she was as good as her word and did not speak again. But she had created an atmosphere that made him reluctant to break the silence. What had Rosamund been saying to her? Had she lied about what had taken place on their journey to London? He felt so angry that he was tempted to storm out of the parlour and go to stay with Walther and Maud. He glared at Rosamund, who flushed to the roots of her hair, but there was an expression in her lovely eyes that kept him glued to his seat.

Rosamund was all of a-quiver, remembering how she had felt when she and the Baron were caught in that forced embrace in the snow. Were her feelings then love or lust? What was he thinking? It was obvious he was angry and she did not blame him. No doubt he would never ask her to marry him and she realised that she might just enjoy finding out about love in his arms. This despite his having deceived her about his station in life.

By the time the meat course was cleared away and the dessert placed in front of them, Alex and Rosamund had calmed down a little and were able to enjoy the delicious confection set before them. More wine was poured and comments made about the food and weather. Rosamund asked when the troupe would be arriving.

'They will soon be here, as will the musicians,' said Lady Elizabeth. 'You must come and watch the Baron being taught his steps. I swear he will be in trouble if he treads on my toes.'

The words had scarcely left Lady Elizabeth's lips when a servant came hurrying into the hall and whispered in her ear. No sooner had the meal been cleared away than a young woman entered the hall, carrying a black-and-silver gown over her arm. Her eyes alighted on Lady Elizabeth and she hurried over to her. She was followed by several other young men and women. The women reminded Rosamund of butterflies because their skirts fluttered and they were dressed in a variety of colours.

'Lady Elizabeth, I bring bad tidings,' trilled the first woman. 'Lady Joan cannot join us. She has caught a fever and is abed. She begs your pardon for disappointing you.'

Elizabeth uttered a *tsk* of annoyance before saying, 'Poor Lady Joan, I hope she will soon be well. It does make matters awkward. The figures will not be right for the dance and we have so little time to find someone else to take her place. The Baron here will partner me.'

The group stared at Alex and one of the ladies smiled. 'Introduce us, Lady Elizabeth.'

'This is Baron Dalsland from Sweden. His grandfather was a great friend of mine and brought me many precious jewels from his country,' said Lady Elizabeth.

'Has he danced before?' said another lady with bold eyes.

'But of course,' said Alex, smiling down at her. 'I would be of little use as a replacement if I could not.'

'I will take you in hand,' said the bold-eyed lady.

Rosamund, sitting on a chair in front of the fire, watched this light flirtation with startled eyes and more than a little annoyance.

'That will be unnecessary,' said Lady Elizabeth firmly. 'I will allow no dalliance during the dance. I have said that I will partner the Baron.'

'What about this young lady?' asked one of the men, noticing Rosamund.

'Oh, I cannot dance,' she said hastily.

He laughed. 'I do not believe that is true. Everyone can dance.'

'Not me,' said Rosamund firmly.

All attention was now on Rosamund. 'I could teach you,' said the fair-haired man who had spoken. 'The steps are not so difficult and you could fill Lady Joan's place. We do not have to perform for another three days, so you could perfect the steps in no time. May I introduce myself? I am Lord Bude.'

Rosamund could not resist looking at Alex to see what he thought of the young man's suggestion. He was frowning. Obviously, he believed she was not good enough to dance with an English lord before royalty.

'I deem it a wonderful notion,' said Lady Elizabeth, much to Rosamund's surprise. 'May I introduce my goddaughter, Mistress Rosamund Appleby, lords and ladies. Her parents are dead and she has recently come to live with me.'

The party eyed Rosamund with as much interest as they had the Baron. The lady who had broken the news about Lady Joan, said, 'It is fate! You are of the same height and have the same colouring as Lady Joan, Mistress Appleby, and, as Lord Bude has said, the steps are not difficult.'

Alex wanted to disagree. Bude was the name Lady Elizabeth had mentioned earlier as a man who might possibly turn traitor. He was obviously of a flirtatious manner; if he was as poor as her ladyship had said, then he would be on the lookout for a wealthy heiress. Perhaps he thought Rosamund might inherit her godmother's fortune. How was Alex to know that her head would not be turned by this handsome young lord? He could not allow that to happen.

But before Alex could make a move on the young lord, one of the ladies approached him.

'I know something of your homeland, Baron,' she said. 'I admired Lady Elizabeth's amber jewellery and she told me it was made in Sweden. I asked my father if he would buy me such a set, but he refused. He said I needed a rich husband if I wanted such trinkets.'

'Hardly a trinket, Margaret, if your father cannot afford such jewellery,' said one of the other ladies. 'It must be worth a fortune.'

'Enough!' said Lady Elizabeth, clapping her hands. 'We are here to dance. My goddaughter will attempt to fill Lady Joan's position.'

Rosamund opened her mouth to say that she had not agreed, but it was too late. Already Lord Bude was reaching for her hand and her godmother was nodding in her direction. 'You had best try on Lady Joan's costume this evening in case it needs altering, Rosamund, my dear. We will walk through the dance several times to give you and the Baron a chance to familiarise yourselves with the steps without the music.'

Rosamund took a deep breath as Lord Bude's soft, white hand clasped hers. 'Now pay attention, Mistress Rosamund,' he said in her ear. 'No one expects you to be as good as the rest of us, but no doubt your pretty face will make up for any faults.'

Immediately Rosamund wanted to tug her hand out of his grasp and resume her seat by the fire, but the other dancers were already calling out instructions. She did her best to comply with what they said, but there were too many voices telling her what to do and she stepped on Bude's toes more than once.

She glanced up at him, apologizing, and instantly was aware that his eyes were gazing down her cleavage. She lost all desire to do well and made a complete mess of the steps when the music began and she was supposed to dance in earnest. It was a relief when the wheezing Lady Elizabeth eventually signalled a halt.

Concerned about her, Alex led her over to the settle and made her sit down. She whispered to him to tell the others that there would be another rehearsal tomorrow evening at Richmond. He did so.

The musicians and dancers departed, chorusing their farewells. Only Lord Bude lingered. 'Perhaps I could give you a private lesson this evening,' he suggested, taking one of Rosamund's hands and kissing it.

'I think not, Lord Bude,' said Alex, removing Rosamund's hand from the other man's grasp. 'Mistress Appleby has had a long journey and needs her rest.'

Bude scowled. 'Surely Mistress Appleby can make her own decisions? I really don't see what it has to do with you, Baron?'

'But that is because you are unaware that the lady and I are betrothed,' said Alex politely.

Only by a blinking of the eyes did Rosamund betray that she was more surprised than Bude to hear those words. His lordship muttered an apology and with a terse good night left the hall.

'Why did you tell him that we were betrothed?' demanded Rosamund, as soon as Bude was out of earshot.

Alex was asking himself the same question. It would have been wiser if he had allowed Rosamund to encourage Bude to discover if he had any dealings with those with treacherous intent. 'He is a fortune-hunter,' snapped Alex. 'Do not take what I said to heart. I still have no intention of getting married until I am thirty.'

A sharp laugh escaped Rosamund. 'Then you should have remained silent. You are forgetting that not only do you wish to be avenged on my brother, but also that I have no fortune.'

'He knows that Lady Elizabeth is extremely wealthy and that you, her goddaughter, have recently come to live with her. It is obvious Bude smells money when he looks at you.'

Two spots of colour appeared high on Rosamund's cheeks and she tugged her hand free. 'You are insulting. Did you not consider he might find me comely?'

'Bude cannot afford to be swayed solely by a lovely face,' he said harshly.

'Why should I believe you? He is a lord of the realm, whilst you are a foreigner, unable to trust me with your real identity.'

Alex realised that he had hurt her and his voice was gentler when he said, 'I did not trust those lords and ladies with it either.'

She frowned. 'You mean you are not a Baron?'

'Ach! I have that title in my own country. I inherited it from my grandfather, as well as his estate and his business.' He hesitated. 'But I have another name that my father gave me and it is not Nilsson.'

'Are you going to tell me it?'

Alex hesitated. 'Why do you think I am here, Rosamund?'

Her eyes darkened. 'I am in no mood for guessing games,' she said shortly. 'If you are already rich, then I presume it simply amuses you to entertain and to spy on people.' She turned away from him and went over to the chair where Lady Joan's costume had been placed and picked it up.

'Come here, if you please,' said Alex quietly.

She glanced at him and he smiled at her in such a way that her heart seemed to move inside her. 'Give me a reason why I should, Baron?'

He walked slowly towards her and stopped a few inches away. 'If you want to perform before the King and Queen, then perhaps you should practise the steps one more time.'

His closeness was having a strange effect on her. 'You mean with you?' Her voice sounded husky.

'Why not?' He took the costume from her and placed it

on the chair. Then he reached for her hand and clasped it firmly. 'One always starts with the left foot,' he said. 'There are four double forwards and then we face each other and drop hands. Double steps back, and then forwards. Let us do that and then we'll try the next part.'

At first she could not concentrate and she muffed her steps and her fingers trembled in his grasp. 'Relax, Rosamund,' he murmured against her hair. 'This is not a matter of life and death. You are meant to find pleasure in the dance.' She nodded and tried to concentrate on her steps and not on the effect he was having on her. 'That's better,' he said. 'Now we do a quarter-turn left and then double forwards, turn right around and double forward back to where we began.'

Rosamund followed his lead and eventually managed the steps without watching her feet. They came to a halt and she laughed. 'I can do this.'

'Of course you can,' said Alex, grinning.

'What next?'

'We now face our partner as we are doing and I turn on the spot. Then you do the same.' She did so and then he took both her hands and they slip-stepped up the hall.

'I think I remember what comes next,' said Rosamund, and proved she did.

Laughing, they came to a halt. 'Ach! That was good,' said Alex. 'You make an excellent dancer when you stop worrying.'

'Thank you.' Rosamund's eyes were luminous as she looked up into his face.

Suddenly, as if drawn together by an invisible cord, they moved closer until their bodies touched. Gently at first they kissed. Rosamund had never enjoyed anything so much and did not want him to let her go. Then a snore that turned into a wheezing cough caused them to spring apart.

'I must go,' murmured Alex, so aroused that he knew that if he did not cool down then he would not be able to answer for the consequences. He made for the door, only to be stopped by Lady Elizabeth's breathless voice.

'I have been thinking, Rosamund, that I would like to see you married before I die.'

Alex turned and looked at Rosamund and then at the white-painted face staring at them both over the back of the settle. Lady Elizabeth smiled grotesquely. 'What say you to an official betrothal before we leave for Richmond, Baron?' she gasped. 'My lawyer will be here soon. He is to make provision for a dowry for my goddaughter and could draw up a betrothal agreement at the same time.'

Alex walked slowly over to the settle. 'You overheard what I said to Bude? You were only pretending to have dozed off?'

'I cannot sleep without my potion, for I can scarcely breathe,' panted Lady Elizabeth. 'I would like to see Rosamund's child born before I—'

'What child?' asked Alex, frowning.

'There is no child,' cried Rosamund, going over to her godmother.

'There could be,' said Lady Elizabeth in a faint voice.

Alex's eyes narrowed. 'Enough of such talk. You should be in bed.' He went over to the settle and scooped the old woman up into his arms. 'Rosamund, open the door,' he commanded.

She hastened to do his bidding, wondering what the

Baron was making of all this talk of a child. Before she could ask if he knew where her godmother's bedchamber was, her maid suddenly appeared.

'What has happened?' she asked anxiously.

'Lady Elizabeth has over-exerted herself,' said Alex. 'Lead the way to her bedchamber and we will follow.'

The maid nodded and almost ran in her haste to reach her ladyship's bedchamber that was fortunately on the ground floor. Once there, she drew back the bedcovers and Alex laid her ladyship down.

'Bring me my potion, Hannah,' gasped Lady Elizabeth, her eyes rolling in her head. 'And, Rosamund, you stay with me.'

The maid hurried out.

Rosamund glanced at Alex, who was standing the other side of the bed. She knew this was not the right time to try to explain to him her godmother's conviction that he had seduced her on the journey to London.

'Sitting up will improve Godmother's breathing. You hold her whilst I pile up the pillows behind her.'

There was much Alex wanted to ask Rosamund, but knew it would have to wait. He moved swiftly to comply with her request and watched Rosamund deftly heap several pillows behind her godmother. Then he eased her gently against them and Rosamund tucked in the bed-clothes so that she was snug and warm. Then she drew up a chair and sat beside the bed and took one of her god-mother's hands in hers.

'Should we send for your physician?' she asked.

Lady Elizabeth moved her head slightly from side to side and closed her eyes. 'Send for the priest,' she whispered.

Rosamund's heart sank. She did not want to believe

that she was about to lose her godmother when she had scarcely had a chance to get to know her. She glanced at the Baron's stern face, but before she could even ask, he was on his way.

To her relief he was not gone long.

'It is done,' he said, wondering if it was his imagination that her ladyship's breathing seemed a little easier now. He hated to see anyone suffer in such a way and walked over to the window and gazed out. He remained there, thinking about what Lady Elizabeth had said about Rosamund's child. He did not want to believe that she was not the innocent he considered her to be. She had insisted there was no child. But if that was true, then why did her godmother believe there could be? Was he missing a trick here?

He glanced towards the bed and caught Rosamund staring at him. *What was she asking of him?* He turned away and gazed out of the window, wondering with part of his mind if the lawyer would arrive at the same time as the priest. If Lady Elizabeth's condition worsened, then what was Alex to do? She had obviously decided that he was the husband she wanted for her goddaughter. If she was dying, would she expect a wedding instead of a betrothal? This had never been part of his plan when he had agreed to do what his natural father had asked.

Hannah reappeared, carrying a golden goblet on a salver. Alex turned and watched the maid and Rosamund help Lady Elizabeth to drink the potion. Would it ease her suffering and enable her to live a while longer? He could only pray it would be so. They eased Lady Elizabeth back against the pillows and watched her close her eyes.

Rosamund sat back in the chair and took her god-mother's hand in hers once more. She was aware that her godmother's breathing was still audible, making almost a whistling sound. But hopefully the potion and rest would improve her condition. She glanced over at Alex; as if sensing her eyes were on him, he turned. But he did not have a smile for her. Could the kisses they had shared mean so little to him? Did he believe in this mythical child and that she had been impregnated by someone else? She watched him go over to the maid and speak to her, then the maid left the room.

Alex resumed his watch at the window, but his body was turned slightly towards Rosamund. He was remembering how much he desired her and how he had compromised her. She was Harry's sister! Were these three things reason enough for him to suggest making an old lady die happy and for him to possibly father another man's child? Maybe her stepbrother's?

But before he could make a decision, a slurred voice from the bed said, 'I was thinking, if you are both willing you could marry, instead of getting betrothed. The priest would say the words over you for the bequest of a tidy sum for his church.'

Her words caused Rosamund's heart to begin to thud in her breast. She did not want the Baron to be forced into marrying her. 'You are not going to die, Godmother,' she said, a quiver in her voice.

'You cannot guarantee that, my dear,' gasped Lady Elizabeth. 'You are not the Almighty. Is it that you would refuse a dying woman and a fortune?'

'I do not want your money,' said Rosamund quietly. 'But I would make you happy.'

Lady Elizabeth said, 'Good. What do you say, Baron? Or is it that you were only toying with my goddaughter's affections?'

'No!' cried Rosamund.

Alex darted a glance at her and for a moment their eyes met and he knew what his answer was going to be. 'I will ignore that slur on my honour, Lady Elizabeth, and I will take your goddaughter as my wife.' He might not love or trust her completely, but he did believe that if there was a child then Fustian had raped her. He felt sick at the thought.

'No slur was intended, Baron,' gasped Lady Elizabeth. 'As soon as Master Jamieson and Father Thomas arrive, they are to be brought here.'

'It will be done, Lady Elizabeth.' Alex's voice was calm despite his racing heart. It was possible that tonight he and Rosamund would be husband and wife. He gave his attention to the view from the window once more.

Chapter Nine

Alex did not have long to wait before noticing a soberly dressed man of middle years and a younger man Alex presumed was his clerk approaching. He informed her ladyship and she asked him to go and greet them and explain the situation.

No sooner had he gone than Rosamund became aware that her godmother seemed to have gone off into a doze. She felt nervous, hoping this was not the prelude to a deeper sleep. The room was quiet, except for the sound of the sick woman's laboured breathing. Rosamund wished that she and her godmother could have met years ago when she was younger and in good health. It seemed an age before Hannah entered the bedchamber with a flagon of wine and a branch of lighted candles. She placed the candelabra on a table close to the bedside before pouring some wine for Rosamund.

Alex entered the bedchamber a few moments later with the lawyer and his clerk. They were followed almost immediately by the priest. From the lawyer's demeanour, it was obvious to Rosamund that Alex had explained all that was needful. As for the priest, he approached the side of the bed opposite to the lawyer. Instantly, Rosamund rose and gave up her seat to him. She moved over to the window with her goblet of wine, aware that Alex stayed by the bed. Obviously, he intended not missing a word said between her godmother, the lawyer and the priest.

Indeed, that was Alex's intention and he could not help thinking that he and his father had not reckoned on this happening when they had made their plans that had involved Lady Elizabeth. Still, he was determined to ensure that her wishes were carried out where Rosamund was concerned.

He looked around for her and saw that she had gone over to the window and was gazing outside. Her face looked drawn and sad and he wanted to crush Fustian beneath his heel. He prayed that her godmother would live long enough to enable them to plight their troth.

Two hours later, Alex knew that he need not have doubted her ladyship's staying power. As soon as he and Rosamund had spoken the words that would bind them together until death, her ladyship had beckoned Hannah over and mouthed that she must serve wine to all those present. Then she reached out a hand to the newly married couple and congratulated them. 'I hope you will have many happy years ahead of you,' she whispered.

Tears trickled down Rosamund's cheeks as she thanked her godmother. It was difficult to believe that she and the Baron were wed. She found herself twisting her godmother's silver-and-amber ring around her finger in an agitated manner. Tonight would be her wedding night. But even as the thought made her feel apprehensive and excited at the same time, she realised that it was unlikely that she and her new husband would have the opportunity to share a bed that night. How could they both leave her godmother when she lay dying?

The lawyer drank his wine and said he would send his clerk with the papers in the morning for her ladyship. The priest said he would come back later as he had a mass to conduct. Alex saw them out and then returned to the bed-chamber where Rosamund had resumed her place at her godmother's side. She rose when he entered the room. 'What do you wish me to do, husband?' she asked, looking docile.

He was suspicious of such meekness. 'What I wish and what I must do are in conflict with each other,' he said, frowning. 'We must take turns to sit with her during the night.'

'Shall I take the first watch?' asked Rosamund.

'Aye. I will partake of supper and then I will come and relieve you, so you can dine.'

'I am not hungry,' said Rosamund.

His frown deepened. 'You must eat to keep up your strength. It will not do for you to be ill,' he rasped.

'Then I will eat,' she said, wondering about the depth of his concern.

'Good,' he said, and left the bedchamber.

Rosamund returned to her post, but this time she knelt at the bedside and prayed not only for her godmother, but her new husband and herself, as well as Harry. Then she sat back on the chair and, as Lady Elizabeth appeared to be sleeping, Rosamund allowed her mind to wander. She did not need a title, especially a foreign one. How did a

Swedish baroness behave? How should she address her new husband, by his title or—by the name he had spoken in the brief service? Alexander. Was that his real name? She wondered if they were legally married if he had not used his proper one. Had the Baron considered such a possibility so he could have the marriage annulled?

Suddenly she was remembering her dream last night. How long ago it seemed now and yet she could recall it vividly. At least it had not been a premonition. The Baron had not turned into her stepbrother during the wedding ceremony. She experienced a cold feeling in her belly simply by thinking of Edward.

She stood up and went over to the window and saw that it was almost pitch-black outside. On such a night might murder be done. She shivered. What was she doing thinking such thoughts? She drew the curtains and returned to her godmother's bedside.

Shortly after the Baron entered the bedchamber and asked if there was any change in Lady Elizabeth's condition. Rosamund shook her head. 'My fear is that this sleep might be one from which she will not wake,' she whispered. 'But she is in God's hands and we must trust that He will do what is best for her.'

'If she recovers this time, it would make sense if she stopped painting her face,' said Alex.

'Perhaps you should suggest it to her, husband,' said Rosamund, lifting limpid eyes to him.

He stared at her fixedly. 'You are her goddaughter. It is probably more fitting if the suggestion came from you.'

'I doubt she will listen to me as she is accustomed to

having her own way. She was so looking forward to attending the celebrations at Richmond and so was I,' said
Rosamund softly. 'I suppose it will be out of the question
going there now.' She stood up. 'You will wake me if I fall
asleep so I can keep my watch, won't you?'

He inclined his head. 'Of course! But go now and eat
and rest.'

Rosamund nodded. She kissed her godmother's cheek
and reluctantly went to eat her lonely supper.

Alex took her place at the side of the bed. He had no intention of waking his wife if she were to fall asleep. *His
wife!* It felt odd saying those two little words, but they did
mean that he now had the right to protect her. But what
about the child her godmother insisted that she was
carrying? The one Rosamund denied having conceived?
He was in a quandary because he could be completely
wrong about Fustian having raped her. But if he had done
so, then most likely she would find the sexual act repulsive. It made sense not to consummate the match just yet
until her condition was known. What if she was not to be
trusted and encouraged her stepbrother and all that she
had told him was false? He was weary and his head was
in a muddle. He settled himself in the chair for what would
surely be a long night.

Rosamund was tempted to disobey her husband and
return to her godmother's bedchamber after finishing her
supper. She did not wish to go to a lonely, cold bed where
no doubt her thoughts would guarantee she would be
unable to sleep. He had not wanted to marry her and
perhaps he thought that she had deliberately led her god-

mother astray in order to trap him. The notion made her feel angry, but thankfully, after a second goblet of wine, she could scarcely keep her eyes open. She made her way to her bedchamber and got into bed and instantly fell asleep.

Alex started awake. The hard lines of his body were tense—he had been dreaming of Rosamund. Despite the mask she wore, he was convinced it was his wife. Yet every time he drew closer to her, she retreated in a way that reminded him of the movements of the dance. Did this mean he was going to lose her? He rubbed his eyes and looked towards the bed. The candles in the candelabra had guttered out and dawn was not far off. He could see the outline of the lady in the bed and, *thank God*, she was still breathing. He stood up and stretched, wondering what had woken him. Perhaps a noise outside. Had the priest returned and not managed to rouse the house in order to gain entry?

He went over to the window and drew back the curtains and rubbed at the frost on the glass with his sleeve and peered out. He saw a slight, dark-haired figure hurrying in the direction of the stables. Immediately he thought the worst—Rosamund regretted the vows she had made last night and was running away. He had to rouse Hannah so she could sit with Lady Elizabeth whilst he went after his wife.

As he strode along the passage he could smell baking bread. When he reached the hall there was a serving wench sweeping the floor. He called to her and she came scurrying over to him and asked how was her ladyship.

'She is asleep, but I've had to leave her for the moment. Will you fetch Hannah to sit with her?' he asked.

'Aye, Baron!'

Alex left her and hurried to the stables where, to his relief, he discovered that his horse was still in its stall. He was returning to the house when he heard someone hail him. He turned and saw Rosamund.

'You did not send Hannah to wake me as you promised and I know the reason why.' She smiled faintly. 'You dozed off, so I let you sleep. Godmother's breathing sounded so much better that when I heard shouting outside I decided to investigate.'

'I saw you from the window and thought you were regretting last night and had decided to run away.'

She stiffened. 'Where would I run to? I see you still do not trust me. I am not so ungrateful towards Godmother or frightened of you that I would run away,' she said coldly and turned away.

'Forgive me! I woke suddenly and obviously I was not thinking rationally.' He reached out and touched her face. 'You are cold. You must get inside without delay.'

'And what of you?' asked Rosamund, warmed by that gesture. 'You must rest whilst I sit with Godmother.'

'Hannah is with her. You mentioned hearing shouting. Did you find out from whence it came?'

'No. I decided if anything untoward had happened, then the guards would have investigated.'

'You went as far as the gates?'

She shook her head. 'I did not want to be out too long.'

'Then I will go and speak to them after I have seen you to the house.'

'I can see myself indoors,' she replied. 'If you are concerned, go immediately.'

She turned away and hurried to her godmother's bedchamber, hoping that she would be no worse than when she had left her. To her delight she found that Lady Elizabeth was awake and speaking to Hannah. Instantly, she broke off from what she was saying and greeted her goddaughter.

'So there you are, my dear,' she gasped. 'I wondered where you and the Baron had gone.'

'I heard shouting, so I went outside to investigate,' said Rosamund. 'I did not see anyone, but the Baron is making a further search.' She smiled. 'How are you feeling now, Godmother? You sound so much better than you did last even.'

'I realise now that it was foolish of me to dance,' said Lady Elizabeth ruefully. 'If we are to go to Richmond, then I know I will have to be sensible.'

Rosamund was surprised. 'You are still considering attending the celebrations?'

'Of a surety. It could be the last time I have the opportunity to share in such an occasion.' Her voice was mournful.

'But won't you find the ride exhausting?' asked Rosamund with concern.

Her godmother shook her head and then had to straighten her wig. 'No. For I will travel by barge. You and the Baron may wish to ride,' she wheezed, resting against the pillows, 'and you may do so, for I am certain you have much to talk about and would prefer to be alone.'

Rosamund did not deny it. 'But who will take care of you?' she asked anxiously.

'My dear! I never travel anywhere without a whole host of servants. Hannah here will not leave my side.' Lady Elizabeth leaned over and patted the woman's arm.

'If you are certain that is your wish. When must we depart?'

'I must wait until my lawyer arrives. I gave him firm instructions that he must have his clerk and copyist prepare the documents for me to sign this morning,' said Lady Elizabeth.

Rosamund took her hand. 'I have not expressed my gratitude for your generous gift of a dowry. I do appreciate your kindness very much indeed.'

Lady Elizabeth smiled. 'I am glad you were sensible enough to fall in with my wishes by marrying the Baron. Now leave me alone for a while and send him to me as soon as he returns.'

Rosamund marvelled at her godmother's stamina, courage and determination. She kissed her cheek and left the bedchamber. There was no sign of the Baron in the parlour or the hall and so Rosamund went outside, thinking to give him the news of her godmother's decision, but he was nowhere in sight. She decided to put on her boots and a cloak and go as far as the gates.

On arriving at the gates Alex had found only one guard on duty. He was stamping his feet and blowing on his fingers and was a different man to either of those guarding the entrance yesterday.

The guard suddenly noticed him and said, 'Who goes there?'

'I am Baron Dalsland and I am a guest of Lady Elizabeth's,' said Alex.

'Ahh! You'll be the foreigner who came yesterday with her ladyship's goddaughter.' The guard's eyes were alight with curiosity. 'Rumour has it in the guardroom that you and the young lady were wed last night.'

Alex did not deny it.

'And is Lady Elizabeth in better health this morning?'

'I believe so.'

The guard grinned. 'It's not the first time she's had her lawyer and the priest out and us thinkin' she were on her death bed. Always manages to rally round so far.'

'I am pleased to hear it.' Alex asked the man whether anyone had come through the gates that morning or if he had seen anything suspicious during the night.

The man pursed his lips and scratched his head. 'Now there's a question. Josh, who's new and from the north, was checking the perimeter wall earlier. He said there were bits of mortar and brick dust on the ground, as well as a broken branch from a tree. It's as if someone had tried to breach the wall.'

'I'd like to speak to this Josh,' said Alex.

'He'll be here later,' said the man.

Alex thanked him and decided to take a walk and see for himself if aught of interest was happening at the Steel Yard or Fustian's house. Hopefully, by the time he returned, the other guard would be back on gate duty and he could have a word with him.

Rosamund arrived at the gates without seeing anyone. She hailed the guard on duty and asked if he had seen the Baron that morning.

'Aye, Baroness.' He looked at her with interest. 'The Baron, your husband, went out.'

Being addressed as Baroness gave Rosamund an odd

feeling and caused her to feel tied to the Baron in a way she had not done so far. Her dark brows knit and she gnawed on her lip, wondering where he could have gone. She thought of Ingrid and was suddenly uneasy.

'Ahhh! I remember where he was going now. I shall go and find him,' she said brightly, and slipped out of the gateway.

She noticed that there were several pairs of footprints in the snow and had no trouble distinguishing those of her husband's boots from the others. First, they were larger, second there was a jagged cut on the leather of the left one. She had noticed such marks when he had left footprints in the mud near a stream several times. It was also a fact that the footprints looked to be the freshest. She began to follow them and managed to do so all the way to a gateway in the Steel Yard, close to the quayside.

She drew her hood further over her head and gazed at the open gates. There were no guards and few people going in and out. Why had the Baron come here? Was it because he expected to find Ingrid here? She felt desolate and stood a moment, trying to decide what to do. The sun was rising in the sky and there was little heat in it, but maybe it was strong enough to soon melt the snow and destroy her husband's footprints. She made up her mind and headed for the gates.

Once inside, she saw that the Steel Yard was like a proper little village with workshops open for business, shops, houses and a church. Despite the earliness of the hour and the weather, there was much hustle and bustle going on inside, but when people called to each other it was as if she had stepped inside Babbel and she could not understand a word. Dismayed, she realised also that people's feet had already turned the snow into slush here and she no longer knew which direction her husband had taken.

Frustrated, she decided to make for the church to find some peace and pray. Once inside, she stood in the gloomy interior lit by a few candles and sent up a prayer. Then she made for the door, only to pause at the sound of voices. She could not make out what was being said, but one of them was definitely female. She melted into the shadows as two people appeared at the far end of the church. Her eyes caught the gleam of a man's fair head in the candlelight before he put on his hat. He had his back to her so that she could not see his face, but with a jerk of her heart, she realised there was something familiar about him. She heard the woman say something and, although, Rosamund had heard Ingrid speak only the once, she recognised that voice. Even as she stood there, she saw the woman draw the man's head down towards hers and they kissed.

Rosamund could not bear to watch them any longer and blundered out of the church, heedless of the noise she made. She ran towards the gates, sliding in the slushy snow and almost losing her balance a couple of times. She was aware that she drew attention to herself, but did not stop until she was through the gates and heading towards the Thames. There she stopped to catch her breath and gaze out over the river at a yellowy wintry sun reflecting on the surface.

How could Alex kiss Ingrid when only a few hours ago he had sworn fidelity to herself? He might have acted as if he hated the woman he believed to have betrayed him, but obviously the tidings that Rosamund had brought him yesterday had melted his fury, and he had not been able to resist her when he saw her again.

Tears filled Rosamund's eyes and trickled down her cheeks. She wiped them away fiercely with the back of her glove and began to trudge towards the Strand. She felt cheated and utterly miserable and kept her head down so no one could see her tears. She was within yards of the gates of her godmother's mansion when a hand seized her shoulder from behind. She tried to turn round, but that hand was relentless and its fingers bit into her flesh through her cloak and gown. A terrible fear seized her and she was unable to cry out for help as her hood was drawn back.

'So it is true,' hissed a hated voice against her ear. 'What a foolish woman you are! Will you never learn that you cannot escape your destiny? You were mad to believe you could. Accept, Rosie, that one day I will have you. You will be my slave and beg me to be merciful to you.'

'Let me go!' she gasped. 'You are too late!'

'You are talking of your betrothal to that Swedish fool. Don't get too fond of him, Rosie. He doesn't have much longer to live.'

Rosamund felt faint and struggled to stay conscious then suddenly she was free. She staggered and fell over in the snow. Edward's voice came to her on the breeze. 'I'll see you again soon, Rosie, and when I do there'll be no escaping me then.'

She tried to get up, but was trembling so much that her feet kept slipping. Then she heard a voice saying, 'Mistress Rosamund, are thee all right? That man! He reminded me of Master Fustian. What was going on there?' The next moment she was being lifted up by two strong arms and gazed in disbelief at the stocky young man staring anxiously into her face.

'Joshua, it can't be you! Oh, this is all too much.' She burst into tears.

Laughter rumbled deep in his throat. ''Tis me, and I'm right glad to see thee, Mistress Rosamund.'

She clutched his arm and smiled through her tears. 'I never thought I'd see you again. I feared that she might have done away with you.'

'Naw, Lady Monica just gave me my marching orders. If it weren't for thee, I'd have left when thy father died.'

'It's like a miracle,' she whispered. 'What are you doing here?'

'I'm one of Lady Elizabeth's guards.'

She gazed into Joshua's broad face with its broken nose and could not be more pleased. 'How did this happen?'

'When Lady Monica turned me off, I goes to the Earl of Derby and asks can he give me some paid labour. He had nuthin'!' Joshua pulled a face. 'But as luck would have it Lady Elizabeth was staying there with her entourage, so I got gabbing with me mate here.' He jerked his head in the direction of the other guard. 'He told me that one of the other men had taken ill and died. So I just stepped into his shoes.'

'I am so pleased,' said Rosamund, remembering how Joshua had grieved for Harry as much as she had done. She was about to tell him the news about her brother, when the other guard spoke up.

'I hate to remind yer, Josh,' he said, 'but this here lady's husband is the Baron. Best not be too familiar.'

'Lor! Thou's right, Will. I'd best be keeping me

distance.' Josh moved away from Rosamund to take up a position the other side of the gate.

She was now feeling extremely peculiar. She had run the gauntlet of so many differing emotions in the last hour that, having lost the support of Joshua's arm, she needed to rest a moment, so leaned against the gatepost.

'Surely we don't have to stand on ceremony, Josh? I'm still the same person you knew back at Appleby,' she said in a low voice.

'I doubt it, Mistress Rosamund. I mean, Baroness,' he said, standing at attention. 'For thee to be here means thee has changed.'

'I *don't* feel different towards you, but I suppose it is true that I have changed. At least the Baron believes so. I must tell you, though, that—' Her voice broke off at the sound of approaching footsteps. She began to tremble afresh. Was it her husband or her stepbrother returning?

The priest stopped and smiled at her. 'I saw your husband a short while ago, Baroness. He told me that Lady Elizabeth has survived the night.'

'Indeed,' said Rosamund, attempting to put some steel into her spine and a welcome in her voice. 'She opened her eyes and spoke to me and I am sure that she will be pleased to see you.'

'What a strong will she has, but she might yet have a relapse, so I must make haste and pray with her. You will accompany me?'

Rosamund glanced at Joshua, but he was staring straight ahead. She decided to tell him about Harry later. Her legs were feeling shaky, but she managed to walk beside the priest to the house. She lingered in her godmother's bedchamber only until the lawyer arrived. Then she asked to be excused and went upstairs to her bedchamber, where she collapsed on the bed.

She attempted to blank out all thought of the last hour, but it was impossible for her to do so. Her fear and pain was too great. Her husband loved another woman and her stepbrother had found her and was determined to punish her for running away. She thumped a fist into the pillow, thinking she would rather die than be taken by him again. But how had Edward discovered that she was here with the Baron? Had Ingrid told him? Had she had time? Thinking of her husband with her brought tears to Rosamund's eyes again.

Perhaps she should kill herself. Belladonna would do the trick. She gasped. What was she thinking of! What purpose would killing herself serve? She would fight them both, Edward and that woman who would steal her husband.

Chapter Ten

Rosamund sprang off the bed. She also had to consider Harry. She longed to see her brother again—what if he returned to England, only to be told that he'd had a sister, but she was dead. There was also Richmond to see! She was supposedly riding there with her new husband today. Was there any way she could escape being alone with him, knowing that he had betrayed her within less than a day of them plighting their troth? She felt that ache in the region of her heart again and determinedly tried to ignore it. Had she not survived years of lack of love and bullying? Why was she getting so fussed? Their wedding had taken place to please her godmother, so maybe she was expecting too much of him in wanting him to remain faithful. But the thought of him kissing another woman still hurt.

A sigh escaped her. She would go down and discuss the journey with her godmother. Pray God that she had not had a relapse and was well enough to go to Richmond. She hoped the gowns in her possession would be sufficient for her stay at the royal palace. She was apprehensive about what lay ahead. Presumably the troupe would still be part of the entertainment, but with her godmother no longer able to dance, would the Baron still take part? She remembered how much she had enjoyed dancing with him yesterday and the kisses they had shared. Obviously, they had not meant anything to him. It was then she recalled her godmother suggesting that she try on Lady Joan's costume. Would it be worth doing so? She would see if the gown was still on the chair in the hall because, if they were to go to Richmond, she would need to pack it.

Rosamund searched for the black-and-silver costume, but it was not there, so she hurried to her godmother's bedchamber and was pleased to find her sitting in a chair with a metal box on her knee. She marvelled at her powers of recovery.

'There you are, my dear,' wheezed Lady Elizabeth, closing the lid of the box and turning the key in the lock. 'Am I to presume that the Baron has not yet returned?'

'Aye. Surely he cannot be much longer?' said Rosamund brightly. 'He was not clad for outdoors. I hope he does not catch a chill.'

Her godmother smiled. 'You already sound like a wife. As soon as he returns you must have breakfast and set out for Richmond. I still have a few matters to deal with before I can leave. They will have made ready a suite of rooms for me and my entourage. In case I am delayed, I will write a message with instructions that you and the Baron are to have one of the finest bedchambers. After all, you were cheated of your wedding night,' she added with a twinkle in her eyes. 'Tonight I want all to go well for you both.'

'What if the Baron does not return?'

Lady Elizabeth's eyes clouded. 'Don't be gloomy, my

dear. I haven't gone to all this trouble to see you married to have my plans thwarted. If he has not returned within the hour, I will send some of the men to make a search for him. In the meantime, I will give orders to have my barge made ready. As long as there is no trouble with the tides or the river freezing over, then all will be well.'

'Perhaps I should travel by barge with you?'

Her godmother gave her a sharp look. 'There is no need for you to fear being alone with the Baron now you are married. He will take care of you as I intended.'

Rosamund was starting to wonder if her godmother's difficulty with breathing last evening had been feigned, but decided it was best not to speak her thoughts. She did not wish to disillusion the old lady about the man she put so much faith in. Instead, she said lightly, 'I had forgotten that the Thames was tidal.'

'It is, indeed, but we are miles from the sea. The horse ferry at Westminster will take you across to the south bank. Unless the weather worsens, the journey should only be of a few hours' duration. You will arrive there well before nightfall,' said Lady Elizabeth.

No sooner had she finished speaking, than there came a knock. 'Enter!' she called.

The door opened and the Baron entered. He looked at his wife and said without preamble, 'I hear you left the grounds in search of me. You should not have done so. One of the men said you were attacked opposite the gates.'

Lady Elizabeth looked at Rosamund in astonishment. 'You made no mention of this to me.'

She flushed. 'No. I did not want to distress you, as it was, one of your guards came to my rescue.'

'I am truly shocked that you should be set upon so close to my gates.'

'I am sure it will not happen again,' said Rosamund, not wanting to upset her further by telling her the identity of her attacker. 'I had naught to steal.'

Alex frowned. 'Even so, it was foolish of you to go out alone. If the guards had not seen you, then you might have been seriously hurt.'

'I would prefer you not to make a fuss,' she said stiffly, annoyed that he should scold her. Where had *he* been when she needed him, but out meeting his former lover? 'I shall not do it again,' she added, an angry gleam in her eyes.

Alex wondered why she was so vexed with him. Was it not natural for a husband to be concerned about his wife's safety? 'I should hope not. Anyway, I bring tidings.'

'What tidings?' asked Lady Elizabeth eagerly.

'Lady Monica and her party have arrived in London.'

It was just as they had expected, but the news caused Rosamund to feel quite sick. 'How do you know this?' she asked.

'I have been having Fustian's house watched and I was fortunate enough to see his wife, Marion, with an older woman whom she addressed as Lady Monica.'

'She must have ridden like the wind to get here,' said Rosamund, thinking it was not surprising the Baron had been out so long if he'd visited both the Steel Yard and her stepbrother's house.

'Or flew on her broomstick,' muttered Lady Elizabeth.

Alex smiled and pressed his wife's shoulder gently. 'You must not fear them. I have the right to protect you now.'

'Spoken like a true knight,' said Rosamund lightly.

Lady Elizabeth sighed. 'Just the kind of husband I wanted.'

Alex stared at her. 'You certainly seem to have made a miraculous recovery, Lady Elizabeth.'

'The power of prayer,' she said piously, touching the amber-and-silver crucifix hanging from her girdle. 'I deem that God has healed me in order that I can make the journey to Richmond. Hopefully I will be able to leave within a few hours. As I have already said, I will travel by barge, so as not to exert myself too much. I have suggested to Rosamund that the pair of you ride to Richmond as soon as possible. We need to make certain that one of us arrives at the palace to execute your father's plans.'

Rosamund thought she must have misheard her godmother's words. Had the Baron not told her that his father had played no part in his life? So what were these plans they were talking about?

'I see the sense in what you say, Lady Elizabeth, but if you fail to reach Richmond, then I will have to reconsider our plans,' said Alex. 'I say that Rosamund could still be of help to us.'

'I do not know of what you speak,' said Rosamund. 'What I wish to know is whether I will still be taking part in the dance? If so, I must inform you, Godmother, that Lady Joan's gown has gone missing from the hall.'

'Do not concern yourself about it,' said the older woman. 'Most likely one of the servants has picked it up. I will see to it that it is packed with my baggage, along with the masks I have ordered, which are yet to be delivered.' She clapped her hands together. 'Now, enough said, my dears. You must eat before setting out on your journey. Breakfast will be served in my parlour,' she wheezed.

'Baron, your wife can explain to you my plans for your arrival at Richmond. Go now! I must write a message for you to take with you.'

Rosamund and Alex accepted their dismissal without comment and left the bedchamber for the parlour. She sat down at table, but he went over to the fire and held his hands out to the blaze. 'It is still very cold out. You must wrap up well.'

Rosamund wondered how he could speak of such mundane matters when he was such a deceiver. 'God-mother said that we are to take the horse ferry at Westminster and cross to the south bank. We should reach Richmond before nightfall,' she said in a colourless voice.

He slanted her a frowning glance. 'You are still upset by what happened outside the gate, I deem. You must not go out alone again.'

'We have already had this conversation,' she muttered.

'Aye. But where did you go when you went out in search for me? I saw no sign of you.'

She thought he sounded suspicious and her hurt deepened. 'Perhaps you weren't looking for me, but someone else?'

Before he could reply, a servant entered and placed food and ale on the table. It was not until the man had left that Alex said, 'You make that sound as if there was something wrong in doing so. I told you where I have been.'

She reached for bread and salted pork and said firmly, 'Are you certain you have told me all that you did?'

'Is this what marriage is about?' Alex picked up the jug and poured the ale. 'I suspect that you are going to tell me you saw me somewhere else.'

'From what you have just said, you did go somewhere other than to spy on my evil stepbrother,' she said, a flush on her cheeks. 'You certainly missed seeing him when you were seeing someone else.'

Alex was astounded. 'Of what are you accusing me?'

'I saw you with that religious in the church in the Steel Yard. You were in an embrace and she was kissing you!'

'You're mistaken. If I had an assignation with Ingrid, I would certainly not arrange to meet her in her nun's habit in a church,' he said firmly.

He sounded so positive that Rosamund was immediately filled with doubt. 'But he seemed familiar and definitely reminded me of you.'

'It was not me.' His voice was carefully controlled. 'Now I'd like to know what you meant by my missing seeing your stepbrother?'

Rosamund felt ashamed of her suspicions. But if it was not the Baron who had been with Ingrid, who had it been?

'Well?' demanded Alex, slapping the table with the flat of his hand.

She started and looked at him and the expression in his eyes caused her to take a deep breath. 'It was Edward who attacked me. He-he threatened me and you.'

Alex's expression altered. 'Did he hurt you?' he rasped.

'No doubt I shall be bruised where he seized me, but he was more intent on—on telling me that I would never escape him and you were going to die.'

Alex swore. 'How did he know I was here? I was so careful.'

'He seemed to know there was something between us.'

'You mean he knows that we're wed?'

'No, I feel sure he did not know that and I did not enlighten him. He did think us betrothed, though.'

Alex was silent and then said, 'Eat your breakfast. We need to leave soon.'

'Might it not be best if we travelled by barge with Lady Elizabeth?' asked Rosamund.

'No. It is possible that she might have a relapse and be unable to make the journey. It is vital that we reach Richmond as soon as possible.'

'Because of these plans to do with your father?'

He did not answer, but carried on eating his breakfast.

She took a mouthful of ale and forced some food down. At least she could be glad that he had not been unfaithful to her so soon. The ache in her heart had abated and she felt much better. 'You said that you spoke to the guards.'

'One of them.'

'You did not speak to Joshua?'

'No. He must have been the other one.' He cocked an eyebrow. 'Why?'

'What is your opinion of him?'

'He seemed a sturdy fellow. Why do you ask? Do you think he could be the spy in the camp?'

'No! Joshua is no thief.'

Alex frowned. 'You know this man?'

She smiled. 'I have known Joshua all my life. He is the man I pretended to be—Master Joshua Wood, woodcutter. He taught Harry about woodcraft and they used to practise swordplay together with wooden swords. That was until Father bought Harry a short-sword. He grieved with me when we believed Harry to be dead.'

'Why did you not tell me this earlier?' he said mildly,

not wanting her to suspect that he was a little envious of the obvious affection that she bore this man.

'I only discovered he was here a short while ago. You may ask the other guard about our meeting.' She reached for the honey.

'Did you speak of Harry to him?' Alex bit into bread and smoked pork.

'I would have done so if the priest had not arrived just then,' replied Rosamund.

He nodded. 'Best that you do not tell him. If he was such a friend to Harry, we do not wanting him taking off in search of him.'

Rosamund's expression lightened. 'I had not thought of his doing so. But why should he not help us?'

'Because Lady Elizabeth needs him here.'

Rosamund fell to thinking, remembering him saying, *Is this what marriage is about?* when she had doubted him. 'Do you regret marrying me?' she asked bluntly.

'What a question to ask me,' said Alex. 'Why? Are you regretting the match we have made? It is not too late for an annulment, if that is what you want. I will be honest and say that I believe your godmother tricked us into marriage because she believes you are carrying my child. I only pray that she will live long enough to realise her mistake.'

Rosamund heaved a sigh. 'She might believe that is so, but we both know that I am not carrying your child. Maybe she has regrets about her own childless state and wants me to have a child so she can be a proxy grandmother.'

'That's understandable. She has made you the recipient of most of her fortune. If all she asks in return is for you to provide her with a proxy grandchild, then the least we can do is to grant her wish,' he said, sounding exasperated.

'So *you* don't want an annulment?' murmured Rosamund, aware of a sudden welling of happiness.

'Not at the moment,' he said, shaking his head. 'Perhaps it makes sense for me to take a wife now instead of waiting until my thirtieth birthday. I could be dead then.'

Rosamund's happiness faded. 'What a thing to say! You have destroyed my appetite. I will go and fetch my baggage and hopefully I will not have been widowed by the time I return. You will not forget my godmother's message before we leave?' She did not wait for his permission, but hurried from the room.

'Damn!' Alex threw down his own napkin and went after her, but she was already out of sight. She must have run like the wind, he thought. He had no idea of the whereabouts of her bedchamber, but was determined to reassure her of his affection and his determination to stay alive before they left for Richmond. He could so easily imagine the atmosphere between them on the journey if he did not put matters right.

He tried several vacant bedchambers on the first floor before he reached one that was locked. From inside came the sound of pacing feet and a voice muttering, 'If I am widowed, what good is it if Godmother leaves her money to me? Edward will find some way to get at me and the money. I might as well be dead now.'

'Rosamund, open this door,' commanded Alex, worried by what he had overheard. 'We must talk.'

There was a long silence before she answered him. 'We have talked enough. It is obvious to me that you do not know how to handle a wife.'

'That is most likely true because I have never had a wife before,' said Alex patiently. 'But there could be that in our future that would make us both happy. Tell me, Rosamund, have you ever slept with a man?'

'Who have you in mind besides yourself?' She laughed a mite hysterically. 'If you suspect that Joshua and I might have had a youthful liaison, then you are mistaken. Joshua never laid a finger on me, unlike that cur, Edward.'

Alex felt a familiar anger at her mention of Edward. 'Unlock the door, Rosamund,' he said in a gentle tone. 'We cannot waste time arguing like this if we are to go to Richmond.'

He heard a bolt being drawn, and the door swung open. He noticed the tearstains on her face before she turned away and picked up her baggage. He experienced a rush of compassion and wanted to protect her not only from other men's angry attentions, but his own.

'Give that here,' he said.

She handed the bag to him. 'Are you going to beat me when we get to Richmond?'

Alex dropped the baggage and kicked the door shut behind him. He seized her by the arms and drew her against him. 'How can you believe that I would beat you?'

'A husband owns his wife. He is free to do with her what he wills,' she said on a sob. 'Edward beats Marion and he would have done the same to me if Father had not forbidden it.'

Alex had difficulty controlling his rage, thinking she was in a real muddle, but knew it would be a terrible mistake for her to see his anger explode. 'Rosamund,

Rosamund,' he whispered against her ear. 'I would not treat you so cruelly. When I hold you in my arms like this, I want to make love to you, not beat you.' He nudged up her jaw with his chin and covered her lips with his own and kissed her gently. He wanted her, but was certain that whilst she was in such an emotional state that matters between them could go badly wrong. 'But now is not the time,' he said softly, releasing her and reaching for her baggage. 'I will meet you downstairs.'

Rosamund was mollified, but she would have preferred him to go on holding her and speaking in that gentle, caring voice. 'You will not forget to ask Lady Elizabeth for the missive you are to hand to the controller of the royal household?' she reminded him.

'I had forgotten,' he said wryly. 'I can see it is going to be useful having a wife. Thank you.'

He left her alone to collect herself and returned to the bedchamber that had been allotted to him last night. He put on his hat and cloak and picked up his gauntlets and saddlebags and went downstairs.

After saddling up his horse and fastening on the pillion seat, he led his steed to the front of the house and went inside in search of Rosamund and Lady Elizabeth.

Her ladyship was not in her bedchamber, but he found her in the parlour eating bread and honey. He half-expected to be asked why he had taken so long preparing for the journey. Instead, she simply handed him a sealed parchment and wished him a safe journey. He thanked her, but paused to ask whether she knew that one of her guards had worked as a woodcutter on Appleby Manor.

'No, I did not know that,' she said, showing interest. 'I

presume you are talking about the man that my captain of the guard hired while I was staying at Lathom House.'

'Aye. Joshua Wood. It has occurred to me that you have a man here who would recognise Rosamund's stepfamily on sight.'

'What are you suggesting?'

'If he is the man Rosamund believes him to be, then he will have their measure and warn us if he should discover anything that could be a threat to us.'

She nodded. 'I will send for him as soon as you and Rosamund have left for Richmond and speak to him. I pray God that we all have a safe journey.' She offered him her hand.

He raised it to his lips and kissed it.

As he turned away, Rosamund entered the parlour. He thought she appeared much calmer. 'So you both are here,' she said. 'I have come to say farewell for the moment, Godmother. I look forward to seeing you at Richmond.'

'Come closer, my dear,' wheezed Lady Elizabeth. 'I would kiss you farewell.'

Rosamund did as asked and was aware of her godmother's close scrutiny as she kissed her cheek. 'Have faith, my dear,' said Lady Elizabeth. 'Now go and enjoy each other's company.'

Rosamund thanked her and followed in Alex's wake. When they arrived at the gates, Rosamund was disappointed not to see Joshua on guard, but she made no mention of him. However, they had not travelled far when Alex said, 'I spoke to Lady Elizabeth about Joshua Wood.'

'What did you say to her?' She could not conceal her apprehension.

'I told her that you trusted him and that he could be

useful. If Fustian were to return here or his mother or brother, he would recognise them and know what to do.'

Relief flooded her being. 'Thank you. I beg pardon for misjudging you.'

'I have misjudged you on several occasions, so I ask your forgiveness.'

'It is important that we trust each other,' she said awkwardly.

Alex nodded, considering being more open with her. Sooner rather than later he would need to tell her that he was the bastard son of a Scottish earl—he was not looking forward to doing so.

Chapter Eleven

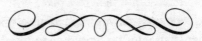

Despite having visited London once before, Rosamund had never travelled as far as Westminster and she was determined to enjoy the experience despite her worry over Edward's threat. Her husband, on the other hand, seemed unconcerned about what her stepbrother might do and also appeared to know exactly where he was going and who lived where. He pointed out the riverside residences of the bishops of Exeter, Bath and Wells, as well as the palaces of the prelates of Carlisle, Durham and Norwich.

'One expects a king to live in a palace. But there is something amiss with the church, whose task it is to preach a gospel of self-sacrifice and love for the poor and needy, when its leaders are living in such luxury,' said Rosamund. 'I don't suppose you will agree with me.'

'Why should I not?' asked Alex. 'It is true that as we near Westminster you will see the hospital of St Mary Rouncelwell, but then comes the Archbishop of York's manor. There should certainly be more provision for the homeless, sick, elderly and poor and I believe change is coming.'

Rosamund was glad that they saw eye to eye on what she considered an important matter, but was curious to know more. 'What do you mean by change? Is it that you believe the rich and proud will repent of their ways? I find that difficult to believe.'

'Some will, but it is those who are educated and can read and want change that will foment it. Holy writ is being printed in such great numbers that there will be those who will speak out against the church and demand reform.'

'It has already begun,' said Rosamund with a stir of excitement. 'I remember Joshua's father talking about the hedge priests that his grandfather had told of to his father. They wandered the country preaching equality for all men and an end to war. They had read the gospels for themselves and paid a terrible price for saying the church was corrupt. Many were burnt alive.' She shuddered.

Alex was surprised that his wife knew of such horrors and should be willing to talk about them. 'From what I have learnt from history, it is that change nearly always involves bloodshed,' he said. 'I doubt if even a king could reform the church without rebellion and suffering. Shall we speak of other matters? I would that you were not made unhappy with such thoughts.'

'You would have me blind to the truth?' she asked.

'No. But we have talked enough of such a disturbing subject,' he said firmly.

Rosamund was silent for a while, but felt rejuvenated by their conversation so far. 'Tell me, have you ever been to Richmond before?' she asked.

'I have not been inside the palace, but I have seen it from a distance. It is similar in design to Lathom House.'

'Is there a reason for the palace's similarity?'

'I have forgotten who told me that the King so admired Lathom House that, after the Palace of Sheen was severely damaged by fire six years ago, he decided to have a new one built to a similar design. He renamed it Richmond because he and his father were once Earls of Richmond.'

'I presume they were named after the Richmond in Yorkshire,' said Rosamund. 'I am glad I will be able to compare the two buildings for myself.'

He nodded. 'Look, there is the ferryman. Fortunately the boat is on this side of the river, so there will be no delay in his taking us across to the other side.'

It was as he said and soon they were set ashore on the south bank of the Thames. Here was St Thomas's Hospital, as well as Bermondsey Palace whose lands stretched as far as Lambeth. They took the road to Putney and rode in silence for a while, busy with their own thoughts.

Rosamund determined not to think too far into the future because that meant worrying about what steps Edward would try to take to punish her and destroy her husband. Of course, she should not be underestimating the Baron and remembered thinking that here was a man strong enough to deal with her stepfamily. She really should have more faith in him.

She allowed her mind to drift into imagining what it would be like travelling to Sweden to begin a completely different life in a foreign country. She would need to learn Swedish if she was not to be solely dependent on this rich, well-travelled husband with an estate and a business to oversee. This Baron whom she had known less than two weeks. It was a daunting prospect. And what about Harry?

What if he did not return to England by the time the Baron decided they should visit his homeland? Perhaps she should discuss that with him when the time came.

She glanced at Alex. 'You said earlier that you have seen Richmond Palace from a distance. For what reason did you travel upstream away from the sea, and the business affairs that might interest you there?'

Alex wished that Rosamund had not asked that question. He sensed that she would know if he prevaricated and he had a growing conviction that his wife could match his grandmother for intelligence and courage. She was no mad girl, but a woman who thought deeply about important matters.

'I have some knowledge of the area due to having travelled by boat as far as Thistleworth,' he said.

'What is at Thistleworth?' she asked.

'Syon House. It is an abbey of the Bridgettine Order and but a league or so from Richmond.'

'I have not heard of that Order before,' said Rosamund, her interest roused. 'I would hear more.'

'It was founded by St Birgetta of Sweden and is open to both men and women.' He did not add that it was there that he and Harry had taken Ingrid last year. She had told them that she was one of the saint's true descendants, despite Birgetta's line having died out with the death of her granddaughter, Lady Ingeborg Knutsdotter, the Abbess of Vadstena. He remembered Ingrid staying at the convent, saying it was a place she liked to retreat to when possible.

'Is Birgetta the Swedish name for Bridget?' asked Rosamund, rousing him from his thoughts.

'Aye.'

Rosamund was reminded of the girl destined to marry William. 'I wonder if my stepbrother's intended bride travelled to London in Lady Monica's train,' she said. 'Her name is Bridget McDonald.'

'It could be useful meeting her,' said Alex. 'But first we need to have our thoughts fixed on events at Richmond.'

Rosamund felt her stomach tighten with nerves at the thought of performing in front of the royal family and their guests.

'What if I am still expected to dance with Lord Bude?' she asked.

'Then you will do so and see what you can glean from him,' said Alex. 'It is surprising how much information a person can drop when they are not thinking about what they are saying.'

Rosamund said, 'You want me to act as one of your spies?'

'I would rather you had naught to do with him, but it would be useful to know what is in his mind,' he replied.

Rosamund nodded. Then she forgot all about Lord Bude—suddenly she caught her first sighting of Richmond Palace. She gasped in admiration.

'What a fairy-tale place. It looks far grander than Lathom House. See how its white stone walls gleam in the sun and how its towers are capped with pepper-pot domes and cupolas. I can easily imagine a damsel in distress imprisoned by her cruel father calling down to a brave knight to rescue her. Is there a moat?'

Alex laughed. 'I didn't realise you could be such a romantic. I have heard there is the remains of one, although a bridge now links that part of the palace to the fountain courtyard. You'll gather from its name that it has a water fountain, which it was once described to me as a pleasure to listen to on a hot day. Apparently the courtyard is flanked by a great hall and a chapel.'

Rosamund said, 'One presumes that the proxy marriage ceremony between the Princess Margaret and the King of Scotland will take place in the chapel?'

'One would think so, but according to Lady Elizabeth the event will be in the royal apartments that are separated from those housing the officials and guests.'

'It is a huge place. I should imagine several large kitchens will be needed, as well as huge butteries, wine cellars and everything else that is necessary to tend the needs of such a huge household,' said Rosamund, her eyes wide with the wonder of it all. 'And what of the gardens? I used to escape to the herb garden whenever possible at Appleby.'

'I believe there are very special gardens here. A large one encircled by two-story galleries, open at ground level and enclosed above. There the court can walk and play indoors when the weather is foul. During fine weather there are flower beds to admire and there is also a tennis court.'

A memory surfaced of Harry and Josh hitting a ball back and forth over a rope stretched between two trees. 'I remember my father telling Harry and me that King Henry discovered a liking for the game in his youth whilst exiled in France.'

'I have played it on occasions, but more for the honour of winning than purely to wager money on a game of chance.' Alex remembered a perspiring Harry determined to trounce him and win the favour of Ingrid, who was watching on the sidelines.

'You have painted a fascinating picture of the palace for

me. You must have listened well to all that was told you,' said Rosamund lightly.

'I have a great interest in architecture.' Alex had no intention of being drawn into telling her that it was Ingrid who had somehow managed to get herself invited to Richmond—he did not want his wife dwelling on events in his past that were over and done with. It was true that he had listened avidly to Ingrid's description of the palace. In the past there had been times when his life had depended on his prior knowledge of a building and he had learnt much that could prove useful.

'Perhaps you would enjoy a walk along the river before we go inside,' he suggested. 'You will get a different view of the palace from there.'

Rosamund agreed and they dismounted. The sun was shining and the snow was beginning to thaw. She was of a mind that the river was a pretty place to take a stroll. His shoulder brushed her arm and she felt a tingle of pleasure at that brief bodily contact. They walked for a while. Then she noticed a barge being rowed upstream.

'Do you think that craft has come from London?' she asked.

'It is possible.' Alex's eyes narrowed against the sun as he gazed at the boat. Suddenly he placed an arm around her shoulders and drew her away from the river's edge. 'If I am not mistaken, that is your stepbrother leaning over the side!'

Rosamund experienced a cold feeling in the pit of her stomach and was glad of the comfort provided by her husband's strong arm. 'What is he doing here? I had thought we could escape him! Surely he could not have been invited?'

'We shall soon find out if the barge ties up at the royal quayside.' Alex ushered her over to where their horses cropped the grass beneath the bare branches of a willow tree.

'What does he have that the King might want?'

'It is well known that King Henry loves gold and silver. Fustian might have provided the King with a costly gift out of his own purse to present to one of his Scottish guests,' said Alex. 'By doing so he wins the King's favour and is invited to the celebrations, although by taking this step he will have given the King the impression he is a very wealthy man.'

'Wealth that my father amassed and which really belongs to Harry,' said Rosamund in a tight voice. 'At least Edward has to pay heavy taxes on the merchandise he brings into the country.'

'Only on that which he imports legally,' said Alex.

Rosamund stared at him. 'You suspect him of smuggling?'

Alex's expression was grim. 'Aye. I also believe that he is probably involved in piracy himself. He could use his ships to attack other ships that sailed out of London. It would not be difficult for him to discover what cargoes they would be carrying and when the ships would leave port. He could have the merchandise smuggled in farther north along the coast. I was lacking a reason as to why he should take such risks, but when you spoke of him wanting to be Lord Mayor of London, that provided me with the information I wanted. All I need is proof.'

'Just like I need proof that he killed Father. You know what makes what he is doing so much worse?' She did not wait for Alex's answer. 'Not only has he stolen what is my brother's, but the motto of the Royal Company of Mercers, of which he is a member, is *Honor Deo*! Honour God! Edward is not a man of honour and deserves to be shunned by that noble company.'

'Ssshhh! Calm yourself.' He brushed his lips against hers. 'It looks like the barge will soon be tying up and its passengers disembarking. I do not want him to see us.'

'Why? He knows that we already know each other and that I must be aware that Harry is alive, so what is the use of us hiding? He would not dare to try to destroy us in full view of people.'

'I need to know if he has another purpose in coming here. Maybe to meet one of his mother's kinsmen. If I am right in my suspicions, then Fustian will not wish the peace pact to go ahead,' said Alex. 'It is best if we avoid coming face to face with him for the moment.'

She understood; besides, the less she saw of her stepbrother, the better she would like it. They walked on in silence, leading the horses. A thought suddenly occurred to Rosamund. 'When do we dance before the royal family?'

'Not for a couple of days and we will be masked,' said Alex. 'There is no need for you to fear Edward. If he were to catch you unawares, remember, I will not be far away.'

'Of course.' She was determined not to be frightened of Edward any longer. At that moment she could have said honestly that, with the Baron by her side, she no longer feared her stepbrother. No doubt it would be a different matter if she was to encounter him in a dark passage.

They retraced their steps and, much to their surprise, were fortunate to arrive at the palace at the same time as Lady Elizabeth and her entourage came into sight. She was being carried in a litter by four strong-looking men and only her eyes betrayed her weariness.

'So there you both are. I am so glad to see you arrived safely,' she said. 'I left within the hour after your departure.' She stretched out a hand to her goddaughter. 'So, Rosamund, my dear, what do you think of the King's palace?'

'It is indeed impressive,' answered Rosamund. 'I cannot wait to see what it is like inside.'

'There is much to see that is fine.' She added in a low voice, 'There are those who say that the King is miserly but, believe me, he was not frugal when it came to decorating Richmond. It is now the finest palace in the kingdom. I was here with my kinsman and his mother, the Countess of Beaufort, for poor Prince Arthur's wedding. Now that was a sumptuous affair. Whilst I doubt that Henry will part with as much gold and silver as he did then, nevertheless, I am certain he will not stint on spending what is necessary to impress our Scottish neighbours.' She indicated that they ride beside her litter and so they led her entourage along the red-brick outer wall to the main gateway that looked out over the Green.

Men-at-arms stood on guard, but as soon as Lady Elizabeth was announced, she and her party were allowed inside the walls. It seemed no time at all before an official was welcoming them and minions were summoned to attend to their needs. Lady Elizabeth asked whether certain people had arrived and the replies she received seemed to please her. Then she asked if a chamber could be made available for her troupe to rehearse in that evening.

Rosamund lost sight of the Baron in the throng and

decided he would be able to find his way to the suite of rooms set aside for Lady Elizabeth and her entourage. A servant showed her to the bedchamber that was to be the Baron and Baroness Dalsland's for the duration of their stay. Rosamund experienced that odd sensation at being addressed as Baroness again and thought, for the first time, that along with her title came responsibility. She now had the power to help those so much poorer than herself. Lady Elizabeth had put one of her maids at Rosamund's disposal and she felt slightly ashamed of the few clothes she had for her to stow away in the oak armoire and chest. She thanked the girl and dismissed her.

Then she spent a few moments admiring the craftsmanship of the beautifully carved furniture and richly embroidered hangings and coverlet on the bed. A fine bed. She eased off her boots and hung up her cloak and hat before lying down. She decided the mattress must be stuffed with feathers and fell to dreaming of her husband making love to her as she listened to the crackling of the log fire. If only he really could love her, then she would be happy. But of course, their marriage was no love match, but one conveniently arranged by her godmother.

'Are you comfortable?'

Rosamund started at the sound of her husband's attractive tones and sat up.

'No, don't disturb yourself.' Alex tossed his hat on a chest and removed his outer clothes and boots before lying down on the bed beside her. Rosamund was intensely aware of him and felt her insides quiver as he reached out and took her hand. 'Your godmother plans to take a nap before the evening meal. She has decided we will take our

meal here in her own apartment and it will be prepared by
her own cook. She has already discovered that the King and
Queen are to sup with their Scottish guests in their private
apartments, no doubt in preparation for the ceremony
tomorrow. After supper there is to be rehearsal for the performance the day after tomorrow.'

She glanced at him. 'Did you tell her that my stepbrother is here?'

'Didn't you?' He rolled onto his side so that he faced her.

'No. There was no opportunity to have a private word.
She was speaking to her servants and having them take
messages to the troupe and the musicians.'

'Then we will tell her later. In the meantime, perhaps
we should also rest after our disturbed night—'

Alex drew his wife towards him. He was expecting a
little resistance on her part, but she snuggled up to him like
a kitten. 'Rest, you say,' she murmured, tentatively placing
an arm across his chest. So trusting, he thought, stroking
her hair and fondling her ear. After the shock of seeing
Fustian, he had immediately wanted to challenge him and
fight with him to the death. Instead, he had known he must
wait until he got him alone.

He planted feather-light kisses down the side of her
face and then kissed her mouth in a leisurely fashion. She
returned his kiss and then rubbed her cheek against his
unshaven one. He sensed she winced and reminded himself
that he must shave later. He lightly touched the outline of
her breast in the blue gown. He felt the peak tighten and
he plucked it gently. A sleepy sigh escaped her and he unfastened the buttons on her gown and slid his hand inside
and caressed that perfectly shaped orb. Several moments

passed before he realised with a rueful smile that she had drifted into sleep. He made himself comfortable and within a short time he also was asleep.

Rosamund woke slowly and realised with part of her mind that someone was moving about in the bedroom. She sat up suddenly and cried, 'Who's there?'

'No need to fear,' said Alex, coming and sitting on the bed. 'It's time to get up and join Lady Elizabeth for supper.'

Rosamund yawned and stretched. 'How long have I been asleep?'

'Do you feel rested?' he asked.

'Aye.' She stared up at him with a puzzled expression.

'Then you have slept long enough.' He smiled and helped her off the bed. 'Do you wish to change your gown?'

'Perhaps.' She glanced at the bed and wondered. 'Did you sleep?'

'Aye.'

Supper was almost over by the time Alex and Rosamund had finished telling Lady Elizabeth about Edward Fustian's arrival at Richmond Palace.

'He will not be the only one hoping to gain the prize of Lord Mayor of London,' she wheezed. 'Several will have paid a pretty penny for the honour of attending the celebrations in the hope of winning that role. You can be sure that the King will be watching them all and have courtiers strategically placed to listen to conversations, so as to deduce which of them is willing to pay the highest price for such a position.'

'The Baron thinks that he and I should keep out of

Edward's sight until we have proof of his infamy,' said Rosamund.

Lady Elizabeth's eyes nearly popped out of her head. 'Don't tell me you suspect Fustian of having something to do with the other business, Baron?'

Alex and Rosamund exchanged looks.

Immediately, Lady Elizabeth said, 'Forget what I said. Time is moving on and we have the rehearsal to attend.'

Easy enough to say *forget,* but Rosamund could not do so. Her husband had asked for her help and she intended giving it to him. She resisted looking his way as they rose and left the apartment to go to the place where several musicians were already in position and tuning up their instruments. The room was adjacent to a much larger chamber from whence came the sound of laughter and loud voices.

'I wonder what is taking place in there?' asked Rosamund of no one in particular.

'Go and see, my dear, and come back and tell me,' said Lady Elizabeth. 'Then we shall close the door so we will not be disturbed.'

Rosamund did so and decided that it was another party rehearsing for their part in the pageant. She noticed the livery on a banner and closed the door and turned to see her godmother in a low-voiced conversation with the Baron.

Rosamund sat down a little away from them, close to a curtained alcove. She tapped her foot in rhythm to the music and tried not to feel excluded. After all, her father had not shared every part of his life with his wives and had often spent time away from home. Besides, it was possible that Alex was telling Lady Elizabeth what they had discussed earlier or perhaps not. She felt insecure again, but waited until she was certain they had finished their conversation before making her way towards them.

'The company next door have a banner displaying the livery of the Royal Guild of Mercers,' said Rosamund.

Alex glanced at her. 'Did you catch sight of Fustian?'

'No, although, perhaps he will attend later.'

Alex nodded. 'We will just have to stay alert in case he should pass through here.'

'I have heard that the Mercers' Guild is financing a grand finale to the pageant,' said Lady Elizabeth.

'I wonder what it will entail,' said Rosamund.

'There is bound to be a tournament with young knights joining the lists to prove how brave they are,' replied her godmother. 'I have never particularly cared for jousting since my brother was killed.'

At that moment members of the troupe began to arrive.

'Where is Lord Bude?' asked Lady Elizabeth.

'None of us has seen him,' said one of the ladies. 'What shall we do?'

'We shall go on with the rehearsal without him,' said Lady Elizabeth. 'I will sit out and the Baron will partner my goddaughter.'

The lords and ladies lined up for the dance.

Alex took Rosamund's hand. 'You remember the movements of the dance?'

'I am certain you will put me right if I have forgotten them,' she replied.

He gazed at her intently. 'I deem you are vexed about something?'

She almost said, *how perceptive of you*. Instead, she shook her head and then gazed down at her feet.

Alex drew in his breath with a hiss, but there was no chance to sort the matter out. The musicians struck up. This time when they danced together she went through the motions without enthusiasm. She expected her husband to mock her performance, but he did not say a word.

'Excellent,' said her godmother, stifling a yawn. 'Perhaps a little more picking up of the feet, Rosamund. But no doubt you are tired. There will be too much making ready for the proxy ceremony in the morning for another rehearsal. And by evening, I doubt any of you will be fit to dance after the celebrations. So we will have a dress rehearsal the following morning.'

They all agreed and the musicians and the troupe drifted away.

Lady Elizabeth turned to Rosamund and Alex. 'I was too kind to you, my dears. Both your performances were leaden. Why do you not go through the steps again? There is plenty of space for you to practise now the others have left.'

Alex raised his tawny eyebrows. 'Well?' he said.

'It is what Godmother wishes,' replied Rosamund, her cheeks flushed.

So once again they performed the movements of the dance and this time Rosamund concentrated on picking up her feet and humming the music. Her husband surprised her by beginning to sing in his own language and slowly she relaxed and began to enjoy herself. They repeated the dance until she was quite out of breath and then he called a halt.

It was in the following silence that they heard voices on the other side of the door. Alex caught his wife's eye and suddenly he seized her hand and drew her into the alcove close by and pulled across the curtain. She stood trembling in the curve of his arm with her cheek pressed against his chest. She could hear the steady thud of his heart as the door opened.

'So you agree the plan should work if the other fails?' asked Edward.

'I don't see why it shouldn't, laddie. I shall have a wee word with yer kinsman. He feels much the same as we do about this damned alliance—and there are others who share his sentiments and will do what they can to prevent it from succeeding. But if we can put some money into our own pockets, who is to gainsay—?' The voice stopped abruptly. When it spoke again, it was in a whisper. 'Who's this?'

'I can't say, but she looks a perfect fright,' sneered Edward. 'Although…wait a moment. This must be Lady Elizabeth Stanley. I have heard that she paints her face.'

'Do yer think she might have heard us talking?' hissed the Scotsman.

'At her age—she's probably as deaf as a post. I did hear that she would be here,' muttered Edward.

'Why's that?'

'She's kin to the King's stepfather, as well as being godmother to my stepsister. Mother was supposed to deal with Rosie, but I will have to do the deed myself.'

Rosamund drew in her breath and instantly Alex pressed her head against his chest.

'What was that?' asked the Scotsman.

Rosamund could scarcely breathe and was aware that Alex was reaching for the dagger at his belt.

Chapter Twelve

Before Alex could release Rosamund and face the two men, there came a sudden break in the snoring and a sleepy voice said, 'Where am I? You—you two men! Who are you?' wheezed Lady Elizabeth.

'You are in the Palace of Richmond,' said Edward loudly. 'Am I correct in believing that you are Lady Elizabeth Stanley?'

'You are. But you have not answered my question. Who are you?'

'Ma name is Sir Andrew Kennedy,' said the Scot.

'You are a Kennedy. Now why does that surprise me?' said her ladyship in a vague tone. 'And you, sir, are obviously English. Have we met before?'

'No, Lady Elizabeth,' said Edward.

'Well, it is of no matter. You can help me up, seeing as how they all appear to have gone.'

'Who have gone?' asked the Scot.

'My troupe of dancers. You will see them perform the day after tomorrow.' There was the sound of rustling silk and Lady Elizabeth's rasping breath. 'Now you, Sir Andrew, can give me your arm. When you get to my age, a woman needs a man to keep her on her toes.'

There was the sound of retreating footsteps and Lady Elizabeth's breathless voice and then silence. Rosamund tugged on Alex's arm and looked up into his shadowy face. 'We must follow them. What if they were to hurt her? You heard what Edward said.'

Reluctantly, Alex set his wife aside and opened the curtain. 'We will not approach them unless it is absolutely necessary,' he said firmly. 'We are Fustian's intended victims, so I doubt they will hurt her.'

'They might do so if they decide she heard them plotting,' said Rosamund, glancing at her husband's face in the light of the wall lantern. 'I wonder to what plan they were referring. If Godmother had not chosen that moment to wake up, we might have found out.'

'She deliberately made a show of being wakened to distract from the noise you made,' said Alex, leading the way along the passage. 'I wonder if your stepmother's treacherous kinsman is another McDonald, working for the previous chieftain of the clan, John of Islay, one time Lord of the Isles and Earl of Ross? I doubt the present lord would be involved in such a plot.'

'How do you know of these people?' whispered Rosamund.

'I keep my eyes and ears open,' he said smoothly. 'You know how to do that, do you not, Rosamund?'

'By not asking so many questions, but just staying quiet and listening,' she murmured. 'There are more people who wish England and Scotland to stay divided than I thought. What do you deem is their plan?'

'That is something we have to find out,' said Alex, caressing her cheek with the back of his hand.

'We?' she asked. 'You still want me to help you?'

He nodded. 'Although there is a certain amount of risk involved.'

'It cannot be any more dangerous than Edward plotting to get rid of me.'

Alex nodded. 'We will discuss this later.'

Rosamund felt a lift of the heart. It seemed that he was going to take her into his confidence after all. Right now she was curious to know why her godmother had considered it strange to see a Kennedy at Richmond.

They arrived at the apartment to find Lady Elizabeth sitting in a chair, drinking from a steaming goblet with Hannah in attendance. She looked up and smiled. 'So there you are, my dears.' She turned to her maid. 'I'll call you when I need you.'

'I am so glad you are safe,' said Rosamund, kissing her godmother.

'You are a good child.' Lady Elizabeth stroked her cheek. 'So smooth.' She sighed. 'I presume you two were hiding behind that curtain and heard what took place?'

'Aye,' said Alex, closing the door and putting his back to it. 'How much of their conversation did you hear?'

'We decided that you were only pretending to be asleep when those men entered the chamber,' added Rosamund.

Her godmother did not answer, but took a sip of her potion before saying, 'What an ill-mannered fool your stepbrother is to insult me and to talk so openly about his plans for you. I will speak to Derby about him and he will quash his ambitions.'

'Not yet,' said Alex firmly. 'We need to discover what his and the other's plans are.'

Lady Elizabeth deliberated. 'The King could have them tortured,' she said with relish.

'But surely that would damage the peace agreement and play into their hands?' said Rosamund. 'Too long our countries have waged war across our borders. We are neighbours and should be allies.'

Lady Elizabeth sighed. 'You are right.'

'Tell us what you know about this Kennedy,' said Rosamund.

'I think you should go to bed,' said Lady Elizabeth, 'and leave this to the Baron and I.'

Rosamund glanced at her husband.

'I say she stays,' said Alex.

His wife gave him a dazzling smile and he felt a catch at his heart, wanting to take her into his arms again.

Lady Elizabeth frowned. 'But what about her safety? What about the child?'

Rosamund was about to say there was no child when her husband indicated with a slight shake of the head that she be silent. 'A man should not have secrets from his wife,' he said smoothly. 'I see no harm in Rosamund knowing what you have to say.'

Lady Elizabeth appeared slightly flustered by that remark. 'If that is what you think, but I am depending on you to keep them both safe.'

'Trust me.' He waved Rosamund to a settle and sat beside her. 'Begin,' he said.

Lady Elizabeth sucked in her cheeks, cracking her paint. 'The King of Scotland has a mistress, Janet Kennedy. No doubt her family would rather a proxy marriage did not take place between James and Princess Margaret. Perhaps in their wildest dreams the Kennedy clan imagine that the son Janet Kennedy bore King James could follow in his father's footsteps. After all, the King has given the boy the title of Earl of Moray.'

Rosamund glanced at Alex to see what he thought of this information.

'I doubt King James would legalise his affair with Janet Kennedy. To favour them would cause war amongst the clans,' he said.

Lady Elizabeth nodded. 'You are probably right. I have heard that she has had other lovers amongst the Scottish hierarchy. One of the powerful Earls of Douglas has been rumoured to have shared her bed.' She fixed Alex with a stare. 'One wonders if he could have fathered more than one bastard.'

Alex scowled at her. 'I think it would be best if we did not discuss the Earls of Douglas.'

'Why? It was your grandmother who insisted that she was the best person to—'

'Enough, Lady Elizabeth,' said Alex, ruthlessly cutting through what she had to say. 'This has naught to do with the matter under discussion.'

'Is it possibly that the Kennedys, Douglases and McDonalds might work together to destroy the peace?' asked Rosamund.

Alex sighed heavily. 'Definitely not. It was a McDonald chieftain, the previous Earl of Ross, who behaved treacherously towards the border Douglases in the present King of Scotland's father's reign. The McDonalds committed murder after signing a treaty with the Yorkist King Edward. They would help him regain his throne and in return he promised to help them defeat the Scottish king, as well as give them land and gold. Edward never kept his side of the bargain and the Earl of Ross suffered defeat at the hands of the present King of Scotland, lost his lands and title and vanished into obscurity. It is possible that he is behind this plot to destroy this chance of peace between England and Scotland.'

'Such intrigue between our countries,' said Rosamund, shocked, but fascinated none the less. 'Do either of you believe that my stepbrother and Kennedy's plan is to prevent the proxy wedding taking place?'

Alex shook his head. 'It presents too much of a risk with so many people around. Kennedy spoke of them lining their pockets. It sounds to me that our plotters' aim is not only to destroy the peace pact, but...' He paused for several moments before continuing, 'Let us consider the costly gifts that King Henry will give to his guests. The plot could include them relieving the homebound Scots nobles of those treasures.'

'But that might not destroy the peace,' said Rosamund.

'That's true,' muttered Alex, 'and from what the Kennedy said about lining their pocket, that was just an afterthought.'

The three of them fell silent, pondering on what their enemies' plan might be. Then Rosamund said, 'The marriage!'

Alex stared at her. 'What do you mean the marriage?'

'If the marriage was not to take place, the alliance would

fall apart,' she said. 'I mean the proper marriage between the new Queen of Scotland and King James. Where will it take place?'

'Edinburgh,' informed Lady Elizabeth, her eyes gleaming. 'Are you saying their plan could be to prevent Margaret from ever being joined to James?'

'She could mean murder,' said Alex, gazing at his wife as if bewitched. 'They could be planning an attack on the young Queen's train as soon as they cross the Scottish border. Her murder would destroy any chance of peace between the two countries. Either side of the border would do to destroy the peace pact. I am stunned, wife, by the sheer breadth of your imaginative powers.'

Rosamund beamed at him. 'Then I haven't wasted the time spent locked up by my stepmother, when all I could do to occupy myself was to think and think and dream of what I would like to do to her if I was free.'

'We should inform the King,' gasped Lady Elizabeth, who was looking exhausted.

Alex shook his head. 'We have no proof. It is naught but guesswork on our part. We must wait and find out when the journey to Scotland is to take place and set a trap.'

'If you insist, Baron. I am for my bed,' said Lady Elizabeth, 'but I tell you now that I might have other ideas on the morrow.'

Rosamund rose to her feet. 'I am sorry that we have kept you awake. You've had an exhausting day.'

'It cannot be helped, my dear.' Lady Elizabeth patted her hand. 'God put me in the right place so that we could hear those villains plotting. If you could assist me out of this chair, Baron. And, Rosamund, please, call Hannah.'

Alex helped Lady Elizabeth to her feet and Rosamund summoned her maid to come and attend to her. Immediately Hannah came running. Alex and Rosamund went to their bedchamber. There a fire still glowed on the hearth and several candles provided more light.

Alex locked the door, thinking that this would be the first night they would spend together as husband and wife. He watched Rosamund wander over to the bed and push aside a hanging. Then he heard her draw in her breath noisily.

'What is it?' he asked, alerted by that sound to reach for his dagger.

'Someone has been in here.'

He hurried over to her.

Rosamund laughed. 'I don't think you will need the dagger. Most likely it was the maid who put the costumes on the bed.' She held up a black gown and flourished a black mask. 'Yours is here, too. Shall we try them on?' she asked.

'No. It is late and we will be able to see more clearly how we look in daylight.' Alex tossed his costume on a chest at the foot of the bed.

Rosamund placed hers beside his and then shot him a tentative glance. He interpreted that look as one of nervousness and thought how she would have delayed getting into bed with him by trying on the costumes. It was going to be a long day tomorrow and they would need to have their wits about them.

'What would you have me do on the morrow?' she asked. 'Would you like me to pay heed to Kennedy's whereabouts and with whom he talks and eavesdrop on their conversation?'

Immediately alarm bells rang in Alex's head. 'No, I

would not. You will stay with Lady Elizabeth and keep out of trouble. You heard what she said about not risking your life and that of the baby.'

Rosamund's face fell. 'But there is no baby, so you do not need to worry too much about me. What about these Earls of Douglas? If you point them out to me, then perhaps—'

'No. They are not here.'

'Is that because King James is not pleased about having a rival for Janet Kennedy's favours and does not trust them?'

'I am not in the Scottish king's confidence,' rasped Alex, turning his back on her.

Rosamund stared at his back and wondered what she had said wrong. Slowly, she began to undress. 'Is it that you do not approve of the Douglases? This talk—'

'Enough, Rosamund!'

'I don't understand. I thought you trusted me now you're allowing me to be involved in gathering information?'

He did not respond, but blew out the candles and marched over to the bed. Disappointed, it was several minutes before she joined him there. He had allowed her the same side as that which she had occupied during their journey to London and he was not facing her. She swallowed a sigh and climbed into bed. She remembered now that he had cut off her godmother when she had been about to say something about the Earls and their bastards, which meant that it was not only herself with whom her husband was annoyed. Hopefully he would be in a better frame of mind on the morrow and she might discover what it was about the Douglases that put him in such a mood.

Alex was furious with himself. Why couldn't he just accept that his father had not wanted the inconvenience of a baby bastard son after his mother had died? It was not as if he had suffered because his grandparents had provided for all his needs. He should not have behaved so ill mannered either to his wife or Lady Elizabeth. Her words about keeping his wife and baby safe played over and over in his head. He felt a sudden longing for it to be true that Rosamund was carrying his child. He thought about his doubts about her chasteness when Lady Elizabeth had spoken of Rosamund carrying a child. How many times had Rosamund denied the truth of her godmother's words? Surely there would be no need for her to do so once she had his ring on her finger if all she had wanted was a father for Fustian's child?

He turned over, but Rosamund had wrapped herself so tightly in the bedcovers that it was obvious that she did not wish to have aught to do with him that night. He sighed and knew that he would have to wait until tomorrow to sort the whole matter out.

Rosamund was the first to wake. Perhaps it was a cock crowing that disturbed her. Instantly, she was aware that her husband was snuggled up against her back with his arm about her. So he had recovered from his bad mood and she rejoiced in it. She remembered longing for him to hold her like this on the journey to London and relaxed against him. She realised he was wearing his shirt, but it had ridden up so that she could feel his naked thigh pressed against the back of her thigh. It gave her a delicious thrill. She had no idea when the proxy wedding would begin, but was certain her godmother would tell the maid to wake them in plenty of time.

She closed her eyes, but could not get to sleep again, so she deliberated over which gown to wear for the ceremony. Eventually she decided on the dark blue one with the fur-lined blue velvet cloak, fastened with her brother's silver brooch. She wondered how Harry would feel about her being alive and married to the man who had saved his life. She did not doubt he would be pleased. If only she could see him again, he would be able to answer all the questions that no one else could. She prayed for his safety and then hummed a snatch of the dance music. She had a feeling of warm contentment. Was this akin to happiness and would it last?

'What are you thinking?'

Her husband's question startled her into saying, 'What should I be thinking? How did you know I was awake?'

Alex caressed her calf with his big toe. 'You were humming. I always think, when someone answers a question with a question that they are avoiding telling the truth.' His voice was light.

Her brow puckered. 'You think I'm not being honest with you?'

'How can I tell if you do not answer my question?'

She thought about that and said cautiously, 'I was thinking about what to wear for the ceremony and decided on the dark blue gown and the blue velvet cloak.'

'Could you not have told me that straight away?'

'I thought you might have considered me frivolous.'

'Deciding on what you are to wear for an important occasion is not frivolous. It shows sense.' He lifted her dark hair and kissed the nape of her neck. 'Besides, why should I disapprove of you being frivolous on occasions? From what you have told me of your previous life, you were seldom light-hearted and you showed good sense in what you had to say in our discussion last night.'

Rosamund turned in his arm and smiled at him. 'Thank you. I am glad that you have forgiven me for overstepping the mark. I should not expect to know all your secrets.'

A smile cleaved his cheek. 'But you would like to do so?'

She thought about that and replied, 'I think it depends on the secret, but I will not press you. I—I must learn to do well all that a wife must do. Lady Elizabeth spoke of your grandmother and I wish I could have met her. I would like to be like her.'

He frowned. 'I would rather you be yourself than someone else. My grandmother was not perfect.'

'You expect me to be perfect?'

'No!' he exclaimed vehemently. 'For I am not perfect.'

Rosamund wanted to ask why he thought that, but did not have the courage. As it was there was a knock on the door that brought their conversation to an end.

'Time to get up,' said Alex.

He would have liked to have stayed longer in bed with his wife and risk bringing up the subject of babies. Instead, they turned away from each other and climbed out of bed.

The fire had gone out and it was cold in the room. Rosamund picked up the jug and hurried over to the door and opened it a few inches. She was about to ask the maid to bring some hot water, but saw a jug of steaming water had been placed on the floor. She carried it inside. 'No doubt all the servants are rushed off their feet this morning.' Her eyes alighted on their dance costumes. 'Do you think we have time to see if they fit?'

Alex rasped a finger along his unshaven jaw. 'You can try yours on whilst I shave.'

'Don't you normally have a man to do that for you?' she asked, watching him take a leather package from a saddle-bag.

'At home in Sweden,' he answered.

'What is your home like? Is it large and well furnished, fitting for a Baron?' She felt in such a good mood that day that she was not going to torture herself with thoughts of Ingrid. She picked up the black silk gown sewn with silver stars and saw that there was a sleeveless surcote to wear over it. She had not noticed it before.

'My grandfather once had a house in Visby, but now trade has dropped off so I sold it after Grandmother died. I have yet to buy another town house.' He glanced round at her. 'There is no rush for me to do so as I have a manor house in the country.'

'When will we go there? Is it possible that Harry might sail to Sweden rather than return to London?' Rosamund eased the gown over her head and pulled it down over a fresh white linen undergown. She tied up the silver ribbons that tightened the bodice and smoothed the sleeves down to her wrists.

'It is possible,' said Alex cautiously. 'It depends on the cargo he is carrying. If he does not return to London by the time spring is here, then we will cross the northern sea in May in the hope of finding he has made landfall there.'

'You said that his ship was given to him by your grand-father,' she said, fastening the surcote. 'That was very generous of him.'

'Aye, it was, but Harry had worked hard for the

business.' Alex wiped his chin with a cloth and turned to look at her. A slow smile lightened his rugged features. 'You look enchanting. I'm reminded of a night sky.'

She gave him a delighted look. 'Do you think that was what Godmother was thinking when she designed the costumes?'

'Perhaps. Let me see you wearing the mask?'

Rosamund complied with his request, but had difficulty fastening the strings at the back. Alex performed the task for her and then twirled her round so that she faced him. 'Would you recognise me?' she asked.

His eyes narrowed. 'If I were not expecting to see you and it was by candlelight and there were other ladies dressed the same and moving in the dance? I think not.'

'I'm not sure the same could be said of you,' she added, removing the surcote. 'You're taller than the other men and your hair is longer and fairer.'

'I am not cutting my hair,' he said firmly.

'You could wear a wig,' she suggested as she tugged at the strings of the mask.

'Here.' He untied it for her and murmured against her ear, 'You are not suggesting I borrow one from Lady Elizabeth?'

Rosamund chuckled. 'I would like to see her face if you were to do so. Have you worn a wig in the past?'

'On occasions when I have needed a special disguise.' He picked up his mask and held it against his face. 'What is your opinion?'

She met the glitter of his eyes through the eyeholes. 'How different a mask makes one appear.' A shiver ran through her.

'There is naught to be frightened of,' he said sharply. 'Now we must stop wasting time and get ready for the ceremony.'

'I beg your pardon. I did not mean to waste time, but—'

'Quick, Rosamund! Out of that gown and on with the one you are wearing for the ceremony,' he said, slapping her lightly on the bottom.

She feared that she had displeased him, for he was still frowning when he picked up the velvet cloak and swung it about her shoulders and fastened it at the throat with Harry's brooch. Once that was done, he escorted her from the bedchamber.

'Do we stay together? Edward is sure to be there and might see us,' she said, a tremor in her voice.

'Perhaps it is wiser to put a little distance between us during the ceremony,' said Alex, taking her hand. 'But do not look so anxious. All will be well.'

She determined to smile more often and told herself that she was looking forward to the day's events. After all, how many of the King's subjects were able to attend such an occasion?

Lady Elizabeth was waiting for them and Rosamund thought she looked regal, dressed as she was in a pale green satin gown sewn with pearls. She suggested that they partake of bread and honey and wash it down with ale before making their way to the Queen's great chamber. 'One just does not know how long these occasions will last,' she said hoarsely. 'What a pretty gown, my dear,' she added.

Rosamund thanked her. 'You look magnificent.'

Her godmother shrugged. 'I would swap all my gowns to be your age again.'

She sat at table with them and gossiped about those who would be at the ceremony, mentioning names she considered obedient to the King. There were others that she would not trust an inch. Alex listened, but spoke little. As for Rosamund, she tried to commit to memory as much as she could of her godmother's revelations.

'Has Bude arrived?' asked Rosamund.

Alex darted her a glance.

'Indeed, he has,' said Lady Elizabeth. 'He sent a message asking me to forgive him for not attending the rehearsal last night. He added that I could depend on him on the day.' Rosamund and Alex exchanged glances. 'No need to look like that, my dears,' continued Lady Elizabeth. 'I have told him that you are partnering each other, so he will be dancing with me.'

Rosamund looked concerned. 'I thought you had decided not to dance again. Remember what happened the other evening.'

Her godmother pouted. 'Stop fretting. Nothing is going to happen to me.'

Chapter Thirteen

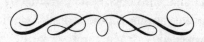

Rosamund was determined not to be nervous as they made their way to the Queen's great chamber. There, a dazzling array of men and women was gathered. She had never been in such illustrious company. She had no idea where her stepbrother was and could only pray that he could not see her, squashed as she was between her godmother and an unknown lady. She wished it was her husband the other side of her, but respected his decision to keep his distance for the moment.

Rosamund watched with lively interest as the twelve-year-old Princess Margaret entered with her five-year-old sister, the Princess Mary, as well as the Queen, who was large with child. There was a fanfare of trumpets as the King and Henry, Prince of Wales, followed them into the chamber. Accompanying them were the Archbishops of Canterbury and York and the Scottish lords and clergy who had their parts to play. Her godmother whispered in Rosamund's ear that it was Patrick Hepburn, the Earl of Bothwell, who would act proxy for the King of Scotland.

He was accompanied by the Archbishop of Glasgow and the Bishop Elect of Murray.

The purpose of the ceremony was announced with great pomp and the proceedings began. As it was asked whether there was any impediment why the alliance should not take place, Rosamund found herself holding her breath, remembering what her godmother had told her about the King of Scotland's mistress. Perhaps Kennedy would speak out at this point, but the moment passed without incident.

Soon after Princess Margaret spoke her vows loudly and clearly to the Earl of Bothwell, finishing with the words, 'Therefore I plight and give to him in your person, as procurator aforesaid, my faith and troth.'

There was a burst of music from the royal trumpeters and in the adjoining chamber minstrels began to play. Rosamund pitied the new Queen of Scotland. She was so young to have to leave her family and country without having met her husband. Terrible to be a pawn in men's games and for her life to be at risk. But before Rosamund could be completely overcome by a fit of the dismals, her godmother told her that they would have to be making a move now that the royal family had led their Scottish guests to another chamber where a sumptuous banquet was spread for all.

Rosamund had barely sat down next to her godmother when she caught sight of her stepbrother. She was filled with a familiar dread. Fortunately, he was not looking her way, but talking to a nun in a white habit. Immediately, she thought of Ingrid and wondered was it her. If so, what would the Baron make of the two of them sitting next to each other? Suddenly, as if he had sensed her eyes upon him, Edward turned his head and stared directly at Rosamund.

She forced herself not to look away and reminded herself that her husband was somewhere in this hall, keeping his eye on her. Edward smiled his wolfish smile and she continued to stare at him dispassionately, despite her throat feeling so tight she felt as if about to suffocate.

The nun placed a hand on Edward's arm and put her mouth against his ear. There was something so intimate about that gesture that Rosamund's suspicions were roused. She watched his lips move and then the nun looked in Rosamund's direction with a startled expression on her lovely face that turned to fear.

Rosamund was so surprised that she could not look away. Then she felt a hand on her shoulder and looked up into her husband's face. 'Do you see her? That is Ingrid sitting at Fustian's side,' he said.

'Aye. I see her,' said Rosamund, her trauma intensified by the anger in his face. 'They must have been together in the Steel Yard that evening I was lost.'

'Aye. Your swine of a stepbrother and the woman I was fool enough to allow to worm secrets out of me,' he said. 'I am glad I know her now for what she is—untrustworthy and an adulteress.'

Rosamund was relieved to hear that was how he felt about his erstwhile lover. 'Does she ever wear anything other than a nun's habit?'

'Aye. She is a woman of many guises, is Ingrid.'

'What is she doing here with Edward dressed as a nun?'

'If there is gain to be made, then I deem she has a part to play in the conspiracy,' said Alex in a low voice, sitting next to Rosamund. He placed his arm about her shoulders, despite continuing to stare at Edward and Ingrid, and brought his head close to Rosamund's. 'I am convinced now that she did play me false.'

'You mean with Edward instead of Harry?'

'Aye.' Alex's eyes glinted. 'I am glad I changed my mind about keeping my distance. I decided I was not having him smirking at you and believing you defenceless. I want him to know that I am your husband.'

His solicitude was comforting. 'Why is she dressed like a nun here?' she whispered. 'How did she get an invitation?'

'It is for us to find out,' said Alex. 'I remember her telling me that she was placed with the nuns after her Danish mother died, but as soon as she was old enough she escaped the convent walls because she found she had no gift for the religious life. It was too dull. Besides, she could not bear women *en masse* day after day.'

'Did you not mention there were the nuns at Syon House, not far from here?'

He nodded. 'Obviously Fustian must have summoned her here for a purpose dressed in such garb. We need to discover what it is.'

Rosamund gazed at his taut profile and her heart ached for love of him. 'Perhaps I should go and make conversation with her and Edward. I could act like a lack-wit and that way they might reveal more than they would to you?'

'No. Your stepbrother knows you are not crazed, however much he might have said so in the past. He also must know you detest him and I am certain by now he suspects that I am aware of his illegal activities. Let us just keep our eyes on them and wait for them to make the first move.' He kissed the side of her face. 'In the meantime, let them see that we are enjoying ourselves in each other's company.'

'If that is the game you want to play,' she said, wondering if the kiss was part of it.

'This is no game, sweeting. This is deadly serious. So, what shall we talk about? You choose.'

How could she start a conversation when her head was in a whirl? But, hesitantly at first, she began to talk about the proxy ceremony and of the clothes worn by the royal family. Whilst they ate, they discussed the food and he told her of the great fish that he and Harry had pulled out of the waters of his own country. In between courses, they discussed jewellery and furniture, dancing, music and architecture.

Every now and again, she noticed he would look surreptitiously at Edward and Ingrid to see what they were doing. And all the time Rosamund wondered why it should still hurt that her husband had once loved Ingrid. She felt so tense that her head ached as she strained to make her voice heard and catch his words against the background noise of music and other chattering voices. She wished the banquet would end.

Fortunately there came the moment when the King gave permission for people to move about whilst the royal family retired for a short while. It was then that Alex noticed Edward leaving the hall and told Rosamund that he was going to follow him.

'That might be what he wants,' she said. 'He might lie in wait for you and—'

'He generally gets someone else to perform his foul deeds,' said Alex, his eyes hard and bright as gemstones. 'You stay here and keep your eye on Ingrid. I also need to send a message.'

Rosamund watched him stride from the hall. Her godmother and the lady on her right had risen as soon as the royal family had left the chamber and now she was alone at the table.

A group of tumblers entered the hall and began to practise their moves. She watched one of them perform a double-back somersault and then several cartwheels. She marvelled at his agility.

'Mistress Appleby?' said a rich, deep voice with a light foreign accent.

Startled, Rosamund looked up and saw Ingrid standing a couple of feet away. The light was better here than it had been in the church and outside the Steel Yard and the face was older than she had thought. There were creases at the corners of the pale blue eyes and lines between nose and mouth. Even so, Ingrid was still a lovely woman.

'Sister—?' enquired Rosamund politely.

'Sister Birgetta.' She inclined her head. 'I would like a word with you, if I may?'

'If you are acting as my stepbrother's emissary, then you can tell him that I do not wish to hear what he has to say,' stated Rosamund, proud that her voice was steady.

Ingrid sighed. 'Master Fustian told me it was hopeless, but I refused to believe him. He said that you were obedient to the church's teaching, so I thought I could act as peacemaker between the two of you.'

'What would you have me do?' asked Rosamund lightly. 'Agree to meet you in a quiet place where he would creep up on me and carry me off to his mother, who would lock me up, then poison me?'

Anger flickered in Ingrid's eyes, to be replaced almost immediately by sadness. 'He told me you needed taking care of because you were a crazed woman. I see it is true, for we saw you in company with a dangerous man. Unlike Master Fustian, who is a good man and wants to look after you.'

So Edward has already told Ingrid that I am crazed. 'You obviously do not know my stepbrother as well as you believe you do,' said Rosamund. 'I have known him a lot longer than you, Sister. He is a cruel thieving cur and he has stolen what belongs to my brother.'

Ingrid appeared to not have heard what Rosamund said because her eyes were fixed on the silver brooch at her throat. 'Where did you get that brooch?'

'The Baron gave it to me. It belongs to my brother, Harry.'

'But what is this you say?' Ingrid gave a tinkling laugh. 'Your brother is dead.'

'Have you proof of that?' said Rosamund with disdain. 'His body was never found, you know. I am certain he still lives.'

Ingrid laughed. 'Because the Baron has told you so? I would not believe him if I were you. He is a spy and is for ever deceiving people.'

If Rosamund had not already known her husband was a spy, then this revelation might be expected to shock her. 'And what is your reason for deceiving people? Linger here a while and tell my husband to his face that he is a deceiver.'

Ingrid's face blanched. 'Your husband! I deemed you were only betrothed.'

'Then you have been wrongly informed. Baron Dalsland and I are married.'

'I don't believe it. There has been no time.'

Rosamund's eyes gleamed with a sapphire light. 'I

married him two days ago in front of a priest in my god-mother's bedchamber.'

Ingrid's lips tightened into a thin line. 'Your godmother! She is the one with the white painted face? Why did you marry the Baron in her bedchamber? Perhaps she has not long to live and thought to provide you with a protector,' Ingrid said in pitying tones. 'You cannot really believe a real baron would marry you without some incitement. Besides, he should be arrested and thrown into a deep, dark dungeon. He is a pirate and has attacked English ships. I will see to it that he is arrested,' she said passionately.

Rosamund could feel a megrim coming on, but her curiosity was roused. 'How can a nun have my husband arrested?'

Ingrid smiled. 'Now you ask a sensible question and I will give you an answer. I will speak to the new Queen of Scotland and ask her to deal with the matter.'

'You are acquainted with her Majesty?' asked Rosamund with genuine surprise.

Ingrid drew herself up and there was an odd expression in her pale blue eyes. 'I am a representative of the Bridgettine Order at Syon House, where prayers have been said for the Princess Margaret daily. They will continue, even though she is now Queen.' She smirked. 'I was appointed to bring her a wedding gift because I have royal blood in my veins. It is a specially printed copy of the gospel of St Luke. She was delighted.' Ingrid tucked her hands in her wide sleeves. 'Now I will go and have a word with the Queen and you may come with me.'

'I would rather not,' said Rosamund, wondering what the Baron would make of this news. 'I can see my husband coming. You had better go.'

Ingrid's self-satisfied expression altered and she hurried away, only to collide into one of the tumblers and send him flying. She steadied herself and suggested loudly that he pick himself up, then she left the hall.

'Frightened her away, did I?' said Alex, looking grim.

'She as good as said that she has the ear of Princess Margaret—I mean, the new Queen of Scotland.'

Alex's expression was suddenly alert. 'Did she say how she managed that?'

'Apparently the nuns pray daily for the Princess Margaret and Ingrid was chosen to bring a present for her from the convent.'

'She has retreated to the convent in the past, so perhaps some of what she told you was true.' Alex sat down next to his wife and grinned at her. 'I don't know how you extracted that information from her, but it is possible that she could worm herself into the royal confidence and end up in a position where she is able to discover the date of departure and the route Queen Margaret and her entourage will take to the border.'

Rosamund was warmed by his praise. 'I am glad I please you. I can add to the information I have already given you and tell you that she was going to ask the new Queen to have you arrested for piracy.'

'Did she now?' Alex whistled. 'She would need to provide proof and no doubt she believes Edward could do that due to his own involvement.'

'He did tell her I was crazed and she wanted to take me to him.'

Alex's gold-brown eyes flamed with anger and he took Rosamund's hand and held it firmly. 'You have given me at least two reasons why I should kill him. The pair of them remind me of the mythical serpents who inhabited the underworld Isle of Naastrand, dripping venom on suffering sinners.'

Rosamund gazed down at their linked hands. 'Mockery and criticism and cruelty over a long period does poison one's confidence and could drive them crazy.'

He raised her hand to her lips and kissed it. 'But those hurts are now in the past. Right now our concern must be that the new Queen of Scotland does not come to any harm.'

'We will tell Godmother and she will warn her,' said Rosamund.

'No,' said Alex firmly. 'We need to catch our conspirators in the act and must have definite proof. Those involved are people of position and power.'

'So is my godmother.'

'I would not deny it, but despite her position and her connection to the royal family, some regard Lady Elizabeth as being a little mad. She has admitted as much herself. We must be patient.'

She nodded and winced with the pain in her head. 'Tell me—were you able to follow Edward?'

'Aye. I saw him in conversation with Lord Bude.'

'Lord Bude! Could you hear what they were saying?'

'Unfortunately, no. Why do you ask?'

Rosamund felt the colour flood to her face. 'I have just realised that it is possible that I mistook him for you in the Hanseatic church in the Steel Yard.'

'You mean he and Ingrid were locked in an embrace?' He laughed. 'Now, is he being ensnared by Ingrid to work for the conspirators or is he already one of them and she has a fancy for him? Even I would admit he is a handsome man. He also has a title, which always impresses Ingrid. I wonder what Fustian would make of it if he knew of that embrace?'

Rosamund thought he did not sound the least bit jealous of Bude. 'Do you still want me to indulge in conversation with Lord Bude at the dress rehearsal?'

'If you can, but don't worry if you can't.'

She nodded and then frowned, giving a little shiver before massaging her forehead.

Alex looked at her with concern. 'Are you cold? Do you have a megrim?'

'Aye. The noise and the smoke and…there is a draught.'

'Then let us slip away before the royal family returns. I, too, have had enough of people and noise.'

A relieved Rosamund said, 'What about Godmother?'

'If we see her on the way out, we can explain that you are not feeling well.'

'Do we tell her about Edward and Ingrid?'

'Of course. But that can wait until later. Right now you need a quiet, dark room to lie down in.'

As they made their way to their bedchamber, Rosamund was aware that her husband's hand was on his sword hilt. It was as if he was prepared for any sudden attack on them. Fortunately, they arrived at their destination without any unwelcome surprises. It was pure joy to kick off her shoes and stretch out on the bed and close her eyes.

The fire was still burning. Obviously, a servant had put more logs on it and there was a bucket of them at the side of the hearth. Not wanting Rosamund to get chilled, Alex put a couple more on the fire. Anxiety gnawed at his innards. He had never felt this worried about anyone before. Neither his grandparents nor Harry or Ingrid. What if this megrim was a sign of a serious illness and she died? He remembered her being out in the snow without a cloak and how her teeth had chattered.

'Are you cold still?' he asked.

'I do feel a little shivery.'

He hurried over to her and sat on the side of the bed and placed a hand on her forehead. He was relieved to find that it was not burning hot.

'Perhaps you would be better sitting by the fire.'

She sat up as if he had given her an order. 'If that is what you want me to do?'

He smoothed back her hair from her forehead. 'I want you to do whatever makes you feel better.'

'As long as I do not have to open my eyes.'

Alex slid an arm beneath her and lifted her up and carried her over to the chair by the fire. He sat down with her on his knee. 'How is this?'

'Fine.' Rosamund rested her head against his shoulder. 'Are you comfortable?' she murmured.

'Aye.' He was aware of the soft curve of her breast beneath the velvet cloak against his arm and the silky hair brushing his chin. 'We have been married only two days, but it seems longer,' he murmured.

'Is that good or bad?'

He smiled. 'I do not believe it is a bad sign.'

'Is it not strange that some days go by like a flash and others, like today, have so much fitted into them? Ingrid was angry when I told her you were my husband. She said a Baron would need much inducement to marry me. I should have mentioned Godmother's dowry.'

'I have no need of your dowry, but it would have impressed Ingrid. I would have liked to have been there when she told Edward that we were married.'

Rosamund opened her eyes to look into her husband's face. He was grinning. She touched his cheek. 'You have a good face.'

He took her hand and brushed her knuckles with his lips. 'You have a lovely face.'

She smiled and lowered her eyelids again. 'Edward will not like it that I am a Baroness.'

'The new Baron and Baroness Dalsland. I can hear us being introduced at a masque in Stockholm.'

'Were the old ones happy?' asked Rosamund.

'They respected each other and seemed content,' he replied. 'Although it was a grief to them that only my mother survived infancy. Sadly she must have been a disappointment to them.'

'Why do you believe that?' She yawned and closed her eyes. 'Did they say so?'

'No. But she presented them with only one grandchild and he was the illegitimate son of a foreigner.' Alex's voice sounded sad.

Rosamund's eyelids fluttered open and she stared at him. 'What are you saying?'

'I should have told you before we were wed, but there were others present and I did not want them to know that I was a bastard,' he said in bitter tones. 'Neither could I risk them knowing the name of my father.'

'Is this the secret you would not tell me?'

'Aye. My father is a Scottish earl, but I did not know of his existence until six months ago.' Alex found it easier to say than he had ever imagined. 'My mother was his mistress for several years and I was the result of their union. She died soon after my birth and I was sent with a wet nurse to my grandparents' home in Sweden. I grew up believing my father was a Swedish hero who had been killed in battle. It was his name I used most of my life. My grandmother did not tell me the truth until she was on her deathbed.'

Rosamund was moved almost to tears. 'How terrible for you to believe yourself one person and then discover you are someone else altogether.'

Her sympathy warmed his heart and he hugged her close and covered her mouth with his and gave her an enthusiastic kiss.

Rosamund felt her megrim ebbing away as she returned his kiss. She was aware of a tide of pleasure creeping over her. Of their own volition her arms wound themselves around his neck.

He lifted her off her feet and carried her over to the bed, where he placed her down without breaking off the kiss. He lay beside her and when he did bring the kiss to an end, it was so he could press kisses down the line of her throat. His fingers undid the fastenings on the front of her gown. She stilled, but when he proceeded to kiss her lips once more and he made no move to remove her gown then she relaxed. He nibbled her ear. A tiny giggle escaped her and he flicked his tongue around its shell-like rim whilst undoing the ribbons at the neck of her undergown. He eased the garment from her shoulders. Aware of his arousal, Alex prayed she was not. He must keep himself under control and concentrate firmly on giving his wife pleasure.

He had to make certain that she was unable to think of anything else but the sensations she was experiencing.

He kissed her again and darted his tongue along the inside of her lower lip. Immediately he sensed their mouths had all her attention and took the opportunity of lightly caressing her upper left breast before circling its centre with a single finger. He felt her breath catch and chose that moment to lower his head and nuzzle her nipple. She gasped, but did not pull away. He was glad, for he was receiving as much pleasure as she appeared to be. For a while his mouth lingered in this area that caused so much gratification for them both whilst he removed her clothing.

Rosamund was in a daze of delight by the time she realised she was stark naked and her husband's tawny head was pressed against her belly. The words *what are you doing?* died on her lips as he kissed her hip bone and she felt his fingers penetrate that part of her that she had been determined once not to surrender to any man. She protested, but he reached up and silenced her with a kiss as his caresses began to work a subtle magic within. Her breath came fast as she felt a gradual build up of pleasure. Her body was still thrumming when he moved away.

She reached out to him in silent protest and watched him remove his clothes. She had never seen a man naked before and she told herself it was to be expected that her gaze would fix on that part of him that proclaimed his manhood. But he did not allow her time to wonder at its size because he returned to her, but this time he slowly and carefully eased that part of him inside her. She gasped, but the pain of his entry was not as great as she had expected. This time there was little gradual build up as he gained possession of her and she heard him groan as he seemed to explode inside her, creating a pleasure so exquisite that she thought her body would not be able to contain it.

Chapter Fourteen

Afterwards Alex and Rosamund lay in a tangle of arms and legs, reluctant to move. He knew now for certain that she had told the truth about the woodcutter not having touched her; also, his fear that Fustian might have raped her was completely allayed. Whilst riding astride on horseback might have stretched her a little, her maidenhood had been intact.

Rosamund stirred beneath him and he lifted his head from her shoulder and gazed down at her as she opened her eyes. He waited for her to speak, but she seemed only able to stare at him and he did not doubt that he had pleasured her. He smiled wryly, guessing she would not know how to thank him for it. No doubt she might be feeling a little discomforted by finding such delight in carnal behaviour. He was tempted to thank her because it had been as good as he had hoped and would be even better next time. His eyes searched for the washstand and drying cloth and he removed himself.

Rosamund watched surreptitiously as her husband washed that part of him that now lay limp. She marvelled at the wonders of the human body. How was it that a child could grow from the act that they had just performed? A child! Lady Elizabeth might get her way after all. Now she was tied to the Baron for fairer or fouler until death parted them. She could not wait to repeat what they had just done. She had not expected to be swept away on such a tide of— of carnal pleasure, and she was certain he must have enjoyed it, too.

There was something about this Swedish baron husband of hers that called to something inside her and it had overcome any resistance that might have lingered from knowing that they had both been tricked into marriage. She felt that she had reached a oneness with him that almost convinced her that she would never feel lonely again. It was only as she was drifting off to sleep that it occurred to her that he had not told her the name of his Scottish father.

The following morning, they were roused by Lady Elizabeth. 'Come on, lie-abeds,' she wheezed. 'I wish I could sleep the way you two do. You'll need to put on your costumes for the dress rehearsal. Not that I'm expecting everyone to turn up.'

'Why not, Godmother?' asked Rosamund, wishing she could share with her the pleasure she had felt in having the Baron make love to her for the first time.

'I shall tell you over breakfast. It will be on the table in my parlour within half an hour. I also wish to know what happened yesterday that caused you to disappear without a word to me. And, Baron, a message has been delivered for you.'

Alex drew Rosamund close and kissed her before reluctantly releasing her and getting out of bed. He wished there was time to make love to his wife again, but other matters demanded his attention. He wrapped the bedcover around him and delayed long enough to go over to the window, draw back the curtains and gaze out.

'What can you see?' asked Rosamund, reaching for her undergown and slipping it on.

'I can see little at the moment due to the mist. Hopefully it will lift.' He turned and faced her. 'You have not forgotten I wish you to try to draw Lord Bude out to talk about your stepbrother?' His expression was sombre.

'I have not forgotten.' Rosamund had not expected to suffer that sinking feeling whenever Edward was mentioned again. Somehow she had believed that what had happened last night between her and her husband had completely destroyed her fear. 'I meant to ask you…' She paused, watching him sluice his face in cold water.

'What is it, Rosamund?' He looked at her.

'You did not tell me the name of your father.'

Alex stilled. 'Can you not guess?'

The question prevented her from asking him again and instead set her thinking about who could his father possibly be.

Alex turned away and began to put on the black-and-silver costume. 'I never wanted to meet him. I only did so because my grandmother insisted on my doing so before she died. It is he who asked me to find out what I could about those whom he suspected of plotting to destroy the peace pact. In return, I am to have the house and land on the Scottish coast that he gave to my mother.'

'That is indeed generous of him,' she said drily. 'I

presume if I am in a position to be able to guess his name that it has been mentioned?'

He smiled. 'Clever Rosamund.'

Rosamund was pleased by the compliment and reached for the black-and-silver gown and pulled it on over her cream linen undergown. 'I presume your natural father was already married when he had an affair with your mother.'

'Aye. To my shame.'

'Why your shame? It was not your sin,' said Rosamund firmly. 'I suppose one could say that at least he was being considerate of his wife if you weren't there as a constant reminder to her of his adultery.'

'I have never viewed my rejection in that light before,' said Alex, staring at her with dawning comprehension. 'Do you really believe that was his reason for sending me away?'

'It does not matter what I believe. What is important is what can make you feel better about yourself and your father,' said Rosamund, searching for a comb to tidy her hair. 'If you are to spend time in the house he has handed over to you, then surely it would be more pleasant if you could accept your father for what he is. After all, he must have been very fond of your mother to have given her a house and land and she must have been fond of him to have not requested of the Queen to return to her own home.'

'I never thought I would hear anyone say such words to me,' said Alex. 'My grandmother only thought of what he might give me.'

'Did he give you the name Alexander?'

'I believe it is one of his baptismal names.'

'There you are, then,' said Rosamund cheerfully. 'He must have accepted that you had a right to it.'

'I believe he is a doughty fighter, as was his father before him. I suppose it's possible he was named after the great Alexander of Macedon who conquered a large part of the known world in his day.' He glanced at Rosamund as he picked up his mask. 'He travelled as far as India in Asia. Harry thought that a great adventure.'

Rosamund looked at her husband in dismay. 'You do not think that he has gone to India?'

Alex looked taken aback. 'The thought had not occurred to me.'

'Then I pray that it did not occur to him either.'

'Aye. Now we *must* go. I am not accustomed to such long discussions before breakfast.' He softened the words with a smile.

'Neither am I,' she said.

They entered her godmother's parlour where Lady Elizabeth confessed to feeling a little groggy that morning. She handed Alex a missive.

'Are you certain you are well enough to dance, God-mother?' asked Rosamund, watching her husband move over to the window to read his message out of the corner of her eye. 'After all, you already know the steps and I suspect it is only for my sake that this rehearsal is necessary.'

'You could well be right, my dear,' said Elizabeth, ad-justing her wig. 'Do you know there is to be the first of many tournaments this morning? No doubt our young lords and ladies will wish to watch the jousts.'

'I find no amusement in watching men seeking to maim or to kill each other for a purse or to prove their manhood,' said Rosamund, spreading honey on bread.

'I am glad we agree on that,' said Lady Elizabeth.

She turned to Alex. 'So, what news do you have for me?'

He placed the missive in a pocket and told Lady Elizabeth about Ingrid and Edward and Lord Bude. The old woman listened carefully, wheezing an exclamation every now and again. When he had finished she was silent for what seemed a long time. Eventually, she said, 'I will speak to my kinsman later today about what you have told me. I will leave it to him to decide whether the King should be informed. A watch will be kept on those we suspect. I doubt this Ingrid will have been able to win Margaret's confidence so swiftly that she would attempt to persuade the King to have you cast into a dungeon.'

Soon after that decision was made they left the apartment, wearing their masks. Her ladyship had said that it would spoil the air of mystery and the dance if anyone were to recognise them beforehand. Despite her conviction, several people wished Lady Elizabeth a good morn. She ignored them. Obviously it took much to disguise such a well-known personage. But Rosamund was of the opinion that the mask made her almost invisible.

They reached the rehearsal chamber and, although the musicians had arrived and a few people had drifted in dressed in costume, it was as Lady Elizabeth had foretold and several members of the troupe were absent. Lord Bude was one of them.

Lady Elizabeth said, 'I wonder what has delayed him this time! Rosamund, you will dance with the Baron and I will save my strength.'

Rosamund was glad that Lord Bude had failed to make an appearance because she had not amassed that much confidence that she felt at ease attempting to glean information out of a young English lord. Still, she experienced pleasure dancing with Alex.

It was as the group was dispersing, having arranged where to meet for their part in the pageant later, that Lord Bude arrived with Edward. Rosamund was taken unawares. She was a girl again, wanting somewhere to hide from her stepbrother.

Alex reached out a hand and caught hold of Rosamund and drew her to his side. She felt strength flow into her and switched her gaze from her stepbrother's arrogant features to Lord Bude's face.

'Damn you for keeping me up so late, Fustian,' he said loudly. 'I have missed the dress rehearsal.'

Rosamund wondered if his annoyance was a pretence. She noted that he was not in costume and his ordinary clothes were rumpled as if he had slept in them.

'Why have you brought this man here, Lord Bude?' demanded Lady Elizabeth. 'These rehearsals are private.'

'I am also interested in your answer,' drawled Alex.

His lordship flushed. 'I beg pardon, Lady Elizabeth, but we played dice well into the night and Fustian would insist on accompanying me here.'

'That is because you were a little worse for drink, your lordship.' Edward's smiling dark eyes embraced the company, lingering on Rosamund. 'My dear Rosie, how lovely to see you. How pale you look. I have been concerned for you, my dear. I heard that you have married this—this foreigner,' he said disdainfully. 'Your father would not have approved. I really should have taken you in hand after he died.'

Rosamund felt the words of protest stick in her throat and then Alex squeezed her hand. 'Tell me, Edward, was it my stepmother who taught you which plants to use if you wished to be rid of someone, such as my father?'

Her stepbrother's smile vanished and he looked furious. 'How dare you besmirch my mother's good character! Here is another sign of your madness. You really are not safe to be let out alone. You should not have run off in that foolish way to marry a man who is a liar, a pirate and a spy.'

'Really, Master Fustian, you are a fool, as I told my god-daughter and her husband two nights ago, to insult my god-daughter and the Baron in such a way,' said Lady Elizabeth.

'Aye,' said Alex icily. 'You will pay for your insults and lack of gallantry towards my wife.'

'You had no right to marry her without my permission,' said Edward hotly.

'I did not need your permission,' said Rosamund, her voice quivering. 'If I needed anyone's, then it would be that of my brother, Harry, whose inheritance you and your mother stole.'

Edward stiffened. 'You really are crazed. Your brother Harry is dead.'

'You know very well that is untrue. As a boy Harry was abducted and smuggled aboard a ship.'

'Where is your proof?' he snapped.

'Six months ago my father caught sight of him in London and thought he recognised him. He spoke of this to my husband and what happens next? Alex is attacked and left for dead and my brother vanishes. I have no doubt you were responsible for these deeds.'

'Is that what your husband told you and you believed

him?' said Edward pityingly. 'You should have listened to Sister Birgetta. She would have told you the truth—that your husband was jealous of any man who looked at his lover, Ingrid Wrangel. I know the mariner whom you refer to and I'll admit that he bears a certain likeness to your brother, Harry, but he is not Harry. Both he and Ingrid disappeared around the same time.'

Rosamund paled. 'I don't believe you. My husband has been searching for Harry and that is why he wished to see my father at Appleby Manor, not knowing that he was already dead.'

Edward shook his head. 'The Baron deceived you. He looks for this other man so that he can kill him, just like he killed his lover.'

The next moment Alex had Edward by the throat and was lifting him off the ground. 'It is you that is a deceiver and are crazed. Ingrid and Sister Birgetta are one and the same. Admit it!'

'You will die for this,' croaked Edward.

'I don't think you are in a position to issue threats,' said Rosamund jubilantly. 'We know things about you and—' She stopped abruptly.

Lady Elizabeth tapped Alex's arm and gave him a warning look. 'Release him.'

Alex opened his hand and Edward dropped to the floor. 'Proof! Where is your proof?' he gasped, rubbing his throat. 'Unless you produce Harry, you have none. You will regret this, Baron!' He stumbled from the chamber.

His parting words were greeted by silence. Alex and Rosamund realised they were the focus of the attention of the dancers who had lingered in the doorway.

'Are you really a spy, Baron?' asked one of the ladies.

Alex's mouth curled up at the corners below the mask. 'I am a wealthy man in my own country, so why should I risk my life as a spy?' He sounded amused. 'Besides, Lady Elizabeth will vouch for my good character.' He paused. 'I add only that my wife's stepbrother and stepmother have been stealing what was rightfully hers and that of her brother after their father died. Is it any wonder Master Fustian resents her having a husband who is going to delve into these matters?'

There were murmurs of agreement and then Lady Elizabeth clapped her hands. 'Come, my lords and ladies. We must go our separate ways. I have messages to send before we meet again.'

The company dispersed and Rosamund noticed that Lord Bude was amongst them. She turned a strained face towards her husband. 'What a terrible scene! Edward was determined to try to convince those here that we were in the wrong.'

Alex said grimly, 'I should not have lost my temper. He was right about us having no proof.'

'It is too late for regrets now,' said Lady Elizabeth.

Alex removed his mask and his expression was stern. 'Aye. We'll need to be even more on our guard than before. Unfortunately, I must leave you both for a while. I will return in time for the performance. If I am late, I will meet you in the antechamber outside the hall.' He reached for his cloak. 'You should be safe enough here in the palace. Just make certain you lock the door of the apartment. There is someone I must see.'

'Who is this person?' asked Rosamund.

'Your friend, Master Wood. I have need of him here.'
He hurried away.

'Come, my dear,' said her godmother. 'We will return to the apartment and change out of our costumes and have some food and wine. There is still much I have to do— but what a scene, as you said. I only pray that your step-brother did not guess what you were going to say and does not warn his fellow conspirators and they escape.'

Rosamund said guiltily, 'I hope so, too. I should have been more discreet.'

'It is difficult to show discretion in the heat of the moment, what with him accusing the Baron not only of dishonesty, but murder.'

'I did not believe it for a moment,' said Rosamund stoutly.

'I should think not,' said Lady Elizabeth. 'But it would be helpful if Harry returned in the next few days.'

Rosamund could not agree more. She desperately needed to see her brother—he was the only one who could prove that Edward's story was a complete fabrication.

They dined simply at midday on bread and smoked fish and a glass of wine and still Alex had not returned. Lady Elizabeth had written several messages and gave them to Rosamund to deliver. She wasted no time in doing so, but was delayed on several occasions by the recipients not being in their chambers and having to go in search of them. Several times she was stopped and asked by people mulling around in different parts of the palace and gardens about the altercation between her husband and stepbrother. She marvelled at how swiftly the news had spread and was expecting when she returned to the apartment to discover that the King wished to speak to them.

But when she unlocked the door of the apartment it was to find her godmother sitting all alone, having already changed into her costume. She appeared to be dozing in a chair. Rosamund asked if she was feeling well. She mumbled a reply, but seemed a little groggy. 'Are you certain you can perform the dance, Godmother?' she asked.

Again the reply was indistinct, but Lady Elizabeth managed to heave herself to her feet. Rosamund turned to enter hers and Alex's bedchamber to put on her own costume. She heard a smothered giggle, then felt a blow to the back of the head and crumpled to the floor.

Alex arrived at the antechamber, out of breath with running from the stables to reach there in time. He could hear the musicians playing the introductory music and was aware of an uneasy murmur from the masked dancers. He looked about him for Rosamund and Lady Elizabeth; realising they were not there, he was filled with a sense of foreboding. Their late arrival would have been unusual if this had been just a rehearsal, but to perform before the royal family, their honoured guests and the whole court, meant something must have gone wrong. 'I'll go and see what has delayed them,' he said.

He was about to leave the antechamber when two black-and-silver clad figures entered the room. He noticed that Lady Elizabeth's wig was askew, but felt a rush of relief at their appearance. She signalled to the other dancers to go on ahead and beckoned Alex over to her. He smiled at the woman by her side. She fluttered her fingers at him as she passed him by. Only then did he realise that she was too tall for his wife; besides, Rosamund had never made such a gesture to him.

He sprang forward and dragged the veil from her head to reveal blonde hair. Ingrid! He should never have left Rosamund and felt heartsick, wondering what Fustian had done to her.

Ingrid wrenched herself out of his grasp and then he heard a woman call, 'Beware! Behind you, Baron!'

Alex turned and would have received the full force of the knife in his chest if Lady Elizabeth's maid had not rushed forward and gripped his assailant's arm with both hands and rested her whole weight on it.

The other dancers had stopped in their tracks at the sound of Hannah's voice and were now witnesses to the altercation happening before them as Alex grappled with the figure who at first glance had appeared to be Lady Elizabeth. The red wig had slipped and Alex was curious to know the identity of his attacker. Brown eyes widened in alarm behind the mask and then suddenly a strangled gasp issued from the painted lips and the eyes widened in shock.

Alex felt his body go slack in his grasp and blood welled between his fingers as he lowered him to the floor. Only then did he see the knife sticking out of his attacker's back. He glanced over at Ingrid, who had backed away towards the door. Had she killed him? If so, for what reason? Alex had been convinced she would like to see him dead. He bent over the man on the floor and removed the mask.

To his amazement the dead man was not Edward Fustian, but a complete stranger. Alex glanced around him. 'Does anyone recognise this man?'

'He's Master William Fustian,' said Hannah. 'Joshua and I came just in time to prevent his brother from carrying off the Baroness. I left the two men fighting. She told me I must go like the wind and warn you.'

'Thank you, Hannah,' said Alex, presuming that his wife was unharmed if she was able to give orders. But he must return to Lady Elizabeth's apartment to make certain and help Joshua in his struggle with Edward. But first—

He gazed about him for Ingrid, but she was no longer there and he realised she must have slipped out of the antechamber whilst he was distracted. But before he could make a move a courtier appeared. 'The King wants to know what is the delay,' he said.

'Master Edward Fustian's brother tried to kill the Baron,' said Lord Bude, 'but he in turn was killed in the struggle. I saw what happened with my own eyes.' He pointed a finger. 'See! He dressed up as Lady Elizabeth.'

The troupe gazed down at the sprawling figure on the floor and one of the ladies shuddered and another asked, 'Where is the real Lady Elizabeth?'

Hannah said, 'Baron, we must go! I had no time to see what had happened to my lady and she might be hurt.'

'What are we going to do about the dance?' asked one of the lords.

'You will have to perform without us,' said Alex.

'But that means there will only be six of us,' said a lady in dismay.

'Just do your best,' he said impatiently. 'I am sure the

King and Queen will understand once they know what has happened. You must tell the Earl of Derby what took place and that I will wait upon him after I have discovered what has happening to Lady Elizabeth.' He hurried from the antechamber, followed by Hannah.

As the door of the apartment came into sight Alex could see Joshua holding a struggling Ingrid captive. 'Where's Edward Fustian?' demanded Alex.

'I am sorry, Baron, but he escaped,' said Joshua, 'but Mistress Rosamund is safe, if a little dizzy from a blow on the head.'

Alex swore beneath his breath. 'Bring her into the apartment.' He entered the chamber and at first could see no sign of his wife and then he noticed her over by an armoire. 'What are you doing?' he said more sharply than he meant and hurried over to her. 'You should be resting.'

'I believe Godmother is in here,' replied Rosamund, steadying herself by resting a hand on the side of the armoire.

Alex gazed into her face and was relieved to see that she appeared to be little the worse for her ordeal. Then, hearing a low moan coming from the armoire, he unlocked the door and flung it open.

'Praise St Jude that you have come,' wheezed a bald Lady Elizabeth, stretching out a trembling hand. 'I thought I was going to die in here.'

Alex helped her out. She was unsteady on her feet and he half-carried the old lady over to a chair and ordered Hannah to find a blanket to wrap around her shivering form. She hurried to do his bidding and he returned to Rosamund and swung her up into his arms and carried her over to the settle. Only when he had seen to her comfort did he deign to give Ingrid some attention.

'Lock her in the armoire, Joshua,' he said tersely, 'until I have time to question her.'

Ingrid spewed forth a string of words in her own tongue, which caused him to respond with a short sharp sentence that silenced her. Then he faced Lady Elizabeth and Rosamund. 'What happened to William?' asked Rosamund before he could speak.

'He's dead.'

Rosamund stared at him in disbelief. 'Did you kill him?'

'No,' replied Alex, kneeling in front of her and chafing her hand. 'Are you sure you are all right?'

'Aye. I don't think I was unconscious for long.' Her fingers clung to his and she added, 'If you did not kill William, then who did?'

'I am not sure if it was Ingrid,' he replied.

Rosamund was baffled. 'But why?'

'What happened about the dance?' ask Lady Elizabeth fretfully.

'It is taking place now, so you are not to worry,' said Hannah.

'I should have been there,' she said, tears rolling down her cheeks. 'I want my potion,' she added.

Alex turned to Joshua, who had bundled Ingrid into the armoire. 'Edward must not be allowed to escape.' He held out his hand for the armoire key and pocketed it. 'Go and tell the captain of the King's guard what has taken place and ask him to organise a search.'

Joshua nodded and hurried out.

Chapter Fifteen

Rosamund said, 'I am so glad that Joshua and Hannah arrived when they did.'

'I beg pardon,' said Alex, frowning. 'I should never have left you.'

'I am not blaming you for what happened,' said Rosamund sincerely. 'You were not to know that he managed to get a key to the door.'

'Even so, I should not have been away so long, but I convinced myself that you would be safe in here with the door locked.'

'Begging your pardon, Baron,' said Hannah, 'but it was one of Master Fustian's men who is to blame. I was fetching something for her ladyship when I was grabbed from behind and mishandled disgracefully and my key was taken from me. He locked me in a cupboard, but I yelled and yelled and eventually Joshua came along and let me out.'

'We have much for which to thank that young man. Unlike that young madam in the armoire,' said Lady Elizabeth, rolling her eyes. 'Can't someone stop her from ca-terwauling? She should be locked in a dungeon and the key thrown away.'

'I will speak to her and see what she has to say,' said Alex, taking the key from his pocket. 'Hannah, make her ladyship's potion and fetch us some food and wine, if you please?'

'Aye, Baron.' Hannah went to do his bidding.

Rosamund turned her attention on her husband as he opened the door of the armoire. Ingrid fell into his arms and clung to him. Instantly Rosamund sprang to her feet, enraged. But before she could ask Ingrid to unhand her husband, Alex disentangled himself and held Ingrid at arm's length.

'You will behave yourself,' he said sternly.

'Alex, how can you speak to me in such a way?' she said in a silky voice. 'I saved your life.'

'How did you do that?' he asked, frowning down at her.

'I killed him for you.' Ingrid bent her head and rubbed her cheek against his arm.

'Stop that,' he ordered, releasing her abruptly. 'You have admitted to murder and you could be strung on a gibbet and hung by your neck until you are dead.'

Ingrid gasped and put a hand to her throat. 'You would not let them do this to me? You once loved me, Alex, and I loved you in return. If it had not been for Harry—'

'So you say, but I no longer love you, Ingrid, that's if it was love I ever felt for you,' said Alex frankly. 'Right now I am more interested in what you have to tell me about Edward Fustian's plans.'

Her expression altered and she said sulkily, 'We are no longer lovers and he does not take me into his confidence.'

He stared at her pitilessly. 'You must consider me a fool. You would not have had access to the dance costumes and arrived at the antechamber with Edward's brother if you were not party to his plans.'

Ingrid tilted her chin and said, 'You must release me and then I will tell you.'

Rosamund held her breath. Would Alex free Ingrid despite his having said that he had never loved her?

'I can make no promises,' said Alex, 'but if you know anything about the plot to ruin the peace pact between England and Scotland, then it is possible that the King might agree to putting you in the care of the nuns at Syon House.'

Ingrid's shoulders slumped. 'I would rather tell you how Harry deceived me that day you both disappeared. He said that he would meet me, but did not come. Later I received a message saying that he had gone away to leave the way open for you and I to marry.'

Alex did not know if she was telling the truth or not. He swore beneath his breath. 'I can see we are not going to get anywhere until you get this off your chest. Do you know where he went?'

'I thought he had returned to fighting pirates in the northern seas, but recently I met a girl, half-Irish, half-Scottish, who believed differently,' said Ingrid.

Rosamund drew closer to them and watched her intently. 'What was her name and what did she know about Harry?' she asked.

Ingrid spared her a scornful look and addressed Alex. 'She would not reveal any information despite the fact that I followed Edward's mother's instructions to persuade her.'

Rosamund drew in her breath sharply.

Alex glanced at her and their eyes met and he said softly, 'She will pay for her wickedness.'

Rosamund nodded and returned to the settle. Alex faced Ingrid once more. 'What is this girl's name?'

'Bridget McDonald. Her father is a sea captain and kin to Edward. These McDonalds proliferate,' she muttered. 'There are several of them involved in a plot to destroy the King of Scotland.'

Now we are coming to the heart of it, thought Alex.

'And how are they to do that?' asked Lady Elizabeth, suddenly seeming to come to life.

Ingrid glanced at her. 'What is this information worth to you?'

Elizabeth's mouth tightened. 'And what is your neck worth to you, madam? You will answer me!'

A muscle in Ingrid's throat convulsed and she swallowed. 'They believe the best way to do this is by waylaying the new Queen of Scotland's entourage once it has crossed the border. They will kill her before she can give James children of mixed English and Scottish blood, so joining the two royal houses together. They will also steal what they can and murder the rest of her entourage.'

Alex sent an admiring look Rosamund's way.

'This Bridget,' said Rosamund. 'Will we find her at my stepbrother's house in London?'

Ingrid nodded. 'I think she will thank me when she knows I have killed William. His mother and her uncle were arranging a match between them in the hope of getting their hands on the fortune they believe her father has hidden away.'

'Thank you, Ingrid,' said Alex.

He turned to Rosamund and Lady Elizabeth. 'I will leave for London immediately.'

'Take me with you,' said Ingrid. 'I can help you. They trust me.'

'But do we trust you?' said Rosamund in a honeyed voice. 'I think not.'

She glanced at her husband to see what he thought of what Ingrid had said, but he had left the room for their bedchamber. He reappeared a few moments later dressed for riding.

'You will release me before you go?' asked Ingrid eagerly.

'Certainly not,' said Lady Elizabeth with a sniff.

Ingrid cursed her, but was silenced by a banging on the door. A voice shouted that it was the Earl of Derby and they must open up. Lady Elizabeth told Alex to let him in. This he did, stepping aside to allow the elderly Earl and two guardsmen into the chamber.

'I hope you can give me a thorough explanation about what is going on, Beth?' The earl's rheumy eyes gazed into her face before looking at the others in the room. 'I have to inform you that so far Master Fustian has not been found, but the search goes on.'

'A word in your ear, my lord, if you please?' said Alex.

'And you are?'

'Baron Dalsland.'

'Ahhh!'

There followed a whispered conversation, after which the guards were ordered to take the prisoner away and lock her up. Ingrid struggled and told Alex that he was an ungrateful dog and that she would put a curse on him.

'It is very difficult trying to keep that woman quiet,' said

Lady Elizabeth. 'Perhaps she should have her tongue ripped out.'

'Godmother!' Rosamund could not help but be shocked by the remark, despite her own antipathy towards Ingrid.

'That would be a foolishness, Beth, if we want to discover if she has any more information that would help us.' The Earl sat down and asked Lady Elizabeth to tell him her story.

She began her tale and, as Rosamund listened, she grew hopeful that she and Alex would be heeded when they recited their part in the events that had taken place. It came to her turn and she had began to relate what had happened when her voice suddenly faltered.

'What is it, my dear?' asked Lady Elizabeth.

'I was just thinking how close we all came to death.'

Alex broke in that point. 'My wife is extremely upset by all that has happened, my lord. I would take her away from the palace back to London immediately.'

'She has done well so far,' said Earl Derby, his brows bristling. 'And the King will most likely want to hear your story himself, Baron. You cannot leave just yet.'

'Aye, but—' began Alex.

Lady Elizabeth placed a hand on the Earl's arm. 'Have pity, Thomas, my poor goddaughter is confused and worn out with all that has taken place. She is with child and it would be terrible indeed if she were to lose the babe due to the deeds of murderous, thieving traitors. Besides, I am ill and I would have my goddaughter accompany me home by barge as soon as possible.'

'Is this true, Baroness, that you are with child?' asked the Earl.

How could Rosamund deny it? She would be seen to be accusing her godmother of lying.

'Of course it is true,' said Alex.

The Earl smiled. 'My best wishes to you both. I will speak to Henry and no doubt he will agree to allow the Baron and Baroness to leave with you in the morning, Elizabeth. Well done, all of you. I am certain it won't be long before we have Master Fustian under lock and key.'

The door closed behind him.

Rosamund looked at Alex and saw that he was looking frustrated. 'What is it?' she asked.

'I must leave now if I am to arrive in London before news reaches your stepmother that William is dead and that Edward faces ruin.'

'But you cannot,' said Rosamund, going over to him. 'You heard what the Earl of Derby said.'

'I know, but if she hears the news before I get there, then she and her kinsman and possibly Edward could take Bridget McDonald and go into hiding. I must leave now,' he said firmly. 'She is the only one who might be able to tell us where Harry is.'

'I understand that, but you would leave me behind?' said Rosamund with a sinking heart.

His face was grave. 'It will not be an easy journey and I will not risk your safety.'

'We have ridden together through the darkness before.'

'But not when you were with child,' he said, against her ear.

'It is not true that I am with child,' she whispered. 'I told you, I have never lain with another man.'

'No. But you have lain with your husband. You could

now be carrying our child. You must keep him or her safe. God willing I will see you when you arrive in London tomorrow.'

His hand was on the door when Lady Elizabeth said, 'You take a risk, Baron, disobeying Derby. What if the King sends for you this evening?'

'I am certain you and Rosamund will be able to vouch for my good intentions,' said Alex.

He was through the door when Rosamund called, 'Wait! You would travel alone? What if Edward has escaped the palace with some of his men and they waylay you?'

Alex did not hesitate. 'I should imagine his men have already been put under guard. But I will not go alone. If it makes you happier, I will take Joshua with me, with your permission, Lady Elizabeth?'

'Of course.' Her chest wheezed as she sighed. 'You are quite mad, Baron, just like your grandfather. I was extremely fond of him, you know? May God be with you.'

Alex smiled, blew a kiss at his wife and closed the door behind him.

Lady Elizabeth exchanged glances with her goddaughter. 'I think it is going to be a long night, my dear.'

Rosamund did not deny it.

It seemed an age before Hannah, accompanied by a couple of servingwomen, brought food and drink. There was a suppressed air of excitement about the maid. But it was not until the food was set on a table and the servingwomen had left that they were to be told her news.

'You will never guess, my lady, what has happened,' said Hannah.

'I am in no mood for guessing games.' Lady Elizabeth yawned. 'I am sleepy, so do not delay, Hannah.'

The maid hastened to tell her tale. 'Apparently, the King sent for one of the Scottish knights, but he could not be found, this despite a search of the palace being made. It is said that the King was angry about that, but he was even more so when it was reported that the woman the Baron questioned has also disappeared.' Her eyes widened with excitement. 'Rumor has it that she was a nun in disguise, but the truth is that she is a witch. They are saying she cast a spell over the guards and flew over the walls on a broomstick.'

Lady Elizabeth made an angry noise. 'Nonsense! Even if the woman were possessed of magic powers, where would she get a broomstick?'

'Easy enough to pick up one of them, my lady,' said Hannah roundly.

'I do not believe it. Someone must have helped her to escape.'

Hannah stiffened. 'I'll say no more, my lady, except that he and she cannot be found anywhere.'

Lady Elizabeth waved her away and, affronted, the maid walked stiff-legged from the room.

'Flying broomsticks,' muttered Lady Elizabeth, reaching for a chicken leg.

'I have heard that belladonna mixed with certain spices and oil can give one the feeling of flying,' said Rosamund in a careful voice. 'A supposed witch could have some mandrake ointment to hand. It can kill if not used with caution.'

'What are you saying, my dear?' Lady Elizabeth glanced across at her. 'You are not eating.'

'I seem to have lost my appetite.' She was thinking a

terrible thought about Alex adopting a Scottish accent and helping his erstwhile lover to escape. Surely it was madness to even harbour such a notion? This was what love did to one. It filled a person with such anxiety concerning the loss of the object of that love.

'I am rather of the mind that the Scottish knight could be Sir Andrew Kennedy. Maybe he freed her, or perhaps it was Master Fustian? We do not know.'

'I have thought of someone else who might have helped her,' said Rosamund. 'Lord Bude. Perhaps he is able to adopt an excellent Scottish accent. If it is him, then maybe they will flee the country.'

'It has not been proved that Lord Bude has committed any error yet,' said Lady Elizabeth. 'This is purely conjecture, my dear. If our Scottish knight is a Kennedy, then he will not be concerned about the Ingrid woman. He will head for the border. If it is Fustian, he would be wiser to avoid London. Myself, I believe the Ingrid woman seduced one of the guards to let her go. Now, eat some of this excellent chicken and then it is bed for us if we are to return to London in the morning.'

Rosamund could see the sense in Lady Elizabeth's words. Much better to believe Edward would head north to Appleby and then on to Scotland. She helped herself to chicken and ham and forced herself to eat. If she was already carrying Alex's child, then it must be fed. The coming night would seem long, but dawn would come and hopefully bring with it a bright tomorrow.

The following morning, after a brief conversation with the Earl of Derby and the King, Lady Elizabeth and

Rosamund were allowed to leave for London. A mist hung over the river and Rosamund was glad of her warm cloak as she boarded the barge. All her doubts and fears had resurfaced as she woke from a nightmare of her husband having played her false. Fortunately, the tide was with them, and by midday they had passed the Palace of Westminster. Soon she would know if dreams had any substance, but, God willing, Alex would be at her godmother's mansion to welcome them with good news.

Believing there was no time to delay, a weary Alex left Joshua at Lady Elizabeth's mansion to tend to their horses. His mount had thrown a shoe and this had slowed them down, so that they had arrived in London much later than hoped. As Alex made his way through the foggy streets of London to Cheapside, he could only hope that Walther had ensured a watch was still being kept on Fustian's house. On reaching the area, Alex did not immediately approach the house, but looked about him for Walther or one of his men. There were few people about, but he had not been standing on the corner for long when Walther approached him.

'I did not expect to see you back in London so soon,' said Walther in their own tongue.

Alex explained what had taken place the evening before and his friend let out a low whistle. 'I have been here several hours and have seen no sign of Master Fustian or of anyone going in or out. But I do know that Mistress Fustian left yesterday afternoon with her two daughters.'

'So Bridget McDonald could still be inside with her uncle and Lady Appleby,' said Alex. 'You will stay here and continue to keep watch. I will try to gain entry. Have you someone watching the back of the house?'

Walther nodded. 'If you need a helping hand, there will be more than two of us as I am expecting another man to take over my watch.'

Alex thanked him and then crossed the street and knocked on the door. A voice from within enquired who was there.

'I have news from Richmond and wish to speak to Mistress Fustian,' he answered.

The door opened and immediately he recognised the woman whom Mistress Fustian had addressed as Lady Monica. She had green eyes that slanted like that of a cat and wrinkles at the corners of her mouth. She was dressed in a russet woollen gown and her hair was concealed beneath a veil. Anger threatened to overcome him, faced as he was with the woman who had caused Rosamund so much suffering. It was with difficulty that he managed to rein in his temper and adopt a vague expression. 'You are not Mistress Fustian.'

'No. She has gone away for a few days to stay with her sister. I am Lady Appleby, the mother of Master Fustian. What is it you want?'

Immediately Alex adopted a grave look. 'In any other circumstances I would have been delighted to make your acquaintance, Lady Appleby. As I said, I am newly come from Richmond.'

Her eyes narrowed. 'What do you mean in *any other* circumstances? What news do you have of my sons? Hasn't the King granted Edward his wish? Is he not to be Lord Mayor of London?'

'It is doubtful. Perhaps I may be permitted to come inside to give you my news. You might wish to sit down.'

Lady Appleby looked thoroughly alarmed and seized his sleeve. 'No. Say what you have to say now! Has someone else gained the King's favour?'

Alex brushed her hand from his sleeve. 'Your son is dead.'

The colour drained from Monica Appleby's face and a keening cry left her lips. Then she grabbed his arm and demanded, 'Which son?'

'Your younger son, William.'

Her relief was apparent. 'Why did you not say so first, upsetting me the way you did? What of my son Edward? Is he safe? Why has he not brought me news concerning William's death?'

'Did I hear someone say that William is dead?' asked a voice that held a Scottish lilt.

Alex looked beyond Lady Appleby to the young woman a few feet behind her. 'Aye, mistress. Master William Fustian is dead.'

'You are certain of this?' she demanded.

'Aye.' He estimated her to be sixteen or seventeen summers. She wore a plain brown gown and wisps of auburn hair had escaped her headdress and curled about her heart-shaped face. 'I saw him die, myself. There can be no mistake.'

'This obviously means that the wedding will not take place,' she said, beaming at him.

'Be quiet, Bridget! Have you no sense of what is fitting?' said Lady Appleby in a cold voice. 'Return to your bedchamber immediately.'

Bridget made no move to do as she was told, but instead said, 'Who are you, sir, so that I know whom to thank for this news?'

'I am Baron Dalsland,' he replied, amazed by her self-possession.

Lady Appleby started back. 'Get in, girl! Go fetch your uncle.'

'I would rather not,' said Bridget.

Lady Appleby brought up her hand and smacked the girl's face. Alex moved swiftly and seized her wrist. 'Do not do that again,' he warned.

'What's going on?' demanded a man's voice in a thick Scottish accent.

Immediately, Bridget ducked beneath Alex's arm and made her escape.

'Now see what you have done,' cried Lady Appleby. 'Unhand me at once, you swine!'

'You heard the lady,' growled the Scotsman, advancing on Alex.

Alex shoved Lady Appleby towards the man, whom he presumed to be her McDonald lover, and turned swiftly on his heel and went after the girl.

He caught a brief glimpse of Walther's surprised face and then it vanished in the mist. He ran on and became aware of the sound of thudding feet to his rear and presumed that McDonald was giving chase. Alex put on a spurt and soon the sounds of pursuit receded into the distance, but in that short time he had lost sight of Bridget McDonald. He came to a sudden halt in front of St Paul's Cathedral.

Could she have gone inside? He did not hesitate, but plunged into its interior, only to find that a mass was taking place and he had no choice but to adopt an attitude of worship whilst out of the corner of his eye, he tried to search the congregation for Bridget. But with so many heads bent in prayer he had an almost impossible task. He could only wait until the service ended and then he hurried to the entrance in the hope of finding the girl on her way out.

Alex stood there, watching all those that left the cathedral, but he could not see her. His expression was grim as he accepted that his reunion with Rosamund would be blighted by the news that he had been within an arm's length of Bridget McDonald, only to lose her.

Chapter Sixteen

'If all had gone well, then surely he should have been here by now,' said Rosamund, trying to remain calm as she planted another stitch in a tear in the hem of her blue gown. She could not bear to lose Alex now when there was a real chance of happiness ahead for them.

Lady Elizabeth said, 'The Baron is no fool. He is not going to walk into a trap. You heard what Joshua said about them arriving in London later than hoped. No doubt the Baron will walk through that door any moment now.'

The words were scarcely out of her mouth when the door opened and Alex entered the parlour. Rosamund's heart leapt in her breast and her relief was so intense that she felt dizzy.

He said without preamble, 'I have bad news. In my haste I lost her and now have no notion of her where-abouts.' He removed his hat and ran a hand through his tawny mane of hair and then went over to the fire and stood gazing into its flames.

'We are talking about Bridget McDonald?' asked Rosamund.

He lifted his head and stared at Rosamund. 'Who else would I mean?'

'No one else,' she said hastily, banishing the unworthy and foolish thought about Ingrid.

He sensed she was not being completely honest with him. 'If you were thinking about your stepmother, then she is still at Fustian's house with McDonald.'

'What happened?' asked Lady Elizabeth.

He told them and both looked relieved. 'At least Bridget McDonald is alive and no longer their prisoner,' said Rosamund, touching Alex's arm. 'You must not blame yourself for what happened. You could not have foreseen her escaping the way she did—also, the weather was against you.'

He smiled wryly. 'That is true, but it might not be easy to find her again.'

'She definitely seems a resourceful girl,' said Rosamund.

'We can organise a search,' said Lady Elizabeth, her eyes brightening. 'Sooner or later the mist will lift and, with the help of my men and your friend Walther and your other accomplices, we will find her.'

Alex warned, 'We are not going to be the only ones searching for her, so we must act swiftly.'

'Do you not think it possible that my stepmother and McDonald will decide to cut their losses and leave the city?' asked Rosamund, presuming he referred to them. 'The news of William's death must have given them some indication that Edward's plans have gone awry.'

'Aye, but it's possible they may linger, hoping for word from him,' said Alex.

'You will never guess what happened after you left,' said Lady Elizabeth, a mischievous glint in her eye.

Alex contained his impatience. 'Tell me,' he said politely.

'Sir Andrew Kennedy and that impudent madam you questioned both vanished from the palace.'

Alex's eyebrows shot up. 'What do you mean— vanished?'

Rosamund bent her head and toyed with the amber-and-silver ring on her finger. 'Someone released Ingrid and, although a search was made, just like Edward, she was not found.'

He stared down at her bent head and wondered if she had allowed herself to doubt him and, despite his words to the contrary, still believed that Ingrid had some power over him. Soon he was going to have to convince his wife without a measure of a doubt that she meant much more to him than Ingrid had ever done.

'Of course! Rumours were flying around that she was a witch and they had flown over the walls on a broomstick,' said Lady Elizabeth. 'I, myself, firmly believe that Sir Andrew and this—this so-called witch will ride for the Scottish border.'

'Whereas I was convinced she would come to London,' said Rosamund, glancing up at him.

'Why?' asked Alex bluntly. 'Do you not deem it possible that Edward could have freed her and set out north for Appleby Manor and from there head for the border?'

'Aye, that could be a possibility,' said Rosamund, 'but I cannot accept it. I do not believe Edward would abandon his mother. There is a bond between them that I now consider quite unhealthy.'

'Rosamund thinks that Lord Bude could have freed Ingrid,' said Lady Elizabeth breathlessly.

Alex slanted a smile at Rosamund. 'Now that is a more likely scenario for me. But let us not be distracted from our purpose—finding Harry, and Bridget McDonald is our key to doing so.'

'You do not deem she might return to Fustian's house?' asked Lady Elizabeth.

'I greatly doubt it, despite her having no cloak or gloves to keep her warm in this freezing fog,' said Alex. 'But if she were to attempt to sneak into the house by a back door, then she will be seen. A watch is being kept in case Lady Appleby and McDonald consider making a run for it.' He looked at Rosamund. 'I was repelled by the way she accepted the news of her younger son's death. It was as if it only mattered to her that Edward lived, so no doubt you are right in your estimation that he will come to London.'

Lady Elizabeth leaned forward and hugged her knees. 'You are presuming that he has not been captured. My kinsman, Derby, is bound to send word to me in the next day or two—that is, if he does not come himself. I will inform him of what you say.'

Alex nodded. 'I must change my garments and I need some refreshments before I go out again.' He left the parlour without a backward glance.

Rosamund wished he had asked her to go upstairs with him. They could have talked in private, but he obviously believed he had no time to waste and considered that she had no part to play in the search for Bridget McDonald. It was possible that he was correct in his presumption, but she resented being expected to just meekly stay in the background with her godmother.

Rosamund stood up. 'Will I ask a servant to bring food and wine here for the Baron?'

'Certainly, my dear. Then we must discuss what is to be done when this young woman is found. It is possible that she will be reluctant to divulge to us the whereabouts of your brother if her own father—who is a McDonald, don't forget—and treasure are involved.'

As Rosamund arranged for refreshments for Alex, she considered her godmother's words. She could see the sense in her reasoning, but deemed there was little point in discussing it before Bridget was found. She would rather be involved in the search.

'I wonder what she was wearing when she escaped and whether she had any coin with her,' said Rosamund, picking up her sewing again.

'Ask the Baron,' said her godmother.

'I will,' she murmured.

Alex did not waste much time in eating and drinking, and talked not at all but to answer Rosamund's question concerning Bridget McDonald.

'She wore only a brown homespun gown and a plain headdress. I doubt that she would have any coin with her. Can you see your stepmother and the uncle providing her with money?'

Rosamund could not, but if Bridget was as resourceful as she estimated, then it was possible she might have had the wits to obtain pennies from somewhere and sown them into the hem of a gown. Surely she would have given some thought to escaping during her captivity?

When Alex took his leave of Rosamund, he warned her against going beyond the perimeter walls of her godmother's mansion. 'If your stepbrother does reach London, then he will be determined to have his revenge on us. I hope to return before nightfall,' he added, 'but if it so happens that I deem it necessary to follow McDonald and Lady Appleby, then I will do so. If they can lead us to your stepbrother, all the better. This might mean my being absent for a day or more.'

'You will take care,' she said, unable to conceal her concern.

His face softened and he touched her cheek with a gentle hand. 'Trust me, Rosamund. I do care about our future.'

She felt tears prick the back of her eyes and nodded wordlessly before pressing her lips against his palm. He kissed her and then, with a nod in Lady Elizabeth's direction, hurried from the parlour.

Rosamund spent a few moments composing herself before facing her godmother again. 'I have been thinking that instead of worrying about what to do once Bridget McDonald is your guest, perhaps we should play our part in trying to solve the puzzling question of where she could be hiding.'

'Certainly,' wheezed Lady Elizabeth. 'We have a young woman of some sixteen summers with no cloak or gloves to keep her warm.'

'She might have a little money.' Rosamund divulged her thoughts about coin to Lady Elizabeth. 'We do not know if she has any friends in the city. It is possible that Edward's wife, Marion, would have befriended her as she was staying in her house, but we know from what the Baron told us that Marion has taken her daughters to stay with her sister.'

'Are we to presume that the girl arrived in London on horseback or by ship?' asked Lady Elizabeth.

'Horseback, if she travelled here from Appleby Manor.' Rosamund paused to consider her poor, misled but unpleasant younger stepbrother, who had been intended for Bridget's husband and prayed God would have mercy on his soul. On a more cheerful note, she thought that at least when Harry did return to reclaim his inheritance he would not have William to contend with and he would certainly appreciate it if their stepmother and Edward were also out of contention. She felt an old familiar chill thinking of them, but then thought of Alex and determinedly did not give way to that paralysing fear of them.

'Is her father not a pirate?' asked Lady Elizabeth.

Rosamund nodded. 'Although, perhaps it is best if we do not use that term when speaking to Mistress McDonald about him, but it does mean that he must have a ship.'

'Would he risk sailing into London?'

'That we cannot know, but it is possible that father and daughter would have means of getting in touch with each other if it was needful.'

'I am convinced, Rosamund, that would be difficult. Ships can be blown off course and end up God only knows where,' said Lady Elizabeth.

'Aye, that is true. But if I were Bridget McDonald, I might be tempted to haunt the quaysides and taverns were mariners abound and make enquiries concerning my father's ship.'

Lady Elizabeth shook her head. 'It would not be seemly for a young woman of her age to do so and it would also be dangerous. No, Rosamund, if she is a young woman of sense, then she will seek aid from those who have her well-being at heart.'

Immediately, Rosamund felt deflated. Who could Bridget McDonald turn to if she had no friends in London? Again she considered what she would do if she was in the Scottish girl's shoes and came up with an answer—one that she decided to keep to herself.

To her relief, Alex did return to the house several hours later. Over supper he informed them that a man had arrived on horseback and entered Fustian's house. He had remained inside and after a short while a wagon had drawn up at the front door and several items had been loaded onto it, including a large trunk. It had departed, taking with it the first man, whom Alex and Walther had presumed to be a messenger. A couple of men had been despatched to follow the wagon whilst Alex remained on watch so that Walther could slip home and have a meal and rest. He had returned to relieve Alex, so he could get some sleep after what had been an extremely long day.

Rosamund had planned to talk to her husband about some of her thoughts concerning Bridget McDonald once they had retired to their bedchamber. As it was, her hopes were not realised; no sooner had Alex's head touched the pillow than he fell into a deep sleep. She spent a restless night, only to drop off just before dawn.

When eventually she awoke, it was to find that she was alone in the bed. She performed her *toilette* swiftly, dressed and hurried downstairs, only to discover that Alex had already left the house.

Frustrated by his lack of communication, she was tempted to follow him, but she remembered what happened last time she had gone out alone behind the perimeter walls and changed her mind. As it was, that proved to be the sensible course; no sooner had Rosamund and Lady Elizabeth finished breakfast than they had a visitor in the elderly person of the Earl of Derby.

Her ladyship welcomed him warmly and Rosamund would have excused herself if he had not waved her to a chair. 'Sit down, my dear. I hope you are both well and recovered from the attack on your persons?'

'Indeed, we have, Thomas,' answered Lady Elizabeth. 'What news do you have from Richmond? Have you caught those villains yet?'

He grimaced. 'I am not here to talk of them, Beth, I bring other tidings. But I will tell you, while I remember, that Kennedy's reason for leaving so precipitously was due to news that his son is dangerously ill and his wife requested his presence at the bedside,' he said drily. 'As for the Fustian fellow, there has been no sighting of him, but his barge was seen being rowed away yesterday just after noon. It was out of sight before anyone thought to report the incident.'

'Now that is interesting,' said Lady Elizabeth. 'Have you discovered yet if it has tied up here in London?'

'The matter is being looked into, but I expect naught to come of it. The Fustian fellow is not going to hang around waiting to be arrested.'

'Well, I can tell you, Thomas, that the Baron has not been slow in visiting Fustian's home and is having a watch kept on the building,' said Lady Elizabeth, 'but so far he has not shown up.'

Derby nodded sagely. 'I tell you, ladies, that the Baron is wasting his time. Fustian will be heading for the border. I must be on my way.' He rose to his feet. 'Oh, the other news I had for you. It is the Queen. She is at her apartments in the Tower for her confinement. We are all praying that she will be safely delivered of a son.'

'I, too, will pray for her,' said Lady Elizabeth. 'I suppose this means that the celebrations have come to an end and your Scottish visitors are preparing to depart for their northern lands?'

'Aye. But Margaret will not be accompanying them. She awaits news of her mother and the child.'

Lady Elizabeth looked relieved and went with him to the front door, leaving Rosamund sitting by the fire. She wondered what Alex would say when he heard the latest tidings from Richmond.

Rosamund did not have long to wait as he arrived back at the house in time for the midday meal. He greeted her with a smile and asked when they were alone whether she was feeling any after-effects from the blow on her head.

'It aches a little, but otherwise I am well,' she answered, warmed by his solicitude.

'Good.' He took her hand and nursed it in his own. 'I beg your forgiveness for having spent so little time with you since returning to London.'

Rosamund assured him that she understood why he was so occupied. 'But while you were out we had a visit from the Earl of Derby. He told us news that will be of interest to you.'

His expression sharpened. 'Tell me!'

'Edward's barge was seen being rowed away yesterday afternoon. No one thought to report it immediately because the Queen was making her departure to the Tower for her lying-in.'

Alex's eyes gleamed with satisfaction. 'This is indeed good news. The wagon that left Fustian's house yesterday was taken to a warehouse close to a wharf the other side of London Bridge. It would not surprise me if today we were to discover Fustian's barge tied up at a quayside close by.'

'You think you will find Edward there?'

'Possibly,' he answered, 'but it could be that we only find his mother and McDonald. It is likely that Fustian sent the message yesterday and no doubt they have passed on the news to him that not only has Bridget McDonald escaped their charge, but that they've had a visit from the Baron Dalsland.'

'But where would they go in a barge? Surely it is not made for sea travel? They would need a real sailing ship for such a journey.'

'That is true, but I deem that it is most likely their intention to leave London by sea,' said Alex, 'despite the risk of serious storms at this time of year.'

'But you will be paying a visit to the barge?' said Rosamund.

'Certainly, but you need not fear that I am fool enough to walk into a trap of Fustian's making again. He would have to use exceptional bait to lure me this time. So do not disobey me, Rosamund, and remain within these walls,' he said strongly.

Rosamund grimaced. 'I did so want to visit St Paul's to pray for the Queen's safe delivery. I had even thought that I might see Bridget McDonald there. Surely she will want to pray for deliverance from her enemies and the safe return of her father.'

For a moment Alex was silent, and then he said, 'I will escort you there. I can understand your frustration in having to stay here when you are anxious to discover if she really does know Harry's whereabouts.'

'Indeed!' Rosamund's face lit up. 'I will go and fetch my cloak.'

As she fastened the ties on the plain brown cloak, one of the ties came loose. Knowing that she had no time to sew it back on, she took Harry's silver brooch and used that to pin it together. Then she joined her husband and hurried from the house.

For a while they walked in silence and then Rosamund said hesitantly, 'A thought has occurred to me, regarding your search for Bridget McDonald.'

Alex gazed into her rosy face. 'I am listening,' he said gravely.

'If she were to have even a single penny on her person, she would be able to purchase some used clothes. I am thinking of male garb. Dressed as a youth, she would be able to enter taverns and saunter along the quayside without too much fear of being spotted. She could ask questions of mariners as to whether they have seen her father's ship in a far-flung port—or even a harbour in these islands of ours.'

Alex stilled. 'Now why did I not consider her taking such measures?'

Rosamund smiled. 'Because you have never been a woman in desperate need.'

'There is that, of course,' he said drily. 'I will speak to Walther and ask him if Maud has had an auburn-haired Scottish lass for a customer.'

'Perhaps it would be best if you did that immediately,' said Rosamund. 'I will go to St Paul's alone.'

'No,' said Alex firmly.

'Then I will not go! There is no time to waste.'

'I will escort you back to the house and then visit Maud myself, and if her answer is as you suggest, then I will scour the taverns and the waterfront,' he said, his eyes alight with determination.

Rosamund opened her mouth to ask, *could she not come with him?*, but already he was dragging her by the hand through the crowded streets.

There came a moment when Rosamund's arm was tugged from Alex's and she lost contact with him. She looked for him and became aware that she was the focus of a pair of curious hazel eyes. The hooded figure drew closer and briefly touched the brooch at her throat. Instantly Rosamund covered the silver cross of Thor's hammer.

'That is a rare gift,' said the youth.

'It belongs to my brother,' responded Rosamund.

The youth backed off as Alex appeared, looking anxious. 'What happened to you? I feared that Fustian had—'

'I'm safe,' she reassured him, 'although, a moment ago, I thought I was in danger of having Harry's brooch stolen.'

'You were not hurt? Who did this?'

Rosamund turned to where she had last seen the youth, but he was no longer there. Alex wasted no time escorting her back to Lady Elizabeth's mansion. He did not linger, but left immediately. Rosamund retired to her bedchamber, for she wanted to be alone so she could ponder on the events of that day and spend some time in prayer. Then she lay on her bed and fell asleep.

On waking, Rosamund swilled her face with cold water and then wandered over to the window and gazed out, hoping to catch sight of Alex approaching the house. There was no sign of him, but she stayed there, watching and hoping. Suddenly she saw movement close to the perimeter wall. Instantly, her heart seemed to climb into her throat and she drew back behind the curtain. Her pulse was racing because she feared that, despite all Alex's determination to protect her from her stepbrother, Edward could reach her even here and steal her away from her husband.

She peered around the curtain, but there was no sign of anyone. Were her eyes playing tricks on her? Then, as she watched, a figure appeared from out of the trees. She was relieved to see that it was much too small and slight to be her stepbrother. It moved cautiously away from the trees and then suddenly stopped and dived into the shrubbery. Could it be a burglar out to steal Lady Elizabeth's jewellery?

Anger and curiosity overcame Rosamund's fear and she left her bedchamber. Outside the door in the passageway there was a chest. Just as she had hoped, there was a lighted lantern and several unlit candles on top of it. She lit a candle and went downstairs. All was quiet, except for voices and clattering coming from the kitchen. She slid silently past it and out of a door at the far end. There was only the slightest breeze, but it blew out the candle.

She stood a moment, letting her eyes become accustomed to the starlight and then she made for the trees close to the perimeter wall. She had not gone far when, sensing someone behind her, she turned. The blow caught her on the side of her face. A rag was stuffed into her mouth and a sack pulled over her head. She was heaved on to someone's shoulder and carried away.

Chapter Seventeen

Rosamund woke. Her head throbbed and her eyelids fluttered open on to pitch darkness. Panic spiralled inside her and she kicked out, only to discover that she was enclosed in the confines of some coarse material. Only one person could have done this to her and that must be Edward. She clawed at the sacking in an attempt to find a break in the fabric so she could pick at it and make a hole.

'Keep still, Rosie,' said a hated familiar voice. 'You are wasting your time.'

'Where are you taking me?' Her heart thudded in her chest and she hugged herself in an attempt to stop herself from trembling.

'Wouldn't you like to know? If you stay quiet and listen, then you might be able to deduce where you are,' said Edward.

Wherever I am, I am in danger from you! she thought. Nevertheless, she remained still and listened. Gradually, she became aware of rocking and the muffled sound of what she presumed were oars propelling them through water.

'Hazard a guess,' he said.

'You are taking me to your barge,' she said breathlessly.

'Now that is a good guess, but wrong.' He laughed and the noise terrified her because it was so similar to the sound that haunted her nightmares.

Rosamund told herself that she must not show fear. 'I don't believe you. My husband will soon realise it is you who has abducted me and then you'll be sorry.'

'Not if he's dead he won't,' said Edward. 'He destroyed all my plans and this time he won't be coming back from the dead.' She felt as if ice encased her heart and her mouth went dry and she was unable to speak. 'Lost your tongue?' asked Edward with another of those insane giggles.

'I wish Ingrid had killed you instead of William,' she managed to say.

'What do you mean, Ingrid killed him? It was the Baron who did so.' There was no laughter in his voice this time.

Rosamund smiled in the darkness. 'Is that what she told you?'

He was silent for a long time and she wished she knew what he was thinking. No doubt he was plotting something evil to happen to Ingrid now.

'No matter,' he said abruptly. 'The Baron really has proved himself a nuisance. I tried to get rid of him once before, but, just like Harry, he refused to die. I wish I knew where your brother is, but irritatingly I don't. He sailed away, not knowing his father had recognised him, leaving a farewell note to the Baron, saying he did not want to lose his friendship because of Ingrid. Your fool of a father came to me and told me he had seen a man he believed to be Harry. He had no idea that Mother was behind his disappearance, but had this notion that someone had rescued

Harry from the river where he had received a bang on the head and lost his memory.'

'So you decided you had to get rid of Father?'

'What else could I do? He was going to give all that would have come to me to Harry. I couldn't have that now, could I?'

She heard the sound of liquid splashing about and then of swallowing. Was he drinking and getting soundly drunk?

'Of course, I still hoped that Harry's ship would founder somewhere and he'd end up at the bottom of the sea, but I couldn't guarantee that happening. Also, your father told me that he'd spoken to the Baron, so he had to be silenced, as well. He still needs silencing, because Harry might just return. I regret I'll have to close your mouth for good, too. But first we will enjoy ourselves together, Rosie. At least I will find great pleasure in our times together. You might not. What do you say?'

She remained silent.

'Perhaps it's best you save your voice for screaming. I do believe we're here.'

Rosamund fought her fear, wondering where *here* was—no doubt she would soon find out. Wherever it was, she was determined to fight Edward to her last breath, even as she prayed that somehow Alex would find her.

She heard another man's voice and the next moment she was lifted and dragged over something hard. She suspected it was wood. When she heard the creak of ropes and was emptied out of the sack as if she was a hunk of meat, the smell of the sea came to her on the breeze. She looked up and saw a mast with a furled sail and stars twinkling in a midnight-blue sky. *He was going to take her out to sea!*

Then waves of fear swept over her and she almost gave up hope of Alex ever finding her.

'Take the boat over to the barge where Ranald McDonald and my mother will be waiting. I expect you to return within the hour with the news that the Baron is dead.'

Rosamund struggled upright, having no intention of being forced to go where she did not want to. Almost immediately she collapsed on to the deck because her feet were so cold that they could not hold her. She cursed Edward.

'Devil take you, Rosie, do you have to swear? Remember you are a Baroness, and show some dignity.' Edward seized her by her hair and dragged her along the deck. She fought all the way, gritting her teeth as she dug her fingernails into the planking. He lifted her head and thrust his face into hers. 'When are you going to learn it does not pay for you to resist me?'

'Is it not time you learnt that my wife is always going to resist your evil intent?' said the voice that Rosamund had begun to believe she might never hear again.

The curse died on Edward's lips as Alex plucked him by the back of his cloak and heaved him upright. He spun him round and smashed his fist into Edward's face. The strength from the blow sent Edward skidding across the deck.

Rosamund heard the hiss of her stepbrother's breath escaping as he crashed into the side of the ship. She let out a yell of pure joy. Alex bent over her and lifted her upright. Her fingers clutched his doublet and her lips found his and they kissed briefly but passionately. Then he set her aside and faced Edward, who had managed to struggle to his feet.

Rosamund caught the glint of starlight on the blade in his hand and cried out, 'Beware, Alex, he is armed.'

'Aye, love,' he murmured, before moving gracefully as a dancer towards their enemy.

She wanted to join in the fight and clenched her fists and looked about her for a weapon, but could see none. The men warily circled each other and now she could see that Alex had his own blade. Then they were grappling with each other and moments later one of the weapons came sliding along the deck towards her. She bent and picked it up and realised it was Harry's short-sword. How had it come here? Alex must have had it. A despairing cry escaped her and she ran across the deck. As she reached the two men, she heard a gurgling sound and then one staggered back and collapsed at her feet.

Fear clutched her heart, but it lasted only a moment because she realised that the man before her on his knees was her stepbrother. There was an expression of disbelief on his face as his fingers clung to the hilt of the dagger in his chest. She did not hesitate, but placed a foot on his shoulder and pushed him over on to his back.

'At last you have paid for the death of my father,' she said.

Edward made a strangled sound and then his eyes glazed over.

Rosamund looked up and saw Alex standing close by and she dropped Harry's short-sword and threw herself into her husband's arms. 'How did you find me?' she whispered against his shoulder.

'You were seen being carried off,' he replied, hugging her close.

'By Joshua?'

'No! He was with me. Besides, if he had seen what happened, then he would have confronted Fustian and his fellow conspirator. Your saviour was much smaller and she used her wits to the best advantage.'

'She?'

Alex held Rosamund a little away from him so he could see her face. 'Aye. I suppose I will have to become accustomed to having a clever wife around.'

A voice came out of the shadows. 'Baron Dalsland, have you forgotten about me?'

He did not reply, but Rosamund stared at the slight figure standing there. 'Who are you?' she asked, even though she sensed that they had already met.

'Bridget McDonald.' She came forward. 'I never knew Black Harry had a sister until a few hours ago.'

'You're that youth who admired Harry's brooch!' Rosamund held out a hand to her.

Bridget clasped it firmly and smiled ruefully. 'Indeed I am. You can have no idea how I felt when I saw you wearing the cross of Thor's hammer. The last time I saw it was when Black Harry and my father set sail for the New World.'

Rosamund gasped. 'My brother's aim was to cross the Great Ocean? I don't want to believe it. It is such a dangerous journey to make.'

'Oh, it's true enough,' said Bridget, her eyes glinting. 'I wanted to go with them, but Black Harry put his foot down and said he wouldn't allow it.'

'What did your father say?' asked Rosamund, fascinated by this insight into her brother's life.

Bridget said indignantly, 'When I would have argued with your brother, my father took me aside and said, "You don't mess about with Black Harry. He knows what is right for you!" I was furious because in the past I sailed with my father many times and I resented your brother parting us.'

'How long is it since you last saw them?' asked Rosamund.

Before Bridget could reply, Alex drew his wife close to him once more. 'The rest would be better told indoors. You will catch a chill if we linger here any longer.'

Rosamund stayed him with a hand to his chest and looked up into his rugged face. 'During all the days I spent on horseback with you, did I ever catch a chill?' she demanded. 'I need to know the rest about Harry now—' She looked at Bridget. 'But first, am I correct in presuming that you were the figure I saw in the garden earlier?'

Bridget nodded. 'I followed you home. Of course, I had recognised the Baron, but I was not sure whether I could trust him. To cut a long story short, I have since decided that I can trust you both,' she added with aplomb.

'I deem I can tell my wife the rest of your story later, Mistress McDonald,' said Alex firmly. 'Despite her protestations, I find standing on this deck exceeding chilly. Let's away to Lady Elizabeth's and a warm fire and a hot drink.'

This time neither of the women argued with him. Rosamund picked up her brother's short-sword and thrust it through her girdle. Alex spoke to one of his accomplices and left him to deal with Edward's body. Then he helped the two women into a boat and rowed them across the river. On the way, he told Rosamund how he, Joshua and Walther and several other accomplices had raided Edward's barge and discovered not only Lady Appleby and her kinsman aboard the vessel, but also Lord Bude and Ingrid.

'Bude and Ingrid were willing to talk for the price of their freedom,' he said.

'You mean you let them go?' asked Rosamund, astonished.

Alex said gruffly, 'They left empty-handed.'

'What do you mean, empty-handed?'

'Lady Elizabeth has not yet realised it, but a burglary took place at her mansion whilst we were at Richmond. It was Bude who provided the gang of thieves with the information concerning the layout of her house and the kind of valuables she owned. Fortunately she had taken her most precious jewels with her to Richmond, but amongst the booty I found Harry's short-sword. I thought you'd be happy to have it returned to you.'

'That was exceedingly generous of you,' said Rosaund, smiling now. 'I almost had an apoplexy when it came sliding across the deck to me. I thought Edward had stabbed you.'

He shook his head at her in reproof. 'You should really learn to trust me more.'

'I do now,' she said with a twinkle.

He grinned. 'Good. When I allowed Bude and Ingrid to escape, I believed at the time that I had no choice if I was to discover where Fustian was taking you. As it was, Mistress McDonald had seen you being abducted and had followed as best she could. But she had no boat, so she decided to seek me out.'

'But how did she find you so quickly?'

'It was pure chance or fate, call it what you will,' said Alex. 'Walther spotted Bridget, recognised the youth's clothes that you had worn when he first set eyes on you and realised that Maud must have sold them to her. He told Joshua, who swiftly had the message relayed to me. So all's well that ends well.'

Rosamund wondered whether he felt he owed Ingrid a kind gesture for misjudging her six months ago. It was probably best if she, herself, put the Danish woman out of her thoughts and concentrated instead on thinking about what she and Alex would have to say to each other once they were alone.

When they arrived back at Lady Elizabeth's mansion, it was to learn that her ladyship had retired for the night. Rosamund took it upon herself to direct one of the servants to prepare a bedchamber for Bridget. Over cups of mulled wine the young Scottish woman told the rest of her story.

'It was six months ago since *Thor's Hammer* set sail. My father had lost his own ship in a battle with Irish pirates, along with his treasure. Fortunately, we escaped with our lives. Still, when he met Black Harry and they recalled the days they had spent together in Harry's youth, Father declared himself ripe for an adventure that would regain him his lost fortune, but honestly this time. So they set sail and I have not heard from them since.'

'But they could be dead,' burst out Rosamund.

The corners of Bridget's mouth drooped and her shoulders slumped. 'I know,' she said forlornly. 'Yet my instincts tell me that they are still alive. Besides, what I knew of Christopher Columbus's voyage across the great ocean to the New Indies convinced me that they should be on their way home by now. Working on that supposition, I decided to make enquiries amongst the mariners to be found in the taverns and boats down by the river. Anyway, when I saw you wearing Black Harry's amulet, or one I thought similar to it, I went in search again of a mariner who told me that he had seen *Thor's Hammer* in the harbour of Ilha da Madeira.'

'Where is that?' asked Rosamund, her hope of finding her brother renewed.

'It is an island off the coast of Africa and I am determined to go there,' said Bridget firmly. 'Somehow I will find the money and a captain who will take me there.'

'God grant you your wish,' said Rosamund, glancing up at her husband with a question in her eyes.

Alex knew what she was asking of him, but decided that the hour was too late to discuss the matter now. He dragged her up from the settle. 'Let us go to bed. You have been through a frightening time and need your rest.'

Bridget also rose. 'Thank you for your kindness in listening to me. I would also like to go to bed now.'

'I'll have a servant show you up,' said Rosamund. 'I would do so myself, but I do not know where all the rooms are here.'

Bridget smiled. 'It is of no importance. God grant you a good night's sleep.'

When Alex and Rosamund reached their bedchamber, he drew her towards him. After the shock of nearly losing her, he wanted her in his arms again. He had not expected that in such a short space of time she would have become so vitally important to his well-being. He kissed her with mounting ardour and she responded with an eagerness that inflamed his senses. He tore at her clothes with impatient fingers and in no time at all she was naked. Only then did he pause to look with blazing eyes at the smooth contours of her body, the skin of which appeared molten gold in the firelight.

'You are beautiful,' he breathed.

'Am I?' Her voice was just a husky thread.

'Are you? You still need to ask me that? My God, Rosamund. Accept my word, for I speak the truth,' he said fiercely. 'I could not bear to lose you.'

Alex began to unfasten his shirt and then suddenly she was on her knees on the bed up close to him. She brushed aside his hands and took over the task. She eased off his shirt and together they removed his woollen vest. She could feel his stomach quivering as she touched the hard muscles. But she hesitated when her hand rested a moment on the fastenings of his hose.

'Too much, too soon, to expect you to—touch me—there,' he croaked.

She lifted her gaze and stared into his face and such a desire to please him welled up inside her. 'You saved me from Edward's foul attentions. If it would give you pleasure, my husband, may I continue?'

'Aye to both questions, wife,' he answered in a throaty whisper.

She seized his face between her hands and kissed him hard. Then she unfastened his hose and peeled them down the long corded muscles of his shanks and calves and dropped them beside his shirt. It would have been impossible for her to ignore his manhood, but she only had enough courage to touch it once lightly with a fingertip. That was enough for Alex. He flung her on the bed and kissed every delicious curve and sensitive spot of her body before taking her in a storm of passion. Afterwards Rosamund lay in a relaxed state curled up against her husband's back and almost immediately she fell asleep.

* * *

When they woke it was morning and they could hear the patter of rain on the window. Alex got up and drew the curtain and looked outside. It was a dreary day. He smiled at Rosamund. 'Shall we go back to bed?'

Rosamund held out her arms and he went into them.

Later, whilst they were having breakfast with her godmother and Bridget, they told Lady Elizabeth all that had taken place yesterday. Alex also returned to her the iron box that they had found on the barge. It might not have contained her most expensive jewellery, but there were still many items of value in it. She was delighted to see it and immediately decided to send for her lawyer.

'No doubt you will need a man of good sense to deal with your stepmother's lawyer,' said Elizabeth. 'Now your stepbrothers are dead, Rosamund, and we have some notion of Harry's whereabouts, then matters can be put into motion to see that the business and property they claimed illegally is made over to him.'

Alex agreed, but added, 'Harry has yet to be found and so preparations must be made for a couple of ships to make the journey to Ilha da Madeira to discover if *Thor's Hammer* is still there. It would make sense to talk some more with the mariner who gave the information to Bridget.'

Bridget leaned forward across the table. 'I beseech you, Baron, that you will allow me to travel on one of these ships?'

Alex said seriously, 'I will give your request much consideration, Mistress McDonald. It will take a little while before they can be made ready for such a long voyage.

Besides, it would be best to wait until the storms of winter are over before setting sail.'

'But what if Black Harry's ship was to leave Ilha da Madeira before then?' cried Bridget.

Alex said, 'Harry is too good a sailor to risk setting out in such inclement weather, although it is possible that he might set sail for Sweden or England as my ships head in the opposite direction. It makes sense to wait at least until April to see if he returns. If he does not do so, then my ships will set sail at the beginning of May. God willing they reach their destination—if it is discovered that *Thor's Hammer* had already departed before they arrived there, then surely someone on that island will know Harry's destination.'

'It seems a long time to wait,' said Bridget, frowning.

'I know,' said Alex, 'but it is just as difficult for Rosamund to contain her impatience. Even so, you must both do so.'

Rosamund said, 'What Alex says is true, Bridget.'

'In the meantime you must stay here, Mistress McDonald,' said Lady Elizabeth.

Bridget's relief was apparent. 'That is kind of you, Lady Elizabeth. I admit to not having come to a decision about what I was to do before setting sail. Thank you.' She turned to Alex. 'What will happen to my uncle and Lady Monica?'

'They will be brought to trial for treason and attempted murder,' he said.

'As is just,' she murmured.

'What of Bude and Ingrid?' asked Rosamund. 'I presume you had them followed, Alex?'

He nodded. 'Aye. I am now of the opinion that they will either take refuge at Bude's place in the country if they decide to stay together, or, if they decide to separate, then it is possible that Ingrid will seek sanctuary at Syon House and Bude might go north of the border.' He rose to his feet. 'In the meantime, if you will excuse my wife and me, Lady Elizabeth…' he inclined his leonine head in her direction '…Mistress McDonald, there are matters we need to discuss,' he said.

'Of course, of course,' said Lady Elizabeth. 'There is still much I would hear from Mistress McDonald about her father and I would know why Harry is called *Black Harry.*'

'I have no idea,' sighed Bridget. 'It would be interesting to have that explained.'

Alex tugged on Rosamund's hand. 'Come, let us go,' he said in a low voice.

She went with him. 'Are we to speak of lawyers, business and property for Harry's sake?' she teased.

He smiled. 'Hopefully Edward has not bled the company dry, but I am certain we will be able to turn it around again if that is so. But rather what is on my mind is that I need to visit my father and report to him my findings at the Palace of Richmond.'

'May I come with you?'

'I was not planning on going without you. I would like your opinion of my father.'

'One of the Earls of Douglas, is he?' she asked, raising an eyebrow.

Alex smiled. 'I said you were clever.'

She chuckled. 'Perhaps he'll give you the opportunity to get to know him better this time. What do you think about us living in your Scottish house until Harry reappears?'

'I am glad you can speak so positively of Harry's return. If it would make you happy then of course we will spend some time in the Scottish house. My father did tell me that he and my mother spent many happy hours there.'

'Perhaps you will find a sense of your mother's presence in that place,' said Rosamund.

'That thought never occurred to me.' He sounded surprised.

'Then think of it now,' said Rosamund.

He drew her towards him. 'I will. Perhaps my father will fill in the gaps of my knowledge of her that my grandparents couldn't.'

They were comfortably silent for a while. Then he said, 'How long ago it seems since we met.'

'Yet it is less than a month ago,' she murmured, raising her head and gazing at him. 'This time when we set out on our travels I will not run away from you.'

His eyes twinkled. 'I would only bring you back if you did. I am never going to let you go now you are mine. I love you, Rosamund.'

Rosamund was extremely glad to hear those words. 'And I love you.'

They kissed, and for a while there was naught else in their heads but the desire to show the other just how much they loved. Their lives had changed so much within this past month and now they had a future together. Yet, although Alex had completed the task that his father had asked of him and he had found the love of his life, he had not completed his self-appointed task of finding Harry.

As if his wife could read his thoughts, Rosamund

suddenly said, 'Harry must be found. I want him to feel as loved as we both do.'

'Aye,' said Alex, remembering that Harry had sailed away in the belief that he was leaving the way open for Alex to be happy. He had achieved what he had set out to do, but not in the way he had intended. Still, if it had not been for Harry's noble gesture, Alex would never have gone in search of him and found Rosamund. He felt a surge of happiness, but mingling with that emotion was the longing to see his dearest friend. There was so much he had to tell him and he determined to waste no time setting in motion all that was needed to find him.

Epilogue

'Are you sure about this, Godmother?' asked Rosamund worriedly for the umpteenth time.

'As sure as one can be of anything in life, my dear,' wheezed Lady Elizabeth, tying a scarf over her hat so the sea breezes would not carry it away. 'Sea air is supposed to be good for one and Bridget must have a chaperon. I know the Baron has decided Joshua Wood is the right man to act as her protector on the journey and he has supplied her with a maid, but Bridget needs a woman of sense to prevent her from behaving in an unseemly fashion. You never heard some of the tales she told me when she sailed with her father.' The old lady rolled her eyes. 'He sounds an exciting rogue and I have rediscovered my taste for travel.'

Rosamund could not help but laugh. 'All right! I accept that you have made the right decision. I only wish that Alex and I were going with you.'

Lady Elizabeth placed a hand on her goddaughter's belly. 'My dear, I expect you to take care of this proxy grandchild of mine and the Baron to take care of you.

Hopefully by the time I return you will have been delivered safely and I can take him or her in my arms and my cup of happiness will runneth over.'

'I pray that it will be as you say.' Rosamund kissed the old woman warmly and determined to hold her tears at bay.

At that moment, Alex and Bridget approached. 'It is time to go, Rosamund, or the Master will miss the tide.'

Rosamund faced Bridget and thought that young woman looked both excited and scared. Impulsively Rosamund placed her arms about her and gave her a hug. Then she stepped back and her violet-blue eyes shone with tears. 'May our Lord and Saviour, His Holy Mother and all the saints be with you on this journey. I pray that your search will be successful and that you all will come home safely.' Her voice broke and her hand searched blindly for that of her husband's.

Alex gripped it tightly; although there was part of him that wanted the thrill of adventuring at sea and continuing the search for Harry, himself, the greater part of him knew that he belonged at Rosamund's side, that her safety and well-being and that of their child was the more important. He had entrusted the task of finding Harry to Bridget, Joshua and Lady Elizabeth and now he must trust them to succeed.

His arm went about his wife's shoulders and he assisted her down the gangplank. Then they both stood on the quayside, watching and waving until they could no longer see their friends clearly; only then did they both turn and, arm in arm, walk away.

* * * * *

Pirate's Daughter, Rebel Wife

JUNE FRANCIS

This book is dedicated to those readers of *His Runaway Maiden* who e-mailed me wanting to know Harry's story. Also to my dear husband, John, who enjoys my historical romances, in memory of a lovely holiday on the island of Madeira for a special birthday.

Prologue

1504

If she did not act now then she would never be free. Bridget McDonald stood on the slanting deck, her hands gripping the side of the ship. A few moments ago she had caught sight of a tall, dark figure on the cliff, but now he had disappeared as the rain swept in.

Was the landfall ahead Madeira, the island she had been searching for? The master of the slave-trader ship and his remaining crew were frantically busy trying to save the vessel from being blown towards the rocks. This could be her only chance of escape. If they succeeded in saving the ship, then she feared its master would immediately come after her again. He had been eyeing her in a manner that terrified Bridget. Since disease had killed his woman a week ago, she had lost the one person who had provided her with some kind of protection from his lustful nature. She was convinced that if the storm had not blown up, he would have raped her by now. If he managed to save his vessel, she feared that this could still happen.

A wave suddenly drenched Bridget, leaving her gasping for breath, and she clung tightly to the side of the ship, trying to summon up the courage to go over the side. She thought how she might not be in this position if the man she had known as Captain Black Harry had not separated her from her father, Callum, by refusing to allow her on either of his ships, destined for the New World, almost two years ago.

She shuddered, recalling the desperate straits she was in, and knew she had no choice but to trust her fate to the waves. She might yet find her father—and if she perished in the water, at least she would not die as a slave-trader's whore but as a free woman. She took a deep breath and dropped into the sea.

Chapter One

Harry swore loudly, cursing the rain that almost blinded him as he slithered down the cliff path, gaining momentum as earth collapsed with the sheer volume of the rain, sending him hurtling towards the beach. He landed on the black sand on his hands and knees to the accompaniment of falling rocks. He drew in his breath with a hiss, his face drawn with pain, and pushed himself upright. He flicked back dripping dark hair and wiped his sodden face and beard on the sleeve of his doublet.

Had he really seen someone poised to jump into the churning sea from that ship? As suddenly as it had started the driving rain had stopped; he wasted no more time, but strode along the beach, scanning the waves for signs of that lonely figure. He was on the verge of turning back when he spotted something down by the shore. He put on a spurt and, as he drew closer, found a body sprawled face down on the sand.

He knelt down and, to his astonishment, discovered that it was a woman; and, more surprisingly, one who was able to swim—that was a rarity in his experience.

She had girded the green skirts of her gown by tucking the ends into her belt at the back—no doubt so they wouldn't hamper the movement of her legs in the water. He eased her into a sitting position, but the upper part of her body flopped forwards against his forearm. She made a choking sound and he thumped her on the back, attempting to free the water from her lungs. The tension inside him subsided as she began to cough, seawater and mucus staining the sleeve of his already soaked doublet. Eventually her coughing ceased, but the action must have drained any resources she had left after such a swim because she lay limp in his arms.

A single, long braid of sodden, dark red hair dangled against his thigh as he manoeuvred her gently round so that he could see her face more clearly. His heart seemed to lurch sideways. He had the oddest feeling that he had seen her likeness before. But where? Her skin was pallid, but it did not detract from her beauty. She had the daintiest of noses, full sensuous lips and a heart-shaped countenance.

At that moment a raindrop splashed on to her face and then another and another. He thought that the rain would rouse her, but although her cheek twitched, her eyelids remained closed. God's Blood! What was he to do with her? She would be doubly soaked to the skin if he tried to carry her all the way to Machico. It seemed he had no choice but to take her to the house of his Portuguese friend, Jorge de Lobos, where Harry was staying.

His face tightened with concentration as he lifted her higher. Holding her close to his chest, he slowly rose to his feet. For a moment he swayed, but then recovered his balance, gritting his teeth against the pain in his thigh. He decided to keep to the beach as long as possible and prayed that there would be no landslides on his chosen path.

Despite the weight of her sodden garments he was able to make reasonable speed, conscious, all the time, of the woman's ashen face and shallow breathing. He took extra care on the shale when he climbed on to the main path, fearing a disastrous fall. It was a relief when he reached the house and was able to put her down on a wooden settle in the entrance hall.

He eased his shoulders and shouted for Joe. When there was no response he made for the kitchen but that, too, was deserted. By the Trinity, where was the youth? Harry returned to the hall and stared down at the woman in the green gown. He found himself remembering the tales of mermaids that an erstwhile pirate called Callum McDonald had told him when he was a boy.

Harry, too, had been plucked from the sea, although he had only been a child. He had been out of his wits when he had woken on the pirate ship, unable to remember his own name or his age as a result of a blow to the head. He had been told by the pirates that his parents had died in a boating accident that had almost taken his life and it was a miracle he had survived. He scowled at the memory, scrubbing at the beard that concealed a hideous scar on his cheek.

He wondered what to do with this unexpected guest. Normally Harry did not have women in the house, but he knew there was naught for it but to keep her here for now. He drew in his breath with a hiss. She needed to be rid of her wet garments, so Joe must ride to Machico and fetch the widow, old Juanita, to undress her. But first Harry had to find him. He left the house and searched the gardens and the stables, but there was still no sign of the youth.

Exasperated, Harry returned to the house. Immediately, he noticed that the woman had moved because she was now curled up in a ball against the arm of the settle. He shook her shoulder and her eyelids opened, revealing red-rimmed eyes the colour of cobnuts. She squinted at him as if her eyes were sore and she was trying to focus. She muttered indistinctly and shrank back against the back of the settle, lifting her arm as if to shield herself from a blow, but then it flopped weakly across her breast and her eyelids closed.

Harry's heart lurched in that peculiar fashion again and he ran a hand over his still-dripping black hair and beard. He took a deep breath and, without more ado, scooped her up into his arms and headed for the stairs, leaving a trail of water pooling on the floor. He took the marble steps slowly because the soles of his shoes were slippery and was relieved to reach the first floor without mishap. He carried her into the guest bedchamber and collapsed with her in his lap on-top of the chest at the foot of the bed.

A loose damp tendril of auburn hair tickled his chin and he frowned as he gazed into the lovely face pillowed against his arm. 'Mistress, you must rouse yourself,' he said in Portuguese.

She moaned but, irritatingly, her eyes remained closed.

Harry lightly slapped her on both cheeks. 'Wake up!' he commanded.

This time she winced and her eyelids fluttered open and she appeared to stare up at him, only then to turn her face away. He could feel her shivering. 'Mistress, will you wake up?' he urged, tugging on her plait. She lifted a fist and for a moment he thought she would hit him, but then her arm dropped to her side. He smiled grimly. At least he seemed to be getting through to her. Again he lightly slapped her cheek.

'If you—you do—do that again, my father w-will m-make you regret it one day,' she stammered in the same language he had spoken.

Harry raised his eyebrows at her fractured accent and wondered where she had learnt Potuguese, as it obviously wasn't her native tongue. 'You must get out of your wet garments or you will catch a fever,' he rasped. 'There's a bed here. Get yourself beneath the covers and I'll see that food and drink is brought to you.'

She began to struggle. He found her amazingly strong, considering the energy she must have spent swimming ashore. But she could not match his strength and he captured both her wrists and held them above her head. He could feel the rapid rise and fall of her breasts against his chest and was aware of sensations that he had not experienced for a while.

'There is no need for you to fight me,' he growled. 'I will not hurt you. Now rouse yourself, undress and get into bed.'

To his dismay, her body sagged and her head fell forwards on to his shoulder. He flinched and tried to wake her once more, but whatever he did, it failed. He knew then that there was naught for it but to undress her himself.

His hands shook as he unfastened the belt from about her waist, so freeing the skirts she had girded there. Then he loosened the ties on the bodice of her gown. Noticing the design of the garment, he fingered the fabric, certain that it had been fashioned in England. So this mermaid was likely to be no peasant Portuguese woman, but could be English. What was she doing here and where was the father she had mentioned?

After removing her gown and having exposed the perfect roundness of her breasts in the damp, cream silk shift that clung to her skin, he knew that he would have had to have been made of wood, not to be stirred by their loveliness.

'Holy Mary, mother of God,' he groaned, clutching his hair with one hand and holding her off from him with the other, 'What am I to do with you?' There was no reply. Clearing his throat, he said loudly, 'Mistress, you need to remove your shift. I will fetch one of my shirts for you to wear. We have no female apparel in this house.'

'Men are s-s-such d-devils,' she stuttered, her eyes still closed.

'Women are no angels, either,' he replied roundly, getting to his feet, leaving her sprawled out on the chest.

When she did not reply, he presumed that she had slipped into that semi-conscious state again. He dragged her upright and swung her over his shoulder. Then he carried her to the side of the bed and placed her down gently. Seizing hold of the thickly woven coverlet of red and brown, he pulled it over her to ensure she stayed warm before hastening from the bedchamber.

Harry stripped off his wet garments in his own

bedchamber and rubbed himself dry. Then with the cloth wrapped around his nether regions, he went over to the window and pushed wide the shutters, staring down over the sloping garden that was fragrant with the perfume of scattered blossoms after the rain. His gaze fixed on the wide expanse of ocean, but could see no sign of a vessel. For as long as he could remember the sea had been his life and a ship his main home, but on days like this he was glad to be on land since the damage to his leg.

He turned from the window with an impatient movement and limped over to the armoire and chest. He removed all that he needed and donned undergarments, shirt, hose and doublet and pulled on boots before removing another shirt from the armoire. Then, gathering up his gloves and hat, he headed for the guest chamber.

He saw that the woman had managed to divest herself of her shift. She was lying on her side, her head close to the edge of the bed with her braid dangling so that its end touched the floor. He would have liked to have seen her hair newly washed with perfumed water, smelling sweetly of camomile or lavender, and hanging loose. He drew in his breath with a hiss. What was he thinking of, fixating on her hair? He could only be glad that her naked body was mostly covered!

He placed his shirt on the bed and was in the process of pulling up the coverlet further, when he saw the scarring on her back. For a moment he froze and then his fingers gently explored the weals in the soft skin across her shoulder blades and lower back. Anger exploded inside him. Someone had cruelly *whipped* her?

Could a husband have done this? He reached for her left hand that was curled on the sheet beneath and found it ringless.

He peered closer at the scars and remembered the beatings he had suffered growing up on the pirate ship. He scowled as he drew the coverlet over her. Then, gathering up her discarded garments, he left the room. He went downstairs and this time was fortunate to find Joe preparing the evening meal.

'We have a guest,' said Harry in English, placing the clothing on the table where the youth was slicing an onion.

Joseph stared at the sodden green gown and darted a startled glance at Harry. 'A woman?'

'Of course it's a woman, Joe! That's a gown, isn't it?' Harry sank on to a chair. 'And such a woman, Joe. You wouldn't believe how beautiful she is. The odd thing is that I feel I have seen her before.'

'God's Blood! A woman under *your* roof!' Joe's voice rose to a squeak as he reached for the sodden gown and sniffed a handful of material. 'This smells of the sea. Where did you find her?'

'She swam ashore from a ship that was in trouble.' Harry stared at Joe through his fingers. 'Unusual a woman being able to swim, hey, Joe? I saw her drop into the sea and later came upon her sprawled on the sand. She is in the guest bedchamber, so keep your eye on her. I need to go out. I want to find out what's happened to that ship.'

Joe had now found the silken shift and dropped it as if it had burnt his fingers. 'Me!' His blue eyes widened in dismay. 'What's she wearing if her clothes are here? Wh-what if—if she starts wandering around half-naked?'

'Enough of that nonsense,' snapped Harry, not wanting to dwell on the image the words conjured up. 'I've left her one of my shirts and I doubt she has the strength to get off the bed. If she wakes, she'll be in need of food and drink. Some soup, perhaps.'

Harry made his way to the stables and saddled up a horse. He rode in the direction where he had last seen the vessel, wanting a closer look at it if possible. He wondered if it had foundered on the rocks. If so, there was a possibility of there being survivors; if not, then others on the island might have seen the vessel and be planning to steal what they could, before those who owned the rights to salvage arrived on the scene.

Bridget was wakened by the sound of a door slowly opening and then stealthy footsteps approaching the bed. Her heart thudded as into her mind came an image of a man with shoulder-length black hair, angry dark eyes, a scar on his nose and a great black beard. She shivered, recalling the face of the master of the slave-trader ship who also had a great black beard. Her instincts were to sit up and defend herself but, not only did her limbs ache unbearably, her head throbbed and her throat felt raw. She was already aware that someone had taken her garments away and left a clean, soft woollen-and-linen shirt behind.

'Who's there?' she asked in a husky voice.

'I've brought you some soup and bread and a drink, mistress,' replied a cautious young English voice.

Bridget was confused. Hadn't her rescuer spoken

to her in Portuguese earlier? She opened her eyes and stared at the youth holding a tray. He could not have been more different to the other man as night was from day. He had straw-coloured hair and a freckled face that was filled with curiosity.

'You're English,' she stated in that tongue.

'Aye, mistress.'

'What is your name?'

'I'm Joe,' replied the gangly youth.

'Where is the bearded man who was here earlier?'

'That would be the captain. He's gone off to see what's happened to the ship you deserted.'

She prayed that he would find no sign of the ship or that it was wrecked and its master drowned. 'The captain? Is he a mariner, then?' she asked, picking up on what the youth called the man who had rescued her.

'Aye.'

'He—he looked fearsome. Is he Portuguese?'

'No, he's English and you have naught to fear from him.' He gave her a reassuring gap-toothed smile. 'Here, mistress, I'll leave your food and drink on this little table here. You get it down you and then have another little sleep.'

Bridget clutched the open neck of the shirt and managed to ease herself into a sitting position. 'Tell me, where am I?'

He paused in the doorway without looking back. 'You're on the island of Madeira, mistress,' he replied and closed the door before she could ask him any more questions.

Bridget sank back against the pillows. Her relief was such that tears filled her eyes and threatened to overpower her. Praise the Trinity that she had at last reached her destination! Now she must hope that she had not arrived here in vain. She remembered her first meeting with the man she still thought of as Captain Black Harry. She and her father, Callum, had been on the coast of Ireland after escaping from a brigand called Patrick O'Malley and his cutthroats. For many a summer past Callum had set sail with young warriors from Scotland to support his Irish wife's family in their battles with the O'Malleys. That summer two years ago his luck had run out and Callum had lost not only his fortune, but his ship.

When Bridget had met Captain Black Harry, she was alone, having left her father trying to persuade the master of another ship to take them back to Scotland with only the promise of payment when they arrived there. She had been embarrassed due to his need to beg for help. Then she had walked slap bang into the handsomest young man she had ever seen. He had helped her to her feet and she had begged his pardon. He had inclined his head and asked in the Gaelic whether he could be of further assistance to her.

Impulsively she had explained their situation and he had escorted her back to Callum. Only then did she discover that the two men had sailed together when Black Harry was a boy. They had much to say to each other and had headed for the nearest tavern.

Bridget frowned as she reached for the cup on the table and gulped down the drink thirstily. If only she had overheard their discussion, she would have been more prepared for what happened the next day. Her eyes darkened. She would never forget what she considered Black Harry's hardhearted treatment of her.

She placed the cup on the table and reached for the food. She dunked the bread in the soup and, despite being ravenous, ate slowly because it hurt to swallow. As she gazed at her surroundings, her eyes began to feel heavy. The white walls appeared to waver and the blue shutters at the window shimmered. On another wall was a niche holding a statue of the Madonna and Child and they appeared to be smiling at her. She fumbled for the cup, picked it up and sniffed it. Had she been drugged? The lad might have assured her that she had naught to fear from the captain, but could she trust him? She had suffered sorely at the hands of men in the past and she felt a rising panic. Her last thought before she slipped into unconsciousness was of her father.

'You put *what* into her drink?' exploded Harry.

'Only a *little* poppy juice, Captain,' replied Joe hastily, backing away from him. 'It was what Juanita gave to me when I couldn't sleep for my aches and pains after I was attacked in the town. She dosed you with it, too! It's not that long since we returned from Africa with you wounded so bad, and I thought you'd not only never walk again, but smash every looking glass in sight.'

A muscle clenched in Harry's jaw. He would never forget seeing his scarred reflection in the mirror for the first time. Later, when he had rattled in the cart into town, the women who had previously fallen into his arms had shrunk away from him and walked by on the other side of the street. Deeply hurt and also suffering agony from the wound in his thigh, he had grown a beard to conceal the scar and chose to keep away from women altogether.

'What if she suspects you've drugged her?' Harry pointed out.

'Why should she? Surely she'll deem her feeling drowsy is due to exhaustion after swimming ashore? I was only trying to ease any pain she was in.'

Harry gazed at him with exasperation. 'I suppose you thought you were doing what was best, but I wanted to question her. Now I'll probably have to wait several hours before she wakes up. Don't ever do such a thing again without my permission, Joe, or you'll be out on your ear!' He paused. 'So what did you think of her?'

'Comely. Her eyes are hurting her. She could do with a potion to bathe them. More importantly, Captain, is the information that she *does* speak English and there is a lilt to her voice that convinces me that it is not her first language.'

Harry nodded.

'So what happened to the ship?' asked Joe.

'I could see no sign of any wreckage, so it appears that her master managed to avoid the rocks. Perhaps on the morrow I will have a search made for the ship.' He changed the subject. 'Now, Joe, what about supper?'

'I'll have it ready for you, Captain, in no time at all.'

'Then I will dine as soon as I make certain that the lady is still breathing. In the morning you can wash her clothes along with mine.'

Harry climbed the stairs, disposed of his outdoor clothes and went to visit his guest. He drew a chair up to the bed and looked down at her. Her cheeks were flushed and when he placed his hand on her forehead, he found it hot and dry. Damnation! She was feverish. Hopefully her condition would not worsen.

He leaned back in the chair, thinking as soon as she was awake he would ask what was her name and for information about the ship and her father. Now he would have supper and return here later. Perhaps she would be willing to speak to him then.

Bridget felt as if she was floating, drifting in that state betwixt sleep and wakefulness. She was aware of discomfort and of being hot one moment and then cold the next. She had vague memories of a man lifting her and being carried in his arms. He had a great black beard, but he was not the cruel master of the slave-trader's ship who had beaten her for her defiance of him. Even so, could she trust him? There was something that had happened before she fell asleep that worried her, but she could not remember what it was.

She heard a door open and footsteps. A chair creaked and she sensed it was not the lad, but *him*. He must be sitting by the bed and looking down at her. She could feel his wine-scented breath on her cheek and then she felt him lift her damp curls and feel her brow. She struggled to force open her eyelids, but when she managed to prise them apart, the candlelight so hurt her eyes that she swiftly closed them again. Even so that brief moment was long enough for her to catch a glimpse of him: he with the strong nose, dark brows, frowning eyes and that great black beard. She shivered.

'So you're awake,' he said roughly. 'You're feverish and that is an inconvenience.'

'Perhaps you should have left me on the shore to die,' she whispered.

'That's a foolish remark to make,' he growled, 'Why did you swim ashore if it were not because you wanted to live?'

'That is true. I was in fear of the slave trader. Do you know what happened to the ship?' she asked anxiously.

'I could see no sign of it.'

'So that beast could still be alive!' She grasped his arm with a tremblimg hand. 'You must not tell him I am here.'

'His ship could still be in difficulties further round the coast. I shall see what I can find out on the morrow. Now don't fret yourself about him. You are safe here.'

Was she? She gazed into his eyes, but could not read his expression and could only pray that he was telling her the truth. She sank back against the pillows, exhausted.

'How did you come to be on his ship?' asked Harry.

'I was sold to him by a pirate in Africa,' she whispered. 'I deem originally the slave-trader's aim was to sell me to some Eastern potentate, but his woman was utterly against such a plan. She wanted me as her servant. She was very beautiful and he could refuse her nothing. We sailed to different islands with slaves, to Tenerife, the Cape Verde Islands. Sometimes we went ashore for several days and twice we returned to Africa for more slaves. I tried to escape, only to be beaten for my attempts. Then disease struck the ship and one by one people began to die.'

Harry felt anger and pity and knew that she'd had a very lucky escape indeed. But what she had said about disease disturbed him greatly. 'What was this disease?' he asked.

'I do not know its name, but I deem it was not the plague,' she said hastily.

He frowned. 'How do you know? Have you seen people die of the plague?'

'No, but I know someone who suffered from the smallpox and she described its symptoms to me.' Bridget's eyelids drooped wearily despite all her efforts to stay awake.

Harry was relieved to hear that she had not been in contact with that horrendous disease. Still, he hoped that she had not been infected by whatever had struck down those on the ship. 'Sleep now,' he said. 'We will speak again in the morning.'

The door closed behind him and she drifted into sleep. Now her dreams were not of the slave trader, but of her father and how the handsome Captain Black Harry had offered him a berth on his ship that was sailing westwards in search of a passage to the Indies. Her father's conversation to her had been full of plans to regain his lost fortune. His excitement had been infectious and Bridget had been just as eager as Callum to take part in such an adventure. But then Captain Black Harry had refused to have her on board his ship and so, rather than allowing her to accompany the men to the Indies, instead he had paid for her passage to Scotland to the home of her father's brother and his wife.

Now fear stalked her dreams. For her kindly aunt had died and her Uncle Ranald had taken her south to the home of his mistress, Lady Monica Appleby, once a McDonald and twice married. Both wanted to get their hands on her father's hoard and would not believe Bridget when she'd told them it had all been stolen. They had even tried to force her into marriage with the lady's imbecile son. She must escape! She had to get away from them!

Bridget shifted restlessly in the bed and began to cough. She was aware of the sound of footfalls and a door opened. She started with fright, for outside it was now dark and the candle burning beneath the statue of the Madonna and Child cast shadows on the walls. Her heart thudded inside her breast as she watched the captain approach her.

'What are you doing?' she asked hoarsely.

'You will need to sit up if you are not to spill this potion,' he said in a low voice.

She remembered the conviction that she'd had earlier about the drink she had downed and croaked, 'Potion! Are you wanting to poison me? I deem the drink I was brought earlier was drugged.'

'A little poppy juice, that is all,' he said easily. 'Joe deemed it would ease your pain. By the Trinity, why should *I* wish to poison you? I might consider some women cruel and selfish, but the truth is that I heard you coughing. Now drink up and pray to God that in the morning you will be rid of the fever.'

Did he speak the truth? It was certainly true that her body ached all over. She struggled to sit up, but the act was beyond her. The captain perched on the side of the bed and hauled her upright, slipping an arm about her shoulders. He reached for the cup and held it to her dry lips. As she felt warm liquid trickle into her mouth, she was aware of the strength in the arm that held her and hated being in his power. So he considered women cruel and selfish, did he? Well, no more so than she thought some men arrogant and brutal. Even so she had no choice but to suffer the captain's ministrations for the moment. She swallowed thirstily until the cup was empty.

Harry lowered her against the pillows and watched as, with a faint sigh, she drifted back into sleep. He did not immediately leave the room, but remained sitting in the chair at her bedside. There was a definite lilt to her voice and it would not surprise him if her first language was the Gaelic. He found himself thinking of Callum McDonald and his daughter, Bridget. What had happened to Callum after he had disappeared sixteen months ago along with one of Harry's two ships, *Odin's Maiden*?

His eyes darkened with anger. God's Blood! He had made a mistake in trusting that wily old pirate when they had met again in Ireland. He should never have offered him a helping hand or been keen to assist the lovely but hot-tempered Bridget, who would now be a young woman of seventeen or eighteen summers.

He gazed down at the beautiful face on the pillow, trying to imagine how this woman might have looked two years ago, remembering how he had considered Bridget older than her years when he had first set eyes on her. Then he had discovered she was much younger than he'd thought, and knew he must put some distance between them in order to protect her from herself. She had been furious with him and he had likened her to an angry cat, spitting out accusations that he was well-named Black Harry because he had a black heart. How dare he separate her from her father, she had ranted. She had attempted to persuade Callum to get him to budge from his stance, but the old pirate had told her in Harry's hearing that it did not do to cross Black Harry. It was then that Harry realised that Callum also did not want to take his daughter with him on such a risky venture, but did not have the heart to tell her.

So Harry had parted from Bridget with her insults ringing in his ears. If naught else, her behaviour had proved to him that however comely she was, she still had some growing up to do. She knew what shipboard life was like from having sailed with her father after her mother had died. Surely her common sense should have told her that his decision was the right one? He certainly hoped she had come to realise that in the past two years.

He continued to gaze down at the woman in the bed. Was she Bridget McDonald? She certainly had a look of her. If she *was* Bridget, then where was her father? When Callum had vanished along with Harry's ship, he had wondered if the man's intention had been to cross the northern seas and make landfall in Scotland in order to be reunited with his daughter. Yet here she was in Madeira, having just escaped a slave-trader's vessel. Perhaps Callum had never arrived in Scotland and, along with Harry's ship and other crew, was now at the bottom of the ocean?

Harry could scarcely contain his impatience for her to wake up and to provide him with some answers to his questions!

Chapter Two

'You must ride into Machico, Joe, and bring Juanita here,' said Harry, turning away from Bridget's bedside. Two days had passed and he had hardly had a sensible word out of her. 'The fever is getting worse. She needs a draught that is stronger than the one you mixed for her.

Joe gazed down at Bridget's scarlet cheeks and twitching face. 'She does look bad and she's been muttering in her delirium.'

Harry shot a glance at him. 'I know. She mentioned a Lady Elizabeth and pirates and then the rest was just a gabbled stream of nonsense. I want you back here with the widow before midday. I need to visit the cane fields and see how the harvest is progressing.'

Joe nodded and left the bedchamber.

Harry resumed his seat next to the bedside and tried to contain his worry. He must persuade Juanita to stay here at the house; only then would he feel some freedom from anxiety about the sick woman he suspected was Bridget McDonald. He could not afford to change his plans and needed to be on hand to supervise the loading of the sugar cane into the carts that would carry the cargo to his ship.

He gazed down at the shivering, restless figure; as he did so, she flung off the bedcovers and, muttering to someone to get away from her in Portuguese, attempted to get out of bed. Starting to his feet, he caught hold of her and could feel the heat emanating from her body. He lifted her back on to the bed and it was then that he noticed what looked like red pinpricks on her skin. His heart sank. Perhaps her fever was not the result of her soaking, but from that disease she had mentioned?

He considered the consequences if that was true and swore beneath his breath. Yet he had no choice but to accept that if whatever had caused the rash was infectious then it was too late for him to protect himself from its effects. He could only hope and pray that it was just a heat rash.

He left the bedchamber and returned shortly after with a cloth and a bowl of cold water. He soaked the cloth in water before wringing it out and wiping her face with it, bathing her eyes especially. Then he folded the cloth into a wet compress and placed it on her forehead. Carefully, he repeated this action and carried on doing so until she appeared less restless. When he touched her skin, although it still felt hot, it was not burning. Was the fever breaking? Or was she cooler due to his ministrations with the wet cloth? Perhaps it was both.

Suddenly her eyes opened and she stared up into his face. Her hand shot out and her fingers fastened on his wrist. 'What have you done to me?' she croaked. 'Where is my father and Captain Black Harry?'

He stiffened. 'What is your father's name?'

'Callum McDonald. Have you seen him here?'

'No.'

Her eyes showed dismay.

Harry's heart began to thud with heavy strokes. So his instincts had been right and she *was* Bridget McDonald, but it seemed she was expecting to find her father and him together. So was he right in thinking that Callum had never arrived in Scotland? It would do no good him asking her that question now. He prised her fingers from his wrist and said, 'You have a fever, mistress. I have sent Joe to fetch a healer.' He wrung out the cloth and placed it on her forehead once again.

'I need help to find him. I cannot waste time lying here,' she said fretfully. 'I must find my father. Perhaps someone else has seen him.'

She made to push down the bedcovers, but Harry prevented her from doing so by placing his hands over hers. 'You're in no fit state to go anywhere right now,' he said firmly. 'Be patient. I will fetch you a drink.'

'Where are my clothes?' demanded Bridget. 'I must find my father.'

He bit back the words that were crowding to be released and went downstairs. He went to the kitchen and made her a drink of wine and water and poured himself a measure of liquor. He decided he needed some fresh air and carried the drink and the flask outside. He sat on the terrace, moodily gazing out over the ocean glistening in the sunlight. He had survived hunger and thirst, battles and storms since last he had seen Bridget. He had been prepared to confront all these adversaries for himself, wanting adventure, as well as discovering new ways to increase his wealth, but he had refused her passage on his ship, determined that not only would she not have to face such dangers, but that her burgeoning beauty would not distract himself or the crew from the business in hand. Now she had come back into his life, bringing uncertainty and trouble.

Why was she searching for Callum here on Madeira? Who was this Lady Elizabeth she had spoken of in her delirium? On whose ship had she originally set sail before being captured and sold to a slaver?

He downed the drink in one gulp and refilled the cup. He stayed there for a while longer, thinking about the fragments of information he'd gleaned from Bridget so far. Then he went indoors, cut bread and spread it with honey and placed food and drink on a tray and carried it upstairs, hoping that she had recovered her composure and would be able to eat something.

As he reached the upstairs passage he heard a crash coming from the bedchamber and made haste. He was stunned by the sight that met his eyes. The small table had been knocked over and Bridget was writhing on the bed and babbling words he could not make out. He seized one of her hands and clasped it between his own. 'Hush, woman, there is no need for such a commotion,' he said gently. 'You are safe.'

She stared at him, but he sensed she was not seeing him because she was still muttering to herself. He wondered if she had fallen asleep and was having a bad dream. She was defying someone, saying that she would not marry their son. Suddenly she went limp.

Harry took her in his arms and brought her against his chest and spoke soothingly, recalling words in

Swedish that the grandmother of his friend Alex, the Baron Dalsland, had used to comfort him when he'd suffered from his recurring nightmares. He was ashamed by the memory because he had been a youth on the verge of early manhood at the time. He should not have given in to such weakness after he had survived three years on board a pirate ship. He'd finally escaped by sneaking off and concealing himself from his shipmates behind a pile of barrels in the Swedish port of Visby. It was Alex who had found him and taken Harry to his grandparents' home. They had provided him with a roof over his head and fed him until his lean body filled out and grew strong. That first summer he and Alex had become like brothers and they were soon fluent in each other's language. Alex's grandfather, the old Baron, had a merchandising business and owned several ships. Harry had asked if he could work for him and the old man had put him under the tutelage of one of his finest captains. When the old Baron had died he had left Harry the *Thor's Hammer*.

Harry stroked Bridget's dark red hair, remembering how he had grieved for the old man. Suddenly he realised that the room had fallen silent. His patient had fallen asleep again. He waited several moments before placing her down on the bed and pulling up the covers over her. He decided to stay with her until she woke or Juanita arrived in case she should have any more bad dreams.

Bridget opened her eyes and her gaze fell on the man asleep in the chair by her bedside. His bearded chin was cupped in one hand and his elbow rested on a cushion on the arm of the chair. His thick dark lashes would have been the envy of many a woman, she thought, wondering how long he had been sitting there. He shifted suddenly and Bridget started nervously and, clearing her throat, asked, 'Captain, are you awake?'

He yawned, revealing excellent teeth, and then his eyes opened and met her gaze. For an instant she felt as if drawn into the depths of those dark blue orbs and her heartbeat quickened. 'I did not mean to go to sleep, but I've been keeping long hours lately,' he said drily.

'You mean because of me, Captain? I am grateful to you for your care.' Her voice was husky and Harry found it extremely attractive, almost as seductive as her physical beauty. 'I wish to leave as soon as possible. I need to find my father. My information is that he and Captain Black Harry were on this island.'

Harry wondered from whom she had had this information. 'But you are ill. You cannot possibly leave,' he said firmly.

'I am feeling much better,' she insisted.

He wondered if he should tell her that her face was covered in spots, but at that moment there came the sound of voices below. He asked her to excuse him and left the bedchamber.

Bridget gazed after him, wondering if it was the healer who had arrived. She was aware that the shirt she was wearing smelled of her perspiration due to her fever. Despite this she knew it to be a fine shirt of excellent quality, so her rescuer was a man of some wealth. At that moment she heard the sound of footsteps coming upstairs and along the passageway towards her. She decided to pretend to have fallen asleep again, thinking she might discover more about the man who had given her shelter that way.

'I have seen this rash before,' said Juanita in Portuguese, glancing over her shoulder at Harry. 'It is a complaint suffered mainly by children and can sometimes kill, but the fever has broken and I have no doubt this woman will recover.'

'How soon will she be fit to leave?' asked Harry, taking coins from a pouch at his belt.

Juanita's eyes fixed on the money. 'Where would you have her go?'

'She is seeking her father, a Callum McDonald, and she has heard that he has been seen on this island. As far as I am aware he has never set foot on Madeira, but I could be mistaken. I ask that you would keep your ears and eyes open in Machico. I will have a search made of Funchal, just in case he could have anchored there at any time this past year.'

Juanita stared at him from under grey, bristling brows. 'You do that, Captain, but if her father is not here, what will you do with her then? She is young and no doubt beautiful when she does not have this rash, but she is also a foreigner. Surely you will not desert her?'

'I have a cargo of sugar cane to get to Lisbon. She needs a woman to keep her company. If I were to leave her here in Madeira, will you stay with her? I will pay you,' Harry offered.

Juanita shook her head and said firmly, 'No, I wish to leave Madeira. I am getting old and I would return to my family home in Portugal. I still have kin there and would spend my last days with them.'

Harry frowned. 'I understand, but would ask another favour of you. Have you heard aught of a slave-trader ship foundering anywhere off this coast or it may have anchored in Machico?'

'I have heard nothing, but I will make enquiries for you.'

He thanked her and changed the subject. 'Is there aught you can prescribe for her rash?'

The old woman fished in a capacious cloth bag and produced a phial. 'You may give her three drops of this liquid if the rash itches her unbearably and keeps her awake.'

Harry took the phial and handed a coin over to Juanita. 'When do you plan to leave for Portugal?'

'When the signs are auspicious.' She chuckled and patted his arm. 'If you have need of me again, send Joseph to fetch me.'

'I will bear in mind what you say.' Harry glanced towards the bed as a thought occurred to him, but he remained silent and went downstairs. He called Joe to keep a watch over their patient and headed for the fields, knowing that he could not afford to change his plans to leave the island once the sugar-cane harvest was gathered in.

Bridget inspected the rash on her arms and frowned, turning over in her mind the conversation she'd overheard between the captain and Juanita. Unfortunately, she had not been able to understand every word spoken, but she felt certain that he had asked Juanita to make enquiries about her father and for that she was grateful. Hopefully he would also have a search made for the slave trader and his vessel. What if the slave trader was still alive and came looking for her? After all he *had* bought her. A chill ran down her spine. What was she to do if the captain were to sail for Lisbon, leaving her behind here on Madeira at the mercy of any unscrupulous person?

There was a knock on the door. 'May I come in?' asked Joe.

Bridget sighed. 'Aye, please do.'

The lad entered the bedchamber, carrying a tray. 'D'yer know that at one time me and the captain thought you might die, but here you are looking a whole load better despite your rash. The captain reckons it could be caused by the fever making you all hot.' He beamed at her.

Bridget forced a smile, guessing why the captain had not been completely honest with Joe. She was also remembering that it was the lad who had put poppy juice in her drink the first day she was here. 'I am much better so I do not need any potions, Joe,' she said hastily.

'All right. But the captain said you're to eat this bread and cheese and then I'm to bring you a custard apple.'

'Tell me about your captain?' she asked.

Joe grinned. 'He's a hard man to please, but he's fair. His ship is anchored in Machico harbour and he's here to load and transport the bulk of Senhor Jorge's sugar-cane harvest to a buyer in Lisbon. It's the *senhor* who owns this house, but he's gone off with a fleet of warships, led by the explorer Vasco da Gama. They're going around the tip of Africa, hoping to find a swifter passage to the Indies. The captain intended going as well, but we were caught up in a battle with the natives at one of the Portuguese trading stations on the African coast.'

'What happened?' she asked, unable to conceal her curiosity.

Joe's eyes took on a faraway expression and he did not immediately answer, then he said solemnly, 'I don't think the captain would like me to give you the gruesome details, but I can tell you that there were more of them than us. There were spears and arrows flying through the air with us managing to dodge most of them. Then it was hand-to-hand fighting. Unfortunately whilst the captain was fighting three of them at once and winning, a spear came out of nowhere and he got wounded in the thigh. The captain drew out that spear and stuck it in one of the enemy. He has a stubborn streak does the captain. Even so that didn't stop him, but then something even nastier happened and we had no choice but to get him out of there.'

'It sounds as if he was lucky to survive,' said Bridget, admiring the captain's bravery.

'You can say that again,' said Joe, his face alight with enjoyment. 'It was the same when we sailed the northern seas and we did battle with pirates. We often ended up in hand-to-hand combat. The captain only ever used the cannon as a last resort. He's always aware that there might be innocent captives aboard who could suffer along with the sinners.'

'That's very perceptive of your captain,' said Bridget.

Joe grinned. 'I'm not sure what that means, but he's the best captain to work for that I know. Now I'll have to be going or he'll be wondering what I'm up to.'

Bridget would have liked to have heard more of the captain's exploits, but did not wish to keep the youth from his work. 'I would like some warm water, Joe, and if you could fetch my clothes I'd be very grateful,' she said persuasively.

'Certainly, the captain had me wash and dry them.'

She said softly, 'You are kind.'

He flushed to the roots of his hair. 'My pleasure, mistress,' he mumbled, and hurried from the bedchamber.

Bridget ate the bread and cheese and drained the cup of wine and water, marvelling that the captain and Joe had survived such adventures. She wondered why, if the captain was English, was he staying here and plying his trade between this island and Lisbon instead of returning home? If her father and Captain Black Harry were not to be found on Madeira it was possible that they might not be because more than a year had passed since his ship had been seen here—then she must try to persuade him to take her to Lisbon. It was possible that she might find news of her father in that bustling city. She wished Joe would hurry and bring her clothes.

However, it was the captain who knocked at the door before announcing his presence and coming into the bedchamber when she bid him enter. He was carrying a basin and had a drying cloth over his arm.

'Where are my clothes?' she blurted out. 'I want to get dressed and out of this bed.'

'I am glad to hear you say that, mistress, but are you certain you are well enough to do so? I am having a search made for your father, but if he cannot be found, I am at a loss what to do with you once you are recovered.

I will be leaving Madeira soon.' He placed the basin on the table and the drying cloth on the bed.

'When will you be leaving?' she asked, sitting up straight. 'Joe told me that you are here for the sugar-cane harvest. If you are to find my father, surely it would be of help to you to have the name of the ship he sailed on? It is called *Thor's Hammer* and was last seen anchored in the harbour at Funchal.'

Harry shot her a glance. 'So it was only *Thor's Hammer* that your informant saw?'

'Aye!' Her brow knit, thinking it sounded as if he thought there should be another ship. 'It belongs to a mariner known as Captain Black Harry. He and my father set out almost two years ago in search of a north-west passage to the Indies in the wake of the voyage made by John Cabot. I was expecting my father to return last year, but he never did so.'

Harry frowned. 'Who told you that the ship could be found here?'

'A mariner in London.'

Harry drew up a chair and sat down. 'It does not necessary follow that your father was on that ship.'

She gripped a handful of the bedclothes convulsively. 'Are you saying that he could have been on the *Odin's Maiden* instead? That's the name of Captain Black Harry's other ship.'

He hesitated. 'It is possible. You must accept, Mistress McDonald, that ocean voyages hold great risk for mariners and explorers.'

She had paled. 'I am not a fool. But Cabot returned, so why shouldn't my father?'

'Why not, indeed?' said Harry, knowing that Cabot

had not returned from his second voyage. He went over to the window and gazed out. 'But I have to be honest with you and tell you in the light of what you have told me that I do not believe your father to be on this island. I, too, have journeyed to the New World and your father went missing the same time as *Odin's Maiden*. This was fifteen, sixteen months or more ago.'

Bridget stared at the captain's broad back in bewilderment. 'What are you saying? That you knew my father? If that is so, why did you not tell me earlier?'

'You have been ill and out of your mind and I didn't immediately know your identity and that you were searching for Callum.'

'Were you on either ship?'

'Aye, I was a shipmate of your father's at one time and that is how I became acquainted with him.'

'Then you will know Captain Black Harry, too?'

Harry wondered how long it would be before it occurred to her that he and Black Harry could be one and the same. He was not looking forward to that moment and was determined to delay it as long as possible. He would wager a gold coin that she would blame *him* for Callum going missing!

He turned and faced her. 'Your father and the captain quarrelled. The captain was keen to sail further south along the coast of the New World, but your father was not.'

'Why not?' Her eyes were intent on his face.

'I assume it was because Callum had no taste for such a venture. I deem he realised that we were not going to find the passage to the Indies or make our fortunes, so he decided to return home. The captain, on the other hand, was keen to speak to the Portuguese explorers who had knowledge of the southern ocean and its winds and currents. Your father chose to disobey his orders and, I suspect, stole *Odin's Maiden* from the captain to make his own way home.'

'My father is no thief!' she said indignantly.

Harry raised his eyebrows. 'He was once a pirate, woman, so how can you say that? When did *you* leave home? It is possible that you and your father missed each other by a cat's whisker.'

Bridget was mortified that this man knew something of her father's past life and said stiffly, 'I left London last May. I know what you are thinking—why has it taken me so long to get here?' Her expression was strained.

'I know why. You have forgotten that you told me that you were sold by a pirate to the slave trader whose ship you escaped from.'

'That is true. I had forgotten,' said Bridget, putting a hand to her head. 'A slave trader who could be on this island and looking for me right now.' Her voice trembled. 'He paid good money for me and might not wish to lose out on his investment.'

Harry said, 'He could also be dead or have already left these waters. As for your father and *Odin's Maiden*, a mariner can always think of reasons why a ship should be delayed. A storm can blow a vessel miles off course and if a ship survives the storm, it can still be damaged, making repairs necessary. If the materials are not to hand, then the ship would need to limp into the nearest harbour, perhaps to remain there for weeks on end.'

'You're saying that this could have happened to *Odin's Maiden* and my father might have arrived home after I left,' said Bridget eagerly. 'Although, you cannot know for certain that my father stole the ship,' she added swiftly.

Harry said, 'Where else could they have both gone, along with a complete crew of men? No doubt he knew that you would be worried about him and wished to be reunited with you. He told me of his affection for his daughter, Bridget.'

Suddenly Bridget's eyes were shiny with tears. 'I can accept that as a possible reason why my father might have taken the ship. It is also possible that he might never have reached Scotland and be at the bottom of the ocean.' Her voice broke on a sob.

Harry said bracingly, 'You would give up hope so soon? He could have wintered at New-found-land, an island discovered by Cabot, whose waters are teeming with fish. This would have delayed his setting out for home.'

Bridget fought back another sob and wiped her eyes with the back of her hand. 'I will try to believe that is what happened, but if he was to search for me at my uncle's house in Scotland, then he would not have found me. He would need to go to London.'

'Why London?'

'Because that is where I was taken by my Uncle Ranald, my father's treacherous brother, after my aunt died. He decided to visit his mistress, Lady Appleby, in the north of England, and because her elder son lived in London and she wished to see him, they forced me to go with them.'

Harry wondered if this was the son she had mentioned earlier in her delirium. 'Why did they do this?'

'They believed I knew where my father's hoard was and would not accept that it had been stolen by an Irish brigand, Patrick O'Malley.' Her eyes darkened. 'If only we had not met Captain Black Harry in Ireland, who took my father away to the Indies without me, how different my life would have turned out.' Bridget scrubbed at her damp eyes. 'I would that you would leave me now.'

Harry was tempted to say that if she had not met him, then she might have been recaptured by Patrick O'Malley and what would have happened to her then? Instead he left her to her *toilette*.

Bridget so wished she knew if her father was alive or dead. Callum usually drank far too much when life dealt him a blow and then he could be reckless in the extreme. She had believed her presence had helped rein in some of his excesses and that was another reason why she had wanted to accompany him on Black Harry's ship. Yet when Callum was sober, he was an excellent seaman and she had learnt much about handling a ship and commanding men by watching him.

She washed her face and hands and then dried them on the cloth. At least she knew more about her father than when she had arrived here. She must cling to the hope that he was still alive. She was also a free woman, so should rejoice in that and keep her spirits up. She still feared the slave trader appearing on the scene despite the captain telling her that she was safe with him. No doubt in the eyes of the Portuguese she belonged to that beast and the law would be on his side if he were to catch her again. The captain, being a foreigner on this island, might come off worse if he were to defend her.

She had to get off this island as soon possible and look for her father elsewhere. As for Captain Black Harry, she would ask her host if he knew what had happened to him since his ship had been seen in Madeira last year.

Chapter Three

Harry swung into the saddle, determined not to blame himself for all that had befallen Bridget since they had parted in Ireland. Yet it was true that if he had not been prepared to pay her passage to Scotland in order for her to stay with her uncle and aunt, then her life would have been different. He remembered wanting to kiss Bridget's luscious mouth when they had first met. Even later when she had insulted him, he had wanted to grab a handful of that red hair of hers that was aflame as if it had caught fire from the sparks that seemed to fly from her in her rage and disappointment and kiss her soundly. How very different both their lives would have been if he had surrendered to his desire. But he still thought he had been right to not take her aboard his ship. A man needed to be totally focused to survive on such a perilous journey.

Harry frowned. He had little faith in Callum having survived the northern ocean in autumn despite his having told Bridget to keep her hopes alive. He was going to have to take responsibility for her, but if she knew he was Captain Black Harry, he sensed she might do something desperate rather than accept his help. She would very likely run away from him and end up in further trouble. He had to think up a plan that would ensure her safety, not just for the next week or two, but for the future. In the meantime he had to ensure that she did not realise he was the man she appeared to despise.

Bridget stirred, wondering what had disturbed her sleep. She could hear a bird singing and eased herself into a sitting position. She had been dreaming of Captain Black Harry and it was not anger she had felt, but a wild excitement. She supposed it was to be expected that she would dream of him now she was here on Madeira where his ship had last been seen. Where was he now? There had been a time after he and her father had set sail when she could not get him out of her mind.

This latest dream had shocked her and she could only believe that her mind was playing tricks on her. There was no way that she would ever take Black Harry as a lover after what he'd done to her.

Besides, she knew the man's real identity, which was one of the reasons she had set out in search of him and her father, as Harry himself was unaware of it. She had initially been accompanied by Lady Elizabeth Stanley, who had befriended her when she was in London, her ladyship's maid, Hannah, and Joshua Wood, a childhood friend of Black Harry, whose real name had turned out to be Harry Appleby. Shockingly, he was heir to a manor in Lancashire and a house and business in London, so no doubt he would not consider her good enough for him. How could she even imagine him making love to her in the light of all these facts? She must be mad!

Her eyes roamed the room and she noticed that the bowl and drying cloth had been removed. She must have fallen into a deep sleep, indeed, to have been unaware of the captain or Joe's entry. How long had she slept? She needed to speak to the captain. What was his name? Her wits had indeed gone begging for her not to have asked that simple question.

She heard voices outside and looked towards the window. The shutters were wide open, allowing sunlight and a flower-scented breeze into the room, along with birdsong. She wanted to be up and doing and longed to be outside in the fresh air. Suddenly she noticed her green gown and silk shift on the chest and her face lit up. She swung her legs over the side of the bed and stood up.

Her knees shook and she realised that she was still weak from her illness, but, by holding on to the bed, she managed to reach its foot and sank down on to the chest. Her fingers fastened on the skirt of her gown and she drew it towards her, along with her shift. She held them to her face and breathed in the smell of the ocean breeze and that of lavender. She wasted no more time, but dragged off the captain's shirt and hastened to pull the shift over her head. It proved more difficult putting on her gown, due to the weight of its skirts.

Once dressed, Bridget felt much better, so decided to unbraid her hair and let it hang loose. If only she had the company of another female to help wash and comb it. She had spent most of her childhood with women until her Irish mother, Mary, had died and her father had taken her with him on his ship, due to his fear of her being abducted by one of the rival Irish clans. She recalled her excitement and had looked forward to a more interesting life. She'd had to familiarise herself with his ship and become accustomed to all-male company. The crew had spoilt her and she had come to feel less awkward in the company of men, to love the sea and visiting new places. She had admired her big strong red-haired father, but never forgot the long weeks that she and her mother had spent waiting for his return from sea. Tears welled in her eyes as she thought of all that was lost to her. She could very likely be an orphan now.

There came a knock on the door. 'May I come in?'

Bridget recognised the captain's voice and her heart leapt. Swiftly she wiped her face, not wanting him to consider her a weak female. It had been a mistake, thinking of the past. It was the present and future that were important. She must persuade this man to help her further.

'Please do, Captain,' she called.

The door opened and he stood, gazing at her with an expression in his indigo eyes that brought a blush to her cheeks. 'You are dressed and looking much improved in health, Mistress McDonald. I deem that you are almost fit to leave this place,' he said.

The colour drained from her face; it appeared to her that he would be rid of her that day and she was not ready to cope alone just yet. Despite her wanting to be up and doing, this house had proved to be a safe haven. How could she possibly manage alone and penniless in a foreign land?

She cleared her throat. 'I do understand, Captain, your wanting to be rid of me because you have your business to attend to—but I must confess my limbs are still a little weak. I much appreciate your hospitality. I only wish I could reimburse you, but I have no money. Yet if you are prepared to continue to help me, then I will see that you are rewarded.'

'I ask for no reward,' he said abruptly. 'You look pale and still need to rest.'

'I am better than I was,' she murmured, tilting her chin.

There was a silence.

'You are English, Captain, and have told me that you were one of my father's shipmates. Does that mean you were once a pirate, too?'

Harry stiffened. 'Never.'

She flushed with embarrassment for she felt as if she had insulted him. She cleared her throat. 'May I ask why you decided to live here on Madeira? You never thought of sailing home with my father?'

'No, he never took me into his confidence before he disappeared. By the purest stroke of luck, I was able to perform a service to the owner of this villa whilst on the other side of the world. There was a skirmish with the natives and I saved his life. We conversed and discovered we had a common ambition, so that is why I set sail in company with him and his companions for Madeira.'

'What was this ambition of yours?' she asked.

'I wished to sail around the coast of Africa to the Indies. I hope that answer will suffice for the moment.

Right now I would know more about you and how you came to be captured by pirates.

She sighed and plucked at her skirts. 'When I set out from London in search of my father, I had three companions and we were accompanied by another ship. Unfortunately the vessels were separated by a storm and our ship was attacked by pirates. Our captain was killed and so were several members of the crew.'

He frowned. 'And your companions?'

'Certainly, owing to her station, Lady Elizabeth should have been ransomed, but I do not know what might have happened to Hannah, her maid, and Joshua Wood, who was also in her service. I was separated from them, you see. They remained on the captured ship and I was taken on to the pirates' vessel to be sold to the slavers.'

'It is possible Joshua Wood might have been forced to join the pirates.'

'I see.' Bridget sighed. 'Tell me, Captain—do you know what happened to Captain Black Harry?'

Harry's heart leapt. He had been waiting for this moment and he still did not know how to answer the question. His dark brows knit and he folded powerful arms across his broad chest. 'I had almost forgotten you knew the captain. This Joshua Wood, you admired him?'

Bridget gave him a startled look. 'He was a good man. Dependable.'

Harry felt a curl of envy. 'A handsome man?'

'I would say pleasant, rather than handsome.'

'You were fond of him?' he pressed.

She frowned, wondering why he asked such questions

of Joshua. 'I liked him. As I have told you, he was a good man, not the kind to force himself on a woman like some,' she added, dropping her gaze and gripping her hands tightly together.

Harry thought of the slave trader and wished he had him there in front of him, so he could punch him in the face, but all he said was, 'I am glad to hear it. This Lady Elizabeth—what is her full name?'

Bridget pulled herself together. 'Lady Elizabeth Stanley. She is related to the King of England.'

Surprise flared in Harry's eyes. 'A rare prize, indeed, for a pirate. I deem you have no need to fear for her life. She will certainly have been ransomed. It is a pity she did not arrange for you to be ransomed, too.'

Bridget nodded. 'But the fault was not hers that I was taken away by the pirates and I know she was deeply concerned for me. In the past she was exceedingly kind to me. When I escaped from my uncle I was able to help in the rescue of her goddaughter, Rosamund, who was abducted by her stepbrother around that time. After-wards, her ladyship offered to be of assistance to me. I became part of her household and she took my problems to heart and decided to accompany me on my search for my father and Captain Black Harry. Only on the way...' She became agitated and jumped to her feet. 'You can have no notion of what it is like to be desired by men who have you in their power! What I had to do just to survive...'

Harry reached out and was compelled to take her by the shoulders. He gazed down into her face and slowly lifted a hand and stroked her cheek. 'You are very beautiful.'

Bridget closed her eyes and allowed her face to rest against his hand. 'Beauty can be a bane,' she whispered, thinking of the time when even Black Harry had looked at her with a delighted expression on his handsome face. She opened her eyes and looked up into the captain's bearded face. 'Do you know the whereabouts of Black Harry?' she asked again with a troubled look.

Harry released her. 'He no longer exists.'

'What!' Bridget was taken aback. 'When did this happen? Did he die recently or was he lost in the New World and someone else took over his ship?'

Harry was surprised by her reaction. 'You sound like you care what happened to him. Yet earlier I received the impression that you despised him, so why should it matter to you if he is dead?'

'There are those I know in England who will be saddened to hear of his death,' she said.

Harry's eyes narrowed. 'If you talk of his family, he has none.'

'How do you know that? He had lost his memory and could not remember his family,' she said with a toss of her head, causing her glorious hair to swirl about her shoulders. 'If only he had not separated me from my father and gone to the New World.'

Harry's gaze fixed on her hair and he longed to touch it and run his fingers through it. Instead he clenched his fists. 'No doubt when last you confronted each other, you were showing all the signs of burgeoning womanhood.'

Bridget flushed. 'What are you suggesting? That he thought I would have an unsettling effect on his crew?'

He raised his eyebrows in a speaking manner. 'No doubt he was aware that a woman's needs are very different from a man's and to be the only female on a long voyage would have presented you with problems.'

She knew he was right about that, but was not going to admit it. 'I would have coped, Captain. A woman can adapt to difficult situations the same as a man.'

'I am not disputing your courage and stamina, Mistress McDonald, but a woman cannot help but practise her feminine wiles on a man in order to get him to do what she wishes.'

Bridget's jaw dropped and, for a moment, she was speechless and hurt that he could believe that of her. 'Are you daring to suggest that I am a coquette?' she demanded. 'I thought you were different from other men because you have been kind to me, but I see now that I was mistaken. I will seek help elsewhere. I have been called a witch in the past and accused of putting a spell on a man. The slave trader was typical of a certain kind of man who blames the object of their lust, without caring what damage they do to a woman. No doubt Black Harry was the same.'

Harry's jaw tightened. 'You do him an injustice when he cannot defend his reputation. I understand why you were desperate enough to jump into a raging sea, but I am not like that slave trader. Anyway, if you prefer to manage without any further help from me then I will leave you alone to consider your options.' He left the bedchamber, closing the door carefully behind him.

If there had been anything close by that she could have picked up and thrown at him, Bridget would have done so. She wanted to scream at him. How could he not understand how much his words had hurt her? She had done everything possible to hide her feminine charms from the pirate crew but little good it had done her. When she had fought off the advances of the ones who had tried to steal a kiss from her, she had been repaid with a beating.

She dropped on to the bed, wondering how she could get off this island without the captain. She remembered Black Harry paying for her passage to Scotland, so she could leave Ireland as her father had wished her to do. She had to admit that it was strange behaviour on Black Harry's part if he really had lusted after her. She recalled how strong and indestructible he had appeared as he had stood on the quayside last time she had seen him. It seemed wrong that two such strong men as he and her father could now be dead.

A lump filled her throat and she wanted to weep. She must return to Black Harry's friend, the Baron Dalsland, in England, but what sad news she would be taking with her to the Baron and his wife, Rosamund, who was Black Harry's sister—the sister he did not know existed. Joshua, too, would be disappointed, as would Lady Elizabeth—that is if they were still alive. She wondered if they believed she, herself, was lost to them for ever.

A tear trickled down her cheek. Perhaps it would be better if she did not return to England because then she would not have to give them such disappointing and sad news. But that was a cowardly thought and she must consider some way she could get back to them.

She wondered if she were to get down on her knees and kiss the captain's feet and beg his pardon he would extend his helping hand to her again. Her proud nature baulked at the very notion of behaving in the way she had been forced to act whilst in the power of the pirate chieftain when she had rebelled against his orders. Fortunately, where he was concerned her beauty had saved her from rape, because she was worth more to him as a virgin.

A knock on the door and her heart began to race and she felt quite faint at the thought of coming face to face with her host again. He was beginning to have the most odd effect on her. Had he returned to tell her that he did indeed want her out of the house immediately?

'Who is it?' she asked in a trembling voice.

'It's Joe.'

She felt a mixture of disappointment and relief. 'Come in.'

He opened the door and peered round it cautiously. 'The captain said that you were vexed. He told me to make sure not to get too close to you with a knife.'

His words came as such an anticlimax that Bridget laughed. 'Your captain jests. I would not hurt you, Joe. I look upon you as my friend.'

'Honestly?' He pushed the door wider with his hip and came further into the bedchamber. 'I've got no female friends, but I've food here that's real appetising. It'll nourish you and make you strong.'

'I suppose you don't get a chance to become acquainted with a suitable lass being away at sea so long,' said Bridget.

'Aye. But, to be honest, I don't know what to say to lasses, unlike some of the crew. Women and drink are the first things they think of as soon as we drop anchor in port.' He reddened. 'I suppose I shouldn't be talking to you about such matters…' His voice trailed off and he looked even more embarrassed.

Bridget lowered her eyes and toyed with her fingers. 'Does the captain go with women?'

Joe placed the tray on the chest and made for the door. 'No, he steers clear of them. There was a woman he once loved, but she was in love with his closest friend.' Joe looked guilty. 'The captain would have me hide if he knew I was gossiping about him. Now you eat your fish and bread.'

Bridget gazed down at the pure white fillets swimming in a creamy herb sauce as if in a daze. 'What kind of fish is it?'

'Forget its name, but it has a real ugly head. Anyway, you're not going to have to look at that because I chopped it off.'

'Did you catch it yourself?' she asked.

Joe grinned. 'Aye. Captain's too busy to go fishing. Time's money and he reckons the winds will be blowing in the right direction soon to take us to Lisbon.'

The lad's words made Bridget feel almost as desperate as she had felt when she had dropped into the sea. 'Tell me, Joe, what is your captain's name?'

'We call him Captain Mariner.'

'Mariner?' She stared at him in surprise. 'But that is simply another name for a sailor.'

Joe nodded. 'Aye, the captain was an orphan like me, so he chose his own name.'

Bridget supposed it made perfect sense. 'And what's your surname, Joe?'

'I'm Joseph Cook because that's what I am. I'll leave you now, mistress, to enjoy your meal.'

After Joe left, Bridget forced herself to eat whilst she mulled over what he had told her. If the captain had naught to do with women, it meant that she was safe from any advances from him. She wondered about the woman he had loved and recalled the expression in his eyes when he had looked at her earlier. He was all man and no doubt could have made many a woman happy. She regretted speaking to him the way she had done now. He must have been deeply hurt when the woman had preferred his friend. Somehow she had to overcome his misgivings about her and convince him that it would serve him well to take her with him on his ship to Lisbon.

Harry stood outside Bridget's bedchamber. He had calmed down and now regretted upsetting her. He should have taken her sufferings into more consideration and considered his words before he spoke. But he had spoken honestly when he had told her that she was beautiful. He desired her and wanted her for himself, but for the moment he had to keep those feelings under control. She was penniless, far from home and her situation was unlikely to improve if Callum was at the bottom of the ocean along with Harry's ship and its crew. She might speak of friends in England, but that country was thousands of miles away. Her beauty, as she had said, was a hindrance rather than a help, and she needed protecting from other men. He could see only one way of ensuring such protection and security for the future. But if she knew him for who he really was, then she might reject his suggestion. If it were not for his beard, she might possibly have guessed who he was by now.

How long before she realised he was deceiving her? He had not actually lied to her when he'd told her that Black Harry no longer existed but she had reacted to the news as he intended, by believing that he had meant he was dead. Harry had always hated being called Black Harry and no one had called him by that name for years, so in a way he did no longer exist. Now Harry, as his alter ego, Captain Mariner, needed to apologise to Bridget McDonald if he was to lay his plan for their future before her. Taking a deep breath, he wrapped his knuckles on the panel of the door and asked for permission to enter.

'Of course, Captain Mariner, do come in,' invited Bridget.

Perhaps he should not be surprised by the sweetness of her tone, aware how desperate was her situation. He half-expected to find her lying on the bed, resting, but she was standing in front of the statue of the Madonna and Child. He cleared his throat. She turned and their eyes caught and held, and he guessed she was trying not to show how nervous she was of him.

'I hope you will forgive me for having spoken words that were hurtful to you?' said Harry quietly.

Bridget did not drop her gaze, but her insides were quivering. 'I, too, spoke out of turn earlier, Captain Mariner. I really am grateful for all you have done for me and I really do need your help. If I had any money, I would pay you to take me aboard your ship and provide me with passage to Lisbon.'

'And what would you do when you reached Lisbon?'

'I would hope that there would be an English ship whose captain would be generous enough to take me to London. I am sure my friends would willingly reimburse him for his trouble.'

Harry frowned. 'You cannot be as foolish as you sound, Mistress McDonald. I refuse to believe that you have forgotten already your earlier fears about the slave trader still searching for you. I deem what you really want is for me to take you all the way to England.'

She blushed. 'It would certainly be the perfect answer to my dilemma.'

Harry muttered, 'Sit down, Mistress McDonald.'

She hesitated and he rasped, 'I cannot sit down until you do and I've been on my feet for hours.'

Hastily she sat on the bed. 'You are busy supervising the loading of the sugar-cane harvest?'

'Aye. All is nearly ready and I will be departing soon.' He paused and was silent for so long that she thought he was going to refuse to take her. Then he took a deep breath. 'I have a proposition to put to you.'

'What kind of proposition?' she asked warily.

He frowned. 'There is no need for you to look so apprehensive, but you are an attractive woman and could cause havoc on my ship.'

'Joe told me that you—'

He glared at her. 'What did he tell you?'

She changed what she had been about to say. 'That you were an orphan just like him, so you chose your own name.'

Harry said drily, 'I don't believe that was your first

choice of words, but no matter.' He paused, putting off the moment when he would put his proposition to her. 'Would you like to know how Joe came to be in my employment?'

'Aye. I know that he is fond of you and thinks you are the best captain he knows.' She smiled.

Harry scrubbed at his beard. 'I found Joe being tormented by a couple of bigger lads down by the waterfront in London, so I took him under my wing because I knew what it was to have no one of your own to fight your corner. He's been with me ever since. He's like a son to me now.'

Bridget felt a strange warmth inside her. 'Surely you're not old enough to have a son his age?'

Harry gave a twisted smile. 'A younger brother, then. I do not know my exact age, but I reckon I must have seen twenty-four summers.' He paused. 'How old are you, Mistress McDonald?'

'It will be the eighteenth anniversary of my birth in a few months.'

He nodded. 'Then it is time you were wed.'

Her mouth tightened. 'You would tease me, Captain Mariner? What kind of man would marry a dowerless woman?'

'I will marry you,' said Harry simply.

Bridget went still and was convinced that she must have misheard him. 'I beg your pardon, Captain? I didn't quite catch what you said.'

'A marriage of convenience, Mistress McDonald,' he said, meeting her gaze squarely. 'You are a penniless woman alone in a foreign land and in need of a protector, and I have decided that a wife could be useful to me.'

She was stunned by his suggestion. 'I cannot believe you would wish to marry me. I have naught to bring you.'

'You are a beautiful woman and will enhance my life. I have roamed the seas for years and it has seldom bothered me that I have no wife or house to call home when I make landfall. Now I have decided that I will buy a house in some port and you can live there. Will that not suit you? You will not have to constantly tolerate my presence for I will be away on business some of the time. You can make a home for me and Joe. Do you think you can manage to do that? If you feel it is beyond your capacities, then say so now.'

Bridget was still feeling stunned by his proposal, but his reasoning sounded sensible. She had to give it serious thought, because what would happen to her if she turned him down? He might feel he no longer needed to feel responsible for her. He had been kind and tended her when she was ill. No doubt he had saved her life and not once had he taken advantage of her dependency on him. He appeared to be an honourable man. But what did he mean exactly by a marriage of convenience?

She cleared her throat. 'I thank you for your offer, Captain, but does it not bother you that we scarcely know each other?'

He raised those devilishly dark eyebrows of his and drawled, 'Most couples who make convenient matches are barely acquainted.'

Bridget knew this to be true. Even the King of England's daughter, Margaret, had married the King of Scotland by proxy without ever having met him. 'That is certainly true. You speak of a marriage of convenience—does that mean you intend this to be a match in name only or shall it be a proper marriage?'

He hesitated. 'Perhaps we can discuss that when we are better acquainted.'

She could see the sense in that because it was possible that they both might have a change of heart in a few months' time. But even so— She frowned. 'Wouldn't a housekeeper do you just as well?'

Harry blinked at her. 'Am I to presume you would rather be my housekeeper?'

'No! For what security would that give me?' she said honestly, reaching out and touching his arm. 'Yet what if, against all the odds, you were to meet another woman and fall in love with her? You might decide that you'd rather be rid of me.'

'It is hardly likely, Mistress McDonald,' he said ruefully. 'But your point is worth considering, only maybe it will be you who will fall in love with another man. You are lovely. It isn't as if you are stuck with an ugly visage like mine. Maybe you will come to hate looking at my face.'

She hesitated. 'I confess I do not have a fondness for black beards. Perhaps if you shaved it off, I would marry you.'

Harry's hand went to his beard in a defensive gesture. 'Is that really necessary?'

'No, it's just that the slave trader had a black beard and I would rather not be reminded of him,' she said.

Harry did not want her constantly thinking of the slave trader, either, as that would not bode well for their future. On the other hand, when she saw him without his beard and recognised him, as well as getting a good look at the disfiguring scar currently hidden beneath his beard, she would have more than one reason for refusing his offer. 'What if I were to promise to shave it off after the wedding?'

She smiled. 'That is a rare promise. I cannot believe you are as ugly as you say you are. I deem you just hide behind that beard because you wish to keep the women at bay.'

He grimaced. 'I would like to hear you say that when you see me minus this beard,' he said, touching his whiskers.

'I deem you dwell too much on the importance of a person's appearance. Surely it is what one's heart is like that is more important.'

'You can say that because you are lovely,' said Harry, 'not that I disagree with you about a person's nature. I would add that, if you decide to accept my proposal, I will expect your complete loyalty to me once we are married.'

His words surprised her. 'Why should you doubt my loyalty? You are offering me a home where I will rule when you are not there. I have no dowry, so no other man of worth would take me as I am. A home of my own is something I have never had before. Just like you, my home was a ship for several years. Even when I lived on land before sailing with my father, my home was either in my Irish grandfather's keep or my uncle's castle. It is true that there will be much for me to learn about organising a household, but I have seen how it is done and I have certain housewifery skills, such as sewing and cooking.'

'Then you will agree to be my wife?' asked Harry, his heart thudding as he waited for her answer.

Chapter Four

Bridget said hesitantly, 'You are offering me so much. I only wish I had part of my father's hoard to give you, then I would feel more worthy of you. I would that neither of us will regret my agreeing to be your wife.'

'I have no need of a dowry,' said Harry, relieved. He took her hand and lifted it to his lips and kissed it. 'Obviously there will be no time for banns to be read, but I will visit the priest in Machico today and, for a few pieces of silver, I am sure he will obtain a special licence so we can wed before we leave Madeira. I pray that you will feel well enough to make the journey in the next few days.'

'If that is your wish.' Bridget could feel her skin tingling where his lips had touched it. 'How will we travel there?'

'On horseback or you could ride alongside me when I drive the cart into Machico. After the ceremony we will go aboard my ship. I will need to oversee the loading of the cargo and, God willing, we will set sail the following morning on the outgoing tide.'

'You have it all planned,' said Bridget, attempting to conceal her sudden apprehension. Could he have planned this from the moment he had discovered her identity? But why should he have done? He had, after all, given sensible reasons why he wished to marry her.

'Naturally, I gave my proposal some thought before broaching the matter,' said Harry. 'Of course, plans can easily be overturned by forgetfulness or misfortune,' he said idly. 'If you can think of aught I might have forgotten, then I will be glad if you will inform me of it. I will leave you now and speak to you on my return.'

Bridget watched him go. She found it difficult to think of anything other at the moment than this man who had saved her life. She had a fair notion of what life was like being married to a mariner. Lonely, if one did not have a family or friends living close by. She felt a tightness in her chest and a moment's panic. Had she made the right decision? He had made no mention of wanting children. Yet she knew from listening to married women talking that most men wanted a son. Her mother had wanted a son, but it had never happened.

There were footsteps outside in the passage that she recognised and her heart began to thud. 'Is that you, Captain?' she called.

He entered the bedchamber and smiled down at her. 'I have been thinking you might like to sit outside on the terrace. I am certain the fresh air and sunshine will do you good.'

Instantly his thoughtfulness banished her ponderings. 'I would like that,' she said sincerely. 'But I have no shoes.' She lifted her skirts to reveal her bare feet. 'I lost them in the sea.'

He frowned and stroked his beard. 'I should have thought of that earlier. No doubt you could also do with more clothes for the journey. I shall see what I can do about such matters when I go into Machico.'

She thanked him.

'I think it is best if I carry you downstairs as this will be the first time you will leave your bedchamber since your arrival,' he said.

Before she could protest and say that she was quite capable of walking, he scooped her up into his arms and carried her from the room. 'But, Captain, my condition is much improved,' she assured him.

'Aye, but you have been close to death and need to conserve your strength for the journey.' Harry was not going to deprive himself of the pleasure of holding her close to him.

On those words, Bridget decided to remain silent, conscious of the strength in his arms and the beating of his heart. It gave her an odd feeling to be cradled in his arms that was not unpleasant.

He set her down in a chair on the terrace where she could gaze down over the garden to the glistening ocean below. 'How calm the water looks today,' she said.

'Aye, it is hard to believe that it can turn into a raging monster with little warning,' said Harry. 'If you will excuse me. I will be back soon.'

'Of course,' said Bridget hastily, watching him until he was out of sight.

Then she turned and looked again over the garden, determined to make the most of these moments of tranquillity. Soon she would have to strengthen her will to face going aboard ship again. What the captain had said about the sea being a raging monster had struck home. But she would not mention her fear of getting caught up in another storm to him.

'Taste this and give me your opinion,' said Harry, handing a goblet to Bridget.

Grateful that he was treating her as he would a normal guest, she took a cautious sip and then a mouthful of the wine. 'It is sweet and fruity with an unusual flavour. If you could bottle it, I'm sure you could make your fortune.'

He smiled. 'I see you have a business head. The unusual flavour is spirit fermented from the processed liquid sugar for the estate's own use. Perhaps one day enough will be produced to make it worth my client's efforts to turn the liquor into a profitable business. At the moment Jorge does not possess enough agricultural land to do so.'

'Jorge is the man who owns this house?'

Harry nodded. 'You have not had the opportunity to discover that Madeira is a heavily forested mountainous island. A lot of trees have to be felled to clear the land for the plough and many of the fields are on a slope. The sugar-cane harvest makes him a decent profit as it is and he also grows vines.'

'So you ship Madeira wine, as well?'

Harry nodded. 'It is a popular wine.'

'Do you have a buyer?'

'I doubt I'll have difficulty finding one in England.' Harry poured a little more of the drink into her goblet. 'I had, until recently, thought of making my home here, but now we are to be married no doubt you will wish

to live near your friends in England. I have heard that
Lady Elizabeth has a fine mansion near the Strand in
London.'

'That is true.' Bridget gazed at his bearded face and
tried to imagine his profile clean shaven, but it was not
easy and she gave up.

'I have also heard she is an eccentric and prone to do
exactly what she likes if she takes a fancy to someone,
having no husband to rein in her wayward behaviour.'

Bridget smiled. 'She is also extremely wealthy
because he died without issue and she inherited his fortune. She is so droll and says exactly what she thinks,
even if it is insulting. Yet her heart is warm and once
she heard my story, she was determined to help me to
find my father.'

'Kind of her, indeed,' said Harry drily. 'I presume it
was she who provided the ship you sailed on.'

Bridget shook her head. 'No, her goddaughter had
recently married the Baron Dalsland and it was he who
placed two of his ships at our disposal.'

'What!' exclaimed Harry, sitting bolt upright.

She looked at him, startled. 'Of course, you will
recognise the name. The Baron was a close friend of
Captain Black Harry. After we discovered that *Thor's
Hammer* had been seen in Funchal harbour, the Baron
was determined to have him found.' She drew in a
trembling breath. 'As you can imagine I was desperate
to leave England as soon as possible, fearing the ship
would be gone if I delayed, but the Baron insisted that
we wait until the weather improved.'

'Wise of him,' rasped Harry. 'You are fortunate in
your friends.' He longed to ask about this woman whom

the Baron had married, but knew it would be more sensible not to show too much interest, if he was to keep his identity secret a little longer. Yet he was extremely curious to know why Alex had not married Ingrid Wrangel, the woman with whom they had both been in love.

'I sincerely hope that Lady Elizabeth is back in London where she belongs,' said Bridget.

'Would you like to live in London?' asked Harry.

'Surely where we live will depend on your trading interests, Captain?'

He did not dispute it because he had seen Joe approaching with food.

Bridget watched as the youth set a basket of bread on the table, as well as dishes of meat, soft white cheese and fruit. She had regained her appetite and her mouth watered. Joe left for a few moments and returned with plates and knives and a jug of wine. She reached for bread and meat and, for a while, neither she nor the captain spoke, but gave all their attention to consuming the meal set before them. It was a while since she had tasted food so good as that she had consumed in this house.

'Perhaps you would prefer to live in Scotland?' suggested Harry, picking up the conversation where they had left off.

'Not particularly. My memories of life with my kinsfolk are not particularly happy ones. I was happier with my mother's family in Ireland, but I would not like to return there. There are too many memories of her in that place where she died and it would make me sad.' She sighed heavily. 'If only my father had not gone to the New World and she was still alive.'

'You can't rewrite the past, Bridget,' said Harry gently. 'You just have to do your best to redeem it.' He pushed back his chair and stood up. 'I will speak to you again in the morning. I have arrangements to make now. Don't overtax your strength,' he called over his shoulder as he walked away.

As Bridget watched him vanish around the side of the house, she thought how right he was that one could not rewrite the past. She must set her mind on the future. If only she knew what had happened to her father; how she wished that his fortune had not been seized by Patrick O'Malley. She still felt unworthy of the man she was to marry, coming as she was to him dowerless.

It was peaceful sitting there. Joe came out a couple of times and asked if there was aught else she wanted. When she told him that she had finished, he cleared the table. She remained there, watching the sun vanish beyond the horizon and the sky streak with apricot, gold and silver, wondering when the captain would return and if the priest would accept his silver in exchange for a special marriage licence. She felt a stir of apprehension mingling with a tingle of excitement, anticipating the days ahead.

'Christian, I have a task for one of the men,' called Harry from the quayside.

'What is it, Captain?' asked the tall, muscular, blond-haired Swede, leaning over the side of the ship.

'I want the name *Thor's Hammer* painted over with the words *St Bridget*.'

The man screwed up his ice-blue eyes. 'Has the sun got to you, Captain?'

Harry smiled. 'You might believe that even more so when I tell you that I am getting married and my bride's name is Bridget.'

The sailor's mouth fell open. 'You jest!'

'No. She is Callum McDonald's daughter and has come in search of her father. He never arrived home, which means that he and the crew and my ship are most likely at the bottom of the ocean.'

The Swede scowled. 'That is no reason for you to marry her.'

'Isn't it?' Harry frowned.

'No! It is not your fault. I was master of the *Odin's Maiden* and he tricked me into going ashore. If he had not done so, then he would not be missing. You must not forget it was Callum who stole your ship,' said Christian fiercely. 'He showed you no loyalty. *I* would never have behaved towards you in such a way.'

'I know,' said Harry, clapping a hand on his shoulder. 'But she is not to blame for that.'

Christian placed his hand over Harry's resting on his shoulder. 'Neither are you. He knew the risks. He had spoken to the settlers on New-found-land on the outward voyage and even then was hell-bent on returning the way we came. I wonder how he managed to persuade the men to crew the ship and disobey your orders?'

Harry shrugged. 'Perhaps they, too, thought I was mad to want to continue down the coast and preferred to return home, albeit empty-handed. Be that as it may, I still feel some responsibility for Bridget,' said Harry, removing his hand. 'Especially as she is all alone.'

Christian froze. 'Why is she on her own?'

Harry leaned against the side of the ship and his eyes

darkened. 'The ship she was on was attacked by pirates and she was sold into slavery.'

'How did she escape?'

'She swam ashore from the slave-trader's ship and I found her on the beach in a state of exhaustion. She needs a protector.'

'That is still no reason for you to marry her,' the Swede insisted.

Harry's mouth set in a firm line. 'I have not made this decision lightly and I do not wish to discuss it further. I've persuaded the priest to perform the ceremony on the morrow, so there will be no delay.'

'Why such haste? Have you considered that she might have been raped by her captor?'

Harry did not answer.

'You have! Yet you would still marry a defiled woman?'

'You've said enough,' said Harry, a warning note in his voice. 'I will not have you questioning my actions and you will speak respectfully of my future wife.' He felt odd enunciating those last two words. 'You can expect the cargo on the morrow.' He did not linger to see the effect of his words on the Swede, but left the ship.

The following morning Bridget awoke early and instantly remembered that this was to be her wedding day. There was a peculiar feeling in her stomach, but she told herself that it was natural she would feel nervous. She was relieved to see that the rash was fading. Hopefully by afternoon it would be scarcely noticeable. She could only pray that neither the captain nor Joe had caught the disease and wondered if her future husband had given any thought to her infecting his crew. Perhaps he believed she was no longer a threat to anyone.

Not waiting for either of them to knock on her door to rouse her, she dressed swiftly and went downstairs in search of the kitchen. There she found the captain in conversation with an old woman dressed in black. They stopped talking the moment she entered the room and Bridget guessed that they had been discussing her.

'It is good to see you up and about so early, Bridget,' said the captain. 'I want to introduce you to the widow Juanita who came to see you whilst you were ill, but you were sleeping. She will be travelling with us as she wishes to return to her family in Lisbon. I thought you would enjoy the company of another woman.'

Bridget marvelled at his consideration. 'I appreciate your forethought, Captain.'

She turned to Juanita and greeted her in Portuguese, stumbling over some of the words.

A smile flooded the older woman's face and she responded graciously, saying that she was happy to travel with the lady who was to be the captain's wife.

'I was of a mind that if you felt well enough that you might like to go with Juanita into Machico this morning and choose some cloth to make a couple of gowns for yourself,' said Harry, taking Bridget's arm and drawing her aside. 'There will be no need for you to return here. Juanita will take you to the chapel and I will meet you there.'

'As much as I would like to do that,' said Bridget in a halting voice, 'you are forgetting that I have no shoes.'

'Of course!' He looked annoyed. 'Then you'll have

to stay here and wait for my return. You will have to trust Juanita to choose what is best.'

'I can easily suggest the fabrics and the colours I would prefer,' said Bridget. 'Sewing will help pass the time during the voyage.

'What about shoes?' asked Harry. 'Let us see the size of your feet.'

She lifted her skirts a few inches and he gazed down at her slender ankles and small feet and then at Juanita's; the latter's were much bigger. 'I deem what is needed is a template,' he added thoughtfully.

Within a short space of time Bridget found herself standing on a drying cloth whilst the captain drew round her foot with a stick of charcoal. She found the whole operation physically disturbing. Her toes twitched and she wobbled; to keep her balance she had to place her hand on his shoulder. Every time his muscles bunched, she remembered how he had carried her downstairs as if she weighed no more than thistledown. Gazing down at his dark hair, she was tempted to press a hand to its springiness.

'Now the other foot,' he said gruffly, gripping her right ankle.

To distract herself Bridget asked him the name of his ship. He hesitated before saying, *'St Bridget.'*

She was amazed. 'What a coincidence.'

'Not at all. I decided to rename her once you agreed to marry me. I've always had a fondness for the saint. She knew what she wanted and wouldn't allow anyone to get in her way.'

'You make her sound selfish,' said Bridget, hoping that he did not think she was the same. 'But, of course, you must know that what she wanted most of all was to serve God. She even asked Him to take away her beauty so no man would want to marry her.'

'You're right. I do know the story,' said Harry drily, unable to resist tickling her toes.

She jerked her ankle out of his grasp, wondering whether he had tickled her deliberately. If so, what had caused him to behave so frivolously? It was unlikely behaviour for the man she was beginning to get to know. 'If you have a pair of spring scissors, I could cut out the shapes,' she offered.

'No, leave them as they are,' said Harry, knowing that he should not have given in to temptation to tickle her, 'that way the shoemaker only has to place a pair of ready-made shoes on the cloth to see if they fit.'

Juanita was handed the cloth and a chinking purse changed hands. Bridget told her what she wanted and the widow left the house.

Bridget wished she was going with her, wanting some task to perform. 'Perhaps I could make breakfast,' she suggested. 'I am sure you and Joe have much to do.'

'There is no need,' said Harry. 'Joe will be back shortly with fresh bread from the bakery and there is the remains of a chicken to eat. Why don't you sit outside and enjoy the garden whilst you can? Joe will need to go into Machico to oversee the food supplies being loaded on to the ship. Perhaps you could go with him instead of me. You would not have to walk far.'

Bridget nodded, disappointed that he was fobbing her off on to Joe. It was not that she would not enjoy travelling with Joe because she liked the lad. But she would have enjoyed the journey more with her future husband. They could have become better acquainted and there was also the fact that he was an interesting man and could have told her more about the island and his travels.

'Is there nothing I can do whilst I am waiting here?' she asked, a little forlornly.

Harry hesitated. 'I have a tear in a shirt that you can repair.'

Her face brightened. 'I will mend it for you.'

He smiled and had left the kitchen before she could remind him that she would need needle and thread, so she hurried after him, only to have to rest against the banister due to a sudden dizziness.

He found her there a few moments later. 'What is wrong?' he asked sharply, fastening his shirt as he came down the stairs. She thought she caught a glint of a silver chain at his throat and wondered if he wore a medal of St Christopher, the patron saint of travellers.

'I was rushing to tell you I had need of needle and thread and came over dizzy,' she said, loosening her grip on the banister.

'You came rushing upstairs just to tell me that, woman,' he chided. 'It is obvious that you still have not recovered from your illness. You could have slipped and broken a leg. There is a sewing box in the kitchen. Now take my arm and let us take the stairs slowly.'

She slipped her hand through his arm. 'I did not want to be a bother to you, although I suppose it is a little late for me to say that now. I've already caused you so much extra time and trouble.'

'I'll not deny it—but it was my decision to take you in and look after you,' he said. 'Do you know, when I first saw you I was reminded of a mermaid. You must swim like a fish to have accomplished that distance from the ship to the shore and survived. I, too, enjoy swimming, although I have no memory of how I learnt.'

She felt flattered by the admiration in his voice. 'My father taught me as soon as he took me on his ship. He told me how he remembered being thrown into the water as a boy and was terrified he would drown. Somehow he managed to doggy paddle to the shore and after that he determined to become a good swimmer. Besides, he discovered that he enjoyed it.' She swallowed a lump in her throat. 'I cannot believe he is dead,' she said huskily.

'Then do not believe it,' said Harry, gazing down at her from fathomless dark blue eyes.

For a moment she felt quite breathless and as if he was drawing the soul from her body. Then she forced herself to look away. 'I will do as you say. I would not like you to regret your decision to marry me, but if my father is still alive, would you allow him to live with us?'

'He might not wish it. Let us wait and see,' said Harry diplomatically.

They had reached the bottom of the stairs and Joe was waiting there for them. Harry raised her hand to his lips and kissed it before saying, 'Go outside and I will join you shortly. I must have a word with Joe.'

Once outside Bridget did not sit down, but walked slowly past the terrace and into the garden. The sun already felt warm on her face and was drawing out the scent from the yellow blossom of a mimosa tree. There were a multitude of flowers, many she had never seen before. She breathed in their fragrance as she wandered down to the foot of the garden where there was a low wall. She noticed that there was a sheer drop on the other side to the beach, although it was not very high.

She perched on the wall with her bare feet nestling in the grass and gazed over the ocean. She thought how pleasant it would be to swim with the captain in the warm waters of this island. She thought about what he had said about mermaids and tried to imagine them both with tails, half-naked, plunging through the surf and able to breathe underwater. Of them coming together and kissing. She blushed at her foolishness and considered how swiftly her own life had altered since she had met him. She was filled with a sense of unreality. Soon she would wed and become the possession of a man she was only just starting to get to know.

Suddenly she heard her name being called. 'I'm here,' she shouted, getting to her feet and beginning the climb up the sloping garden.

The captain appeared a few yards above here. 'What were you thinking of, wandering away without saying where you were going?' he chided.

She bristled at the tone of his voice. 'Where could I go? I have no shoes, cloak, hat or money and I am unlikely to do anything as foolish as to jump from the wall on to the shore.'

'You could fall and it is not unknown for pirates to land on this coast.' He took her arm. 'Come! I have much to do this day and have no time to waste. I have decided that instead of delaying to break your fast here, you can eat on the journey.'

'What about your shirt?' she protested. 'Was I not to mend it?'

'You can do that on the ship.'

'If that is your command,' said Bridget.

The severity of his expression relaxed. 'You do not like my giving you orders,' he said softly, touching her cheek with a gentle hand.

'You are to be my husband, so I will have to become accustomed to it,' she said, a spirited sparkle in her eyes.

Harry reached up and plucked a blossom from a tree and placed it behind her ear. 'I am glad that you understand that,' he teased. 'Some flowers in your hair and you will look like a bride.' He took more blossoms and handed them to her and then he kissed her lightly. 'I deem I will give myself the pleasure of taking you to the ship. No doubt there will be much of interest for you to watch down at the quayside whilst I am busy.'

Bridget clutched the flowers to her bosom. Never had she expected such *courtly* behaviour from this bearded rescuer of hers, so different to what she expected. Not only did he give her flowers, but he seemed to know what she enjoyed already. She had always found anchoring in a new port fascinating. She went with him, still wishing wistfully that her father could be there to give her away and that she had a dowry to give to her captain.

Chapter Five

Joe was obviously pleased to be going with them to Machico. He was smiling and humming a tune beneath his breath. She was aware of his eyes on her as the captain helped her up on to the wide seat of the cart before climbing up beside her. She placed the blossoms in her lap.

'You might find the journey a little bumpy,' Harry said.

'I'm sure I'll survive. I will hold on tightly.' Her hand sought the metal guardrail at the edge of the seat.

'Good.' He nodded to Joe. 'Now don't drive too fast.'

'Aye, aye, Captain,' responded the youth, touching his cap with the end of his whip. He clicked his tongue against his teeth, flicked the reins and the horse began to move.

The captain placed his arm around the back of the seat, his hand resting lightly on Bridget's shoulder. She was very aware of his closeness as the cart bumped and jerked along the path. He told her a little more about the island and it did not seem long at all to Bridget before they were crossing a bridge over a river, the banks of which were covered in lush vegetation. Then Machico came into view.

The town was backed by steep hills and the captain pointed out to her the Chapel of the Miracles and told her that was where the marriage ceremony would take place. He said that it had been erected over the resting place of a pair of lovers, one of them an English adventurer, Robert Machim. 'Apparently he set sail from Bristol in the fourteenth century with the lady of his heart, Anne d'Arset, to escape the wrath of her father,' he added.

Bridget was surprised that he should know of such a romantic tale. 'I thought Madeira was not discovered until early in the last century by the Portuguese.'

'The lovers' destination was Brittany, but a storm blew them off course and they ended up here.'

'I can understand how that could easily happen,' said Bridget seriously, hoping that they would encounter no such storms on the journey to England. 'Is there another church? The chapel does not look very big.'

'A larger church is being built and there is another chapel to the west of the town,' informed the captain.

She noticed a construction on a headland. 'And what is that building?'

'A fort. The people have to be prepared for attacks from the sea even here.'

'Is nowhere safe from pirates?' She sighed. 'Where is your ship anchored?'

'You'll soon see. Then I will introduce you to Master Larsson.'

'Who is he?'

'My second-in-command. He is expecting you.'

Bridget wondered what Master Larsson had been told about her. Had he approved of his captain's decision to marry and take her aboard his ship?

As soon as she set eyes on the tall Swede with a shock of flaxen hair, she knew that he had not. He might welcome her aboard the ship in his strongly accented English, but he had such cold eyes when he looked at her. His disapproval was even more obvious when he went with her and the captain into his cabin. He removed a cloak hanging on the back of a chair and left without a word.

'I deem Master Larsson does not like me,' said Bridget, looking troubled.

Harry thought how perceptive she was in some ways. Yet she had not recognised *him* beneath the simple disguise of a beard! 'You must not concern yourself about what he thinks. It is nothing personal. He just does not approve of women aboard ship.'

Just like Captain Black Harry, thought Bridget, feeling an odd ache at her heart. She gazed about her at the latticed window and large table with charts and instruments of navigation on its surface. There were a couple of chairs screwed to the floor, as well as lockers beneath a wide bunk bed that would take two people if necessary. Only now did it occur to her that most likely she and the captain would have to share this cabin. His crew would expect it. Her heart began to beat heavily and she knew that she should try to pluck up the courage to say something about their sleeping arrangements.

But before she could speak he said, 'I'll leave you now, Bridget, I have matters to see to,' and he was gone.

Bridget stood motionless for a moment, wondering what to do next, then realised she was still clutching her flowers. If she did not put them in some water, they would soon wilt. She found a bucket of water in the cabin, as well as a pot, and dealt with her blossoms. She decided not to linger here, but went up on deck and padded across to the side of the ship. She took several deep breaths in an attempt to calm herself. Already she knew what it felt like to be held in the captain's arms and to feel the gentle touch of his lips on hers. But what would it feel like if he were not to behave so gently? She chewed on her lip. She had seen cattle in the fields mating so knew what coupling entailed. She only stopped chewing her lip when she tasted blood.

She was not yet prepared to welcome the captain into her body. He had begun to court her, but she still barely knew him. How would he react once he had his ring on her finger? She was filled with trepidation as she rested her arms on the polished wood and gazed down at the quayside.

'Senhorita McDonald!'

Bridget's eyes searched for the owner of the voice and she caught sight of Juanita. The widow was not alone, but accompanied by a man carrying several rolls of cloth. Bridget forced a smile and waved to them. Once they were on board, she suggested that they take the cloth to the cabin. The man dumped it on the bed and left the two women alone.

'I did not expect to see you so soon,' said Bridget.

'No doubt it would have taken me longer if we had discussed at further length what you wanted,' said Juanita, glancing about the cabin. 'This is a great adventure, no?'

'Aye, I suppose it is.' Bridget darted a look at the bed.

Juanita's eyes followed hers. 'There is no need for you to fear him. He might look fierce, but he is a good man.'

'Of course, but—' Bridget hugged herself and paced the floor.

'You do not quite trust him because you do not know him very well. But the captain needs love, so you must give it to him.'

Bridget hesitated. 'Why do you say that? Is it that you have heard that he loved a woman and lost her? He has told me that he wants me only to keep house for him.'

Juanita laughed. 'He would marry you to be his housekeeper? I do not believe it. I remember what the captain was like when he first returned with Senhor Jorge. They caused a great stir amongst the young ladies in Machico.' Juanita set aside the paraphernalia on the table and spread out the cloth. 'Is this not fine?'

Bridget scarcely glanced at the cloth. 'You mean he went with women? I don't believe it!'

'Why? He was very handsome then, so handsome.' She sighed gustily. 'Not handsome, anymore, because of the scar on his cheek and some of the women look at him askance, so he grows a beard, but still I deem he is an attractive man, so big and so strong. Also he is not poor.'

Bridget thought about the captain's reluctance to

shave off his beard. Obviously, he really did fear she would be repulsed by *his ugly visage* if she saw the scar before they were wed. Perhaps she should have insisted that he shave his beard off before their marriage. Yet what right had she to do so when he had offered her so much for so little in exchange?

'You like the colour?' asked Juanita, changing the subject.

Bridget saw that the roll of material was of blue wool. 'Aye, it is what I told you to get.'

'The wool is from Flanders. The seller must have paid a pretty penny for it and the captain even more. He wants you to dress like a lady, so he can be proud of you. This blue, it is the colour of the Madonna's robe. She smiles on you and will bring you good fortune. You will have his child.'

'Who are you that you can foretell such things?' said Bridget, startled. 'Is it that you consider yourself a seer?'

Juanita's eyes widened. 'He is lusty and you are beautiful, so why should you not make fine children?'

Bridget chose to ignore her words. Why should she believe her? Juanita picked up the material and swirled it around Bridget's shoulders. 'Many men have worshipped the Madonna. Children will forge your union and make it strong.' She paused and murmured, 'This is of great importance because I sense there is a woman waiting for him in England.'

Bridget stared at her in disbelief as she felt the material slither from about her neck. Was it possible this woman the captain loved might not have married his friend and still awaited his return? But Juanita could not know this and was surely saying these things to make herself sound important.

'You are talking nonsense. Please, say no more,' said Bridget.

Juanita shrugged. 'You will see. And now what about your shoes? I hope you will like them. I purchased two pairs as the captain ordered. A pair of soft leather slippers and another of strong leather with tough soles.' She displayed them. 'Try on your slippers, my pretty. You do not want to go to your wedding in your bare feet.'

Bridget reached for the slippers.

'You have pretty feet,' said Juanita. 'Sit down and I will help you on with them.'

Bridget hesitated, then sat on the bed. She remembered how the captain had tickled her toes and a pleasant heat pooled in the pit of her stomach. Why was she feeling like this just at the memory of his touch? Then she recalled the strength of his arms and a tremor shot through her.

'A perfect fit,' said Juanita, 'and so pretty.'

Bridget held out a foot and could not but agree with the old woman. What had she been thinking of buying red shoes with tiny flowers painted on them? Yet it seemed a long time since Bridget had worn anything so delightful. She removed the slippers, aware of Juanita watching her. 'You are right. They are pretty. You have made a good choice.'

'Now the other shoes,' said the old woman, smiling. 'You will need them if you are to walk on difficult terrain.'

'What are you forecasting now?' asked Bridget.

'I forecast nothing. There will always be times in one's life when the way is rough. You will see.'

Bridget had had enough of her comments and asked her politely to leave as she wanted to rest. Juanita fixed Bridget with her dark eyes and gave a throaty chuckle before shuffling from the cabin.

Bridget sank on to the bed and stared at the shoes. She picked them up and went over to one of the lockers; finding it empty, she placed them inside. She picked up the slippers and put them on. Then she went over to the table to collect the rolls of cloth, scissors, chalk, needles and thread. She was in the process of placing them with the shoes when she heard the captain's voice. Her heart seemed to lurch sideways and she knew that she did not want him to find her in his cabin, acting as if she had already taken possession of it. She opened the door and went on deck.

Harry was instantly aware of Bridget and thought she looked pale and apprehensive. Briefly, he considered leaving the complete supervision of the loading of the sugar cane to Christian Larsson and making his way over to her side to ask if all was well. He was aware that he had given her little time to become accustomed to the idea of becoming his wife. For an instant their eyes met and she darted him a nervous smile.

God's Blood! Surely she was not frightened of him? The thought angered him. Had he not proved in the last few days she was safe with him and that he had her well-being at heart? If he were to die, all that he possessed would come to her as his wife. He was not a fabulously rich man, but he could provide her with a comfortable lifestyle. He realised that now was not the right time to tell her that. There would be time enough for that after the wedding.

The loading of the sugar cane was finally completed and the cargo of wine stored. Joe returned with a loaded cart and several of the crew helped him to stow everything away, although the coops of live chickens were wedged on deck in a manner that meant they would not be flung about once the ship sailed.

During this time Bridget was aware of the curious glances of the men. Whatever their thoughts of their captain's behaviour, none of them was speaking them aloud. She returned to the cabin and wove the flowers into a garland as best she could and adorned her hair with it. When she emerged into the sunlight again she was aware of the eyes of the captain and the crew upon her. Even when it came time for them to leave the ship and go to the chapel, not one of the crew seemed to think that congratulations to their captain and his future bride were in order. She felt uneasy, wondering if Master Larsson was causing trouble for them both behind the captain's back. No doubt the Swede had also known Black Harry and her father. Was her father the reason why Master Larsson looked so disapprovingly at her? Had he known Callum had once sailed a pirate ship?

She clenched and unclenched her hands, telling herself that she was marrying Captain Mariner, not his second-in-command or the crew. She would behave with decorum and they would realise that, although she was her father's daughter, she knew how to behave. She felt a deep sadness thinking of her father, trying to convince herself that he was alive. Yet her mood was dark and it took an effort to pin a smile on her face.

Juanita and Joe were to accompany them to the chapel. As the captain drew her arm through his, Bridget asked, 'How long will it take us to reach Lisbon?'

'If all goes well, within a sennight,' he answered. 'Hopefully, we should be in England within the month. Is there aught else you wish to ask me?'

She hesitated, remembering that wide bunk in the cabin, but her courage failed her.

'Do the shoes fit well?' he asked, gazing down at her bent head.

She lifted her skirts to show him the soft red slippers.

'Not sensible, but suitable for a wedding,' he said with a chuckle.

The sound caused her to jerk up her head and stare at him. 'Why do you laugh?'

'Because I am pleased to be marrying you. I would that you had a bridal gown to wear, but at least you have pretty shoes for your pretty feet.' He added in a whisper, 'You have naught to fear from me, Bridget.'

Her nod was almost imperceptible, but he took it for agreement and, without more ado, led her through the bustling streets of Machico to the chapel.

Bridget had wondered if at the last minute something would go wrong. Perhaps the priest would not marry them after all or the captain might have forgotten the ring. Possibly she would panic and be unable to say her vows. How she wished her father was beside her! Would he have approved of her marrying Captain Mariner? As it was, she felt as if it were someone else speaking when it came to her playing her part. As for Captain Henry Mariner, his voice was rough but clear when he spoke the words that would bind her to him.

They emerged from the chapel into the evening sunshine. Bridget was conscious of the heavy gold ring on her finger. It spoke to her of his ownership and, for an instant, she was reminded of the manacled African slaves on the trader's ship. Then she told herself that to compare her situation with those slaves was nonsense. The captain had shown her kindness. Of her own free will she had agreed to marry him. At least now she could believe that she legally belonged to him and the slave trader had no remaining claim on her.

They made haste in returning to the ship, where a special meal was prepared for them, accompanied by a fine Madeira wine. It made Bridget pleasantly sleepy, if still a little apprehensive because since Juanita had spoken of the captain being lusty and of her having his child, she did not know how best to behave. Would she have the courage to tell the captain she was not ready to have him in her bed if he should decide that he wanted to consummate their marriage? He was stronger than she and could overpower her if he chose.

She lingered on deck, watching the activity on the quayside. The crew had been given permission to go ashore for a couple of hours, but now they were returning to rest before making ready to sail on the morning tide. She was aware of her husband's eyes on her. What was he thinking? He rose suddenly and, without a word to her, went and spoke to Joe before making his way to his cabin. His actions startled her. She had it in mind that he would expect her to retire before him, so she could prepare for bed and snuggle beneath the covers before he made an appearance. But perhaps he had only gone to fetch something and would make a reappearance, so she stayed out in the fresh air, waiting to see if that was what would happen.

She saw Joe carrying a steaming pot into the cabin and wondered what was taking place in there for he did not immediately reappear. She watched Juanita wrap herself in a cloak and curl up on a pallet beneath an awning on the deck. She was conscious that some of the crew kept glancing her way. She began to feel restless, wondering why Joe was in the cabin so long. Suddenly he reappeared, carrying the pot. He waved to her and then vanished beneath the awning.

The sun had set and the stars were beginning to prick on in the darkening sky. She knew that she could delay no longer and made her way to the cabin. Hopefully her husband would not be angry because she had stayed on deck so long. Her heart beat heavily as she entered the cabin and closed the door behind her. A lantern hung from a hook in the ceiling, but the light it cast was not strong and she could only make out the shadowy outline of the bed and her husband's strong shoulders and profile. She started when he addressed her.

'I thought your curiosity might have brought you here the sooner. You asked me to shave off my beard and Joe has done so for me,' he said in a strained voice.

'So that is why he was in here so long.' Her hand searched for a chair because her legs felt suddenly weak. 'I confess that I had forgotten that I had asked that of you.'

He made a noise in his throat as if clearing it. 'So I could have kept my beard?'

'No. I am glad you have shaved it off and I am curious to see how you look, although, in this light—'

'I can do naught about the light, but if you come closer you might have some notion of how I look without a beard. If you were blind you could read my features with your fingers, although, if you explore my face in such a fashion you will soon discover just how ugly I am.'

'I cannot believe that you are as ugly as you believe yourself to be!' exclaimed Bridget, crossing the cabin towards the bed.

It was darker there, so she could barely see his features. Was that what he'd intended? Taking a deep breath, she sat on the edge of the bed and placed her hands either side of his face. Instantly she could feel the twisted outline and jagged skin of the scar that covered most of his cheek. She could feel him trembling and, despite having been warned of its ugliness, was shocked by the extent of the damage to his cheek.

'What caused this?' she asked.

'A jab with a burning torch during a skirmish in Africa,' he said hoarsely.

'It must have hurt.'

Unexpectedly he chuckled deep in his throat. 'An understatement, my dear Bridget. It burned like hell's fire.' He placed his arms at either side of her waist and drew her closer to him.

'Joe made no mention of a burn although he did tell me of the wound to your thigh,' she said, feeling slightly breathless, still cradling his face between her hands and very aware that he was holding her so that their bodies were pressed against each other. She was relieved that he was still wearing his shirt.

'I wager he made me out to be some kind of idiotic hero.' He brushed his lips against the inside of her wrist and she felt her nerves tingle.

'A hero, certainly,' said Bridget, easing a throat that was suddenly tight with emotion. She felt such sympathy for him that she wanted to bring him some comfort.

'He's prejudiced in my favour.'

'I cannot blame him. You did after all rescue him from being bullied and have taken care of him ever since.' She removed her hands and rested them on his forearms and gazed into his shadowy face. 'In a way, you have done a similar thing for me. You might not have done battle with the slave trader who held me prisoner, but you have rescued me from my fear of him.'

'It was pure chance that I was standing on the cliff and saw you drop into the sea.'

'You do not consider fate meant us to meet?' She found it easier to say these things to him in the dark.

'Fate, chance? What is the difference?'

'I thought you would know that,' she said.

'You are saying I was meant to see you and to find you? I deem you are more of a romantic than I would have thought, Bridget. I wonder if you will feel the same in the morning when you see me in the light.' Leaning forwards, he pressed his lips against hers. 'Now undress and go to sleep. It's been a long day for both of us and no doubt you are still recovering from your illness.'

'My health is much improved now.'

She wondered what would have happened if her lips

had yielded to his. Now he had turned away from her and was lying down. She had no choice but to share his bed. No doubt when he purchased a house for them, they would have separate bedchambers. She was relieved that he had no intention of forcing himself upon her this night, but was also aware of a vague disappointment that he obviously found her easily resistible. She would like to rid him of the memory of that woman who had preferred his friend.

She dragged the garland of blossoms from her hair and removed her gown and slippers. Then, still wearing her shift, she climbed into bed and turned her back on him and tried to settle to sleep. But sleep would not come because she was too aware of his presence, although he made no move towards her and his breathing was steady and even. Obviously he was already asleep and her sharing his bed did not bother him a jot. She closed her eyes and instantly was conscious of a wave slapping against the hull as the ship rocked at anchor. She willed sleep to come, but it did not, and she lay there gazing into the darkness, thinking of Juanita's words to her.

Harry lay awake, listening to the sound of Bridget's gentle breathing and conscious of the swell of her bottom against the small of his back. He longed to turn towards her and take her in his arms and ravish her mouth with kisses and make love to her. Yet he had married her under false pretences and should never have done so. Once she saw him for who he was, then she would not want to consummate their union, and he desperately wanted her.

Why had he agreed to her request to shave off his

beard, so revealing his ugly self to her censure? There was no doubt in his mind that when she saw his face by the light of day, she would feel revulsion as well as fury. Surely she would recognise that side of his profile that was undamaged. She might run away from him as soon as the opportunity arose. He could not allow that and would perhaps have to lock her in this cabin for her own protection. He would not like doing so, but what else could he do to prevent her from fleeing into danger?

Suddenly she turned over and his pulses raced. Cautiously he rolled over so that he was facing her. He caught the gleam of her eyes in the darkness. 'Can't you sleep?' he whispered.

'No.'

She wondered what he would say if she told him what Juanita had said about them having a child. She was tempted to ask him whether the old woman had a reputation as a seer. She remembered how lonely a mariner's wife's life could be when her husband was away at sea, so that when he suddenly drew her close to him she did not resist. He nuzzled her ear and then the side of her face before covering her mouth with his and kissing her gently; when she did not pull away, he kissed her more deeply. Skilfully, he slipped the strap of her shift from her shoulder and then caressed the side of her neck with his lips, easing the garment down until her breasts were bared. Then his fingers gently stroked her nipples.

The breath caught in Bridget's throat because the sensation caused by his caresses was extremely pleasing, but really she should ask him to stop. But then his mouth covered hers again and instinctively hers opened beneath his. He ran his tongue along the inside of her lower lip and all the time his fingers were creating havoc with her senses. Then he lowered his head and took her nipple into his mouth and instantly she felt a warm, pleasant heat pool between her legs as he suckled her. She began to tremble and he lifted his head and kissed her mouth again, but this time his tongue dallied with hers and she felt as if her whole body was a mass of differing sensations. His hands were sliding down her hips, taking her shift with them. She thought that she really must tell him to stop as his gentle fingers began to explore her most private place, only instead the word that she uttered was, 'Please!' for never had she experienced such physical delight, which grew and grew until she was gasping and a voice in her head was saying *don't stop*!

Bliss suddenly flooded her being, so then when he entered her she was unable to resist him. Instead she clung to him as he pushed further and further into her and another wave of ecstasy took her with him as he climaxed.

Chapter Six

When she woke the following morning, the first thing Bridget set eyes on was the silver amulet nestling in the dark hairs on her husband's chest as he lay on his side a few inches away from her. The amulet was fashioned in a cross from a miniature *Thor's Hammer* and she had seen one like it before.

Her heart began to thud in an unpleasant manner as she lifted her head and gazed at his handsome profile, unable to see the scarred side of his face. Only now did she recognise him for who he was and it gave her such a shock that she shot up in bed and banged her head against the wooden wall of the ship, which was dipping up and down in an alarming manner. She yelped in pain. Her husband opened an eye, but said not a word. She was so angry that she lifted a fist and punched him in the chest. 'Captain Black Harry, you *cur*!' she exclaimed, as the full extent of her position and his actions hit her.

He flinched and his eyes darkened. 'Why do you insist on calling me Black Harry?'

'Because that is your name and you have a black heart,' she cried.

'It is *not* my name,' he growled. 'It is the one Callum gave me when I was a boy on the pirate ship and I hated it. I was always given the filthiest tasks to do so was always dirty.'

'You deem by telling me that that you will rouse my sympathy?' Her voice rose several octaves. 'You have deceived me! You told me you were dead and I thought I would never see you again and now I will have to put up with your company until you die again,' she added on a sob, raising her fist once more.

He seized her wrist. 'I know my being alive must come as a shock to you, but surely you cannot wish I was dead again?'

'You were never dead in the first place!' she cried. 'You lied to me! Have you no conscience? If I'd known it was you I was marrying, I would never have taken holy vows and let you near me,' she added, struggling to free herself.

'That is why I never told you. I knew you'd probably do something foolish, such as running away, if I'd been honest with you.'

'You never gave me the option. If you would let go of my wrist, then I will do that right now.'

'Too late, Bridget. We're at sea and there's nowhere for you to run to, so why don't you be sensible? Accept that we are man and wife and be glad that you won't have to worry about where your next crust is coming from and will have a roof over your head.'

'You think that makes your deception acceptable?' she asked incredulously. 'I might as well have stayed on the slave-trader's ship instead of swimming straight into your arms, for I am as much your captive as I was his after last night.'

'Don't talk such nonsense!' he thundered, outraged by her comment. 'I did not force you to consummate our union. I wooed you.'

'You *seduced* me!' she hissed angrily.

'I know you are angry, but how can you possibly compare my actions in any way to that despicable slave trader?'

'You *bought* me,' she accused.

'I *married* you!' he protested.

'I thought you were Captain Henry Mariner, a different man altogether,' she said.

'No, Bridget, he is me,' said Harry softly, 'so get that into your head and perhaps then you will begin to realise that I am not the black-hearted villain you insist on my being.'

'Maybe I would have realised it sooner if you had been honest with me. Instead, you spoke falsely because you had no faith in my judgement. You looked upon my outer appearance and saw a woman you desired, but you believed that inside I was still the girl you refused to have on your ship two years ago.'

He hesitated. 'There is some truth in what you say, but that is because you made it obvious this past week when you spoke about Black Harry that you still held a grudge against him for separating you from your father. I knew then that you would cut off your nose to spite your face if I told you the truth. And you've proved that to me a few moments ago by calling me a cur as soon as you recognised me without my beard. I was right to do what I thought was best for you.'

For a moment his sheer arrogance took her breath away. 'You were not my father that you should make my decisions for me!' she said in a seething voice, wrenching her wrist out of his grasp. 'I am getting dressed and going out on deck. I need some fresh air.' She reached for her gown, only to overbalance and fall off the bed. She went careering across the floor and ended up beneath the table and lay there, winded.

Harry was out of the bed in a flash and hauled her out by her feet. The indignity of her position brought tears to her eyes. She struggled as he lifted her up and staggered with her across the cabin. He dumped her on the bed and kept his arms around her. It was only then that she realised he was wearing only his shirt.

She gasped and tried to hide her eyes, but she could not get her hands free. 'Let me go!' she cried. 'I do not want a repeat of last night.'

His eyes glinted. 'But you found pleasure in it. Still, you're a fool if you deem I would take you in the mood you are in at the moment. Now keep your voice down. We don't want the whole ship knowing we are quarrelling.' He released her and moved away from her.

'I want our marriage annulled,' she said in a shaky voice, rubbing a grazed elbow.

He shook his head. 'Out of the question after last night. Besides, you promised to remain with me for fairer or fouler.'

'And *you* are the fouler.' She tossed the words at him.

She was aware of the weight of the silence that

followed as his hand flew to his cheek. She remembered how the skin had felt beneath her fingers last night and suddenly she was scared and waited for the blow to fall. Only he did not touch her, but instead turned his back on her. She struggled with anger, pain, shame and pity, and part of her wanted to reach out to him and beg his pardon. But the thought that she was his wife and he had such power over her held her back. Why could he not have told her the truth?

A few moments later she heard the cabin door open and close. What was she to do? Escape was impossible. Now frustration was her uppermost emotion. She had been in this position of wanting to escape so many times before that she shook with the strength of the anger that accompanied her frustration. For a moment she considered behaving like the girl he still thought her to be. She would dress, leave the cabin, cross over to the side of the ship and throw herself into the sea. That would show him just how much he had hurt her. It would say to him that she would rather die than have to live with him. Only she did not want to die—rather she would live and find some way to pay him back for his arrogance and deceit!

She should have insisted that he shave off his beard before instead of after the wedding. Only she had been so grateful to him for all that he was offering her: a home, his name.

His name! She paced the floor. She suddenly recalled that even though he didn't yet know it, her new husband was Harry Appleby, heir to Appleby Manor, a business and a house in London. Was their marriage even legal? He had married her under the name of Captain Henry

Mariner, so perhaps it wasn't. Her spirits lifted and she thought that she would go out on deck and tell him that they weren't legally married. When he asked why, then she would tell him it was because he wasn't who he said he was when they had exchanged their vows. She hated him for his deception, when she had been so honest with him. Despised him for his lack of faith in the woman she was now.

She must get dressed. Carefully she made her *toilette* before donning her gown. Then she put on stockings and her sturdy shoes before taking several deep breaths and going outside.

Almost immediately she was aware of Master Larsson, who raked her with one of his frosty glances, and several of the seamen looked her way. Her husband, though, appeared intent on ignoring her, seemingly absorbed in commanding his ship. He held himself upright and from the angle she viewed him now his profile was as handsome as when she had first set eyes on him in Ireland and been charmed by him.

Then he turned his head and she saw that horrific damage to his face. Seeing it in the bright light of day, she sternly suppressed feelings of compassion, determined to remain angry with him. Then his cold gaze touched her face and she knew he was utterly furious with her. Her own grievances rose once more and threatened to choke her and she looked at him with disdain. For a further moment she did consider going through with her plan, only it struck her afresh that their marriage had been consummated and what would that make her if she spoke out and said their marriage was not a true one? His *mistress*? The thought was unpalatable to her.

She was relieved when Joe hailed her and she turned away and carefully made her way across the deck, clinging to a rope that had been slung between two masts. The youth's smile melted some of the ice in her heart and she exchanged a few words with him. She ate her breakfast under the awning and forced herself to converse desultorily with Juanita about the fabrics she had brought her. But all the time she was aware that her husband was only yards away and no doubt listening to every word she spoke.

Harry was deeply hurt, not only because Bridget had spoken her mind about how she felt about his appearance, but also for comparing his behaviour to that of the slave trader. His aim in wanting to possess her was completely different. Bridget was also mistaken about his opinion of her. He had admired the woman he had rescued for her courage, as well as her beauty. He had also not simply married her because he had wanted her for himself, but had done so out of concern for her protection and to make amends for the ills that had befallen her since she had taken her farewell of her father.

It had taken an enormous amount of will-power to keep his gaze averted from his wife's comely figure when she came out on deck, but eventually he had been unable to resist glancing her way and what had been her response? She had looked at him as if he was beneath her. No doubt now she knew him for that sorry boy on the pirate ship whom her father had befriended, she considered him unworthy of her. A boy with no name, only the one that he had given himself. What right had she to consider herself better than himself? She was only a woman. A lovely woman to be sure, but a woman, nevertheless. Her grandfather might have been a Scottish lord, but her father was a pirate and had stolen one of Harry's ships. A ship that Harry had paid for to be built in Sweden when he'd decided to go into business for himself.

He had worked hard to get where he was; although he had often longed to know his family name and background, he had learned to live with the fact that he might never know the truth about himself and to be proud of his achievements. He had been mad to marry Bridget, but it was done now and he was determined that she would learn to accept his rule. After all, she had all to gain and little to lose.

He watched his wife rise from her seat under the awning and go towards the cabin. He thought she might have stayed out longer on the deck, but obviously she would rather not linger where she could see him. He turned away and went to speak to Master Larsson.

Bridget entered the cabin, wondering if her husband would follow her, but thankfully he did not. She took out the blue cloth he'd purchased for her new dress and stared at it for several moments before tossing it aside as her anger rose again. She wanted nothing from him. If only her father had kept his hoard in a sensible place instead of having it all with him on his ship! She wondered where her husband kept his money. There was a chest in the cabin that was locked, so perhaps it was hidden in there.

She went over to the window and stared out over the sea and thought the surface looked a little choppy. She longed for the journey to be over and wished she could wake up on the morrow and be in London. But that was impossible. The voyage would take at least a month and the thought of sharing a cabin for all that time with her new husband filled her with dismay. How was she going to pass the time if she did not occupy herself with sewing? Also she did not fancy wearing the same gown and shift all the way to England. She turned back to the table, picked up the material again and, seizing the shears, took the plunge and cut the cloth.

Bridget ate the midday meal in her husband's company on his orders, but during that time he exchanged no words with her, so she was also silent, thinking that if she began to talk she might say more than she intended. The rest of the day passed agonisingly slowly and she wondered what would happen when they were alone together that night. Would he attempt to force his will on her and make her submit to him?

She need not have worried because he spent only a few brief moments in the cabin that evening before telling her that he would be spending that night on deck, as the weather was on the change and it might be a rough night. She felt a curl of fear in her stomach. No doubt he wanted to make certain the cargo was doubly secure and to keep his eye on things. He said that he would send Juanita to be with her. She thanked him in a cool voice.

Shortly after there was a knock on the door and the

sound of Juanita's voice requesting permission to enter. Bridget told her to come in.

'I wish I had stayed in Madeira now,' said Juanita as the wind took the door from her hand and slammed it shut. She was wearing a black cloak and carried a bag containing her possessions. 'Perhaps it was God's will that I stayed there and I have disobeyed him.' The old woman clung to any object she could get a grip on as she crossed the cabin towards the bed.

'You believe that just because the sea is rough? Perhaps you'd best start praying,' said Bridget seriously.

'That is my intention,' said Juanita. 'Is it acceptable to you that I share your bed?'

Bridget did not see how she had any choice in the matter. She could hardly expect the old woman to sit up all night if the weather was to get worse. 'Of course.'

Juanita thanked her and Bridget organised their sleeping arrangements and suggested they say their prayers once they were in bed. The old woman agreed. Once that was done, to Bridget's surprise Juanita offered her a drink of poppy juice from a flask. She refused as gently as she could, preferring to have her wits about her if a storm were to blow up as her husband predicted. After all she had no reason to doubt his seamanship. So whilst the old woman snored, Bridget lay, listening to the wind and waves and thinking of Harry out in the elements along with the rest of crew.

She remembered being confined to a cabin with Lady Elizabeth and her maid, Hannah, during the storm that had raged last year. Her ladyship had remained calm and tried to soothe their fears by talking of her travels as a young woman after she'd been widowed. It had been a very different case altogether when Bridget had been confined to a cabin with the slave-trader's woman during a ferocious storm. That had raged for days and she recalled the woman's terror and conviction that she was going to die.

Bridget sighed and rolled on to her side and gripped the wooden rail at the edge of the bed. She remembered the storm that had blown the vessel to Madeira and that dark figure on the cliff. How would she have felt if she had known it was Black Harry? Would it have given her hope? It seemed that it *was* fate that had led him to that point that day—would she have survived if he had not seen her and she'd remained on the beach exhausted and soaked to the skin? She did owe him her life, but how she wished he could have been honest with her. She might just have accepted his offer of marriage for that reason alone. But instead he had deceived her. Still, however angry she was with him, she realised that she was going to have to tell him soon that he was Harry Appleby, heir to all that had been his father's, and that in England, his sister waited for his return. He deserved to know his true identity. Perhaps he would decide that their marriage was still legal because Mariner had been the name he was known by? Eventually she dozed off with that thought in her head.

She was wakened shortly after dawn by Harry entering the cabin. Juanita was still asleep by her side. Bridget sat up cautiously as the ship was rolling terrifyingly. All was grey outside of the window with clouds racing across the sky. Her husband staggered towards the bed and she noticed that his hat and cloak were sodden. 'You are soaking wet and will catch a chill,' she shouted.

He shrugged and held out some hard biscuits and fruit to her. 'You don't have to pretend that you care about me,' he yelled. 'You will have to make do with these for now. You must both stay here in the cabin until the storm abates.' He went back outside.

Bridget determinedly quashed her fear and tried to concentrate on anything but the storm, but the noise made it difficult. She decided there was no point in waking Juanita and ate a piece of fruit and then nibbled at a hard biscuit. She prayed silently for the safety of the men on deck and for the ship, that the storm would die down and that they would not be blown off course. She wondered when she would get the opportunity to tell her husband the news of his true identity. Obviously not until the storm had passed—it wasn't exactly a subject she could explain in one short sentence. As it grew lighter in the cabin, she decided to get on with the task of sewing her simple gown in an attempt to take her mind off what might be happening on deck.

Juanita woke a couple of hours later, refused food and downed another dose of poppy juice and lay drowsing on the bed. As she sewed, Bridget could hear her muttering in her own tongue, but could not make out what she was saying. Bridget thought that if Juanita had any supernatural powers that it would make sense for her to use them now.

She thought of her father with tears in her eyes. She tried hard not to imagine him caught up in a furious storm that could have sunk the ship that carried him.

She knew it did her no good to think so negatively. Now Harry filled her mind. Had he been able to forgive her father for stealing his ship? After all, a ship was a valuable commodity and it meant that Harry could not transport as many cargoes as he might have done. She wondered if Callum had been drunk when he had stolen *Odin's Maiden*. Whichever way she looked at it, Harry had every right to be furious with the McDonalds. Still, that was no excuse for his deception over their marriage!

Joe staggered into the cabin several hours later, bringing them more cold food. He looked harassed and sad.

'Are you all right?' asked Bridget, concern in her voice.

'One of the men has been washed overboard. He was swept away before we could do anything to save him,' he shouted. 'The captain's real upset about it, I can tell.'

Her fear soared and it took all her will-power to bring it back under control. She wanted to scream out for the storm to stop and to weep for the man who had lost his life. She wondered if he had a wife and family back home, wherever home had been for him. 'Have you experienced such a storm before, Joe?' she cried.

'Aye, and the captain got us through it then and he'll do so again,' he said stoutly, 'so don't you worry.'

She was touched by Joe's faith in his master and experienced a sudden yearning for those last couple of days at the villa on Madeira when she had not known who Harry really was.

Joe left the cabin and Bridget forced herself to eat another piece of fruit and a biscuit. Fortunately she had never been seasick in her life. Then she prayed again, asking Almighty God and all the saints that no more men's lives would be lost.

It was evening when Harry called in to say that he thought the storm would blow itself out through the night. Bridget thought he looked exhausted and said, 'You need some sleep.'

He looked at her as if he could not credit that she could be concerned for him. 'I shall sleep when I deem it is safe for me to do so,' he snapped. 'In the meantime you will stay where you are.'

'Can't I go on deck for just a few moments?' she asked.

He shook his head. 'It is safer for you here. The deck is slippery and you would be putting yourself and others at risk. Do what I say in this, Bridget, I will not have you disobeying my orders,' he said harshly, and slammed the door behind him.

She knew what he meant by risk, but considered there had been no need for him to add that part about *disobeying his orders*. She was a mariner's daughter and had more sense than he gave her credit for, she thought indignantly.

Bridget spent most of that night listening not only to Juanita snoring but in praying and trying to make out if the sound of the wind was lessening. At least the rain had stopped. It occurred to her that Callum must have really trusted Harry to have agreed to sail across the great ocean under his command. Yet no man was infallible. What if Harry should collapse for lack of sleep and be washed overboard? It did not bear thinking about, especially as Master Larsson would then take over command of the ship. She quashed that thought and managed to doze off as the storm finally began to die down.

She woke to find that dawn was not far off and that Juanita was finally up and dressed and sitting at the table. Bridget put on her own gown and shoes and went out on deck. The sky was a washed-out silver grey tinged with streamers of pale peach clouds. There was all sorts of debris littered across the deck and the sails were reefed as she would expect. She found her husband slumped over the side of the ship and she thought at first he was gazing out over the sea. Only when she brought her face down to his level and he did not move did she realise that his eyes were closed.

'Harry, wake up,' she said, shaking him by the shoulder and discovering that his cloak was still sodden.

'What is it?' he muttered, struggling to lift his eyelids.

'You need to get some sleep,' said Bridget, surrendering to her better self and slipping her arm beneath his cloak and attempting to hoist him upright.

He yawned and then stared into her face. 'What are you doing here?' he asked.

She noticed that his black hair hung lankly about his cheeks and that he had a couple of days' stubble. She avoided looking directly at his scar in case it annoyed him. 'I came to see where you were and it is good that I did, for you might have toppled into the sea.'

'Would you have cared?' he asked quietly.

'That is a foolish thing to say,' she retorted angrily.

'Why? If I was dead then you would not have to live with me and look at this foul visage every day,' he commented drily, having noticed her deliberate attempt not to look at his damaged cheek.

'I suppose I deserve that, but do you have to throw my words back in my face?'

'Maybe, maybe not.' His expression was strained. 'I will not argue with you now. You are right in saying that I must get some sleep.'

'I will have Juanita leave the cabin so you can undress and get into bed.'

He nodded wearily and, removing her arm from about his waist, straightened up and limped across the deck to his cabin. She followed him, realising that the wound in his leg must be causing him pain. Pain was not something that she wished on him. She was aware that several of the crew sat, slumped on barrels, whilst others were unfastening the sails. A couple were staring at Harry whilst Master Larsson was looking at her with an unreadable expression. Suddenly it occurred to her to wonder if he considered it unlucky to have women aboard ship. Her father had told her that there were such mariners who superstitiously believed in such things.

When they entered the cabin it was to find that Juanita was still sitting at the table, but now she was gazing down at a chart.

'What are you doing?' asked Harry.

She glanced up. 'I am trying to make sense of this. Look here, is this Lisbon?' Juanita placed a finger on the chart. 'I pray that we have not been blown too far off course.'

Harry limped over to her. 'Now the skies are clear once more we shall soon find out,' he said.

Juanita stared into his face. 'You are in pain.'

'I will survive,' he said.

'Of course, but you must rest now. You are a clever man and I think your seamanship saved my life and for that I am grateful. I have a little poppy juice still and will leave it for you.'

Harry nodded and watched her place the flask on the table before leaving them alone. He glanced at Bridget. 'You do not have to stay.'

'Why not? I am prepared to help you,' she said stiffly.

'I can manage without your help.'

She was hurt at having her olive branch thrown back in her face. 'If that is your wish, then I will leave you alone.'

'Tell Joe to come here.' His tone remained brusque.

She paused with her hand on the handle of the door. 'Do you not think it will appear odd Joe coming to your aid whilst I am here to wait on you? After all, I *am* your wife.'

'A rebellious wife, at that. I don't care how it appears to the crew. I prefer Joe to do what is necessary for my comfort.' He sat down heavily in the chair. 'Now, please go!'

Bridget felt hot with embarrassment and anger as she left the cabin, determined that if her husband was ever to have need of her help, then he was going to have to beg for it!

Chapter Seven

Harry swore vigorously as Joe helped him off with his hose and then he collapsed on to the bed, perspiration beading his forehead and naked chest.

'You all right, Captain?' asked the lad anxiously.

He did not answer, but lay there, panting.

Joe peered at the red and swollen scar that formed part of Harry's thigh where a chunk of infection had been cauterised, leaving a hole in the muscle. He shook his head. 'You've been on that leg too long,' he said.

'I know, but I had no choice,' he gasped.

'You're going to have to rest it.'

Harry did not answer, but muttered, 'Pass me the poppy juice and the bottle of spirit I brought from the villa.'

Joe did as ordered and also brought a pewter tankard. He mixed the spirit with the juice and was about to add water when Harry said, 'No, give me it as it is.'

'But it'll knock you out, Captain!'

'That is exactly what I want it to do,' growled Harry.

Joe looked uneasy.

Harry said, 'That's an order, Joe!'

'But what of the mistress? She's not going to be pleased when she's seen so little of you these past two days and nights.'

'She said I needed to sleep and that's exactly what I'm going to get and I don't want any pain keeping me awake,' said Harry, propping himself up on an elbow. 'Now hand me the drink and then fetch me a clean shirt.'

Joe followed orders, watching Harry down the drink before helping him on with his shirt. 'The mistress would enjoy doing this,' said the lad.

'Shut up, Joe!' Harry growled. 'You can leave me now and get cooking some hot food for the crew.'

'I suppose you'll do without until you wake up.'

'Aye,' said Harry, lying down and pulling the bed-covers over him. He thought of Bridget and how it had felt making love to her. He would like to experience the pleasure all over again. Yet he still felt stricken by what she'd said to him about being the *fouler* option. He remembered the expression on her face when she had seen his scar for the first time and his hand wandered to his cheek. His fingernails rasped the two days' growth of beard there. Then he finally felt the pain in his thigh begin to ebb and slipped into oblivion.

Bridget quietly opened the door and entered the cabin. This was the seventh time that she had done so since her husband had told her that he had no need of her. Each time she gazed down at his slumbering face, her eyes were drawn to the scar on his cheek. She had come partly due to a conviction that the crew expected it of her and partly because she felt compelled to keep her eye on him despite the hurt and anger he had caused her. The more she was able to peer closely at the savage scar, the more she was becoming accustomed to it. She would have wished it away if she could, but only because it had such an adverse effect on him. He might deny caring what others thought about him, but she did not believe him. The scar made him vulnerable to people's opinion of him. Otherwise, why had he grown a beard? Without this scar she might have recognised him.

She ventured to hold a hand over the scar, blocking it out so that it was easy to see how he had looked without it two years ago. She lightly touched it with her palm, only to start back as his eyes suddenly opened. A sailor's curse tripped off her tongue and she crossed herself. He did not speak, only staring up at her before his eyelids closed again.

She wasted no time leaving his side and sitting at the table. Was he pretending to be asleep or was he awake? Perhaps she should go outside. But she still felt she needed to be here. Joe had told her that the captain's leg was causing him a great deal of pain because he had been on it for most of the storm, so she had to make allowances for his temper. She would remain quietly here and wait and see what he did next. Soon it would be nightfall and the cabin would darken. If he woke, would he leave the cabin and spend the night on deck? If he remained asleep in here, then she could wrap her cloak around her and rest in this chair. Although she would rather he woke. She did not like him being asleep so long with Master Larsson in charge. She preferred

Harry on deck, commanding his ship, not his rather dubious second-in-command.

'What are you doing over there?'

Bridget almost jumped out of her skin. 'You're awake!'

'Obviously I'm awake if I'm speaking to you.' He sat up and wiped his face with his hands.

She did not like it when he made sarcastic comments. 'You'll be hungry. No doubt that is another of my unnecessary remarks,' she said.

'Aye. You can go and tell Joe to bring me some food.'

She rose to her feet and without another word left the cabin.

What had she been doing earlier bending over him? wondered Harry, flinging back the bedcovers. He yawned and ran an unsteady hand over his untidy hair before getting out of bed and searching for his belt that had a pouch attached to it. Having found it, he removed a key from the pouch before limping over to the chest and unlocking it. Way down at the bottom of it beneath his clothes were business papers and a bag of coin, but the bulk of his money was with the bankers.

He took out clean hose and, gritting his teeth, sat on a chair. He managed to pull them on, but had to rest before removing a fresh doublet from the chest. Then he fetched his comb and tidied his hair. He was putting on his shoes when the door opened. He glanced up and saw Bridget enter, balancing a tray on her hip. 'Where's Joe?' he asked.

'Preparing the crew's supper. Surely you do not object

to my bringing your food?' He did not answer, so she closed the door and carried the tray in both hands and placed it on the table. 'You've dressed—does that mean you plan on going out on deck?' she asked.

'For a while, but I will be back here later.'

She nodded, but did not ask if that meant he would be sharing the bed with her. She felt unexpectedly weak at the knees, remembering the bliss she had found in his arms when they had consummated their marriage. She asked to be excused and left the cabin. She took deep breaths of fresh air, trying to ban the memory of that night as she walked around the deck and thinking that she still had to find the right moment to tell him that he was Harry Appleby.

The sun had set by the time he came out on deck and she wondered what he had been doing all this time. She noticed that he was still limping as he went over to Joe and spoke to him. Then he went to different members of the crew and talked to them until it grew dark and the stars twinkled on in the night sky and the moon rose. She gazed up at it in wonder, scarcely able to believe that the last two days of storm had taken place.

'It is time you retired to the cabin, Bridget,' said Harry.

She lowered her eyes and stared at him. 'Do you have any idea if we are far off course?'

'If we are, then it is only by a small margin. If I read the sky aright, then I would not be surprised if we arrived at Lisbon earlier than I estimated.'

'That is good news,' she said, relieved.

'Aye, I am sure you want to reach England as soon

as possible to see your friends.' He turned away and left her standing there.

Impulsively she called, 'Harry, wait a moment. There is something I wish to tell you.'

He turned, but before he could make a move towards her, Master Larsson loomed up out of the darkness and spoke to Harry. He stood, listening, and then obviously answered him. Then the Swede talked a little more and Harry nodded and said something else.

Bridget, realising that they were going to be a while, returned to the cabin where she found the lantern was already lit and, to her surprise, that the bed was divided into two parts by a bolster set in the middle. She felt an odd ache in the region of her heart. What was she to make of her husband's actions? Was he saying that she need not worry that there would be a repeat of their wedding night as he would respect her wishes? Or was he saying that he no longer desired her so and could not even bear that their bodies might brush against each other?

Her mouth quivered with emotion and then hardened as she fiercely controlled herself. Whatever his reasoning, it suited her too, she told herself. She prepared for bed, said her prayers, thanking her Lord, his Holy Mother and the Saints for making the storm pass. She also prayed for the sailor who had been lost and his family if he had any. Then she wrapped herself in a couple of blankets and lay down on one side of the bolster and tried to sleep. At least she would not be bothered this night by Juanita's snores and mutterings. Then she thought of the old woman sleeping under the awning and hoped she was not too uncomfortable.

* * *

It had been some time before Bridget had fallen asleep, but eventually she had done so. When she woke it was morning and there was no sign of Harry, but his side of the bed appeared to have been slept in. The fact that he was already up and about caused her to wonder if he was deliberately trying to avoid her. She could play his game if he wished, but surely they wouldn't be able to keep it up aboard ship for long. If they were living in a house, of course, it would be different. More room to stay out of each other's way.

She wondered why that thought made her feel sad—how could she make a proper home for them if they had no time for each other? *House, home!* She decided that now was the time to tell him that he was Harry Appleby, a man of property. He needed to know the truth, regardless of how she felt about him. She made her *toilette* and dressed before leaving the cabin.

To her annoyance she found that Master Larsson was also up and about and once again in conversation with Harry. It struck her that her husband probably spent more time talking to his second-in-command than he did to her! They both glanced her way and their looks were enough to convince her that Harry had been talking about her to the Swede. The next moment he curtailed his conversation and approached her.

'You are up early, Bridget,' he said.

'You were up even earlier despite losing two nights' sleep,' she countered. 'Tell me, where does Master Larsson sleep?'

'Why should you be interested? Do you consider him handsome?' he said, frowning.

'No! He has cold eyes, and as I have said before, I deem he does not approve of me. I am just curious; he always seems to be hovering and wanting your attention. When did you meet him and where?'

'In Sweden whilst I was working for Alex, the Baron Dalsland, whom you have met. I remember you mentioned that Alex supplied the ships for you to search for your father and myself. Hopefully I will find my friend in London, although, it is possible that he might have returned to his home in Sweden. I have to confess that I was surprised when you said he had married someone other than a Danish woman called Ingrid Wrangel. I believed they were in love and would definitely marry.'

'Mistress Wrangel proved to be an adulteress, a thief and a double-agent spy at the very least,' said Bridget vehemently. 'He would never have married her!'

Harry stared at her with a fixed expression, stunned by the news. 'I don't believe it! You must be mistaken. She, Alex and I worked together for years, collecting information. She would *never* have betrayed him. She loved him.'

Bridget instantly realised that Ingrid must be the woman *he* loved too. Her tone gentled. 'I didn't realised that you knew her so well but I am sorry, Harry, there is definitely no mistake. Yet if you choose not to believe me, that is your prerogative.' She turned and walked away.

'Bridget, come back here!' ordered Harry.

She turned and looked at him, but made no move towards him.

'Now, this instant!' he roared.

She was instantly aware that those on deck had gone quiet and were watching them. She glanced in Master Larsson's direction and saw that he was smirking. She felt degraded and was furious with Harry for making her feel like this, but she knew that she could not ignore her husband's command because it would undermine his authority with his men, so she obeyed him. She kept her eyes down in what looked to be a submissive manner, but really it was so he would not see the hurt and anger in her eyes.

'What is it you want from me?' she asked in a low voice.

'I want to know why you say these things about Mistress Wrangel,' he demanded.

'I say them because they are true,' she said.

'That is not the answer I am seeking. What proof can you provide that would convince me that you are telling the truth? Master Larsson has also known Mistress Wrangel for several years and he would vouch for her character.'

His mention of Master Larsson was enough to increase her anger and hurt. She lifted her head and stared at him. 'Can you not just take *my* word that I know what I am talking about?'

'I knew Ingrid a lot longer than I have known you, Bridget,' Harry pointed out.

'So you are saying that my word is not good enough for you! May I suggest that you did not know her as well as you thought,' she hissed, her anger simmering just below the surface of her voice. 'Perhaps when you reach England, you will discover who are your true friends and who are not. Now may I go? I have some sewing to do.'

Harry's eyes narrowed. 'When I reach London I will find out what this is all about and why you feel the need to slander Ingrid.'

'You do that, Black Harry,' she said insolently. 'Now may I go?'

He dismissed her with a wave of the hand and it took her all her will-power not to slap his face. She returned to the cabin with angry tears in her eyes. There she paced the floor with her arms folded across her breasts, hugging herself and thinking, why, why had it had to be the Danish woman whom Harry had loved?

Eventually she calmed down and told herself that once they reached London, she would be vindicated and then he would realise his error. Yet perhaps he might still feel some love for the beautiful Danish woman with her silver-blonde hair and magnolia skin. The thought caused a further lowering of her spirits and Bridget forced herself to do something to take her mind off such thoughts.

She took up her sewing and made the final touches to the gown. Having done that, she decided to cut out a shift from the plain cream material Juanita had brought her. She moved the charts and instruments of navigation on the captain's table to one side and as she did so she caught sight of the wedding ring on her hand and felt a sharp stab of pain in her breast. How dare Harry speak to her the way he had done? He had deceived her and she must never forget that he had tricked her into this marriage. Sooner or later she knew she would have to tell him the truth about his true identity because she could imagine what such tidings would mean to him. But in light of his accusations towards her, he probably wouldn't believe her! So perhaps she should not bother to try telling him, but instead wait until they reached London and then he would know the kind of company his precious Ingrid Wrangel had kept and he would find out for himself who he really was.

Bridget's stomach rumbled and she realised that she had not had breakfast. She decided to go and see Joe about food. As she left the cabin she passed Harry and Master Larsson on the way in, but chose to ignore them. She guessed that they needed to consult the charts and apply Harry's instruments of navigation.

Whilst speaking to Joe, it suddenly occurred to Bridget to ask him if he had ever met Ingrid Wrangel.

'Aye,' he said, a grim expression on his face.

Bridget had never seen Joe look like that. 'You did not like her?'

'She treated me as if I was dirt beneath her feet, but never in the captain's company. With him her words were always honey sweet and she chose to ignore me then. That suited me because I didn't want to upset the captain by complaining about her. Yet she's no better than I am because she was an orphan like us for all she gave herself airs. She was placed with the nuns as a child and brought up by them.'

'A nun's habit is one of her favourite disguises,' murmured Bridget, glad that in Joe she had someone who knew Ingrid Wrangel for what she was. 'She is a dangerous woman.'

'Aye, I was glad when the captain made the decision

to leave London and her behind, only it also meant severing his ties with the Baron,' he added with a touch of regret in his voice.

'You liked the Baron,' said Bridget.

He nodded. 'I'm hoping he and the captain will heal the breach between them caused by that Danish witch and be friends again.'

Bridget assured him that she felt certain that was a strong possibility. Then she changed the subject and, taking a plate of food from Joe, went and joined Juanita. She was sitting on a barrel, darning hose. 'How are you today, Juanita?' she asked.

'I am happy because the captain tells me that soon we will reach Lisbon,' she replied. 'But the captain, he is not looking happy. You have displeased him.'

Bridget darted a glance in her husband's direction—he had obviously not spent much time in the cabin. 'We have displeased each other.'

'But he cares about your welfare, otherwise he would not have married you. The crew, they often watch you. I have seen them doing so. Of course, most of them knew your father and there are those who sympathise with the dilemma you were in and understand why the captain married you.'

Bridget sighed. 'I do not need their pity.'

'It is better than hate. Maybe your father asked the captain to take care of you in the event of an evil fate overtaking him.'

'If that were true, I don't know why the captain has never mentioned it to me,' said Bridget, thinking that he could have easily done so. After all, as Captain Mariner he had told her that he had sailed with her father in the past.

'A man does not tell a woman everything he knows,' murmured Juanita. 'Soon we will reach Lisbon and I will leave you. You must take care of yourself for the child's sake.'

Bridget blushed and was startled into saying, 'I do not know if there will be a child yet. It is far too soon to tell.'

'It will bind you together.'

'I don't see how that can be. The captain will choose to continue his travels despite having a wife and child, no doubt. We will be parted for months on end and that will hardly serve to strengthen our relationship.'

Juanita patted her hand. 'The wound in his thigh still gives him much trouble. I see change in the air for both of you.'

Bridget thought it did not take a seer to forecast change when one was leaving one country for another and a couple were newly married. Although, if Harry's wound was bothering him, then it was possible he might choose to give up the sea once he learnt of his inheritance.

She thought about that and realised that she would prefer that he chose to stay on land. She might be angry with him about his deception and his defence of Ingrid, but she would rather have him where she could keep an eye on him. It bothered her that he was in pain, and his disability could mean that he was not as fleet-footed as he once was and result in his having an accident aboard ship that could lead to his death.

The thought caused a shiver down her spine. She

glanced in her husband's direction and caught him looking at her with a louring expression. Her mouth tightened and she turned her head away and continued her conversation with Juanita.

Harry was in a foul mood. Why couldn't his wife hold his gaze longer than a few seconds? Was it that she could not bear to look at his scar or was it because they had disagreed so strongly over Ingrid? Well, the latter would be sorted out. But if it were the former, then he would have to grow a beard again to conceal his scar despite her aversion to big black beards. At least back at the villa on Madeira, she had never looked at him with such distaste in her eyes. Despite their disagreements he still desperately wanted her, but whilst she so disapproved of him there was no way he could make love to her. He would never force an unwilling wife.

He shifted uncomfortably from one foot to the other, knowing the only way to ease his pain was to lie down and rest for a day or so, but he could not do so because it would make him appear a weakling in front of his crew. The pain was such that he could not bear his leg being touched and that was another reason why he had placed the bolster in the middle of the bed—in case, by chance, Bridget should kick him in her sleep. He would have taken more poppy juice for the pain, but there was none left.

Bridget gazed at Harry through half-closed eyelids and watched him blow out the candle in the lantern. What was he doing? He had not undressed and she wondered if he was going to sleep out on deck again, but now she could see his shadowy figure approaching the bed. To her astonishment he stretched out fully clothed on his side of the bed on top of the bedcovers. She did not know what to make of his behaviour. What was preventing him from getting beneath the bedclothes as he had done so last night?

She wanted to ask him, but feared if she did so he might snap her nose off, so she lay on her side, gazing at him through the darkness, willing him to say something. Since he had entered the cabin, they had not exchanged a word. Perhaps he was lying there, thinking of Ingrid, she thought with a mixture of irritation and sadness. Ingrid, who had not known Harry's true identity until after he had sailed away without telling her or the Baron where he was going. It was only Bridget who had known his destination, but she had managed to keep that from Ingrid and her lover, Edward Fustian, Harry's evil step-brother, until she was able to inform the Baron and Harry's sister, Rosamund.

Bridget felt a strong conflict of emotions that was holding her back from telling Harry the truth about himself. Perhaps she needed to rethink the decision she had made about letting him discover for himself the truth when he reached London? Whichever way she looked at it, she realised that he would no doubt be even angrier than he was with her right now if she kept the truth from him. She must not forget his feelings for Ingrid in all this. Thinking his deep, even breathing meant he had fallen asleep already and she had once more missed her chance to tell him, she sighed and turned away from her husband and eventually fell asleep herself.

* * *

Bridget was mistaken in thinking that it was Ingrid who occupied Harry's thoughts. His body was afire with desire for his wife despite his aching thigh. He wanted to feel her naked skin against his own, to caress and kiss every inch of it and to bring her to that point of ecstasy again. Hearing her sigh, he wondered what was on her mind. No doubt she was regretting marrying him, but they had to make the best of the bargain they had made. He forced himself to concentrate his mind on what lay ahead: the task of unloading the sugar cane and speaking to the buyer when he reached Lisbon. It had an excellent harbour situated on the right bank of the Tagus River and it was from here that Vasco da Gama had originally set sail on his voyage of discovery to the Indies. Situated on the furthest western point of Europe, the port was ideally placed for trade with northern Europe, London, Scotland and Africa. Now with a new passage to India underway and the discovery of the lands across the great ocean there was no doubt in his mind that the port would increase in power and wealth.

He looked forward to arriving there and no doubt Bridget could not wait to escape him for a while, he thought grimly, remembering how she had struggled to obey him earlier that day. Perhaps he should have insisted on her telling him what she knew about Ingrid that he did not. Instead he had given no thought to how Ingrid might have changed since he had left. What could have led her to betray the Baron? Bridget had spoken of Ingrid being an adulteress. Was it possible that she had fallen in love with someone else and this man had persuaded her to act against her better nature? He needed to know the truth, but could he trust Bridget to be honest with him when she was so obviously cold towards him?

Eventually Harry had dozed off, only to wake again whilst it was still dark. His thigh was no longer aching and he was filled with a sudden restlessness. As Bridget seemed sound asleep, he decided to get up and see how the men on watch were faring.

The air was fresh and filled with the scent of the sea, but mingling with it he caught the smell of vegetation. One of the men on watch glanced his way. 'I deem we should make Lisbon this day,' he said.

'Good!' Harry eased himself down on to a barrel and gazed up at the sky. Suddenly he was filled with a sense of wonder and peace, remembering Bridget being on deck after the storm had blown itself out. She, too, had looked up at the stars and no doubt marvelled at the Almighty's creation. 'I'll be staying on deck if one of you wants to get his head down,' he said.

The men exchanged glances and one nodded. The other thanked the captain and went to catch up on some sleep. The remaining mariner and Harry talked idly until the sun rose and the rest of the crew began to stir.

When Bridget came out on deck she instantly went over to where her husband stood at the wheel. 'You're up early,' he said, without looking at her.

'You were up even earlier. It is a fine morning. How much longer before we reach Lisbon?' she asked, thinking sadly that he obviously had not wanted to remain alone with her in the cabin any longer than necessary.

'Hopefully later this day.' He pointed to what looked like a cloud on the horizon. 'There is the coast of Portugal.'

Bridget's spirits soared and she put aside those things that rankled and said, 'I cannot wait to set foot on land again. Will you allow me to do so, Harry? I need to purchase such items that are essential to a woman's *toilette*. I had thought of going with Juanita. I have been to the city before, but I cannot say that I know it well.' She gazed up at the several days' stubble on his face and, when he did not answer, added impulsively, 'Harry, I pray that you do not intend growing a beard again.'

Harry stared down at her, wondering if her words meant that she preferred the sight of his scar to being reminded of the slave trader. If that were true, then perhaps he had misunderstood her use of the word *fouler* and she'd not meant his appearance, but only how he'd deceived her.

She touched his bristly jaw with the back of her hand and pulled a face. 'Please shave?'

He gazed down at her with a light in his eyes that she had not seen there for several days, but he did not say aye or nay, only took some coins from the pouch at his belt and handed them to her. 'Buy what you need, but promise me that you will be back here before dark.'

Her eyes lit up. 'I promise.'

A couple of hours later Bridget saw Joe carrying a pan of steaming water into the cabin, which Harry had entered a short while ago. Her breath caught in her throat and it occurred to her that perhaps after all she had some influence over her husband. She decided that tonight she would definitely tell him the truth about himself and what she knew about Ingrid's perfidy, which included the attempted abduction of Harry's own sister.

Harry watched Master Larsson supervising the loading of the cargo of sugar cane into wagons. Joe and one of the crew had already gone ashore to purchase fresh supplies and another two were handling the filling of the water containers. Harry had already spoken with the harbour master and his buyer and looked forward to taking aboard a cargo of sherry. He had no buyer for it, but he had no doubt he would find a market for it in London.

Suddenly Bridget and Juanita appeared at his side. 'It is time I left, Captain,' said the latter. 'I am looking forward to introducing your wife to my family and I will show her the best places to buy all that she needs.'

'Make the most of your time here because the journey to England will take us longer than it took us to reach here, Bridget,' he said.

She surprised him by standing on tiptoe and kissing his scarred cheek before hurrying down the gangplank after Juanita. She did not look back.

As he gazed after them, Harry thought of how he would have liked to show his wife his favourite places in Lisbon and buy her some pretty trinket. Yet despite that kiss it seemed obvious to him that she did not want his company, but preferred that of another woman.

He was about to turn away when he noticed a stranger

standing in the doorway of a tavern, looking up at his ship. He was powerfully built and had a rugged, weatherbeaten face. As Harry watched, the man crossed the quayside, apparently to take a closer look at his ship. He walked alongside its length and stopped where the ship's name was inscribed. He stood there so long that Harry's curiosity was about to get the better of him when the man stepped back and returned to the inn and went inside.

Harry left the ship and stood where the man had done and saw that the paint was peeling, revealing the words *Thor's Hammer* in faint letters. Now why should that man be so interested in the name of his ship? He crossed the quayside and went inside the tavern. He spotted his quarry talking to another man, so he made his way towards them. He knew the moment the bearded man saw him because he started to his feet. 'Who are you?' demanded Harry in Portuguese, seizing him by the front of his doublet. 'Why are you interested in my ship? Are you that filthy slave trader who bought my wife?'

Chapter Eight

The man's companion spoke rapidly to Harry. 'He does not speak Portuguese, Captain. He is English and is seeking a woman called Bridget McDonald and a man known as Captain Black Harry.'

At this revelation, Harry released the man and stared at him with interest. 'What do you want with them?'

'Yer've seen the lass?' rumbled the man, smoothing the fabric of his leather jerkin with an unsteady hand.

'You tell me who you are and what you want of them first,' demanded Harry.

'Name's Joshua Wood. Does that mean aught to yer?' he asked, peering at Harry intently.

Names tumbled through Harry's mind. He remembered what Bridget had told him about her companions with whom she had left London and realised this man could be the man she had spoken about.

'Maybe,' he answered.

'Can we get out of here?' asked Joshua Wood, a quiver of excitement threading his voice. 'The light's that bad in this place that I can't quite make out—'

Harry led the way outside and was instantly the object of Joshua's scrutiny once more. He was starting to get annoyed because the man had the audacity to bring his own face so close to Harry's that their noses almost touched.

'What is it that you're looking for?' growled Harry. 'Back off, man.'

Joshua ignored his words and reaching out, touched the bridge of Harry's nose before withdrawing his hand. 'I gave yer that scar, Master Harry, but not that really bad one on yer cheek,' he shouted. 'God's Blood! I thought that I'd never see this day, but here yer are alive, and if not as handsome as yer were as a boy, it—it *is* you!' He choked on the words and wiped the back of his hand across eyes that were suddenly damp.

Harry stared at him in disbelief. He felt light-headed and extremely odd. Such a meeting was something that he had occasionally dreamed about, but never believed would happen. 'You knew me as a boy?' he asked quickly.

'Aye! We used to play together, regular-like. That scar on yer nose, I caught yer a whack with one of them wooden swords me father made us. He was yer father's woodcutter. Fancy yer not being able to remember that! It didn't half bleed and yer were out to spill my blood afterwards.' Joshua chuckled and then sobered up immediately. 'But there, the Baron Dalsland did tell us that yer couldn't remember those days because yer'd been clean knocked out. It's one of his ships that brought me here.'

'Bridget told me about you and her ladyship being captured by pirates and how the Baron had supplied the ships to search for me and Callum McDonald,' said Harry, feeling totally dazed.

Joshua gave him a searching look. 'Is she all right? We feared for her virtue and her life.'

Harry nodded. 'You must excuse me, Master Wood, but I feel a need to rest against this wall. You cannot imagine how peculiar it is to meet someone who remembers that part of one's life that one cannot remember.'

'Certainly, Master Harry,' said Joshua, surveying him anxiously. 'But I'm sure once we have a good ol' chinwag, the memories will come flooding back.'

'You really believe so, Master Wood,' said Harry, leaning against the wall of the tavern, unable to take his eyes from the other man's face. 'I presume the Baron could not come seeking me, himself, because he is now married?'

'Aye, Master Harry. I see yer know about his marrying your sister and I presume yer on yer way back to England to be reunited with them.'

Harry was utterly dumbstruck by the news that he even *had* a sister, but tried to appear as if it came as no surprise to him. Why had Bridget not told him all this? He cleared his throat. 'Aye. As you can imagine it came as welcome news to me. Of course, there were gaps in what she knows and I would be interested to hear everything you can tell me about my sister. For as long as I can remember I've had these nightmares involving a dark-haired girl mouthing words to me from the top chamber of a tower and of a woman falling down some stairs.' He stopped, unable to carry on because it suddenly occurred to him that the girl was very likely his sister. He was overcome by emotion and turned his face away, ashamed to be seen in such a vulnerable state.

'There now, Master Harry,' said Joshua gruffly, patting his shoulder. 'That girl would be Mistress Rosamund.'

Rosamund! He could not understand why Bridget had not told him that his friend Alex had married his sister. She must have realised how much he would have welcomed such news! He managed to gain control of himself. 'You must forgive me, Master Wood,' he said, his voice unsteady. 'I have not mentioned my dreams to Bridget.'

'Name's Josh,' he said, smiling. 'From when we were almost in the cradle I was always Josh to yer. Mistress Rosamund used to trail after us, wanting to join in our games. She grieved badly when you went missing, as did your father.'

Harry wiped his face on his sleeve and took a deep breath. 'My father—' His voice cracked.

'Sir James Appleby of Appleby Manor in Lancashire. Sadly he is dead now.'

Harry rocked on his heels. The name repeated itself over and over in his head very slowly. *Appleby, Appleby, Appleby! Why had Bridget not told him this, either?* But Joshua was continuing. 'At least, yer don't have to avenge his murder. Those responsible have already paid the price, so all yer have to do is come home and claim yer inheritance. Yer shouldn't have any difficulty proving who yer are despite that nasty scar on yer cheek. I'd like to hear the tale of how yer got that. Yer always did want to go adventuring, Master Harry. I suppose now yer'll be thinking of settling down at Appleby Manor.

I'll vouch for yer, and so will the Baron, who's more important, and so will Mistress Rosamund.'

Why had Bridget kept all this from him? Why? Why? Harry presumed as there was no mention of his mother that she was also dead. His mouth felt dry. 'As I said, I saw in my dreams a woman being pushed downstairs. There was another woman there and she—'

Joshua gazed at him in fascination. 'I do believe that was no dream, but could be a memory. The first woman was likely to be your mother, God rest her soul, and the second would be Mistress Fustian, who was supposedly taking care of her whilst yer father was away. Mistress Fustian became Sir James's second wife. She was kin to Bridget's father's cousin and it was she who had you abducted so you wouldn't rightfully inherit and told your father you'd drowned. I hope I'm telling yer things yer already know?' he asked.

'It is interesting to hear it from your point of view,' said Harry hastily. It was obvious then that some of the McDonalds were involved in his abduction, but had Callum known of it? 'I was told by the pirate captain when I awoke aboard his ship with no memory of who I was that my parents had drowned at sea in a boating accident.'

'Well, he would speak falsely to you, wouldn't he?'

Harry agreed. 'Why was my father murdered?'

Joshua looked at him oddly. 'I suppose Bridget might not have known about that because it was before she came on the scene. It was because he spotted you in London, but didn't have a chance to speak to you. Besides, he thought he could be mistaken and so he made the mistake of mentioning it to Edward Fustian, your stepbrother. He also mentioned it to the Baron, but unfortunately you'd sailed away by then.'

Harry's head felt as if it was going to burst with all this startling information. 'I never liked Fustian. In fact, I knew he was a dishonest, unsavoury character as soon as I met him in London. If I had realised then he was my stepbrother...' His voice trailed off.

Joshua gave a grim smile. 'You don't have to worry about him. As I said, he's dead and so is his mother and Bridget's uncle.'

Harry was suddenly beginning to feel suspicious of Bridget's motives in keeping all this from him. He remembered her mentioning her uncle forcing her to go to London and that it was there that she had met Lady Elizabeth.

'No doubt Bridget will be wondering about Lady Elizabeth,' said Joshua, as if he had read Harry's mind.

'We thought a ransom would have been paid for her.'

'Aye, we were convinced that Bridget was lost to us and a captive in a harem. But God's Blood, Master Harry,' burst out Joshua, 'as your sister said, if it weren't for Bridget then we'd never have set sail in search of yer and her father in the first place, so we had to find her. It was she who told us yer'd both gone off to the New World after yer disappeared from London. She was desperate to find you both. So can I see her?' asked Joshua.

Harry was also desperate to see her, but not for the same reason as Joshua! 'Regretfully you have just missed her. She has gone to purchase a few essentials for the journey home.'

Joshua looked disappointed. 'Is her father with her?'

Harry shook his head. 'He decided not to travel with me to Madeira, but to journey across the northern ocean, so it is possible that he did not survive the crossing.'

'That would be sad tidings, indeed, for Bridget,' said Joshua, frowning.

Harry decided it was time to inform Joshua of his marriage. 'Aye, it was and because of that I asked her to marry me.'

Joshua stared at him in astonishment and then a smile broke over his face. 'God's Blood, that is good news.'

'I am glad you think so,' he said lightly. 'I know the thought of waking up every morning to see this face of mine on the pillow next to them might put some women off marriage to me, but Bridget was happy to accept me as I am.'

'I wasn't going to say aught about yer face, Master Harry, but that yer always did have a kind heart. Yer never thought anyone beneath yer. Not that I'm saying aught against Mistress Bridget.'

Harry smiled falsely. 'No doubt she complained of my having a black heart because I parted her from her father, but we have had to deal with our differences. Besides, if I had not found her when I did, God only knows what might have happened to her.'

'It was fate,' said Joshua solemnly.

'Exactly, Master Wood,' said Harry smoothly. 'I am more grateful than words can say for your coming in search of us but I am afraid I must go now. We have not long anchored here in Lisbon and I have business I must tend to, and as I have no notion of the hour Bridget will return, I suggest you come to my ship in the morning when we would both be delighted to see you and to talk some more.'

'Certainly, Master Harry,' said Joshua hastily. 'I didn't mean to keep you from your business.'

'I would much rather continue talking to you, Master Wood,' said Harry sincerely, 'but you understand that I must see to matters here in Lisbon.'

The two men shook hands and parted.

How could Bridget have kept so much from him? wondered a seething Harry. Was she far more vengeful and devious than he ever thought she could be? His thoughts so occupied his mind that as he went aboard his ship, he failed to notice Master Larsson trying to attract his attention. It was not until he planted himself in front of Harry and spoke directly to him that he became aware of his presence.

'Who was that man you were talking to?' asked Christian in a sharp voice. 'You seemed to have a lot to say to each other.'

Harry started. 'You're not going to believe this, Christian, but that man, Joshua Wood, knew me when I was a boy. We used to play together. His father worked for my father and he came here on one of the Baron's ships in search of me and Bridget. He was one of her companions on the pirate ship and he told me that my name is Harry Appleby and that I'm heir to a manor and business in England!'

'No wonder you look so pleased,' said Christian,

his eyes lighting up. 'You will be able to buy another ship.'

Harry was taken aback. 'I have only just received this news; I've had little chance to make plans.'

'But you will consider buying another ship?' urged Christian. 'I have served as your second-in-command since Callum stole the *Odin's Maiden* and I would like to be master of a vessel again.'

'I understand your feelings, but I cannot make such an important decision so soon,' said Harry. 'When we arrive in England will be time enough for me to do so. In the meantime I have much to do and must speak to my wife.'

Christian's expression altered. 'It is always her that possesses your thoughts now. Do you not consider it peculiar that she did not tell you about this? Surely if this man was one of her companions and knew of your new status, then she would have done so, too? Perhaps it is the reason why she married you?'

Harry had begun to wonder about this, himself, but he did not like hearing it from Christian. 'I would rather you did not make such accusations against my wife,' he said coolly.

'Why not? Face up to the truth, Captain. Once she realised that Callum was at the bottom of the ocean, she knew herself to be in dire straits and so played on your sympathy. Knowing you were a man of substance, she'd reason that, if you knew the truth, you'd want a different kind of wife than her. For God's sake, Harry, she's the daughter of a thieving pirate!'

'That's as may be, but there's no way she could

guarantee that I would ask her to marry me,' snapped Harry.

'You think not?'

'Aye! She loathed my very name.'

'All the more reason for tricking you into marriage. Even I can see that she is a beautiful woman. You've been taken for a fool by a devious woman,' he said scornfully.

Harry's anger spiralled out of control and he saw red and punched Christian squarely on the jaw. He went flailing backwards on to the deck. 'You go too far!' thundered Harry. 'You forget your position.'

Christian picked himself up from the deck and stared at Harry from furious eyes. 'She's bewitched you. You are not the man you were, but have grown soft.'

Harry said icily, 'Our friendship is at an end. I will pay you what is owed to you and you will leave this ship.' He walked away from Christian, raging inwardly. How dare Bridget put him in such a position that he looked a fool! What was going on in her mind that she should keep such momentous news from him?

Bridget was later than she had intended and it was dusk by the time she returned to the ship. Juanita had been as good as her word and taken her to visit her kinsfolk and they had insisted on her sharing their meal. Afterwards she had enjoyed herself wandering around the city with Juanita and a couple of her nieces. She had been able to purchase several scarcely used items of clothing as well as bindings for her monthly courses that were due soon. She prayed Harry would not be vexed with her for being late.

There was no sign of her husband on deck, so she presumed that he was still ashore and was relieved. She went immediately to the cabin, thinking to stow away most of her purchases, only to find Harry waiting there for her in the gloom as he had not lit the lantern.

'So you've returned at last,' he said.

Bridget thought that his tone of voice did not bode well for her. Faced with a powerful man who was angry caused flashbacks to the slave ship she'd been on. Her stomach began to quiver and she found herself babbling. 'I beg pardon for being late, only Juanita's sister insisted I share a meal with her family and then I had items to purchase as I mentioned to you. I hope you like the garments I bought with your money.' She placed them on the table.

'What price do I have to pay for the truth from you, Bridget?'

The question took her by surprise as did his suddenly springing to his feet. She backed away from him and felt the rim of the table dig into her waist. 'I—I don't know what you're talking about?'

'Are you certain of that? Think, Bridget! What information might you have that I would be eager to possess? Such glad tidings that I would have given you the moon if I'd heard it from your lips.' He seized her by the throat and punished those lips with a fierce kiss.

Bridget's heart seemed to take a nose dive into the pit of her stomach and she felt sick. She did not struggle, but remained motionless in his grasp. He lifted his head and his glittering eyes seemed to be able to see into her mind. 'Well, what have you to say for yourself?' he demanded in a silky voice. 'And I want the truth this time.'

'Who told you?' she whispered.

'Someone who knows Harry *Appleby*. Don't pretend and tell me that you've never heard that name before.'

She had trouble swallowing. 'I deem it would be a waste of my time, seeing as you already seem to be aware that I have,' she croaked.

'I need to know why you kept my identity a secret from me.'

'I am having difficulty speaking with your hand around my throat.' Her heart was pounding in her chest.

He loosened his grip and pushed her into a chair and moved to the other side of the table. 'Well?' he demanded.

She sighed. 'I did not realise before we married that you were Black Harry, so how could I tell Captain Mariner that he was Harry Appleby?'

'So you say but I don't know if I can believe you any longer. I gave you enough clues to my identity and marvelled even then that you did not pick them up.'

'I was ill! I wasn't expecting Black Harry to take care of me,' she protested.

'That could be a falsehood. Master Wood said that I've always had a kind heart. Surely when you were in his company he must have talked about me and you realised that I was a better person than you had thought?'

'Joshua is here!' she exclaimed with delight and started to her feet.

'Sit down,' roared Harry.

She jumped out of her skin and immediately sat

down, frightened once more of this angry man. 'How did he recognise you?'

'You mean with this damned scar on my face?' He fingered it. 'Suffice to say he did so by the smaller scar on the bridge of my nose. Why didn't you, Bridget?'

'Y-you had a thick beard w-when I first set eyes on you again. Perhaps if I hadn't asked you to shave today then Joshua m-might not have recognised you.'

Harry nodded. 'I will allow you that, but I deem he saw more in my face than that small scar. My hair, my eyes. You barely hesitated before accepting a proposal of marriage from a man you believed to be a complete stranger.'

She was indignant. 'I would have refused, but you persuaded me that I had no choice but to accept your offer. Besides, you'd told me that you knew my father.'

'So you were prepared to trust me because I was acquainted with Callum, an erstwhile pirate and a thief?'

Her eyes flashed with annoyance. 'I was obviously a fool to do so, but I did trust Captain Mariner, especially when he told me that he was ugly beneath his beard when I asked him to shave it off.'

'You could have asked me to shave off my beard because you wanted to make certain that I was Harry Appleby because you had already recognised me,' he said, looming over her.

She shrank back in the chair. 'No!'

'Aye,' he contradicted her. 'You set out in search of me with your companions, knowing that Black Harry was Harry Appleby. No doubt you couldn't believe your good fortune when you woke up and saw me bending over you. When you recognised me and discovered your father was most likely at the bottom of the ocean, you decided that marrying me would be a good idea. After all, you are a beautiful woman and although you said that beauty is a bane, you decided to use it to your advantage. You probably just didn't expect me to ask you to marry me so soon.'

'I don't know how you can say I used my beauty when I was covered in a rash and suffering from a fever half of the time!' she retorted indignantly. 'Anyway, you didn't shave off your beard before we were married, so how could I have been certain it was you? You waited until our wedding night and afterwards I only saw you in poor light, such as now.'

His eyes flickered over her face and she could feel his breath on her cheek as he brought his head close to hers. 'But the next morning you immediately recognised me, Bridget, despite my *foul* scar. You could have told me the truth then. What have you to say to that?'

Bridget felt a familiar anger stir inside her and stared at him stonily. 'When I woke up the day after we were married and realised you were Black Harry all I could think of was that you had deceived me. For days I had believed you to be Captain Mariner, an admirable man who had saved my life. Suddenly you were no longer that person, but Black Harry, who had parted me from my father,' she said heatedly.

'Even if that was true you'd have known then that I was Harry Appleby, a man of property. You must have been very pleased with yourself later when your anger abated and you realised exactly to whom you were married,' he said bitterly. 'Perhaps you thought that Harry with the ugly face should be grateful to someone as beautiful as you for marrying him?'

She was aghast. 'It did not even occur to me. The truth is that I was staggered when I realised who I had married and that I would be tied to you for life. I even suggested we get an annulment!' she exclaimed.

'Yes, only afterwards, when there could be no annulment. *You* had all to gain whilst *I*—'

Her anger erupted and she sprang to her feet. 'If you remember, I pointed that out when you made your proposal! I said that it was unfair that you were giving so much and I came to you dowerless.'

'Very clever of you. You roused my compassion,' he retorted.

'I have had enough of listening to this,' said Bridget.

She made a rush for the door, but before she could wrench it open, he had seized hold of her and dragged her away. He lifted her and flung her on the bed. 'You will stay here.'

'I will not!'

She struggled to sit up, but he pushed her down and put his arms either side of her. 'You *will* obey me.'

'If Joshua Wood is here, then I will leave you and return to England with him,' she said. 'You can forget that you were ever married to me. After all, you married me in the name of Captain Henry Mariner, so perhaps our marriage is not legal anyway.'

'Don't be a fool! It was my legal name for years and is on many a document. You will remain with me whether you like it or not. I will need an heir now I am the owner of a manor and after our wedding night you could be carrying my son. When Joshua Wood comes aboard tomorrow I expect you to behave as if all is well between us. I have no wish for him to realise that you kept my true identity from me.'

She was in agreement with him that she did not want Joshua to know how she had behaved. 'What of your crew—will they not wonder why you didn't inform them of your good fortune?'

'Leave the crew to me. They owe me loyalty and would not dare to question my actions openly,' he said, thinking only Christian Larsson would do that. 'Do you understand, Bridget?'

'Aye, you want me to act as if I am delighted to be married to you.'

He nodded.

'I will try. But if you had told me from the beginning that you were Black Harry, we would not be in this position now.'

'You are putting the blame on me again, I see,' he said vexedly.

'But it is true,' she protested. 'I would have told you that you were Harry Appleby if you had done so.'

Harry wanted to believe her and it was true that he had deliberately set out to deceive her. 'Let us say that is a real possibility, but it still leaves me with the question—why did you delay once you realised the truth? I can only believe it was out of spite.'

'No! The reasons I have given you are the true ones—and, of course, I didn't see you for days after our marriage because of the storm. Then when I did, all we seemed to do was argue and I never got the opportunity to tell you.'

He frowned down at her despite being unable to make out her features. 'I can see that we could continue to argue about this all night.' He rose from the bed. 'I must go. I have a task to perform and must go ashore.'

'When will you return?' she asked.

'I do not know. I have much to celebrate even if you are still my wife,' he said harshly, opening the door and closing it after him.

Chapter Nine

Bridget lay there in the darkness, thinking over what had just taken place. She accepted that whilst Harry's actions in deceiving her were reprehensible her own behaviour did not bear scrutiny, either. She could have told him earlier about his being Harry Appleby and it was true that she had intended doing so on more than one occasion. If only she had told him before going ashore instead of deciding to leave it until this evening, his opinion of her would be so different right now.

How different? While she had delayed telling him, she would have told him sooner if he had not sprung to Ingrid Wrangel's defence in the way that he had. Why could he not believe her about the perfidy of that woman? After all, Bridget had told him that the Baron had married someone else other than Ingrid. Surely that should have given Harry cause to wonder why his friend should have changed his mind about marrying the Danish woman?

Bridget sighed. No doubt she would have more questions to answer later. What if he returned drunk? Her stomach quivered, remembering how uncontrollable her father used to be when in his cups. She could only hope that her husband had more self-control but those words *I have much to celebrate* echoed in her head. She decided to go up on deck and see if anything was happening outside.

Bridget gazed down at the quayside. Some buildings were in darkness, but lights could be seen coming from several taverns and the sound of voices and laughter was being carried on the air. There was the smell of meat and fish being grilled over charcoal and that of fried onions.

'You all right, *Mistress Appleby*?'

Bridget started at the sound of Joe's voice as he sidled up to her. His elbow nudged hers and she turned her head and looked at him by the light of the lanterns on mast, stern and prow. 'So the news is already out,' she said.

'Aye, the captain told me,' replied Joe, grinning at her. 'He explained why he'd kept it a secret until it had to come out once Master Joshua Wood came looking for you both.'

'He did?

'Aye, he didn't want the crew feeling unsettled, wondering whether he'd be giving up the sea. He knows I'm no good at keeping secrets so I was kept in the dark, too.'

So her husband had thought up an excuse to give to the crew, thought Bridget. 'What do you think about it, Joe?'

'Whatever the captain decides is all right by me. He'll not be sending me away if he decides to settle down. He told me that there is a home for me wherever he goes. I'd be content to give up the sea as it's not easy cooking on a ship. I'd really enjoy cooking in a proper kitchen.'

Bridget could understand why Joe felt that way. But would her husband be able to settle down when the sea had been his life for so long or would he hate staying in one place? He'd had little time yet to think much about it and decide where he wanted to make his home.

'You hungry, missus?' asked Joe, rousing her from her thoughts.

Bridget did not have much of an appetite, but decided that at least having a meal would help pass the time. 'Aye, Joe,' she said with a smile.

'Like to eat it up here on deck?'

She nodded.

In no time at all Joe was serving up a platter of grilled fish in a sorrel sauce with fresh crusty bread. He poured her a glass of wine and bid her, *'Bon appétit!'*

As she sipped her wine, she noticed Master Larsson on the quayside. He was staring directly at her with such an unpleasant expression on his face that she felt a chill run down her spine. He called out to her, but she could not make out the words. She stood up and moved closer to the side of the ship and only then did she noticed that his face appeared to be swollen. Then suddenly she saw Harry come into view and expected him to greet his second-in-command. To her surprise, they ignored each other and Master Larsson strode off in the opposite direction.

She watched as Harry came aboard ship, thinking that she had not expected him back so soon. He spoke to Joe before approaching her. 'What are you thinking of sitting here all alone in full view of men passing by, Bridget?' he said sternly. 'What did Master Larsson say to you?'

'I did not catch his words.'

Her husband seemed relieved about that and sat down on a cask the other side of the makeshift table. He tapped his fingers on it and his expression was now so forbidding that she half-expected him to order her to the cabin. She would have liked to have known his thoughts, but no doubt he would consider the question an intrusion.

She had finished her supper by the time Joe placed a plate of food in front of Harry before pouring wine for him and replenishing Bridget's goblet. Harry took a mouthful of fish and sauce, said something complimentary to Joe and then dismissed him.

It was a clear night and in other circumstances she might have found it romantic. But there was naught loving about the way her husband felt towards her and her feelings towards him were not loving, either. They were very mixed and confused. In this light she could not make out his scar and she recalled the first time she had set eyes on him. She remembered his smile and how it had warmed her heart and, unexpectedly, she longed to see him smile at her in such a way again.

'What are you thinking?' asked Harry, glancing up from his plate and gazing at her.

'The first time I saw you,' she answered, taken off guard.

He raised his eyebrows and reached for his wine. 'You trusted me enough then to speak the truth.'

'You listened to me and I believed that you would help me and my father.'

'And I did…' Harry paused. 'Tell me honestly, Bridget, did Callum know of my abduction when I was a child? The fact that it was he who named me Harry when I awoke on the pirate ship causes me to wonder if that is a possibility.'

She supposed in the circumstances that the question should not have come as a surprise. 'I was only a child at the time. If he had mentioned it to my mother, I was unaware of it.' She hesitated. 'Besides, if my father had known who you really were, I cannot see him keeping quiet about it for long.'

'At least you are now being honest and I deem you are right. Callum would not have been able to resist revealing such knowledge when we met up again if he knew me to be a man of substance. He'd have told me and expected a reward for handing me such welcome news.'

'So we can agree that my father was not party to your abduction,' she said, 'And I did not know your true identity until the beginning of last year when I was in London and made the acquaintance of the Baron and your sister, Rosamund.'

Harry's expression darkened. 'How could you keep the news that I had a sister from me?'

'Harry, I honestly tried to tell you on a couple of occasions. During the storm I was going to tell you, thinking you should be aware of who you were in case aught happened to you and you went to the grave not knowing the truth.'

'When was this?'

'When you brought me and Juanita some food, but we could hardly hear the other speak, so I decided it was not a good time.'

'You could have told me afterwards.'

'You mean after the storm when you slept for a whole day.'

'I cannot deny that we saw little of each other during that time, but there has been time since.'

'Not much time,' she pointed out. 'And if you remember, we had that disagreement over Ingrid Wrangel. That was another time I approached you to tell you the truth about yourself and got distracted, which I am very sorry for.'

He was silent. As if from a distance she could hear the sounds of laughter and people talking. A dog barked and there came the gentle slapping of waves against the hull of the ship causing it to rock gently.

'Are you saying you would have told me then if we had not argued?' he demanded. 'I remember you making accusations against Ingrid that I found difficult to accept.'

'I thought of telling you before you doubted my word about that woman,' she replied coolly.

'You only *thought* of telling me, but you did not!'

'Afterwards there never seemed the right moment and you would glare at me so.'

'And you viewed me with disdain!'

'I was angry and hurt because I had believed Captain Mariner a man worthy of my respect and he had turned into the man I—I—'

'Despised,' finished Harry, wanting done with this conversation.

'I do not despise you, but I needed time to adjust, Harry,' said Bridget quietly. 'When I met you in Ireland, we spent but a short time in each other's company before you spoke to my father and then our ways parted acrimoniously.'

'I know what you are going to say—then we met again and I rushed you into marriage under false pretences after only a week. I still deem you should have told me I was Harry Appleby sooner.'

'I would have told you this evening if Joshua had not turned up. I had made up my mind to do so,' she confessed.

'You expect me to believe that?' said Harry. 'I deem you still do not understand how momentous this news is to me. I am no longer that little frightened boy your father named Black Harry or the person I named Captain Henry Mariner because I hated being called Black Harry with its connotations of filth and being subjected to beatings by a pirate captain whose obnoxious trade I hated. It was one of the reasons I felt compelled to fight against piracy in the northern seas along with the Baron and members of the Hanseatic League. Now I have a sister, Rosamund, who is married to the Baron, who was like a brother to me, and you kept that from me too!' He almost choked on the words.

She felt exceptionally guilty and would have asked him to forgive her, only the words stuck in her throat because she could not forget he had deceived her too and believed her guilty of an equally awful deception, that of marrying him for his position and money. 'What are you going to do with me?'

'You're my wife—what do you expect me to do to you? Beat you?' he said bitterly.

'Some would say you have a right to do so. Master Larsson, for instance.'

'I do not hit women,' he said in a low voice that had pent-up anger running through. 'Just go to the cabin and stay there.'

Bridget was glad to escape from his anger and retire to bed. The bolster was still in place, but would he be joining her there? Perhaps he would go ashore again and escape into some woman's arms. In the mood he was in, it was highly unlikely he would want her.

It seemed that she was correct in that assumption because he came to the cabin shortly after she did, but behaved as if she did not exist.

The following morning they both rose early and after breakfast they returned to the cabin. Now she was trying to ignore Harry's presence as he perused one of his charts whilst she inspected the clothes she had purchased.

One of the gowns was dark red and made from what she was certain was silk. She had bought it from a used-garment stall and the hem and sleeves would need shortening. She had also bought a robe of a russet colour that she liked very much. When she was younger, Bridget had not bothered her head about fine clothes and had even worn a youth's breeches and shirt when she had needed to disguise herself after escaping from her uncle and his mistress. But Lady Elizabeth's love of fashion in clothing and jewellery had stirred Bridget's own interest.

There came a knock at the door. 'Who is it?' asked Harry.

'Master Joshua Wood is here to see you, Captain,' called Joe.

Harry gave Bridget a warning look before opening the door. She glanced over and saw Joshua's sturdy figure in the doorway. Instantly she expressed delight at seeing him and invited him to sit down. For a few moments they talked about Lady Elizabeth and then Bridget asked him whether the Baron and Rosamund's expected baby had arrived safely.

Joshua grinned. 'She and the Baron have a fine boy. They have named him Douglas Alexander Harry James and he has the Baroness's eyes and the Baron's flaxen hair and fine nose. Hopefully yer'll see for yerself once yer back in England. They were leaving for Appleby Manor when I left London.'

'This is good news, is it not, Harry?' said Bridget.

Harry nodded agreement and she realised he was in the grip of a strong emotion. Suddenly it occurred to her that he had not known Rosamund was having a child, either. Did this mean as soon as Joshua left that she would receive the sharp edge of Harry's tongue once again?

She watched him as he went and poured wine and handed around the goblets. 'Let us drink a toast to my nephew,' he said.

So they drank to the health of Douglas Alexander Harry James. After doing so Joshua suggested a toast to Master Harry and Bridget and wished them a long and happy life together. 'To my wife,' said Harry, raising his goblet.

'To my husband,' she murmured, following suit, thinking how difficult it was to behave as if all was light and happiness between them.

Yet they must have played the part well because Joshua said, 'It does my heart good to see you both so happy.' Then he turned to Harry. 'So, Master Harry, what do you say to my coming back to work for you at Appleby Manor?'

'You would leave her ladyship's employment?' asked Harry, surprised.

'It is what she will expect once she hears the news that you have been found,' said Joshua, turning the goblet between his hands. 'I only went to work for her because your stepmother dismissed me. Lady Elizabeth was staying at Lathom House, the home of her cousin, the Earl of Derby, and she hired me. She was a friend of your mother and remembered me as a boy. Only my heart is in the north at Appleby, Master Harry,' he said earnestly, 'and I long to be back there.'

In the face of such eagerness, Harry could only say, 'Then I will be happy to welcome you back.'

A grin split Joshua's face. 'It won't quite be like old times, but I'm certain you'll be happy there once you find your feet again. You had a great fondness for the place and used to know every inch of your father's land.'

Harry was looking forward to seeing his old home and wondered if once he set foot on his land whether the memories would come flooding back. Often he had visited places and thought that they reminded him of somewhere. Perhaps it had been Appleby? Then he thought of Bridget and wondered if they would ever be able to turn it into a happy home the way they felt about each other at the moment.

Joshua asked could he make the journey back to London on Harry's ship and he agreed, certain that he would learn much from Joshua about his boyhood on the voyage home. Then they talked of London and his father's house and business, and Harry wished he could remember Sir James and grieved afresh for his dead parents. Joshua asked about his travels and Harry suggested they go up on deck because he did not wish to reveal some of the gory details in front of Bridget.

She did not realise that was his reasoning behind the suggestion that the two men go on deck. It was obvious he did not want to be in her company and much preferred that of Joshua. She wondered what Master Larsson would make of their friendship.

When Harry returned he found Bridget turning up the hem of the gown she had bought. She did not look up at him, but carried on with what she was doing. 'You played your part well,' he said. 'Just make certain that you keep it up in Joshua's company.'

Bridget gave him a speaking glance.

Harry frowned. 'It should not be too difficult. I must tell you that we will not be sailing alone to England, but will have the company of the ship that brought Joshua here and that Master Larsson has transferred to that vessel.'

Bridget was astonished. 'Why?'

'I do not need to explain that to you,' said Harry. 'I have a new second-in-command now, Master Hans Nilsson from that same ship.'

Bridget wondered what had happened between her husband and Master Larsson. Perhaps he had not been as pleased as his captain that Harry had come into an inheritance. Could it be that Master Larsson was jealous? Maybe he had decided that Harry was likely to give up his seafaring life and had made a move to another ship now. Whatever his reasons, Bridget was glad to be finally rid of Master Larsson's cold disapproving presence.

When his wife remained silent, Harry continued, 'The master of the other ship expects to find the Baron or his representative in London and will be looking for fresh orders. It is possible that ship will be ordered to Sweden.'

'Are you saying that Master Larsson is likely to sail with her and that I will never have to see him again?'

Harry nodded. 'I need to go back on deck, but I will see you later. If you decide to leave the cabin, then wrap a scarf around your neck. I regret that there is some slight bruising where I seized you roughly last evening.' He did not wait for her reaction, but went out. Bridget put a hand to her throat and gazed at the door as it closed behind him, thinking that was most likely the nearest she would ever get to an apology from him. She would be glad when they set sail. The sooner they arrived in England, the better she would feel.

They left Lisbon the following morning and in the days that followed little seemed to change between Bridget and Harry. In company they pretended that all was well between them and that they were looking forward to seeing their friends and making their first home together once they arrived at Appleby Manor. They spent scarcely any time alone as Joshua often joined them or Harry was busy discussing the business of the ship with Hans Nilsson. He seemed a good man with a ready smile for Bridget, but when she told her husband so she was surprised that he did not seem pleased with her comment. During the night when Harry was not on deck, the bolster remained in place in their bed.

After a week, Bridget wondered how long they would go on like this. When would they start feeling the need to forgive each other? She stood at the side of the ship, gazing over the sea. Above the slap of the waves and the sound of sawing of wood by the ship's carpenter, Andrew, she could hear the conversation between Harry and Joshua.

'Nothing beats good English oak,' Joshua was saying as he thumped a foot on the wooden deck.

Harry said, 'I would not deny it, but this ship was built in Sweden.'

Joshua chuckled. 'My mistake. Yer have some fine trees on Appleby Manor, Master Harry, not just of oak but chestnut, hornbeam, willow and beech. There's also plenty of hazel that provide a fine crop of nuts in the autumn.'

'You fill me with even more longing to be there,' said Harry. 'Let us talk livestock. I seem to remember you saying that I have no sheep.'

'Aye, that is true.'

'Why not? Their wool would make a good cash crop.'

Joshua grinned. 'You're thinking like a merchant, Master Harry. Trees also bring in the money.'

'I would not argue.' He smiled and took Joshua's arm. 'Come, let us leave Andrew to his repairs.'

As the two men moved away, Bridget sighed and wondered what their life at Appleby would really be like. Despite Harry's enthusiasm for his childhood home, surely he would not find it easy after being accustomed to the feel of the deck rolling beneath his feet as his ship forged through the waves and his eyes being accustomed to the far horizons of the seas. It would be a very different kind of life to that which he had known for so long.

She knew the same could be said for herself. It would be arduous taking the organisation of Harry's household into her inexperienced hands and the thought excited and scared her at the same. No doubt he would be watching her every move, so she must not fail. Yet if she were to have his child she felt he would forgive her much and she, too, could forgive him for what he had done to her, for the child would belong to them both. She prayed daily that she was already pregnant from that one coupling on their wedding night. She tried to think about the pleasure he had given her because it filled her with longing. At least her monthly courses were overdue so it was possible that she was indeed already with child.

Suddenly she noticed the Baron's vessel was near enough for her to see some of the mariners going about their work. She became aware that she was being watched and, with a sense of shock, realised that it was Master Larsson who was gazing at her. Once more, there was that in his expression that filled her with unease.

Then he shifted his gaze to where Harry was talking to Joshua. Was it possible that the Swede might have it in mind to cause trouble for her and Harry in the future despite Harry saying that he would most likely go home to Sweden?

That evening Harry came into the cabin as Bridget was performing her *toilette* before retiring to bed. She was wearing the russet robe and he stopped short when he saw her and his eyes fixed on the upper curve of her breasts. Her hair hung loose down her back and she was polishing it with a cloth.

'You look—' He drew in his breath.

She ran her hands over the robe in a very feminine way and blushed. He was conscious of an instant arousal and carefully sat on a chair to remove his boots.

'You might think I am making a fuss over naught, Harry,' said Bridget after a moment's hesitation, 'but I noticed Master Larsson watching us from the Baron's ship this morning and I deem he will cause us trouble if he can.'

'I don't see how that is possible.'

'Neither do I, but my instincts tell me that he will try to do so. Did you fear you might have had a mutiny on your hands if he had stayed on this ship? I know he did not approve of your marrying me and perhaps several of the men felt the same.'

Harry shook his head. 'I cannot believe my crew would mutiny, especially now Christian has gone, but some might be dissatisfied. We did not leave the New World richer men. The rewards were greater when we were battling with pirates in the northern seas and defeating them.' He paused. 'I am glad that you have mentioned this, though. I will promise them a bonus when we reach London and I come into my inheritance, and that should ensure their loyalty.'

Bridget considered that a worthy idea and told him so. He flushed. 'I am glad I am redeeming myself in your eyes.'

He padded across the floor to where she was sitting on the bed and sat beside her. Her pulses began to race as he slipped his hand inside her robe and caressed her breast and kissed her. The kiss took her unawares and weakened the emotional and physical barrier she had put up against him, but she was uncertain what he expected of her. The kiss deepened and despite her inner struggle to resist him, her lips yielded to his and she did not protest when he eased her down on the bed and unfastened the girdle that held her robe together. His hands roamed over the silk of her night rail and the breath shuddered in her lungs as he bent his head and kissed her breasts through the material. When he finally took possession of her, such was the urgency she felt to respond to him that she could not rein it in. His passionate reaction took her unawares, but it only increased her desire for fulfilment at his hands. Such exquisite pleasure was hers that she clung on to him, kissing his chest, shoulders and his lips as he finally found release in her arms.

Afterwards she felt a deep disappointment when he immediately turned his back on her and fell asleep.

The following morning she woke and instantly knew that something had changed because she felt different. Perhaps at last she and Harry could talk about their feelings. She rolled over only to find that he was sitting up on the side of the bed, getting dressed.

She did not know what made her say, 'Do you miss the excitement of doing battle with pirates and savages?' It was not what she had intended saying at all!

Harry shrugged. 'I came near to losing my life several times and more recently in Africa.'

'I have not forgotten Joe telling me you fought like a lion, battling with several men at once single-handed. He made you out to be a real hero.'

'Joe exaggerates.'

'But I am aware that scar on your face is not your only wound.'

'No.' He hesitated. 'Give me your hand.'

Bridget hesitated and then placed her hand into his. He took hold of it and guided it inside his hose to his bare thigh. 'Can you feel the scar?'

She felt her heart thudding as her fingers found the dent in the muscle of his thigh. 'It must have been a terrible wound.'

'I thought I would lose the leg.'

'But you fought back and survived.' She was about to withdraw her hand, but he stayed it with his own and she was suddenly aware of his manhood hovering so close that she could have touched it. She began to tremble, unsure what he expected of her. Did he want her to take hold of it? The next moment he sighed and lifted her hand and placed it back on her lap.

Bridget was aware of that confusion of emotions she felt towards him. She had believed after last night he would want to couple with her again this morning. Instead he was finishing getting dressed and a few moments later he left the cabin. What was she to think of his actions? Was he regretting giving in to his desire for her last night? Did she wish he had not done so? She could not say that she did, but perhaps if he were to want her again she would not show herself so willing. After all, she didn't want to be rejected again come morning as had just happened to her.

She dressed and went out on deck. Her husband was talking to Hans Nilsson, so she went over to where the carpenter, Andrew, and Joshua were talking. Now Master Larsson had left the ship Bridget felt more at ease with the crew and asked Andrew whether he had a wife and family.

'Aye, I had three lads and a lass when I left home,' he said. 'I'm hoping that they and the wife are still there to welcome me. They live with my father-in-law so she had help with the lads. I will be glad to see them as I have been a long time at sea and pray that they have not forgotten me.'

Bridget glanced at Joshua. 'I know that you did not have a sweetheart in London, Josh, but was there a woman you had a fondness for back at Appleby?'

'Not a woman and not at Appleby, but a young lass who lived in a nearby town. I made her acquaintance when Master Harry and I were boys, but her father wouldn't tolerate me back then; no doubt she'll be betrothed by now.'

Bridget considered that a pity because she believed Joshua deserved some happiness and a woman to take care of him. He had been such a loyal friend to Rosamund and Harry that he deserved some reward.

'Master Larsson, now, he never bothered with the

women,' said Andrew. 'It was always work with him, and he and the captain sailed together for many years. I was surprised when he left and went to the other ship.'

Joshua glanced at him. 'Are we talking about the mariner who is on the Baron's ship now? If so, I can tell you that he was boasting a swollen jaw when he came aboard.'

'You think he'd been in a fight?' asked Bridget.

Joshua nodded.

Bridget was musing over what Joshua had told her later that day in the cabin. Harry had finished consulting his charts and instruments with his new second-in-command and was now sharpening a quill to fill in his log.

'Joshua was saying that Master Larsson had a swollen jaw when he went aboard the Baron's ship. It looked as if he had been in a fight. Do you know aught about it, Harry?'

'Damnation!' he exclaimed savagely.

Bridget looked at him and went over to the table. 'You've cut yourself!'

'Your question startled me,' he said, scowling at her.

Worried at the sight of the blood, she took hold of his hand and sucked his bloodied finger.

He stared at her in amazement. 'What are you doing?'

'Oh, my goodness, what *am* I doing?' Bridget dropped his hand. 'I beg your pardon. I don't know what came over me.'

'Obviously.' A faint smile played round his lips and he lifted his cut finger and put it to his own mouth.

'I only did what my mother used to do when I cut myself,' babbled Bridget. 'She told me that Jesus used spittle for healing. I doubt I've done you any harm. I will bind it for you.' She hurried over to one of the lockers and took out scissors, salve and binding, and returned to him. She looked at the bloodied digit. 'I think I should clean it first.'

He watched her cross the cabin and scoop water into a small bowl from the pail hanging from a nail. She moved with a natural grace that pleased him. His anger and hurt had abated somewhat in the past week, but it still rankled with him that she could have kept so much from him. There were times still when he wondered if she had done so because she wanted to hurt him for deceiving her over his identity before marrying her.

Bridget took hold of his hand and wiped away the blood. Suddenly her limbs felt as if they were turning to water and she was intensely aware of the smell of his herbal soap, overlying that male scent that was particular to him. She felt dizzy and as she tried to take off the top of the jar of salve it slipped from her fingers.

Chapter Ten

'**B**ridget!' Harry's tone was sharp. 'Are you all right?'

She leaned against the table. 'I feel faint. It must be the sight of the blood.'

'You certainly look pale.' He stood up and took hold of her arms and sat her in the chair he had vacated. He felt anxious as he gazed down at her as she rested her head against the back of the chair with her eyes closed. 'You stay there. I'll get you a drink,' he said.

Bridget had no intention of moving, but was thinking that she could not remember the sight of blood ever having this effect on her in the past.

Harry poured her some wine and brought it to her. He held it to her lips and she sipped it slowly. After a few moments she gradually began to feel better. 'I can bind up your finger now,' she said.

'You'll stay where you are,' said Harry, frowning. 'I don't want you falling down and banging your head. I'll deal with my finger. Perhaps you should rest.'

Before Bridget could say aye or nay, he had swung

her into his arms and carried her over to the bed. He sat her down and knelt in front of her and removed her shoes. 'You really should not have to do these things for me,' she said, surrendering to a compulsion to touch his wind-tangled hair and smooth it down.

'I do not mind acting as lady's maid to my wife,' said Harry, glancing up at her. The breath caught in his throat because she looked so lovely, sitting there. Her expression altered and tears filled her eyes. 'What is wrong?' he asked, concern in his voice. 'Do you still feel unwell?'

Bridget did not answer him, but her tears fell thick and fast. He was dismayed and sat on the bed and lifted her on to his knee. He stroked her hair and kissed her cheek. 'Is it that you are thinking of Callum?'

She turned her head and gazed at him through a sheen of tears. 'Are you certain my father didn't ask you to take care of me if aught happened to him?'

Harry glowered at her. 'Do you really think Callum would trust you to a man you believed had a black heart?'

'No, but perhaps he didn't believe you had a black heart,' she wailed.

'Perhaps not. Anyway, Callum believed himself indestructible. He used to talk about how he survived so many adventures.'

'If that is true and he survived crossing the great ocean to the west, then perhaps I should have refused your offer of marriage and had more faith in him.'

Harry's expression altered. 'It is too late to go back now. You are my wife, but no doubt you would have it differently?'

She hesitated and then reached up and clasped her hands behind his neck and drew herself up against him. Her lips touched his as lightly as a butterfly's wing. 'I would not say that. I am thinking, Harry, that perhaps I felt faint not because of the blood but because I am with child.'

Harry's heart began to thud. 'You really think so?'

Her eyes searched his face. 'But if I am, Harry, that will make you happy, will it not?'

'It will.' He cupped her face between his hands and returned her kiss, feeling a stirring in his loins. He so wanted to make love to her, but how could he when she had nearly fainted away? 'We must take care for we do not want to risk hurting the child.' She nodded, and he drew away from her, wondering if he detected regret in her lovely eyes.

A week passed and still the 'curse' did not come and then one morning Bridget rose and felt so nauseous that she vomited into the chamber pot.

Harry gazed at her with concern. 'I cannot believe you're seasick, not after all the time you've spent at sea.'

'No, Harry, I am not suffering from *mal de mer*,' she said, feeling wretched. 'I deem it is the sickness a woman suffers when she is with child.'

'So you are certain that you are with child?'

She nodded. 'My monthly courses are overdue so I deem it is as we hoped.'

'Is there aught I can fetch you? What about break-fast?'

She lifted her wan features. 'Food is the last thing I want right now.'

'Poor Bridget,' he said sympathetically, kissing her forehead. 'I will take care of you. You stay in bed until you are feeling better.'

Bridget did exactly that and prayed that the sickness would soon pass and that the journey home would not be disrupted by storms and be achieved in a winning time.

The next few days only served to convince Bridget even more that her diagnosis of her condition was indeed the correct one. Every morning Harry would rise, look into her pallid face and fetch a bowl. It seemed that for now all that had gone wrong between them was forgotten because they were having a child. Unfortunately, Bridget did not get her wish for a swift journey to England and even more annoying was that the sickness did not confine itself to mornings only; she felt sickly in the evenings, too.

Another storm blew up and their ship was separated from that of the Baron. They were delayed in a French port for several days. By then the crew were aware of her condition. She had always eaten breakfast, so naturally Joe had been the first to notice her affliction and mentioned it to Harry. He told him the happy news.

Joe was delighted and said to them both, 'We'll be a proper family with a baby in the house.'

To have his own family was what Harry had always wanted and he was solicitous of his young wife for the rest of the voyage. Bridget appreciated his care, although there was part of her that would rather he did not feel he had to hold the bowl for her while she was being sick. No woman looked their best at such times, but she kept her thoughts to herself, not wanting to appear ungrateful.

One day Bridget was sitting on deck eating the midday meal with Harry and Joshua, when the latter surprised her by saying, 'No doubt you will be wondering what happened to the Danish woman, Ingrid Wrangel, in your absence, Bridget?'

She was instantly aware that Harry's attention had been caught and it was he who said, 'Aye, we would like to have the latest news of her.'

Joshua glanced at him. 'I was forgetting that you were acquainted with her too, Master Harry. No doubt Mistress Bridget has told yer about her double dealings and how she managed to escape punishment for her crimes. Just before I left London the Baron told me that there were rumours that a nun of the Bridgettine Order has been seen in the vicinity of yer house in London, as well as down by the headquarters of the Hanseatic League near the Thames.'

'He deems it could be Ingrid?' asked Harry, feeling deeply uneasy at Joshua's mention of Ingrid's crimes. 'I know she was placed as a child with that order in Sweden and was reared by the nuns. I remember taking her by boat to one of their houses near Richmond, but why should she now be dressed as a nun?'

'It is one of her favourite disguises,' said Bridget. 'She used it to gain entry into Richmond Palace. Not only was she involved in a plot with Edward Fustian, her lover, to abduct your sister and to destroy the Peace Pact between England and Scotland, but with her other lover, Lord Bude, she stole a jewel box from Lady Elizabeth's mansion. I had hoped to never set eyes on her again,' said Bridget, aware of her husband's stunned expression.

'Yer not alone on that score,' said Joshua, nodding his head vigorously. 'The Baroness feels the same.'

Bridget glanced at her husband again and decided to change the subject, feeling little satisfaction in having her word backed up by Joshua when Harry looked so upset.

Later when Harry and Bridget were alone in the cabin, he sat down at the table across from her and said one word, 'Ingrid.'

Bridget glanced at him. 'You want to talk about Ingrid *now*?'

Harry frowned. 'Aye, from what Joshua said it seems I have not been fair to you. I thought a short while ago that I should ask what you knew about her, but events overtook me.'

Bridget raised her eyebrows, remembering how hurt and angry she had felt when he had doubted her word. 'What do you want to know?'

'Why Ingrid should want to abduct my sister?'

'Two reasons. The Baron had enlisted Rosamund as one of his spies and along with Lady Elizabeth the three of them and Joshua foiled the plot I mentioned. Part of it was to murder the Queen of Scotland.'

'The Baron should not have involved my sister in such dangerous work,' Harry said harshly.

'I would not argue with you, but shall we leave the Baron out of this for now? I can see that you still want to believe that Ingrid is the woman you left behind in London.'

He frowned. 'You're mistaken. How can I dispute what you say when Joshua agrees with you? What else can you tell me?'

'She was in league with your stepmother and my uncle, as well. I can't remember if I told you that they wanted me to marry William Fustian, Edward's younger brother. They had some crazy notion that by doing so they would get their hands on my father's hoard. They could not accept that it had been stolen.' She smiled faintly. 'I will add that Ingrid did me one favour when she killed William.'

Harry swore beneath his breath. 'Why did she kill him?'

'It gets too complicated but, simply, he got killed when she decided to switch sides, thinking that if Rosamund was abducted and eventually killed, then the Baron might just turn to her again. In my opinion Ingrid Wrangel is completely deranged.'

She looked at Harry and saw that he was looking grim. 'How did she manage to escape justice?'

Bridget shrugged. 'There are those who believe she is a witch and used a broomstick, but I think she managed to escape because of her disguise and also because she wasn't as important as she believed herself to be and was allowed to go free.'

Harry was silent. 'A madness in the light of all you have told me.'

'I would agree,' said Bridget. 'But perhaps after all she is a witch and bewitched those responsible.'

'That is superstitious nonsense,' he said.

'Then she used her womanly wiles,' retorted Bridget pointedly.

Harry was silent, just staring at her.

Bridget moved away from him and gazed out of the window. 'I wonder if we will find the Baron's ship when we get to London. Master Larsson just might be having second thoughts about going to Sweden.'

'It will make no difference to me. He and I fell out,' said Harry.

'You did?' She turned and stared at him.

'He was insubordinate and insulted us both.'

A slow smile lit her face. 'So *you* hit him.'

Harry admitted, 'I lost my temper.'

'I wish I had been there to see it.'

Harry managed a smile. 'The outcome might have been different if I had not taken him by surprise.'

'You do yourself a disfavour, Harry Appleby,' she said firmly. 'What did you tell the master of the other ship about him leaving your service?'

'That Master Larsson was a man of good character and an excellent seaman and that we had disagreed on a matter of principle. I could do no less for it was the truth,' said Harry, fiddling with the quill on the table. 'I told him that I would be glad if he hired him and in return if he could let me have one of his crew who could do his job. I am satisfied with the exchange.'

'No doubt you miss him,' said Bridget.

Harry shrugged. 'I do not regret Christian's departure. He was becoming too judgemental. Now, shall we forget him?'

Bridget nodded, although she knew that she would not forget Master Larsson any time soon.

* * *

A few hours later, Harry entered the cabin. 'I have brought you something, Bridget.'

Bridget looked up from her sewing, wondering if this was his way of making amends for not having believed her about Ingrid. 'What is it?'

'The English coast is in sight, so I thought it was the right time to show you a very special gift.' He went back outside and returned carrying a cradle.

Bridget could not believe her eyes. She set aside her sewing and her skirts fluttered about her ankles as she hurried over to where he had placed the cradle on the floor. She fingered a carving of a flower and then that of a bird. 'Did Andrew make this?'

'Who else?' replied Harry, smiling.

'It is a work of beauty. I must thank him.' She glanced up at her husband and caught an expression on his face that moved her. 'It is a lovely gift. Although the baby cannot be due until early next year, it is still best to be prepared.'

'I wanted my son to have the best cradle in the country,' said Harry. 'See how Andrew has made it so that it will swing and rock him to sleep if he ever travels with us by sea.'

'An ordinary carpenter would not have thought of that,' said Bridget, enthralled by the idea. She set the cradle in motion herself. 'See how it will also work on land. How long before we reach London, now that the English coast is in sight?'

'It is the end of May, so there will be light enough for us to sail safely around the coast and anchor in the Thames estuary before nightfall.'

Bridget was delighted and excited by this news. She thanked Harry and the carpenter and looked forward to arriving in London on the morrow.

Bridget gazed through the early-morning haze that hung over the massed roofs of houses, shops and churches towards the towering spire of St Paul's Cathedral.

'Are you ready?' asked Harry from behind her.

She looked into his scarred face and could see how eager he was to go ashore. So much now depended on them finding their friends. Hopefully there might also be news of her father. 'Aye,' she said.

Harry swung down the side of the ship and into the rowing boat below where Joshua waited. He held the boat steady whilst Harry held up a hand to Bridget. She seized hold of his wrist but as she clambered into the boat, she slipped and fell heavily, hitting the side of the boat. The blow knocked all the breath out of her and made her feel sick.

'Are you all right?' asked Harry with concern, putting an arm around her and helping her up.

'Aye, I think so,' she gasped.

Harry settled her on a seat in the stern. He asked her again if she was all right and she nodded, not wanting to make a fuss. The side of her belly was very sore where it had made contact with the wood. She watched as Harry took up the oars and rowed the short distance to the shore. Soon he and Joshua were dragging the boat up the beach.

She found it difficult walking on land again after so much time at sea and staggered about as if drunk. The ground seemed to be moving up and down. Her husband placed his arm about her waist. 'You'll soon get used to it,' he said, helping her up the stone steps that led to the quayside.

She knew he was right, but she still felt sick. After taking several deep breaths she gazed at the scene in front of her. There were warehouses and wooden cranes and goods piled up on the ground. Men stood about talking or hurrying about their business.

Harry had been ashore earlier with his new second-in-command, Hans. They had spoken with the port authorities and discovered that the Baron's vessel carrying Master Larsson had anchored in the river earlier. Harry was now free to give his attention to his wife and his personal affairs. 'I think it best if we visit Lady Elizabeth first. If she is at home she is bound to know of the whereabouts of the Baron and my sister,' he said.

Bridget agreed and the three of them set off in the direction of St Paul's wharf and one of the numerous city churches. Before they reached the cathedral, they turned left to cross a bridge over the River Fleet and then walked along Fleet Street. Eventually they came to the Strand and the gates of her ladyship's mansion.

A guard approached, eyeing Harry's scarred face with suspicion. Joshua called, 'Hoy, Ned, don't yer recognise me, mate?'

The man peered through the bars of the gate. 'Josh, is that you, lad?'

'Of course it's me. Is her ladyship at home?'

'Aye, she's been looking out for yer every day, has been real fretful,' said Ned, unbarring the gate.

Joshua stepped aside, suggesting that Harry and

Bridget go ahead of him. 'This is Master and Mistress Appleby, Ned,' he said.

Ned's eyes widened. 'Is that Mistress McDonald who you went in search of? I thought we'd never see her again. You go and hurry on up to the house, her ladyship will be that pleased to see yer.'

They did not need any encouragement and were soon making their way up the drive to the house barely visible through the trees ahead. As they arrived at its frontage, the door opened and a woman appeared. She was short and stout and was wearing a damson-coloured gown made of a rich satin brocade, trimmed with lace. Her face was pock-marked and on her head was a burnt-orange-coloured wig.

'Lady Elizabeth!' cried Bridget, breaking into a run.

Harry watched his wife fling her arms around the old lady. 'My dear child, you are safe! You can have no notion of how I feared for your well-being,' she wheezed. 'I have prayed morn, noon and night for you. Praise God, that you are here at last.'

Eventually they drew apart and Lady Elizabeth touched the younger woman's cheek with a gentle hand. 'My dear, I fear you have suffered greatly since last we met,' she said in a breathless voice. 'You look pale.'

'All is well now,' said Bridget, wiping her eyes.

Harry stepped forwards. 'May I introduce myself, Lady Elizabeth. I am Harry Appleby.'

The old lady lifted her head and gazed into the scarred face of the man standing before her and her jaw dropped. 'So who have you been fighting, Harry Appleby, to get a face like that?'

Such an honest reaction surprised Harry into a laugh. 'A native brandishing a burning torch in my face.'

'I'll wager it hurt,' she said.

He nodded.

'You might say I have no reason to comment on your appearance when my own is often mocked by the ill mannered,' said her ladyship with a twinkle. 'I used to paint my face to conceal the pock marks, but in the end I gave it up. The paint didn't do my chest any good and eventually one has to accept oneself as one is,' she wheezed, nodding her head so that she almost dislodged her wig. 'Your father was a handsome man, but he was a selfish, thoughtless fool, and you are better off without him,' she continued. 'Your mother, on the other hand, had a lovely nature, and I miss her greatly.' Lady Elizabeth dabbed at her eyes with a scrap of lace.

'You remember her well?' asked Harry hoarsely, deciding to ignore her comments about his father.

The old lady nodded. 'We were girls together. Still, it's water under the bridge now, so what is the point of talking of such times. You must be weary after your journey and have much to tell me.'

Harry wanted to say that he would like to hear all that she remembered about his mother, but decided that perhaps now was not the right moment.

Lady Elizabeth paused for breath before adding, 'You'd best come inside and tell me everything. You will stay here, of course. I will have bedchambers prepared for you both.'

'There is something I need to tell you first,' said Bridget.

'Aye,' said Harry. 'Bridget and I are married, Lady Elizabeth.'

She stared at him and then beckoned Bridget forwards with a beringed hand. 'How did this come about?' she whispered.

'Perhaps we can tell you once we are inside, Lady Elizabeth,' said Harry, who had very good hearing. 'Bridget had a fall earlier and I deem she would be best sitting down.'

Her ladyship nodded and then glanced at Joshua. 'You have my gratitude and will not go unrewarded, but for now you are off duty.'

Joshua winked at Harry, who grabbed his arm and said, 'Return to the ship and bring our baggage. Leave the cradle where it is for now. Tell Hans I will give him his orders in the morning.'

Joshua nodded and hurried away.

Harry turned to face Lady Elizabeth. 'I hope you do not mind, but Joshua wishes to return to Appleby Manor with us.'

'I see you do not intend wasting time, setting your affairs in order. But come, first I would hear everything that has befallen you both, so do not dawdle,' said Lady Elizabeth, leading the way.

Bridget and Harry exchanged smiles and followed her into a parlour. Bridget could tell that her ladyship's honesty about her own disfigurement had had a profound effect on Harry for the better.

'You will not mind dining here?' asked Lady Elizabeth. 'It gets the sunlight at this time of day and is cosier and much easier for the servants.'

'Of course not,' said Harry easily. 'Whatever pleases you, Lady Elizabeth.'

She fixed him with a stare. 'I can see you have not lost the charm you possessed as a boy.'

Harry thanked her. Then he took Bridget's hand and led her to a cushioned settle and sat down beside her.

Lady Elizabeth rang a silver bell and in no time at all a manservant appeared. She gave him orders, including one to have a bedchamber prepared for her guests. Then she sat in a cushioned chair that was like a throne and wheezed, 'Now tell me how you found each other and where you were married? I want to know everything.'

Bridget glanced at her husband. 'I was washed up on the shore in Madeira and Harry found me.'

'I thought she was a mermaid at first because she swims like a fish,' he said. 'She jumped into the sea from a slave-trader's ship. I have never seen such courage.'

Bridget blushed. 'I am not the only one who has courage. You have, too.'

'A slave-trader's ship!' Lady Elizabeth shuddered.

Bridget realised her mistake. 'I should not have mentioned that but, as you see, I survived the ordeal intact.'

Harry gazed at her and realised she was trying to communicate to Lady Elizabeth that she had not been raped.

'I am glad to hear it, my dear,' said her ladyship, looking relieved.

'Perhaps we should leave the telling of our more perilous adventures to another time,' said Harry.

'I agree,' said her ladyship. 'Tell me about your wedding, instead.'

'We were married in Madeira,' said Harry, smiling into Bridget's eyes.

She was transfixed by his smile. Afterwards she wondered if she had been bewitched by it to say what she did. 'Aye, it was very romantic. The ceremony was in a chapel built over the graves of two lovers. One of them was English and the other French. They'd had to flee from the lady's tyrannical father, but instead of landing in Brittany, their ship was blown off course. That is also how the slaver's ship ended up exactly where I wanted it to be. Harry saved my life when he fished me from the sea. He could not have been more caring. I could so easily have died because I caught a disease and was covered in spots.'

'And Harry still chose to marry you. Well!' She beamed at Bridget. 'All's well that ends well. So where is your father?'

The light in Bridget's eyes died. 'We do not know where my father is. It is possible that he arrived in Scotland after I left England in search of him and that he might have come to London.'

'What is his name? I have quite forgotten,' said Lady Elizabeth.

'Callum McDonald,' said Harry, adding helpfully, 'Red-haired with a weatherbeaten, freckled face.'

'I feel I have heard that name recently.' Her ladyship sighed. 'The Baron would know.'

'Where is the Baron?' asked Harry.

'He is staying here, but has gone out on business. It is possible that he is at your house in Cheap Side,' said Lady Elizabeth.

Harry glanced at Bridget.

'You wish to go and see if he is there for yourself?' she said.

'Aye.'

'Would you mind if I stayed here whilst you go?' asked Bridget.

'Of course not,' said Harry, taking her hand and squeezing it. 'It is probably best you rest after your fall.'

She agreed and did not tell him that her side still ached where it had hit the boat and that she felt a megrim coming on.

'You will excuse me, Lady Elizabeth?' asked Harry. 'But it is important that I see the Baron as soon as possible.'

'Of course, Harry. You go. Bridget and I will be happy here on our own.' She waved him away.

Harry kissed Bridget's cheek and left the room.

Chapter Eleven

As Harry approached the house in Cheap Side, he saw a flaxen-haired, strong-looking man standing in the doorway and immediately recognised the Baron. He was having a low-voiced discussion with another man whom Harry had never seen before. Their exchange came to an end and the Baron went inside before Harry could hail him. He hurried across the street and hammered on the door. There was a short delay before he heard footsteps approaching.

'Who is it?' called a voice.

'It's Harry.' He drew a deep breath. 'Harry Appleby.'

He heard a bolt being drawn and the door opened. His Swedish friend stared at him with a mixture of delight and incredulity in his blue eyes.

'God's Blood, it *is* you, Harry! I had almost given up hope of ever seeing you again. What the hell have you done to your face? That must have been some battle you were in.'

'It was,' said Harry grimly. 'I'll tell you all about it some time.'

'I look forward to hearing about.' Alex placed a hand on his shoulder and squeezed it. 'What were you thinking of, disappearing the way you did? If you knew the trouble you've caused us, you wouldn't have gone hiving off across the ocean.'

'I'm pleased to see you too,' said Harry drily. 'Can I come in, Alex?'

The Baron's lips twitched. 'It's *your* house, actually, although there are a few legal details to be sorted out before the deeds can be handed over to you.' He opened the door wide and his expression was sombre now. 'Do you know aught about Bridget McDonald? She went in search of you and her father.'

'Aye, I know,' said Harry. 'She found me, or should I say that I found her. Then we encountered Joshua in Lisbon.'

'God's Teeth!' Alex's fair eyebrows shot up and disappeared beneath his hair. 'That is wonderful news!'

'I'd say it was almost a miracle,' said Harry, smiling.

Alex seized his arm. 'Come in and you can tell me all about it. I must admit that when I sent Joshua chasing after Bridget, I had my doubts about his ever finding her. I was deeply concerned about her safety.'

'And you had need to be. She was sold into slavery.' Harry closed the door behind him and glanced about the entrance before allowing himself to be drawn further into the house. He said in a marvelling tone, 'It was a while before I could believe I had a name that truly belonged to me, never mind a business, a town house and a manor. This is all mine?'

'Aye, I can imagine how you would find it hard to believe,' said Alex. 'No doubt your feelings would equal Rosamund's when she discovered you were still alive. But if it were not for Bridget we would not have known where you went after you disappeared without a farewell. What about Bridget's father? Did he find Bridget?'

Harry flashed him a startled look. 'What do you mean by that? Callum never set sail for Madeira with me but set off alone across the northern ocean back to Scotland. We feared he was at the bottom of the northern ocean.'

'I know about that! The old reprobate was here in London. You'll never believe what he told me,' said Alex.

'You're telling me that he did survive the crossing!' Harry almost shouted the words.

'Aye! And that's not all he did. But first, come and have a drink,' said Alex, opening a door and showing him into a room. 'You've just missed the man I appointed to run the business in your stead, by the way. He's been lodging here. I thought it best not to leave the house empty.'

'Never mind him right now! Where's Callum?' demanded Harry.

'All in good time,' chuckled Alex. 'I'll get those drinks.'

Harry sat down on a plain wooden chair and drummed his fingers on the table. If Callum had returned to Scotland, he could see that he was going to have to chase after him and bring him back. At least Bridget was going to be happy that her father was alive. So was Harry, if the truth was known, because it meant that his ship was safe and he had an odd fondness for the old reprobate.

Alex entered, carrying two tankards of ale. He placed them on the table and sat opposite Harry and raised his tankard, 'To your good health, Harry, and future prosperity.'

Harry drank half the contents and then put down his tankard. 'How is my sister? Is she well?' he asked.

'Aye, she's carrying our second child, so I left her at Appleby Manor, rather than have her endure the long journey whilst she is suffering from morning sickness.'

Harry decided to keep quiet about Bridget's condition for the moment, but maybe he would have to leave her behind in London whilst he made the journey to Appleby Manor. 'Congratulations. I believe you already have a fine son.'

Alex grinned. 'Wait until you see your nephew. You'll be proud of him.'

'I am impatient to see them both,' said Harry gruffly, 'and I'll have more questions to ask you about them, but first tell me about Callum—and is my ship in one piece?'

Alex looked a little uncomfortable.

'What is wrong?' asked Harry immediately, who knew his friend well.

'Callum took the *Odin's Maiden* with him, Harry. I suppose he thought two ships were better than one.'

Harry scowled. 'What do you mean by that and where has the old pirate gone?'

'In search of Bridget. He sailed into London in his

own ship, bringing yours, as well. He left the same way, no doubt believing that if he was going after pirates he would need plenty of men. He had hired a skeleton crew in Ireland and sailed for Scotland, believing he would find Bridget at his brother's castle. Instead he found his nephew who told him that his mother had died and his father had taken Bridget to London. Apparently the nephew is a mariner, too, so Callum put him in command of his ship whilst he remained in command of the *Odin's Maiden* and they both sailed into the Thames.'

Harry was astounded. 'He went to Ireland first?'

'Aye, he only *borrowed* your ship, so he said, having in mind to recover his own vessel and take back as much of his hoard from Patrick O'Malley that he could find.'

Harry downed the rest of the ale in his tankard and wiped his hand across his mouth. 'Why did I not think that he might have that in mind? He went on enough about his hoard and O'Malley.' The question was irrelevant because Harry had believed above all else that Callum's intention was to be reunited with Bridget. 'So Callum managed to get his ship back, but what about his treasure?'

'He enlisted some of Bridget's mother's kin and with their help, Callum took what was his with interest and set fire to O'Malley's ship.'

Harry let out a long low whistle before saying, 'If Callum ever reaches Madeira, he'll be better staying there. He could have the whole O'Malley clan after him.'

'He reckons they would not know it was him because they wouldn't be expecting him. Besides he says it was dark and he was in and out in no time.' Alex shook his head. 'I should have had the river authorities impound your ship until you could reclaim her, but I never expected him to leave so suddenly. His first reaction to the news that Bridget was a prisoner of pirates was to get drunk, but when he sobered up he wanted to know where she'd last been seen. Then he started blaming himself and saying he'd have to go and find you both.'

Harry swore. 'Bridget's here in London with me. I've left her at Lady Elizabeth's mansion. She slipped getting into the boat and hurt herself, so I thought it best to leave her behind.'

'I hope she is all right,' said Alex, looking concerned.

'She's strong, Alex,' Harry said with a hint of pride in his voice. 'She's had to be to survive what she's been through. I admire her courage as well as her beauty. This will come as a shock to you, but Bridget and I are married and we are expecting our first child.'

Alex slammed down his tankard. 'God's Teeth! How did you persuade her? She was mad as an angry bee with you for separating her from her father. It's not that she was—?'

'What? Raped by the slave trader and needed my good name? No, nothing like that, although I reckon there was a danger of it after the slave-trader's woman died of disease. That is when Bridget jumped into the sea and swam for shore despite how stormy it was.' Harry took a mouthful of ale.

'She did what? And what slave trader?'

Harry told him.

'I should have gone with them,' said Alex, frowning.

'Don't you start blaming yourself,' said Harry. 'Your presence very likely wouldn't have affected the outcome.' There was a silence and then he continued, 'Putting all this aside, I confess I received the shock of my life when I was told you were married to my sister. I thought you were mad for Ingrid or I wouldn't have left the way I did.'

'Ingrid is not the woman I believed her to be,' said Alex, his eyes clouding.

'So I have heard. I'd like to know what your experience of her ill doings are some time.'

Alex nodded. 'Your sister is worth ten thousand of her.' A smile tugged at the corners of his mouth. 'Rosamund is another such as Bridget. She has much courage and she is as lovely inside as she is out. We love each other dearly.'

Harry experienced a pang of envy. He wasn't certain what real love was, but had to admit that he would hate Bridget not to be part of his life now that he had found her once more. He cleared his throat. 'I'm glad you and Rosamund found each other and are happy.'

'I, too.' Alex stared at him. 'But tell me more about you and Bridget.'

Harry told him as much of the truth as he wanted Alex to know and then said, 'I can imagine what Bridget is going to say about her father.'

'As long as she doesn't expect you to go chasing after him all the way to Africa and Madeira.'

'No chance of that,' said Harry firmly. 'The next travelling I do will be to Appleby Manor.'

'On horseback or by ship?' asked Alex.

Harry hesitated. 'I haven't considered travelling there by ship, but where is the nearest port?'

'Preston. It is situated inland on the River Ribble that flows into the Irish Sea. You could anchor there and travel by horseback to Appleby Manor. But it would probably take longer than travelling from London on horseback because you would have to sail right round Land's End and up the coast of Wales.'

Harry rubbed his scar. 'How are you travelling?'

'By horse,' replied Alex, 'although one of my ships will be setting sail for Preston in a day or two. It'll be picking up a cargo there and then Rosamund and I will join her and sail to Scotland before returning to our house in Sweden.'

'When?' asked Harry, displeased to hear this news.

Alex sighed. 'I know how you must feel, Harry, about having such a short time with Rosamund before we have to leave, but we have spent little time in my own country since our wedding.'

'I understand that you have been tied up looking after my affairs and I am exceeding grateful,' said Harry. 'It is just that I am concerned about Bridget travelling by horseback in her condition. Perhaps I should leave her with Lady Elizabeth whilst she is still suffering the sickness and travel north with you.'

'You can't do that, Harry!' exclaimed Alex. 'I'll be leaving London tomorrow with Lady Elizabeth. I promised to escort her to Colleweston, the Countess of Richmond's mansion in Northamptonshire, on my way north. You have matters to attend to here and will need at least a few days to sort out the legal paperwork.'

Harry frowned. 'But if you and my sister are to depart for Scotland soon, then I cannot spare more than three days in London if I am to spend any time at all with her.'

'I agree. Besides, the sooner she knows that you and Bridget are both alive the better. It is not good for her to fret in her condition.' Alex rose to his feet and changed the subject. 'So what about *Thor's Hammer* and your seafaring life? I presume you are prepared to give it up?'

'If you'd asked me that two years ago, I'd have said never, but now my circumstances have changed, I must settle down.' Harry's dark brows knit. 'But what am I to do about my ship now I am a landowner? I am reluctant to part with the gift your grandfather gave me.'

'You'll be able to make use of her in your business still. What about Christian Larsson—surely you can promote him to master?'

'He is no longer a member of my crew.'

'What happened? Is he dead?'

'No. He is now working for you, Alex,' said Harry with a wry smile.

'Why?'

'He resented Bridget and was insubordinate. His replacement seems a reliable man. I think I can safely leave the *Hammer*—or the *St Bridget* as I renamed her—in his care,' said Harry. 'As for the *Odin's Maiden*...' he sighed '...I will have to leave her to her fate and pray God that Callum returns with her intact.'

Alex nodded. 'Now shall we return to Lady Elizabeth's? I would like to see Bridget and tell her how glad I am to see her safely back and to congratulate her.'

Harry agreed, thinking that he was not looking forward to telling his wife about what her father had been up to in Ireland.

Alex said, 'I'll take you to meet your father's lawyer and your man of business before this day is out. In the meantime, can you tell me how you came by that scar?' he added, opening the front door.

Harry thought with a sinking heart how his scar could never be ignored, even by his dearest friend, but he set aside such a depressing thought and began to tell Alex about his adventures. They were still deep in conversation when they came to the gates of Lady Elizabeth's mansion.

Bridget had given up watching out for Harry as soon as she spotted Joshua trundling a cart towards the house. She had a niggling pain in her belly, but dismissed it as of no importance and was about to go outside when Lady Elizabeth bumbled into the parlour.

'So I didn't imagine you were here,' she said, beaming at her. 'And Harry Appleby, where has he gone?' She gazed about as if expecting him to suddenly pop out from behind the settle.

'To visit his house in Cheap Side. I was just on my way outside. I have noticed that Joshua has arrived with our baggage. Will you excuse me?'

'Certainly, my dear,' said Lady Elizabeth, settling herself in her chair. 'You'll want to go upstairs and unpack. I'll have one of the maids to show you the way.' She reached for the bell and a maid came running.

In no time at all the cart had been emptied and Bridget and Joshua were following the girl upstairs. She opened the door on to a bedchamber that was luxurious by any standards. Bridget took a deep satisfying breath and went inside, followed by Joshua. She wasted no time unpacking, trying to ignore the fact that the niggling pain in her side had become a positive bellyache. She undressed, washed her face and hands and donned her robe, thinking to have a rest on the bed. But first she went over to the window, hoping to see Harry coming back to her.

Her heart lifted as she set eyes on his familiar, well-built figure walking up the drive. She saw that he was not alone, but accompanied by the Baron. She wondered what he had told his old friend about their marriage and the baby. She was about to go downstairs when she felt suddenly wet underneath. With a sudden sense of doom, she unfastened her robe and saw a trickle of blood running down her leg. Her heart began to bang with fright as she realised what was happening.

Blindly she reached for the door handle, but then draw back her hand. She couldn't go rushing for help, trailing blood all over the place. She remembered the bindings she had purchased in Lisbon and where she had put them. Having recovered them from the chest, along with the belt to tie the ends to, she bound herself up.

The tears were rolling down her cheeks as with shaking hands she removed her bloodied robe and donned a clean shift. Only then did she place a drying cloth on the bed and lay down. She could not stop crying. How big would her baby be? Only a tiny creature. No one could even tell if they looked at her that she had been carrying it. *Had!* Was she really miscarrying, then? She did not want to believe that was happening. She prayed that by lying down the blood would tail off and her child would be saved, but the pains in her belly were growing stronger and she groaned as they intensified.

There was a knock on the door and it opened and Harry stood there. 'How are you feeling?' he asked. She pushed herself into a sitting position and could do no more than stare at him. 'You've been crying,' he said, hurrying over to her. 'What is wrong? You look as if you are in pain. Do you have a megrim?'

'I—I—I deem I am miscarrying the baby!' A sob burst in her throat. 'See the blood on my robe.'

'What! Oh, dear God!' Harry had not expected this and was shocked to the core. Bridget was strong. She had endured so much. How could she be losing their child?

She clutched his sleeve. 'God must have decided that we don't deserve to have a baby.'

'Nonsense,' said Harry, feeling sick inside. 'You must be mistaken.'

'About what?' she cried. 'God's intentions or about my miscarrying the baby?'

'I suppose I mean both. What should I do?' he demanded, running a hand through his hair. 'Should I ask Lady Elizabeth to send for a midwife or a physician?'

'I don't know.' Another sob burst from her.

'Don't cry!' said Harry, unable to bear to see her in tears. If she were to die—! He did not know where the thought came from because it was not as if she had gone full term and was giving birth. He felt a chill run down his spine. 'I'll speak to Lady Elizabeth, she's a woman.'

Bridget tried to pull herself together. 'Aye, and no fool. She has had no children of her own, but she will know what to do.' She gazed up at her husband from tear-drenched eyes. 'Oh, Harry, hold me for a moment!'

Harry hesitated, deeming he should fetch help, but there was such sadness in his wife's face that he could not deny her. He put his arms around her and rocked her, resting his damaged cheek on her hair. 'It will be all right,' he said.

Bridget could only cling to him and cry against his shoulder. He could feel tears in his own eyes and knew he had to be strong and leave this bedchamber and fetch help. 'If I let you go, you'll be all right, won't you?' he said huskily.

She nodded, but a sob caught in her throat as she let him go. He kissed her quickly and almost ran out of the room. He raced downstairs with his heart thudding in his chest. Only for a moment when he gazed down at Lady Elizabeth with her ridiculous wig and pock-marked face did he wonder how he was going to put into words the tragedy that was taking place upstairs.

'Something is wrong, isn't it, Harry? Tell me!' she demanded.

He told her.

She wasted no time in ringing for a servant and sending him to fetch her physician and a woman she knew of good repute. Only then did she ask Harry to help her upstairs as she wished to see Bridget for herself. She told him to make haste and he complied with her wishes.

As soon as her ladyship set eyes on Bridget, she told

Harry to leave them alone together. Reluctantly he did so and went in search of Alex with a heavy heart.

'I am so sorry, Harry,' said his friend, putting an arm about his shoulders. 'But perhaps if Bridget rests, the bleeding will stop and the baby will be saved.'

Harry was silent. Bridget's tears had convinced him that the baby could not be saved. What if he was to lose her as well? He felt helpless in the face of what was happening and could only pray that she would not die, too. At the moment that was all he could do for her.

Harry sat at Bridget's bedside, gazing down at her slumbering pale face. He remembered how he had felt when she had been ill in Madeira and he had watched over her. Fortunately she had recovered and he had to believe she would do so now. Both the physician and the midwife had tried to reassure him by telling him that she should be up and about in a few days' time, but until then she should rest as much as possible.

The midwife had told him that it was not unusual for a woman to miscarry a first child in the early months and that there was no reason why they should not have another child. Her words were of some comfort to Harry because he had begun to worry that not only might Bridget not be able to conceive again, but that he was to blame for the miscarriage. He remembered her slipping and hitting the side of the boat. If he'd had a firmer grip on her that would not have happened. He was convinced that the fall had caused Bridget to lose their baby.

Bridget suddenly opened her eyes and gazed up at Harry. 'You're still here,' she murmured.

'Aye.' He took her hand and squeezed it. 'How do you feel?'

'As if I have been kicked by a horse,' she murmured. 'The physician gave me some poppy juice to help with the pain, so I am still a little sleepy. I am sorry I lost your baby.' Tears filled her eyes.

'It is not your fault,' said Harry hastily, needing her to be the strong Bridget—the one who had jumped into the sea and showed such courage. 'The midwife assures me that there can be other babies,' he continued. 'But for now I will ask Lady Elizabeth for the use of another guest chamber, so as not to disturb you. You need to rest if you are to make a swift recovery.'

She did not want him to leave her, but could see the sense in his words knowing that he wanted to go to Appleby Manor as soon as he could. 'If that is what you wish. I regret that I will not be able to travel for a few days, but if you wish to go to Lancashire without me, then—'

'Shall we wait and see how you fare?' interrupted Harry. 'I have business to do in London that will take a couple of days and I need to purchase horses and what is necessary for the journey. I would prefer not to leave you behind.'

Reassured by his words, Bridget drifted into sleep. Harry remained there a while longer, just gazing down at her, thinking that some time soon he was going to have to tell her about Callum and worried about how she would take the news.

He went downstairs and found Alex and Lady Elizabeth in her parlour, conversing together. They looked up as he entered the room. 'How is dear Bridget now?' asked her ladyship.

'She is sleeping,' said Harry.

'Sit down, dear boy,' bid Lady Elizabeth. 'You look exhausted.'

'Well, that is not for any work I have done,' he said with a wry smile, seating himself on the settle. 'It is oddly tiring just sitting and waiting and worrying.'

'Your priority at the moment is Bridget, so Lady Elizabeth and I have decided to postpone our departure and will leave the day after next. Tomorrow, if Bridget's condition is improved, I will take you to meet your man of business and your father's lawyer.'

Harry thanked him.

'Also, dear boy, you may stay here as long as you consider it necessary,' said Lady Elizabeth. 'Treat my home as you would your own.'

Harry thought about how he and Bridget had never had a proper home of their own. 'Thank you, Lady Elizabeth, your offer is much appreciated. I fear the house in Cheap Side is a gloomy place and in need of renovation.' He grimaced. 'Besides, I would not wish to uproot my man of business. After all, at least for the summer, I do intend to make our home at Appleby Manor.'

'You will find much to keep you occupied there,' said Alex, 'although you will probably need to spend some time in London before autumn.'

Harry agreed, although he was hoping that would be unnecessary and he could leave the bulk of the business in his man's hands. If Alex had chosen him then surely he could be trusted until then. He did not wish to leave Bridget alone in an unfamiliar house when there was much that she had to learn, too. He remembered the moment she had told him that she thought she was with child. He felt so sad that they had lost this baby that had helped bring them together again and set aside their hurt and anger. He had so looked forward to the three of them being a family.

Chapter Twelve

The following day Harry and Bridget were sharing breakfast on a tray in her bedchamber. She was looking more herself, but was still pale and there was a sadness in her face that made his heart ache. He insisted that she stay in bed at least for another day.

'I will do as you say, Harry, but you do not have to stay with me all the time. Go and have some fresh air.'

'I will. I shall go now and walk in the garden and then I will back for a while because I will be going out later with Alex on business.' He smiled down at her. 'Is there aught I can get you before I go?'

'If you could ask if I could have some hot water?'

He nodded and went downstairs and relayed Bridget's request to one of the maids. Then he went out into the garden. The gardener was already up and about and impulsively Harry asked whether there were any roses in bloom.

'Aye, there are some early ones,' replied the gnarled old man, gazing at him intently. 'Is it that yer wanting them for Mistress Bridget?'

Harry nodded and resisted the temptation to cover his scar with his hand. 'Indeed, I do.'

'I'll cut some for her while yer have a stroll round the garden. I'll have them ready for yer when yer get back here.'

Harry thanked him and continued his promenade, thinking that if Bridget's condition improved even more by the morrow, then he would begin to make arrangements for them to travel to Appleby Manor. He would also have to make time today to visit his ship, and that reminded him that he must tell Bridget about her father. He had very mixed feelings about doing so because he did not want her to get all tearful again.

He collected the roses from the gardener on his return, had one of the maids place them in water in a vase, then he carried them upstairs.

'Good morning again, Bridget,' he said, slightly anxious because she was worrying her lower lip with her teeth.

She lifted her gaze and smiled hesitantly. 'What have you there? Did you enjoy your walk around the garden?'

He placed the bowl of roses on the table by the bedside. 'The gardener allowed me to have these for you.'

She touched one of the velvety dark pink petals and sniffed the flower's heart. 'How—how beautiful they are, and so different from the blossoms you plucked for me when we were in Madeira.' Her eyes were shiny with unshed tears.

'Please, Bridget, don't cry,' he pleaded. 'Or I will

never bring you flowers again,' he teased, sitting down on the bed and taking hold of her hand.

A small laugh escaped her. 'You are too kind, Harry. I love you bringing me flowers.'

I wish you could love me. The thought seemed to come out of nowhere and he forgot what he was about to say. Then he collected himself together. 'They're only a few roses from her ladyship's garden,' he said casually. 'Wait until you're gathering armfuls from our own garden.'

'I would like that,' she said softly. 'I have never had a garden of my own and no one has ever given me flowers before but you.'

'No? I admit that I've never given flowers to anyone else but you,' said Harry, toying with her fingers.

She clung to his hand and blurted out, 'Harry, I am worrying that there might not be another child. I was an only child. My father would have liked a son but—what if I cannot conceive again?'

Harry felt a peculiar sinking feeling in the pit of his stomach. 'You conceived the baby we lost quickly enough. I don't see why it shouldn't happen again. Besides, Callum was at sea for long stretches of time. It is possible that is one of the reasons he and your mother didn't have any more children. I am giving up the sea so there will be opportunity enough for us to—' He wanted to say make love but the words wouldn't come.

It seemed it was not necessary for him to say them aloud because her colour was suddenly heightened. 'I am glad you will not have to battle with such storms as we have experienced at sea.'

He agreed.

Then they both fell silent.

Harry knew the moment had come when he had to tell her about Callum. 'Bridget, I have some tidings about your father—and before you think the worst,' he added swiftly, 'he is not dead. At least—'

'Where is he?' asked Bridget.

'He's gone in search of you. Alex told me that he came here with his own ship and *Odin's Maiden*.'

Bridget felt quite light-headed. 'With his *own* ship! I don't understand. How did he get it back?'

'Think, Bridget,' said Harry gently. 'I have lost count of how many times Callum told me the story of Patrick O'Malley stealing his ship and you both narrowly escaping death. Over and over he spoke of having his revenge. I did not give it serious thought until Alex told me that your father used *Odin's Maiden* to strike at O'Malley and get back his ship. He waited until nightfall and took back all that was his and extra. Then he set fire to O'Malley's ship.'

Bridget was dumbfounded and for several moments she could only stare at Harry. Then she found her voice. 'How *could* he?'

'You mean how did he get away with it or why didn't he go to you first and tell you of his plans? You must have still been in this country when he was busy doing that. If he'd come to find you first, you'd never have left on your voyage to try to find him,' Harry pointed out.

'I know why he didn't come to me first! He knew I'd most likely try to persuade him not to take such a risk. No doubt he bribed your men to crew *Odin's Maiden* for him with promises of a reward if they helped him regain his treasure,' she said waspishly.

'I did always wonder how he persuaded them.'

'I wager he had been drinking when he attacked the ship,' said Bridget.

Harry said, 'Highly unlikely. He'd need a clear head to achieve what he did.'

She was silent for a long time and then, with eyes glinting, said, 'How dare he have me worrying all this time! If he had come straight home to me, I would never have gone in search of him. I would never have been taken by pirates and captured by that filthy slave trader! You would not have asked me to marry you because I was penniless and in need of a protector and I would never have miscarried,' she said bitterly.

'Are you regretting our marriage?' asked Harry bluntly.

'I was thinking of it from your point of view. I really didn't marry you because I knew you were Harry Appleby, you know. I did so because you suggested it and provided me with a way out of my predicament. I just wish I had my father in front of me now. I'd tell him what I thought of him.'

Harry scowled. 'If I had him here right now, then I would shake him like a dog would a rat and make him grovel and beg your forgiveness for the inconvenience and suffering he has put you through. As it is I do not know what you expect me to do about him, but I—'

Bridget looked taken aback. 'I expect you to do *nothing*, Harry! You have your own affairs to tend to and so I can only wait and see if he returns. It could be that he will lose his life in another battle with pirates or in Africa and I will never see him again. As for his treasure, that will be gone for good, unless he has put it somewhere safe this time.'

'Let us try to not be pessimistic, Bridget. He is likely to anchor at Lisbon for fresh water and supplies. It is possible that he will ask for information about both of us and someone will inform him that we left for England.'

'But he mightn't get that information and then he'll sail for Africa and—' She shrugged, feeling angry and helpless in the light of her father's latest venture.

'Let us not waste time worrying about what might or might not happen to him. We have been through all this before where he is concerned.' He reached out and drew her close to him.

She sighed and closed her eyes, wanting nothing more than to rest in his arms, but the moment did not last because after a short while he released her. 'I must leave you and go with Alex,' said Harry, getting to his feet. 'Is there anything you wish me to bring you?'

Bridget shook her head. 'I only need to know when you plan to leave London. If you feel you must go sooner, then I could stay here and follow you on. Perhaps you could leave Joshua and he could accompany me.'

He stared at her, wondering why the sudden change of heart. Yesterday she had not wished him to leave without her. It had to be because of what he had told her about her father. Surely she wouldn't be foolish enough to wait until he was out of the way and then set out in search of her father?

'I need Joshua with me, and what kind of husband would I be if I were to leave you after the trauma you have suffered?' he said firmly, not giving her time to consider answering that question, but leaving her to ponder on what he'd said.

Bridget thought about Harry's parting words for several moments before she pushed back the bedcovers and slid her legs out of the bed. She stood up, only to discover that not only was she all a-tremble, but she felt a rush of menstrual blood. She resigned herself to having to change her bindings and remaining there in the bedchamber for at least another day.

Weak tears filled her eyes. She was foolish to have even considered for a moment staying here in the hope of her father returning in the following week or so. There was much she wanted to say to him, but not in Harry's company. Her husband had been very forbearing when he had told her about the latest episode in her father's adventurous life. He had not even hinted that his own ship could have been blown out of the water by Patrick O'Malley if the raid had gone wrong. She wanted some of her father's hoard to give to Harry as a dowry—he deserved it. If she could do that, she would feel much happier. Harry might have deceived her before marrying her, but she had not lost by it and she wanted them to be on a more equal footing. Perhaps it would not matter so much if she had not miscarried her precious baby. Tears threatened again, but she blinked them back.

Bridget was sitting by the bedchamber window in her night rail, gazing out as the daylight faded. Stars were twinkling on in the sky and the fragrance of roses perfumed the air. A dog barked in the distance, but otherwise all was still and quiet. Then she heard the door open behind her. She turned her head and looked at her husband. 'You've been a long time.'

Harry gazed across the bedchamber to where he could make out Bridget's shapely silhouette by the light of the dying sun and yearned to make love to her. 'Shouldn't you be in bed?'

'I have not been up long and have only sat here, gazing out of the window and thinking of all that has happened since I last saw my father.'

'There are things you would change, of course?'

'Naturally.'

He waited, but she said no more, and he wondered if one of them would be his shaving off his beard before they had taken their marriage vows. Involuntarily he touched his scar and then dropped his hand. 'I have spoken to my man of business and intend to introduce him to Hans on the morrow. If you feel strong enough, do you wish to go into the city and purchase a new robe and aught else you might need?'

'I do not like taking your money,' said Bridget, walking carefully over to the other side of the bed to Harry and sitting down. 'I have been thinking that my father must have gone to Scotland before he came to London as he would have not known I was here. He might have left some of his hoard up there.'

'Perhaps, but let's not talk of your father's money,' said Harry. 'I just came in to see how you fared and to let you know I have seen the lawyer.'

'No doubt the lawyer was surprised to see you?'

'Aye. Documents are being drawn up even now and will be copied during the night. As Alex will be leaving London in the morning and is unlikely to return for several months, it was decided that the business of signing everything over to me would be dealt with straight away.'

'That is good news,' said Bridget.

'Aye, but now you must get back in bed as the days ahead will be wearisome.'

'You will still sleep in the other bedchamber?' asked Bridget, barely able to distinguish his features.

'If that is what you prefer. I would like to stay in case you need me during the night.'

'Then you must stay,' said Bridget, climbing into bed.

His decision pleased her because, despite her ladyship coming to sit with her for part of the day, she had felt bereft, unable to stop thinking not only of the baby but of Harry being absent for hours. On board ship she had been so accustomed to his being in close proximity, even when they were not speaking and angry with each other.

He climbed into bed clad in a nightshirt. Her leg brushed his and he rolled over, giving her space. Bridget would have appreciated his cuddling her because suddenly she felt low spirited and the ready tears pricked the back of her eyes.

She had no idea how long she lay there before stretching out a hand to touch him. When he did not react, she slid her hand further around his body. A fingernail caught on one of the curls on his chest and she had difficulty freeing it. She drew herself closer to him and slid her other arm around him so she could free her fingernail. It was when she was withdrawing her arms that she felt the scars on his back and remembered his mention of being whipped on the pirate ship. She pressed her lips against his back, believing him to be asleep. Then she closed her eyes and drifted into slumber.

Harry wondered if he had imagined that light caress on his back. But if he had not, what was he to make of his wife's behaviour? A faint smile played about his lips as he closed his eyes.

The bedchamber was filled with light when Bridget woke to find herself alone in the bed. She sat up and realised that physically she was feeling much better. She could smell Harry's roses and sat up and looked for him. Then she saw him, clad only in a drying cloth slung about his hips, gazing out of the window. She could not take her eyes from the way the sun played on his skin, so that it seemed to glow, and thought what a fine body he had.

She cleared her throat. 'Good morning, Harry.'

He turned and his gaze rested a moment on her bare shoulder where her night rail had slipped down. 'Good morning, Bridget. You sound better today.' He reached for his shirt. 'I beg pardon, but I cannot linger. Alex and Lady Elizabeth are leaving today and I want to wish them Godspeed.'

Immediately Bridget said, 'Then I must also do so. If you would be so kind as to wait until I am dressed.'

His brow puckered. 'Are you certain you feel well enough to go downstairs?'

'If I do not try, I will not know. You will wait for me?'

'Of course I will wait for you.' He paused before

saying, ' I have decided you must have a personal maid now we have a position to maintain.'

'Could that not wait until we arrived at Appleby Manor?' she asked, startled.

'No. It is best you have a female with you in the circumstances.'

'If that is what you wish.'

She climbed out of bed and for an instant she swayed. Harry was there in a moment to steady her. 'Are you certain that you are well enough to go downstairs?' He frowned.

Bridget was touched by his concern and was glad to rest against his chest for a moment. 'Aye, I am sure I only felt odd for a moment because I stood up so suddenly. If you could fetch me the scarlet gown and cream shift from the armoire, that would be of help.'

Harry removed his arm from about her waist and she placed her hand on the bedpost and watched him carry out her request. What did it matter if her father had disappointed her? She had a husband who was proving himself far more worthy and who was prepared to fetch and carry for her and who had brought her flowers.

'See,' said Harry, placing the garments on the bed, 'you do need a maid. Do you wish me to help you dress?'

'I—I deem I can manage,' she said, remembering she would need to change her bindings. 'If—if you could turn your back?'

Harry turned away and finished dressing himself.

'I would appreciate your arm, Harry,' she said a short while later.

He turned and the breath caught in his throat. 'That is an unusual gown and suits you admirably.'

She blushed and thanked him, holding out a hand to him. He opened the door before sweeping her off her feet and carrying her out of the bedchamber. She would have protested, but from previous experience guessed she would be wasting her time, so, placing her arms around his neck, she allowed him to carry her downstairs. Yet when they reached the bottom, she requested that he set her on her feet. 'I do not want her ladyship thinking that I am not fit for her to leave and delay her journey again.'

'I hope to see you at Appleby in ten days' time if the weather stays fine,' said Alex, embracing his brother-in-law.

Harry returned his hug and then they drew apart. He would have been happier travelling north with the Baron, keeping them company as there was safety in numbers. Yet his worst fears were not that they would be attacked by footpads or be delayed by bad roads, but rather that Bridget might find the journey arduous and fall ill and that his sister would take one look at his scarred face and be repulsed by him.

Alex turned to Bridget and kissed her on the cheek. 'I cannot wait to see Rosamund's face when she sees the two of you together. It will be a blessing to her that she will not be leaving her brother all alone at Appleby when we depart for Scotland.'

'But we will see each other again?' said Bridget anxiously. 'I know that Sweden is far away, but you will visit England often?'

'As often as we are able and you must visit us, too.'

'Come, Baron, we must be on our way,' interrupted Lady Elizabeth, touching his arm. 'I wish that I could accompany all of you to Appleby, but my old bones and this chest of mine cannot cope with such a long journey on the road. You must take care that you do not overtire Bridget, my dear boy,' she said, holding her cheek up for his kiss. 'I look forward to a happier outcome for you both in the future.'

He kissed her and then she and Bridget exchanged kisses before her ladyship accepted the assistance of both men into her carriage. Alex would be riding along-side the vehicle with another four outriders.

Bridget and Harry waved until they were out of sight before going back inside the house. He suggested that she sit inside her ladyship's parlour whilst he went to have a word with her ladyship's housekeeper, Mistress Tyler, about hiring a young, respectable and reliable girl who would be willing to travel with them to Lancashire.

'I will make enquiries for you, Master Appleby,' she replied, 'but I must warn you that there are some, I know, who'd like the position, but who would be alarmed at travelling to northern parts, believing folk up there to be no better than savages.'

'Just do your best, mistress, and I will make it worth your while,' said Harry. 'Tell the one you choose that I will pay her well. If she finds after we arrive there that she is not happy, then we will hire a local lass so she can return to London.'

'Now that is a generous offer, Master Appleby, and should make my task easier,' said the housekeeper, her eyes alight.

'Then waste no time and go to it.' Harry went to tell Bridget what he had done.

She was warmed by his thoughtfulness. 'I was wondering, Harry, if when we reach Appleby it will stir memories of your boyhood?'

'I, too, have thought of that. In the past I often asked myself how is it that I have not forgotten how to put on my shoes or to remember how to string words together that make sense, but could not remember my own name and scarcely anything about my family?'

'At least you now know the truth about yourself and how you came to be on that pirate ship,' said Bridget, hesitating before adding, 'I hope you can forgive me for not telling you sooner about your being Harry Appleby?'

'Let us forget the past,' he said. 'I know now who I am and just wish that the seas could be rid of pirates. They are a scourge.' He thought how there would be no peace whilst so many men believed it was their right to raid ships that traded in their waters. He only hoped that Callum's luck would not run out and that he would return safely. It would do Bridget no good at all if after more days and weeks or even months of worry about her father, he did not return.

Mistress Tyler was as good as her word and later that morning informed Harry that she had found a girl whom she thought might be suitable for his purpose, although she hadn't had much experience, but she was willing to go north. Was it possible for him to see her now? He agreed and, as Bridget was present, suggested that she stay whilst he interviewed the girl in case she should have questions that she would like to ask her.

Shortly after the housekeeper returned with a maiden of perhaps some twelve summers, whom the woman informed them was an orphan. Once the door closed behind the housekeeper, both Harry and Bridget turned their attention to the girl. She was slight of build with a slender face that would have been pretty if her nose had not been broken at some time, as it gave her a belligerent look.

Yet when Harry asked her name, she answered in a voice that belied that impression, for it was soft and hesitant. 'My name is Dorcas Saddler, Master Appleby.'

'Mistress Tyler has explained to you what this position involves?' Harry asked.

'Aye, sir.'

'And you have no qualms about travelling north with us?' asked Harry.

'I wouldn't say that, sir, but it can't be any worse than the life I'll be leaving behind. I'll be glad to get away, to tell you the truth.'

'Your last employer treated you roughly?'

'No, it was me father who did this to me.' She touched her nose. 'But he got killed in a brawl last Monday when the landlord gave us notice to quit. If it hadn't been for ol' Tyler I'd have been living on the streets.'

'Your mother is dead, then?' asked Bridget.

'Aye, she's well gone and deserves to be with the angels for all she suffered from me father.' Her eyes filled with tears and she sniffed and wiped her face with the back of her hand.

'Then this job must appear fortuitous to you,' said Bridget, pitying the girl.

Dorcas stared at her. 'What's that mean, mistress?'

'That this job is just what you need,' said Harry.

The girl's face lit up. 'Aye, it's that all right. I'm all alone in the world now. Me brothers ran away because me father was beating them up and I don't blame them, although I wish they'd taken me with them.'

Bridget was filled with pity for the girl. She might have had little experience of being a lady's maid, but she could train her to do all that she would need of her. Besides, she needed a home and looking after herself. She darted a look at her husband. 'I think Dorcas will suit us, Harry.'

Harry thought he knew what was going on in his wife's head. In the short time she had been with child, her maternal instincts had been roused and taking this girl under her wing could go some way in helping her recover from her loss.

'As you wish, but you must make certain that Dorcas has all that is necessary for the journey. No doubt she will need another set of clothes and a pair of shoes.'

Bridget's eyes brightened. 'I know of a used-clothes dealer, not far from St Paul's Cathedral. We will pay them a visit.'

The girl beamed at her. 'I know the place. Yer talking about Walther and Maud's place. Yer can have no notion of just how grateful I am to yer both for giving me this position.'

Bridget smiled, remembering how she had been feeling quite desperate when Harry had proposed marriage. 'When we reach Appleby Manor, then we will see about having new clothes made for you. That is, of course, if you do not change your mind about staying in Lancashire.'

'Those barbarians can't be any worse than me father,' said Dorcas stoutly. 'And it's an adventure, isn't it, Mistress Appleby? I've never set foot outside of London in me life, so I'm really looking forward to it.'

'Good,' said Bridget, delighted. 'And we can be thankful, Dorcas, that we are making the journey whilst the days are long, the weather is clement and the countryside looks its best.'

Chapter Thirteen

Not long after, Harry accompanied his wife and Dorcas to the used-clothes dealers. He had used their services in the past when he had needed a disguise for his under-cover work with the Baron. They were delighted to see the newly married couple and Harry conversed with Walther for a short while before leaving his wife and Dorcas in their capable hands and going off towards Cheap Side.

Maud produced suitable clothing for Dorcas and Bridget sat on a chair provided and was glad to par-take of a cup of Maud's homemade mead and a bun. She found pleasure in watching the expression on the girl's face as she tried on different items. For once she did not worry about spending Harry's money and even bought herself a cloak, a robe, a gown, a hat and gloves of fine quality.

After leaving the shop they made their way to the shoemakers' row where they were able to buy ready-made shoes for Dorcas. Then Bridget decided there were several other purchases she wished to make for the journey, so they hired a lad to carry all that they had bought back to the house.

By then Bridget was feeling tired, so she lay on her bed and told Dorcas to put away the items they had bought and discussed what she expected of her. Afterwards they had a light meal. Then Bridget decided to sit in the garden and have Dorcas keep her company whilst the girl shortened the hem of the gown Bridget had purchased. She wondered how much longer Harry would be out and hoped he would not be late.

Harry had gone down to the Thames with his man of business, having sent a messenger to arrange with his second-in-command, Hans, to meet them at a local tavern. They had discussed those customers who remembered Sir James and would be willing to do business with his son. They had talked about luxury goods and how his father had had dealings with the wool merchants in Preston and debated whether to rekindle that line of business.

When the meeting was over, the three men parted company. Harry was about to visit his lawyer when a once-familiar voice stopped him in his tracks. 'So you have returned, Harry.'

He whirled round and stared at the woman standing in the shadows. His eyes narrowed. 'What are you doing here, Ingrid? You're taking a risk, aren't you?'

She responded with a tinkle of laughter. 'I am flattered you recognised me so easily despite my disguise. Now I am known as Sister Birgetta,' she said, dancing out of the alley next to the tavern into the light and within a couple of feet of him. Instantly she started back.

'I was told about your disfigurement, but I did not expect it to be so ugly,' she gasped. 'Master Larsson was right. You are not the man you used to be.'

The muscles of Harry's face tightened. 'You should have stayed in the convent, Ingrid. Then you might not have turned out so cruel, murderous and treacherous.'

She fixed him with cold pale blue eyes. 'I see you have been discussing me with that conniving, crafty Scottish witch you married. No doubt she tricked you into it, but now you know who you are, Harry, you must realise your mistake?'

'Don't refer to my wife so rudely,' said Harry in a dangerously low voice. 'If you think because you are dressed as a religious that I won't treat you as you deserve for that insult, then it is *you* who are mistaken.'

Ingrid laughed. 'Why so angry, Harry? Is it because you know I am speaking the truth? I'm surprised at you for allowing yourself to be fooled into marrying a thieving pirate's daughter. But perhaps it was because Bridget told you that she could lead you to her father's treasure. You can't trust her, Harry.'

'You're the person I cannot trust,' said Harry, seizing Ingrid by the front of her white habit and lifting her off her feet. 'Another remark like that and I'll throw you in the river. What are you doing snooping around here, anyway? You should have more care for your life, Ingrid. You should be punished for your actions, especially your involvement in my sister's abduction.'

'Bridget speaks falsely! I order you to put me down,' screamed Ingrid, clawing at his hand.

'And if I don't? What will you do?' He raised her higher in the air.

Her screams now began to draw attention to them, but Harry ignored those who were watching. She cursed him and Bridget in her own tongue and Harry decided enough was enough. He carried her over to the edge of the quayside. 'Do you really want me to put you down, Ingrid?'

Fear caused her face to twitch. 'You wouldn't, Harry. Remember the good times we had when we were younger. You loved me then.'

'What I felt for you was not love, but the foolish longings of a youth.'

'I don't believe you!' She spat in his face.

He noticed that there were a couple of men tending their nets on the shore not far away, so he opened his hand and released her. She seemed to float in the air for several moments and then she landed in a patch of mud a few feet beneath with a splat. She scrabbled to gain a foothold and her white habit swiftly became smeared with filth. Obscenities streamed from her mouth. Harry saw that the two men had paused in their task and were now watching Ingrid's struggles.

'God's Blood, captain, yer've done it now,' said Joe, appearing at his shoulder. 'She'll be putting a spell on yer next. I heard from a lad I know who works in one of the taverns that she talks to some right unsavoury characters.'

Harry wiped his face on his sleeve and turned round. 'You recognise her, Joe?'

'Aye, Captain. She's Ingrid Wrangel who yer were friendly with once. I saw her talking to Master Larsson early this morning.'

Harry frowned. 'Where is the Baron's ship anchored? I would speak with Christian myself.'

'She's already set sail for Preston, Captain.'

'Do you know if Master Larsson was aboard?'

'I couldn't say. Do yer want me to keep an eye on the so-called nun down there? I wouldn't like her to cause yer trouble. According to Josh, she was hand in glove with one of those hard-up lords whose father was killed at Bosworth. They stole her ladyship's jewellery box from her mansion, yer know. The lord then went and got himself killed in an attack with several ruffians on a party of pilgrims.'

Joe's words gave Harry cause for serious thought. 'Aye, Joe. You do that for me. I must speak with Hans again and tell him that I want him to set sail for Preston as soon as possible. He might even catch up with Alex's ship that's heading that way.'

'So what will you be doing, Captain?'

'I want to get my wife away from London. Who knows what Ingrid might have been plotting? After I have spoken to Hans and seen my lawyer, I will return to Lady Elizabeth's mansion, and Josh and I will make ready the horses. I would like to set out for Appleby Manor early this evening. We will travel only as far as that inn we stayed at in St Albans a few years ago. A horse will be left for you if you are not back by then. Follow us as soon as you are able and meet up with us there.'

'I remember the inn,' said Joe, his eyes bright with excitement.

'Good. Keep your head low and I will see you later.'

'Aye, aye, Captain.' Joe saluted.

Harry clapped him on the shoulder and strode away.

'How are you feeling, Bridget?' asked Harry.

Bridget looked up into her husband's face and instantly rose from the garden seat. 'What has happened?'

'Naught for you to fret about,' he said easily. 'I have decided that I would like to spend a little more time in my sister's company, so we should set out early this evening. That way you will be on horseback only for a short time and I have bought a pillion seat for you. You will be able to rest at the inn in St Albans. Do you feel well enough to agree to that plan, Bridget?'

Bridget hesitated, wondering if he was being completely honest with her about his reason for setting out this evening. She knew him well enough now to know when he was keeping something from her. Still, she decided not to waste time asking him again. Instead, she said, 'It sounds a sensible plan. I shall have Dorcas help me to pack our belongings.'

'Good!' He looked relieved and wasted no time in hurrying to the stables.

Bridget turned to Dorcas, but the girl was already on her feet and it was obvious that she had overheard Harry's words. They wasted no time going inside the house. It took them scarcely any time at all to pack their belongings, but it was only at the last moment that Bridget remembered her husband's shaving gear. She pushed it down the side of the leather bag.

Dorcas carried the larger bag downstairs and dumped it outside the front of the house, and Bridget followed with a smaller bag. Already Joshua had brought round one of the horses and he began the task of tying the baggage on to the beast.

Mistress Tyler came outside to see what was happening. Bridget explained to her about Harry's reason for them leaving that evening. She suggested that although they should be able to have supper at the inn, that they should take some bread, cheese and cold meats, as well as a flagon of ale, just in case they couldn't. 'No doubt the roads will be dusty and you'll get parched.'

Bridget thanked her.

In no time at all Bridget was accepting Harry's help up into the pillion seat. She settled herself into it and when he asked was she comfortable, assured him that a cushion would not go amiss. Instantly he sent Dorcas to fetch one.

It was only as Dorcas was handing up the cushion that she confessed that she had never ridden a horse in her life. She glanced up nervously at the other beast.

'Then you will have to ride with the baggage,' said Bridget, smiling encouragingly. 'Hang on tightly and Josh will ride his horse and attach a leading rein to the baggage horse. You should be safe enough as we will not be doing any galloping.'

Mistress Tyler appeared with food and the flagon of ale, and Harry placed it in one of the saddle bags. The housekeeper wished them Godspeed. Bridget thanked her for her assistance, and soon they were riding down the drive and out of the mansion gates.

They travelled in the direction of Fleet Street, but instead of heading into the city centre, Harry turned up Shoe Lane which led to Fleet Hill and eventually out into the countryside. There they paused to look down on London. Suddenly Bridget realised that Joe was missing and asked why he was not with them.

'He'll follow us on,' said Harry, tossing the words over his shoulder. 'He had a task to do for me, but hopefully it will not delay him for long and he will join us at the inn in St Albans.'

Bridget wondered if this task had aught to do with her father. Suddenly it occurred to her that Harry might have discovered that Patrick O'Malley had found out that her father was to blame for torching his ship and had set out to revenge that act. He could be in London and looking for her. She had hoped that she and Harry could be honest with each other now, but perhaps she was mistaken. Of course, it was possible that he was keeping such a secret from her because he did not want her worrying. Perhaps he realised that she was still fretting over losing the baby and would do so for some time to come. She decided to keep quiet about her suspicions for now.

Bridget was weary and stiff by the time they arrived at the inn in St Albans. Harry helped her to dismount before going inside the inn to make enquiries about a bedchamber. When he returned, Bridget was relieved that he had managed to bespeak one. He suggested that she go upstairs immediately with Dorcas and rest. He had arranged for a supper to be sent up to them.

'But what about you?' she asked.

'I'm going to retrace some of our journey to see if there is any sign of Joe.'

'Could Joshua not do that?'

'He is seeing to the other horses. I will not be long, so do not fret.' The next moment he was gone.

Her husband's attempt to stem any worry she felt only served to make her believe that there could be some truth in what she had thought earlier. She had no doubt that if Patrick O'Malley could not get his hands on her father, then he would like to capture her. Harry obviously considered it his primary duty as her husband to protect her and that is why they'd left London so swiftly and so late in the day. She decided that she had no option but to do as he suggested and retire to the bedchamber and partake of supper when it arrived. She would leave the provisions that Mrs Tyler had provided for the morrow.

Bridget woke from a dream in which she was cradling a baby in her arms and realised that she must have dozed off. She felt that ache of loss inside her chest and sighed. Then she opened her eyes and saw to her amazement that dawn was not far off. There was a scratching at the door and she heard her husband's voice whispering her name. She felt a burst of unexpected joy and scrambled out of bed and went and unlocked the door.

Harry was leaning against the door jamb, looking windblown and weary. He smiled down at her. 'I beg your pardon for arriving so late.'

She took hold of his arm and drew him inside. 'You are safe and that is all that matters. Did you find Joe?'

'Aye. His horse had thrown a shoe.'

'As long as that is all it was that kept him.'

'What else could there be?' asked Harry, gazing down at her sleep-flushed cheeks.

She hesitated and then said, 'I thought you might have had tidings about my father.'

'No, I would have told you if I'd had news of him.' Harry glanced in the direction of the bed where Dorcas was curled up fast asleep. Bridget's eyes followed his and she said, 'I am sorry. She kept me company and she was telling me about her mother and of how she had looked after her younger siblings who sadly died young when she suddenly fell asleep.'

Harry frowned. 'You should have discouraged her from telling you such tales. They will only upset you. I suggest you wake her and we make an early start.'

'I know children can die at such an early age. One cannot close one's eyes to the realities of life,' she murmured, reaching out and picking a length of cotton from his doublet. 'But Dorcas and her brothers survived, so I am not downcast.'

'Joe brought me news that the *St Bridget* has set sail for Preston in the wake of the Baron's ship. It could take her two weeks or more to reach there.'

'Is the cradle still aboard?'

Harry nodded and thought he caught the sheen of tears in her eyes. He felt a sudden lump in his throat, wondering if the child had been a boy or a girl as lovely as her mother. He reached out and placed his gloved hand against her face. She rested her cheek there a moment and then drew away from him as there came a sound from the bed. Both glanced in that direction and saw the humped shape of Dorcas moving.

'We'll talk some more later,' he said, and pressed a kiss on his wife's mouth before leaving her alone with Dorcas.

Bridget ran a finger over her tingling lips and would have liked to have had the chance to kiss him back. Then she remembered the need for haste and went over to the bed. 'Up with you, Dorcas. My husband has returned and we must be on our way.'

The maid poked her untidy head out of the bedcovers and blinked at her like a drowsy cat in the dawn light. 'So what kept the master?'

'Joe's horse threw a shoe. You've yet to meet Joe. He is an orphan the same as you. Now we must be out of here before the master returns and hammers on the door, asking us why we are taking so long.'

A few hours later Bridget was feeling reasonably cheerful. The sight of so much greenery and trees in blossom as well as wild flowers growing in meadows and rampantly in the hedgerows was wonderfully uplifting after being at sea for so long.

'Do you think you will ever become accustomed to the countryside as you were to gazing out over the sea, Harry?' she asked, resting a hand on his muscular shoulder and bringing her head close to the back of his.

'I wonder,' he murmured, overwhelmingly aware of her physical presence and enjoying the *frisson* of pleasure caused by her breasts pressing against his back. 'What are *your* feelings about living in the countryside? It is not as if you have done so in the past. I remember Callum telling me that your grandparents' home in Ireland was near the sea.'

'That is true and it is also true that my Scottish grandfather's castle overlooks a sea loch.'

'Appleby Manor is miles from the sea, but I have been

told that the Irish Sea can be seen from a tower that is part of the manor house.'

'I suppose Josh told you that or perhaps it was the Baron,' said Bridget.

'They both told me of it,' said Harry, 'and I was reminded of a recurring dream of mine that Josh has now convinced me is no dream, but a memory.'

'Tell me about your memories?' asked Bridget.

So Harry told her and she listened intently and eventually said, 'I agree that these are memories. It is possible, Harry, that you cannot remember everything about when you were a boy because one does forget places and faces and events if they are commonplace and one is not seeing them constantly.'

'That does make sense,' said Harry.

'Perhaps when you have spent a few days at Appleby and ridden about your fields and woods you will have that sense of having been there before.'

'That is what I am hoping,' said Harry. 'But you have not answered my question. What are your feelings about living in the countryside?'

I would be content living anywhere with you, said a little voice in her head. That thought had only come to her recently and she did not yet have the courage to speak it aloud. For it could only mean that she had grown to love him despite that which had threatened to keep them apart.

'I accept now that my place is by your side and I am looking forward, a little apprehensively, I confess, to making our home there.'

He glanced over his shoulder. 'I, too, am apprehensive. What if those in my employ take a dislike of me and consider me a complete lackwit? They will know that I have been a mariner for most of my life and that I come to the role I am to fill knowing so little.'

'I am certain if you confess that to them, then they will know you are not an arrogant man, but a master prepared to learn and do your best for them,' said Bridget. 'Besides, it is my opinion that they will be glad to welcome you. They must have known for some time that Rosamund will eventually have to leave with the Baron and wondered what would happen to Appleby Manor if you were not found. It could be that they thought the manor might be sold to someone who has no real attachment to the home where you were born.'

Harry nodded. 'I had not thought of that.'

She smiled. 'Then consider it now and do not worry so much.'

'I will do what you advise, but it would have been so much better if—' He stopped, about to say *you had not miscarried our child*.

'If what?' asked Bridget. 'If you had never been abducted and been able to grow up in the place where you belonged?'

'Aye,' said Harry, relieved that she could not read his thoughts.

'Yet, Harry, so much that is good would not have happened if you had remained at home. Most likely you would never have made the acquaintance of the Baron and other folk who I am sure enriched your life.'

He could see the truth of that and fell silent, thinking back over his life and thinking that Bridget had not mentioned the most important person in his life. Herself.

'Did you get to see Master Larsson?' she asked, taking him by surprise.

'No, I did not,' said Harry. 'Why do you ask?'

'It just occurred to me that he might still be serving aboard the Baron's ship. If that is so, then he will be in the north at the same time as we are,' said Bridget. 'Do you think he will want to see you?'

'For what reason?'

'Perhaps he has had time to regret what he said to you and would like to ask your forgiveness and be friends again? I do not like the man, but you knew each other for such a long time.'

'I'd like to believe that,' said Harry, thinking that in the light of what he knew of Christian Larsson's behaviour since reaching London, he was more inclined to believe the opposite.

'But you don't,' said Bridget.

'No,' admitted Harry.

After their exchange about Christian Larsson they were silent for a long time. She thought that he thought she was foolish to have made such a suggestion, while Harry wondered if he should have told Bridget his reason for feeling the way he did, but then he would have to tell her about his meeting with Ingrid, and just thinking of that encounter left a bad taste in his mouth. He would also have to tell her what Joe had told him about the company Ingrid was keeping lately, and he would rather not worry Bridget about that.

Their small party halted only for a short while to take refreshment at an inn, then they were on their way again. Now Bridget rallied and they passed the time talking about what might need doing at the house and the proximity of the nearest market town and port. They discussed furniture, something that neither of them had ever had need to do before. Bridget still found it difficult to believe that she was to be the lady of the manor. She thought about her father and what he might say if he returned and learnt that she was married to Harry Appleby, alias Black Harry. She would have felt pleasure to have been able to tell him that he was to be a grandfather. She wished for the umpteenth time that she had not miscarried their baby.

Soon after Harry insisted on Bridget having a rest and during that time there was a heated exchange between Joe and Dorcas. Changes had been made when they had set out again, which resulted in Dorcas having to sit behind Joe, holding on to his belt, whilst Joshua led the baggage horse and kept a watch out to the rear for sign of any trouble. The problem was that Joe was not pleased about Dorcas sharing his horse.

'She never stops talking,' he told Harry. 'I called her a lackwit and had to tell her to shut up.'

'And what did she say to that?' asked Harry, trying to look severe.

'That she was no fool and stuck her tongue out at me, so I caught hold of it and she didn't half get annoyed.' He grinned at the memory. 'She's got plenty of spirit. If it weren't for her broken nose, she wouldn't be half bad looking.'

Bridget was amused but said, 'Be kind to her, Joe. She had a tough life even before she became an orphan. Her father was cruel to her and she is not to blame for her appearance. It is what comes from our heart and thoughts that matter, not what we look like.'

Her words caused not only Joe to look thoughtful, but Harry, too. Did his wife really mean what she said and was it possible that she accepted the way he looked? Perhaps she now believed that the sad loss of their baby was the foulest thing to happen to them since they exchanged their vows. He could only pray that was so as he watched Joe helping Dorcas on to his horse with a kind word and a smile.

They set out again and Harry thought what a great responsibility it was rearing children, so that they were able to cope with all that life threw at them. Despite Dorcas's father's treatment of her, the girl had not lost her spirit. He wished he could remember those early years of his life when he had known his parents. Joshua had spoken of them at length, but he had not been there with Harry during those times he was alone with his father or mother and his sister. He could only pray that when, if, he and Bridget did have other children, he would be able to make a decent job of being a father. At least the begetting of them would be a pleasure. Just the thought of making love to Bridget roused him, but he decided it would be sensible not to allow his thoughts to wander along such paths whilst on horseback!

Chapter Fourteen

It was early evening on the fifth day that they arrived at an inn in Leicester. The road had been busy because it was that time of year when people were going on pilgrimage and the only spaces available were in a communal sleeping chamber. They spent that night sleeping fitfully on pallets. Harry was concerned about Bridget's comfort and safety.

The following evening the next inn was just as busy, so that Harry felt it necessary that he, Joe and Joshua took turns to keep watch during the night. In such a situation one never knew whether there was a thief or even a cutthroat amongst those lying on the floor.

It was Dorcas who hinted that they could be being followed the following evening. 'Why d'yer think that?' asked Joe, helping her down from the horse. 'There's that many folk on the road yer'd have trouble spotting any one person unless yer'd seen them before.'

'It's just a feeling I have,' said the maid with a sniff. 'Me mother used to have these feelings, too.'

'I think the captain will need more than just yer feelings before being convinced,' said Joe.

Dorcas jutted her chin. 'Yer can say what yer like, but I'm going to keep me peepers open. I don't want to wake up with me throat cut in the night.'

Joe chuckled. 'Yer'd have a job doing that.'

She giggled. 'See what yer mean.' She hurried into the inn in Bridget's wake, leaving him staring after her.

Joe knew that he couldn't just ignore her words and so, with an air of embarrassment, he mentioned what Dorcas had said to Harry. 'I know it sounds daft, Captain, but do yer consider there is a possibility of us being followed?'

'Maybe,' said Harry, stroking his scar. 'You take the horses to the stables and I'll have a word with Dorcas, yourself and Josh later. Now I must see what accommodation is available.'

He knew that Bridget was beginning to flag and that she needed some privacy and a good night's sleep, so he hurried inside the inn and spoke to the innkeeper. He was smiling when he came out of the inn and found Bridget leaning against the wall. 'I have bribed the innkeeper to let us have his own bedchamber,' he said.

Her face lit up. 'Thank you, Harry. I know if I had to lie on a hard pallet on the floor again I must, but I am so glad I do not have to listen to people coughing and shifting about tonight.'

He wondered if she thought that he should have done more for her comfort and felt as if he had proved less than the best of husbands. 'I must speak to the others. You go inside and the innkeeper's wife will show you the room. I will join you as soon as I can and we will have supper together in private.'

Bridget walked wearily into the inn and Harry's eyes followed her. He would be glad when they reached Appleby Manor. He only spoke briefly to Dorcas before suggesting that she go to see if her mistress needed her help. Then he told Josh and Joe that he wanted them to take turns keeping a watch that night and to let him know if they saw anyone they recognised.

When Harry entered the bedchamber not long after, Bridget had already changed out of the clothes she had worn day after day and was wearing her night rail and robe. She had loosened her hair and he could not resist kissing her whilst twisting a strand of her wavy auburn hair between his fingers. 'You are so beautiful,' he said.

She blushed and briefly touched his cheek. He wondered what she was thinking when she touched his scar. Was she remembering the first time she had done so in the darkness of the cabin on the ship? How he had deceived her? Had she forgiven him for doing so? Perhaps she could forgive, but never forget. She had wandered over to the table and now sat down. 'We must be sensible and eat this supper that the innkeeper's good wife has prepared for us,' she said.

He sat down at the small table and soon they were making short work of the stewed rabbit in an herb, onion and barley broth with crusty brown bread. The food was washed down by an excellent ale and they talked little, content to be alone and tired after the day's travelling.

Once the food had been cleared away they went to bed. Bridget was drowsy and appeared to have fallen asleep to Harry, who lay with an arm across her. He wanted her, yet found it comforting just to cuddle up close. Completely relaxed he was not, because he had to keep under control his desire for her and also part of his mind was occupied with thoughts of those who might be following them. He gave serious thought to Ingrid's wish for revenge because of his losing his temper and dropping her in the mud. At least Bridget was safe here in this bedchamber with him.

Bridget felt the aches and pains and tensions of the day drifting away as she relaxed beneath her husband's protective arm. She had a sense of well-being because at last it seemed that all was coming right between them. Harry might not love her, but she believed that he cared for her, and for the moment that was enough. Whether in the days to come that would prove to be so, she was not going to worry about now. Sleepy with fresh air and exhausted with travelling she fell asleep.

When Harry woke it was dark and at first he had no notion of what it was that had woken him. Cautiously he sat up in bed, so as not to disturb Bridget, and could not resist pressing his lips against her bare shoulder where her night rail had slipped down. She did not stir.

Suddenly he became aware of whispering voices outside the window. He strained his ears, hoping to be able to make out what was being said, but when he couldn't, he slid out of bed and carefully parted the curtains.

Harry was just in time to see a robed figure go over to the stables. There was no sign of whoever it was he or she had been conversing with, but Harry's suspicions were aroused. He wondered where Joe or Joshua were and whether they were aware of what was happening outside.

As he turned away from the window, there came a tapping on the door of the bedchamber. He snatched up his hose from the floor and dragged them on before tiptoeing across the floor. 'Is that you, Joe?' he whispered.

'No, Master Appleby, it's Dorcas. I thought I'd best let yer know that neither Joe nor Joshua have come to their pallets.'

'All right, Dorcas. Go downstairs and unlock the back door if need be. I'll join you in a few moments.'

He wondered if Joe had fetched Joshua because he needed his help, both having decided not to disturb him and Bridget. He dressed swiftly and was fastening his doublet when Bridget's sleepy voice said, 'I've been dreaming and a thought has occurred to me.'

'Tell me later,' said Harry.

He crept downstairs and when he reached the bottom, Dorcas came out of the shadows. 'Is them being missing aught to do with what I told yer, Master Appleby?' she whispered.

'Aye, most likely.'

Harry opened the outside door cautiously, looked about him and, seeing no one, went outside. Dorcas followed him as he headed for the stables. The door was open. He paused and listened and thought he heard groaning. He ordered Dorcas to wait and slipped inside.

There to his relief he found Joe still alive and trying to sit up. He left him a moment and searched the stables, but found no one hiding there.

Joe had sank back on to a heap of straw. Harry shook his shoulder and the lad tried to sit up again, but had trouble doing so. Worried, Harry hoisted him on to his shoulder and carried him outside and leaned him against the wall. The lad's knees sagged and Harry said, 'Come on, Joe, wake up!'

'Is he gonna be all right?' asked Dorcas.

The lad opened his eyelids, only to close them again. He winced and then peered between his eyelids at Harry and Dorcas. 'God's Blood, Captain, I should have seen her coming. I've a terrible head.'

'I shouldn't have left you to keep watch alone,' said Harry.

'Not your fault, Captain. I shouldn't have allowed myself to be distracted by the sight of the Danish witch.'

'Ingrid!'

'Aye, Dorcas was right and we were being followed by one of the bully boys she recognised as living in her street. He was with Ingrid and there was another man dressed as a monk. I didn't see his face,' said Joe.

He staggered away from the wall and, before Harry could prevent him, doused his head in the horse trough. 'That's better,' said the lad, shaking his dripping head and wiping his hand over his wet face. 'I tell you what, Captain—'

But Harry was not listening; he had already whirled round to make his way back to the inn. He had remembered that he had not locked the bedchamber door and was worried in case Ingrid or either man reached Bridget. He was stopped in his tracks by the sight of his wife hurrying towards him.

'What is happening?' she called in a low voice.

Harry seized her arm. 'You shouldn't have left the bedchamber, but stayed there and locked the door.'

'Too late for that now. Is it Patrick O'Malley?' she asked, gazing up into her husband's shadowy features.

'What has he to do with this? Don't answer that right now,' he said swiftly. 'Explain later. I want you back inside. You shouldn't be outside in your robe and slippers. Dorcas, go with your mistress back to the inn.'

Bridget did not move. 'If Patrick O'Malley is not following us, then who is?' she asked.

Harry hesitated. 'Do as I say, Bridget! This isn't the place for such a conversation.'

For a moment he thought she was going to disobey him but then she turned quickly and walked away with her robe fluttering about her ankles. Dorset followed her.

'So what do we do next?' enquired Joe. 'And where's Josh?'

'We'll think about that after we've seen the women to the bedchamber,' said Harry. 'I wouldn't put it past our enemies to have slipped inside whilst we've been talking.' Without more ado he and Joe followed Bridget and Dorcas across the stable yard towards the inn.

Bridget glanced over her shoulder once and then disappeared inside. Harry wasted no time in following her and Dorcas upstairs, but when they reached the bedchamber, he pushed them aside and went in first. He could see no sign of entry via the window and after a quick search knew there was no one hiding in the room. 'You and Dorcas remain here until I return,' he said to Bridget. 'Lock the door after me.'

Bridget opened her mouth to protest, but he was gone.

Joe looked up at Harry, but he held his finger to his lips and the lad was silent until they were downstairs. Only then did he whisper, 'What do yer think has happened to Josh, Captain?'

'We'll make a search for him. He's either followed them or is unconscious and concealed somewhere.'

'Yer don't think he's dead?' asked Joe, a tremor in his voice.

'Let's not think the worst,' said Harry, looking down at the lad. 'Perhaps you'd best stay here and rest after that knock on the head.'

'I'd rather watch yer back, Captain.'

They went outside and instantly Harry became aware of the sleepy chirruping of birds and realised that dawn was not far off. He made a quick search of the outhouses and the surrounding area and found a man sprawled under a tree. For a moment his heart misgave him, but then he realised that it was not Joshua. He felt for a pulse and discovered the man was dead. Had Joshua killed him, or someone else? He would inform the innkeeper and leave him to deal with the corpse.

'I'm going to check our horses, Joe,' he said quietly, for he had not done so earlier whilst in the stables.

He did so and discovered that Joshua's mount was missing. 'He's followed them,' said Harry, coming outside.

'What do we do?' asked Joe.

Harry's dark brows knit. 'We continue with our journey. Ingrid and her companion must have realised that we're aware of their presence and won't try anything here again.'

'What do yer think was their plan, Captain?' asked Joe.

'Murder, abduction?' Harry's expression was grim.

'What are yer going to tell the missus?'

'If she hasn't already wormed the truth out of Dorcas, then I will tell her the truth,' said Harry, who was not looking forward to doing so.

He rapped his knuckles on the panel of the door and spoke his name in a low voice. A few moments later he heard the door being unlocked and it swung open to reveal Bridget dressed for travelling. She did not look at him, but moved further back into the room that was filling with daylight. There was no sign of Dorcas.

'So—' said Bridget, looking him squarely in the face as he closed the door behind him.

'What has Dorcas told you?'

'Enough for me to realise that you have kept secret from me an encounter with Ingrid.' She struggled to keep her voice steady, not wanting to reveal how hurt she felt.

'Dorcas could not know the whole of it,' said Harry, rubbing his scar.

'I knew *none* of it,' cried Bridget, turning her back on him and going over to the window.

'I did not want you to worry. I dealt with her as I saw fit.'

Bridget whirled round and her eyes glinted with anger. 'Why did you not hand her over to the sheriff?

She is a known felon. Is it that you could not bring yourself to do so because you still feel something for her despite what I and others have told you about her?'

'Now you are talking nonsense,' said Harry, his temper rising. 'I would have thought that by now you would know me better. I despise her as much as you do.'

'I cannot believe that is true.'

'Why? Because I once believed myself in love with her?'

Bridget was silent, sensing that this was an argument that neither of them was going to win. She began to gather her belongings together and put them in a canvas bag.

'Anyway, what is this about Patrick O'Malley?' asked Harry. 'Did something happen whilst I was away from the house that causes you to believe he might have been in London and followed us?'

'No! I sensed that you were keeping something from me and mistakenly believed it concerned him,' said Bridget in a low voice. She changed the subject. 'Will we be making an early start? The sooner this journey is over the better.'

'At least we can agree on that,' said Harry. 'Joshua is missing, but there is little point in us waiting for him. He knows our destination and will follow us on if he has not returned before we go.'

'You think he has followed her?'

'Aye. We found the dead body of a man. Hopefully, Dorcas will be able to identify him before we go.'

'But Ingrid is not alone, is she?' said Bridget, her voice rising. 'Dorcas mentioned a monk.'

'That could be a disguise,' said Harry.

'My exact thoughts.'

'So who do you think it might be?' asked Bridget.

'I cannot say for certain. Maybe we will have an answer before this month of June is out.'

Harry gathered his possessions together and unlocked the door. 'Shall we go?' he said.

Bridget nodded and swept out of the bedchamber, recalling the meal they had shared and how she had felt secure and content beneath his arm in bed. Now that contentment was shattered by Harry keeping secrets from her about a woman he'd once had strong feelings for.

Joshua had still not made an appearance by the time they were ready to leave. They could all only hope that he was safe. Harry especially had come to value his loyalty and common sense since they had met in Lisbon and would not like to lose him. He decided he must have faith in the other man's abilities to survive as his own priority was Bridget's safety.

Both Harry and Joe were very much on their guard as they travelled further north, keeping a lookout for anyone who seemed to be taking too much interest in their small party. He and Bridget barely spoke to each other. She wondered if she would ever be able to trust Harry to be honest with her.

They crossed the Cheshire border and it was now that Harry became obsessed by thoughts of his reunion with his sister. Joshua had told him that Rosamund had been broken-hearted when she had been told that he was dead. He longed to see her, yet still feared that he might be a disappointment to her because the boy she remembered no longer existed, and she would be confronted with the scarred face of a man who was a stranger to her.

Two days later they had crossed the border into the Palatine of Lancashire, and it was now that Harry began to ask the way to Lathom House, one of the homes of the Earl of Derby. It was a well-known landmark, and only a few miles from Appleby Manor. After a couple of hours they began to pass fields of growing wheat and peas and greens. There were orchards on which the blossom was fading and all seemed peaceful. As they drew nearer to the house that now appeared amongst the trees and shrubs, Harry saw that it was built of sandstone and that sunlight reflecting off latticed windows. He noticed a tower jutting up at one side and knew that this was Appleby Manor house. He felt a leap of the heart and turned to look at Bridget to see what she thought of it, but her eyes were looking straight past him.

The front door opened and a woman emerged. Behind her came a man with a child in his arms. Harry's heartbeat quickened and, within moments, he had brought his horse to a halt. He gazed down upon the dark-haired woman standing a yard or so away from him. She was smiling up at him through the tears that shimmered in her violet eyes.

'Harry, it has to be you because you are as Alex described you,' she said, stretching up a hand to him. 'I am your sister Rosamund and I have longed for this moment.'

Harry forced down the lump in his throat and removed his riding glove. His strong fingers curled about those of his sister and still he could not speak for the emotion he felt.

'Well, Harry, it's not like you to be lost for words,' teased Alex.

'I am remembering a dream in which a dark-haired little girl waved frantically to me from a tower,' said Harry in husky tones. 'The mind is truly strange in what it chooses to remember and what to forget.'

'I was that girl,' said Rosamund, tears trickling down her cheeks. 'It was the last time I caught sight of you and you were shouting a warning to me. Welcome home, my dear, dear brother.'

Harry slid down from his horse and he and Rosamund hugged each other, his scarred cheek resting on her dark head.

Bridget bit down hard on her lower lip to control its trembling as she gazed at her husband and his sister. She almost felt envious of their feelings for each other. She looked away and caught Alex's eye. He winked at her and she brushed away a tear and forced a smile.

Alex summoned one of the maids who had suddenly appeared and handed his son to her. Then he helped Bridget down from the pillion seat.

'I am glad to see this day,' he said.

'I, too. It feels as if we have been waiting a long time for it to arrive,' she murmured, telling herself that envy must have no place here.

At the sound of his wife's voice, Harry lifted his head and gazed at Bridget. As they stared at each other something unexpected happened. In the light of their quarrel over Ingrid, it seemed almost magical. They exchanged smiles and Harry felt such a swell of emotion that he knew that he had to make matters right between them. He held out his hand to her. She moved forwards and clasped it and he drew her close, so that he encapsulated both Bridget and Rosamund in his embrace.

'I am so glad to see you both happy,' said Bridget, knowing she must forgive him for keeping his encounter with Ingrid from her.

The two women kissed each other and then both kissed Harry before bursting out laughing with exultation.

'Can I join in?' asked Alex, grinning.

'Of course! Come, dearest,' said Rosamund, drawing him in to the circle. 'Let us savour this moment before all too soon—' She did not finish what she was about to say because a baby began to wail. She pulled a droll face. 'Is that not typical? Do you not find just when you are in the middle of something that needs saying, it is interrupted?'

Bridget watched as Rosamund took her child from the maid and hushed him. 'So this is your son,' murmured Bridget, gazing down at the child with a tender expression on her face and firmly suppressing her own feelings of loss. 'May I hold him?'

'Of course, but I warn you that he is damp,' said Rosamund.

Bridget took the wriggling baby and gazed down into his handsome features. Then she felt Harry's hand on her shoulder. 'He has your eyes, Rosamund,' he said.

'I wish that you both could have been here when he was born,' said his sister. 'We would have liked you to be Douglas's godparents. Harry, he wore the robe that we wore when we were baptised. You will not remember, but it is made of silk and has tiny seed pearls sewn into it. Perhaps when you and Bridget—' She stopped short. 'I beg your pardons. Alex only arrived a few hours ago and told me of your miscarriage, Bridget. I am so sorry. Let us pray that it will not be long before you conceive again,' she added, touching both her brother's and Bridget's arms with a gentle hand.

Bridget thanked her and darted Harry a glance. 'May I hold my nephew?' he asked.

'Of course,' she said instantly.

Their hands brushed as she passed Douglas to him and she gazed into his face as he clutched his nephew to him and saw it through a sheen of tears.

'Greetings, nephew,' said Harry unsteadily. 'It is a pleasure to meet you.'

Douglas stilled a moment and then, seizing a handful of the sleeve of Harry's doublet, dragged himself up so that he was able to perch on his uncle's other arm. He peered into Harry's face and patted his scarred cheek.

'Don't do that, Douglas!' exclaimed Rosamund.

'It is all right, sister,' said Harry, seizing the boy's hand and pretending to nibble his fingers. Douglas chuckled and Harry grinned. Obviously his nephew did not find him repulsive.

'Well, I never,' said Alex. 'Never did I expect to see you so swiftly adept at entertaining my son, Harry.'

'Nor I,' said Bridget, thinking about what Rosamund had said about her and Harry conceiving another child. She wanted that so much but worried that she might do so and have her hopes raised, only to miscarry again.

Rosamund said, 'It is obvious that my brother has an affinity with children, but it cannot be comfortable for him to have a damp *derrière* sitting on his arm. I will give Douglas to his nursemaid and she can change him. Then he will be in a more pleasing condition to entertain his uncle.'

Harry handed his nephew over to his sister. 'I hope to see a lot of you both before you leave for Scotland.'

Rosamund sighed. 'It is a sadness to me that we will have to leave only too soon, but we cannot delay the journey for much longer.'

'I understand that you and Alex have been putting off the moment for my sake,' said Harry. 'I appreciate all you have done here.'

'It was the least we could do for you,' said Rosamund, her voice husky. 'But let us not mar this time with anticipating the moment of parting. This day is one of the happiest of my life. I feel that we are at last a complete family and, wherever we are, there is naught that can change that now.'

'I thought of you often when I was in places where I was unable to receive word of you,' said Bridget.

'Aye, you, too,' said Rosamund softly.

Alex said, 'You have all suffered greatly, but it is over now. Let us forget the difficult times and rejoice in the present.' He paused and said, 'So what do the two of you think of your new home?'

Bridget and Harry gazed up at the house. 'I find it difficult to believe that this interesting edifice belongs to me,' he said, experiencing pride and emotion.

'It needs renovating inside,' said Rosamund. 'Our stepmother used to complain that Father was always reluctant to spend money on the house. Most of it went back into the business and the land.'

'You'll get a better view of your property from the tower,' said Alex.

'Later,' said Rosamund. 'I deem that Bridget is impatient to see what it is like inside. You lead the way, Harry.'

Harry hesitated and then did as his sister told him. Bridget was only a few feet behind him.

Chapter Fifteen

The hall was far grander than Harry had imagined, with a double flight of stairs leading to the first floor at the far end. The walls had obviously had their spring whitewash to rid the place of the grime caused by the winter fires. There were no hangings, so he presumed they had been taken down to be beaten.

'The house dates back to the time of Edward the Second,' said Rosamund.

'A hundred and fifty years ago,' he murmured. 'Hence the need for the tower and thick walls, necessary during those unruly times. The Scots were known to raid this far south.' He exchanged glances with Bridget and smiled.

'Did Josh tell you that?' she asked.

He did not answer, but continued to gaze about the hall, as the memories came flooding back. It felt most peculiar, remembering the fireplace and the chimney being built. 'No, I remember.' He grinned. 'I deem it is time for a toast. If you could summon one of the servants, Rosamund.'

His sister gazed at him with a wondering expression on her face and did as he requested. The man who responded to her call gazed wide-eyed at Harry.

'Master Harry!' he exclaimed.

'You recognise me?' asked Harry.

'Aye, that I do. Yer've changed somewhat, been through the wars by the look of that scar, but yer've got a look of the old master. It's good to see yer back.'

'Is it, Will?' asked Harry, putting a hand to his head.

'Aye, Master Harry.' He beamed at him.

Harry asked him to bring some wine for the ladies and tankards of ale for himself and the Baron. Will hurried away and Harry was aware that he was the focus of four pairs of eyes. 'I know what you're going to say,' he murmured, and sat down suddenly on a chair.

'Your memory really is coming back,' said Bridget, sitting on a chair and gazing at him in delight.

'How much do you remember?' asked Rosamund.

'I don't know. Information about this hall came to me in a flash.'

'How strange,' said Bridget.

'Isn't it,' said Harry, puzzled himself. 'How could I forget so much about myself, family and this place and now remember it?'

'Most likely it is one of those mysteries that we'll never know the answer to,' said Alex. 'I mean your forgetting all that you did and now remembering it is a puzzle.'

Rosamund smiled. 'So you will not need me to act as your guide and to tell you tales of our childhood and parents that Joshua could not tell you.'

Harry returned her smile. 'I would not entirely agree with what you say. I am certain there is much that I have simply forgotten due to the passage of time.'

There was a silence and suddenly Rosamund asked, 'Where is Joshua, by the way? I did not notice him earlier.'

Bridget and Harry looked at each other and before either could decide what to say in way of a reply, Will and one of the maidservants appeared with their drinks. The girl looked askance at Harry, but all his attention was on Bridget as she asked him in a low voice, 'What are we going to tell Rosamund? In her condition I do not wish to upset her by mentioning Ingrid.'

'Then we will not do so,' said Harry. 'I will say that Josh was delayed on a matter of urgent business and hopefully will arrive soon.'

This Harry did and Rosamund accepted his reason for Joshua's absence. Alex was not so easily satisfied. He took Harry aside whilst Rosamund talked to Bridget about household matters. At some point during their conversations, Dorcas and Joe came into the hall with the baggage, and Rosamund suggested that she take Bridget upstairs to show her the bedchamber that she had prepared for her and Harry.

'I do hope Harry likes this bedchamber. It belonged to our mother and it has a lovely view,' said Rosamund.

'I like it already,' said Bridget, gazing about her with smiling approval.

'Of course, you will most likely wish to choose your own furnishings once you have settled in here. Most of those were here when my mother was alive.'

'In that case, Harry might wish to keep them,' said Bridget.

She joined Rosamund at the window and looked out over the front of the house to overgrown flower beds and a lawn that looked newly scythed. Fields stretched out to woodland in the distance and she thought she caught the gleam of an expanse of water beyond.

'Is that the Irish Sea?' she asked.

'Aye, but it is a good few hours' journey away,' said Rosamund. 'From the tower you get a better view of the landscape. I will take you and Harry up there, so you can see for yourselves. It used to be Harry's bedchamber before our stepmother decided to shut me away up there.'

'I am glad she is dead.'

'You're glad who is dead?' asked Harry, entering the bedchamber,

'Our wicked stepmother,' replied Rosamund, smiling at him. 'Come and see the view.' She held out a hand to him.

Harry joined them at the window, and both women made room for him between them. He leaned out over the sill and his gaze searched the meadows where he could see a few cattle grazing and long grass rippling in the breeze.

'Soon it will be time for haymaking,' said Rosamund. 'You must speak to your steward and the reeve. The land is not used as it should be. Several fields lay fallow because we could not pay the wages of the labourers you need.'

Harry nodded. His intense scrutiny encompassed the

woods and the gleam of water in the distance. 'That is the Irish Sea?'

Rosamund nodded. 'Bridget asked that question, too. Is it that you now remember being taken there when you were abducted?'

'No,' said Harry. 'That I still cannot remember.'

'What about this bedchamber?' asked Rosamund.

He turned and surveyed the room. 'I presume there is something special about it. Did our mother sleep here?'

Rosamund nodded. 'Aye, although this bed was not hers. Our stepmother persuaded Father that there was some evil at work in this room and he had the bed burnt. He certainly never came in here afterwards. Maybe his conscience bothered him due to his marrying that woman so soon after Mother's death.'

'I think she killed our mother,' said Harry abruptly.

Both women stared at him.

'The nightmares I have had for years, I sincerely believe now that they were not dreams, but memories I buried deep because I could not bear the pain they caused. If I am right, it was not in here that she died. but on the staircase to my bedchamber in the tower. That woman pushed our mother down the stairs and she caught her head on the stone wall. I went to her, but she never got up again. That hag seized me and made certain I could not speak of it to my father.'

'I was told she had died of a disease, but I always wondered whether she had quickened Mother's end with the potions she gave her,' said Rosamund.

'Perhaps she did both,' said Bridget, 'but she is punished now and maybe it is time you both laid your ghosts to rest.'

'I would like to visit my mother's grave and lay flowers upon it,' said Harry quietly.

Harry and Bridget stood in front of the grave in the churchyard where his mother's body lay at rest, watching as his sister removed the flowers she had placed in a container there only the other day. She beckoned Harry forwards, and he knelt on the ground and replaced the fading flowers with a posy of myrtle, heart's-ease and pink roses that Bridget had gathered for him.

He bent his head and said a silent prayer and remained in that position for several moments. He gave thanks for the woman who had given him life and whom his sister and Lady Elizabeth had spoken of with such affection. He grieved that he had not been able to save her life.

Bridget rested her hand on his shoulder, understanding some of how he felt. She thought of her own mother buried beneath Irish skies. She felt his hand cover hers briefly as if he knew what she was thinking and then he rose to his feet.

None of them spoke as they left the graveside and made their way out of the churchyard. Harry asked Bridget to excuse him and his sister for a short while as there were questions he wanted to ask her.

Bridget would have liked to have listened in on their conversation, but it was obvious that Harry did not want her there. 'I will have some hot water brought up to our chamber. I am feeling filthy,' she said.

'I will see you soon,' called Harry, as she walked away.

Bridget thought that after all the emotions that had been revealed since they had arrived here that she and Harry might have been able to share their feelings more openly. Perhaps she had misread the expression in his eyes earlier. She went inside the house and, after requesting a pitcher of hot water, went upstairs.

She hurried along the dimly lit passage to their bed-chamber, only to trip over an uneven flagstone. She managed to prevent herself from falling by putting a hand against the wall. She must tell Harry that more light was needed here. At last she reached the bedcham-ber and went inside and searched for what she needed in the armoire and chest. Then she walked over to the window and gazed out towards the Irish Sea, thinking about the *St Bridget* and whether she had arrived at Preston yet.

At a knock on the door, she went to open it, hoping it was Harry, but it was only one of the maids with her hot water. She washed, changed into a fresh gown and then sat waiting for her husband to come.

'So do you remember this place at all, Harry?' asked Rosamund, coming out from beneath the trees and on to the river bank. 'Do you think it was from here that you were abducted and taken to sea? Your clothes were found on the banks of the river, after all.'

Harry smiled faintly. 'I wonder how many times people will say that to me now I have returned.' His sister had talked and talked about their childhood, and he had felt the years slipping away in the same fashion they had done when Joshua Wood had reminisced. 'Josh described the river to me, but I can't see how it would eventually flow into the sea or the Ribble from here. I know seagoing vessels anchor at Preston where woollen cloth is exported.'

'Aye, Flemish weavers came over during the last century,' said his sister. 'I can understand your interest, and you're right in thinking that you couldn't get from here by boat to the Irish Sea further south or Preston in the north. The port that is mainly used for ships going to and fro between Ireland is Liverpool. It is only a small place, but it has its own charter.'

'I suppose it is possible I was drugged and taken there. I wager I probably wasn't even near this river when I was abducted. My clothes would have been planted on this bank to give the impression that I'd been swimming.'

Rosamund agreed.

Harry changed the subject to talk now about one that was close to his heart. 'You know Bridget well,' he said. 'Do you deem that she can be happy here with the occasional outing to Preston or Ormskirk?'

'She loves you, so she will be happy wherever you are,' said Rosamund.

Harry froze. 'How can you tell that she loves me? Has she told you so?'

'Any woman would love a man who found her on an alien beach and saved her life. Especially one who was prepared to marry her despite her father having stolen one of his ships,' said Rosamund, her eyes twinkling. 'In my opinion Bridget had strong feelings for you even when she ranted against you as Black Harry.'

She linked her arm through Harry's. 'I only wish that we could spend more time with you and Bridget and watch all your plans for Appleby come to fruition.

It will always hold a special place in my heart. I pray that you and Bridget will have many sons and daughters and that you will find great happiness here.' She hugged his arm. 'Shall we return to the house? You must be famished after your journey.'

It had seemed to Bridget that she had been waiting an age for Harry and could feel herself getting tenser every moment that passed. Eventually she decided that she had waited long enough and went downstairs. Alex was there and immediately offered her a glass of wine. She thanked him and wondered what was keeping Harry and Rosamund so long. She was ashamed that she still could feel envious of their newfound close relationship.

She was sipping her wine when they entered the hall. Harry glanced her way and for a moment their eyes caught. He smiled, accepted a glass of wine from a servant and raised it to her. She saluted him with her own. But there was to be no time for them to talk privately because within minutes they were joined by the priest, steward and reeve.

In no time at all they were seated at table and a meal of pork, roasted apples, onions and spring greens was set before them. After the introductions were made the men discussed the husbandry of the land. Harry broached the idea of rearing sheep and selling the wool to the weavers in Preston. 'Although I suppose we could employ our own weavers,' he added as an afterthought.

'You'd need to build cottages for them, Master Appleby,' said the steward.

'Aye, but we have the land, don't we?'

Bridget listened to the conversation with interest,

feeling herself drawn in to that which so interested Harry now he was home.

'Certainly, Master Appleby, and it would give work to some of the local villagers,' said the reeve.

'Then that is settled,' said Harry, smiling.

The men grinned and they began to discuss which fields to turn over to sheep and where would be best to build the cottages.

Harry wondered whether to broach the subject of planting sugar beet, but then decided, as it was only at the experimental stage on Madeira and most likely the climate here would not be suitable, that he had best remain silent. Thinking of Madeira made his thoughts turn to the time he had spent there with Bridget. He remembered that even before he had asked her to marry him, he had feared losing her. He guessed that Callum had coped with losing his wife by turning to drink. Where was the old pirate now? Had he arrived at Lisbon or Madeira? Could someone have given him the information that Bridget was Harry's wife and that they had already set out for England? If he arrived safely, there was much Harry had to say to his father-in-law. He glanced in Bridget's direction, caught her eye and wanted to be alone with her on this, their first night in their own home.

The door to the hall suddenly opened and a man appeared in the doorway. His garments were travel stained and for a moment he just stood there; then he begged pardon and turned and went right out again. Instantly Harry pushed back his chair and asked his guests to excuse him. He hurried across the hall and went outside.

'That was Joshua Wood!' exclaimed Rosamund, turning to Bridget.

'Aye, I am glad he has arrived safely. I wonder what news he has for Harry.' Bridget would have liked to have followed after the two men, but knew she would have to wait until the meal was over and the priest and other men had departed. Only then could she rise and go after them.

Bridget hurried outside, but there was no sign of the two men, so she made for the stables, thinking that she might find them there, only to discover the stable void of their presence. She had no notion where else they could be, so decided to return to the house, hoping Harry might have gone there during her absence.

The hall was occupied only by the servants clearing away after the meal, so Bridget went upstairs to their bedchamber, considering it possible that Harry believed that she had retired for the night. To her disappointment he was not there, but someone had lighted several candles and the bed had been turned down. Had one of the maids done that or had it been Dorcas or Harry?

Where was he? For him to be missing this long, Joshua must have had a lot to tell him. She was disturbed by a knock on the door and hurried to open it. To her disappointment it was Rosamund.

'I wondered if my brother was here,' she said.

Bridget shook her head and invited her inside. 'I have searched, but cannot find him,' said Rosamund.

'I, too, have done so,' said Bridget.

Rosamund went over to the window and Bridget followed her. 'Can you see any sign of him?' she asked.

'No,' replied Rosamund. 'I suppose it is possible that they have gone to Joshua's old home in the woods if they want to talk in private. I wish I knew for certain,' she added.

'You are behaving as if…' Bridget's voice trailed off.

'As if I am anxious about my brother?' Rosamund moved away from the window and sat in a chair. 'He has been abducted before and I have only just been reunited with him.'

'I deem you worry unnecessarily,' said Bridget firmly. 'But if you give me directions to Joshua's house in the woods, then I will go and see if he is there.'

Rosamund shook her head. 'It will soon be dark. You could easily get lost, and Harry would be very vexed with me if that were to happen. No doubt he will return soon. I will speak to Alex, and he will wait up until Harry returns. I will see you in the morning.'

Bridget wished her a goodnight and closed the door behind her. She could not prevent herself from thinking of Ingrid. Perhaps when she had left with her companion they had met others. Maybe Joshua had scarcely managed to escape with his life? Could they have followed him here? She paced the floor, praying for Harry and hoping she was worrying unnecessarily. Then weariness suddenly swept over her and she sank on to the bed, kicked off her shoes and lay down. Despite all her attempts to remain awake, her head nodded and she dozed off.

It was the sound of a door opening and stealthy movements that wakened her. The candles must have burnt down because the room was in darkness. Her heart began to beat heavily and she wished she had a weapon to hand. Then she heard a muffled curse.

'Harry, is that you?'

'Aye. What are you doing awake, Bridget? You should have long been asleep.'

'I was worried about you. What did Joshua have to say? Where have you been all this time?'

'There's no need for you to worry. Go to sleep.'

Bridget was hurt. She had expected this first night at Appleby Manor to be spent not simply sleeping. 'You sound as if you are not coming to bed.'

He did not answer, but the next moment she felt his arms go round her. She sensed a suppressed excitement about him, and then his warm breath was on her mouth and he kissed her long and hard before releasing her. 'Trust me that it is naught for you to worry about. All will be well,' he replied. 'Now go to sleep, and that is an order.'

Bridget heard the sound of the door opening and closing. For several moments she remained where she was, and then she rose from the bed and padded over to the door and went out into the passage. Her eyes had become accustomed to the lack of light in the bedchamber, but it was darker here and she could see no sign of Harry and only the slightest glimmer of a dying flame from a sconce on the wall. Even so she decided to try to follow him.

She had not gone far when she stubbed her toe and lost her balance. Only by the sheerest good fortune did her hand hit the wall, so she was able to steady herself. Even so this second accident along this passage unnerved her, and when she tried to continue, her toe hurt abominably. She had no choice but to return to the bedchamber. It was a relief to arrive at the open door and go inside and find her way over to a chair. She sat down and lifted her foot and discovered that, as she suspected, her big toe was cut and bleeding. She fumbled about in the unfamiliar room in search of what she needed to deal with the injury. By the time she had finished with salve and binding, she was glad to undress and climb into bed, worn out by the exertions of the day.

Bridget started awake at the sound of knocking on the door. 'Mistress Appleby, wake up! The hour is late and the Baroness has sent me to see if all is well with you.'

Bridget noticed with a sinking heart that there was no sign of Harry in the chamber. She climbed out of bed and went and opened the door. Where was he? Had something happened to him despite his reassurances? 'Forgive me, Dorcas, I did not get to sleep until the early hours.'

'I was starting to think yer'd both been murdered in yer bed,' said the girl, looking about her. 'Where's the master?'

'That I don't know.'

'I wager Joe will know,' said Dorcas, her eyes bright as she placed a pitcher of steaming water on the wash-stand. 'Shall I help yer with yer *toilette* or shall I go and see if I can find him?'

'The latter,' said Bridget. 'I will get dressed and wait here for you.'

* * *

Dorcas wasted no time going in search of Joe. When she returned she did not come empty-handed, but brought some bread and honey and a cup of small ale for her mistress. Bridget accepted them gratefully, for she had regained the appetite she had lost after the miscarriage.

'Did you speak to Joe?' she asked.

'No, I could find only the Baroness. Apparently the master, Joshua and Joe have gone to Liverpool whilst the Baron has gone to Preston,' said Dorcas.

'How odd,' said Bridget. 'Did she explain why?'

Dorcas shook her head. 'She said you're not to worry.'

Easier said than done, thought Bridget, unable to understand why Harry had needed to leave in such haste whilst it was still dark if there was naught for her to worry about. She forced herself to eat some bread and honey and drink the small ale, wondering how long she would have to wait before Harry returned.

As soon as Bridget went downstairs she went in search of Rosamund and found her in the herb garden, picking mint. She greeted her friend and then asked did she know why Harry had gone to Liverpool, whilst the Baron had travelled up to Preston?

'The two are not related,' said Rosamund, smiling. 'My brother had already left for Liverpool. A messenger came this morning with the news that Alex's ship has anchored at Preston, so that is why he has gone there.'

Bridget frowned. 'I can only think that Harry's ship has encountered a squall or some such difficulty and has been damaged and that is why it has taken shelter in the Mersey. It would be the first port in Lancashire on the journey up from the south, so the ship could be repaired.'

'It sounds like the most likely explanation to me,' said Rosamund. 'Now what would you like to do today? I can show you round the house and introduce you properly to Cook and the rest of the servants.'

'Later, if you do not mind, Rosamund? First I would like to see Harry's tower.'

'As long as you do not expect me to climb up to the top,' said Rosamund, smiling.

Bridget agreed.

Shortly after, she stood at the top of the tower, getting her breath back and gazing out over fields and woods towards the Irish Sea. She wished there was some means of being able to get a closer look at places so far away, but as that was impossible, she decided to come up here as often as she could during the day and watch out for Harry's return. If she was a man and knew the way, then she would have ridden to Liverpool herself. As it was she was going to have to be patient.

So it was that Bridget spent her first full day at Appleby Manor without Harry there to share that precious time. She felt anxious and more than a little annoyed that he had not told her his plans. Evening came and still there was no sign of the three men. She barely slept that night.

Bridget rose early the following morning and within the hour she was climbing the tower once more. But there was no sign of any riders. Her anxiety increased as the hours passed and still they did not return.

The following morning Alex arrived back from Preston and was surprised and disappointed that Harry was not there. Yet he showed no sign of anxiety.

Whether that was because he believed there was no need for concern or because he had complete faith in Harry to get himself out of any fix, she did not know. She found it difficult to believe that all was well with her husband when he had so wanted to spend these days in his sister's company. Obviously something unexpected had happened, but what?

It was early morning on the fourth day that Bridget climbed the tower again. The air was still, with a promise of heat later. She watched as several birds took noisy flight from the trees and then she thought she caught the sound of men's voices. She had no notion of how far away they were, but it was enough to send her hurrying towards the staircase.

She had barely started on her way down when she heard the sound of footsteps coming up towards her. She thought it was Harry and that he might have caught sight of her and had come running to her. She turned the first corner, expecting to see him, only when she saw the figure there, she knew the shape was all wrong.

Her heart began to thud and it was several moments before she found her voice. 'What are you doing here, Ingrid?'

Ingrid threw back her hood and stared up at her with hatred in her eyes. 'So there you are,' she said. 'I've been looking for you.'

'How did you know where to find me?' Bridget wished Harry was here right now.

'Patience, Bridget. I am really very annoyed with you. You are one of those people who will not stay out of other people's affairs. Here was I impatiently waiting for Harry to return. I knew him to be heir to Appleby Manor and thought I could probably bewitch him long enough to persuade him to marry me. Only you reached him first, so my plan was ruined.'

'You must be mad if you think that Harry would have married you after he discovered you were party to his sister's abduction!' exclaimed Bridget. 'He knows you for what you are.'

'That's as may be, but he once loved me, you know.'

'Not any longer he doesn't.'

'I know that now. The ugly fool told me so, but I could have given him a love potion to bewitch his senses. Although, when he dropped me in the mud, I was not very pleased with him.'

Bridget did not know Harry had done such a thing, only that he had encountered Ingrid and kept that meeting from her. But it certainly didn't sound as though any romance had been involved! 'My husband is *not* ugly. Now, if you would get out of my way…' she said haughtily.

Ingrid's eyes narrowed. 'I did not come all this way, Bridget McDonald, to do what *you* say.'

'Why did you come? You were not invited.'

'Master Larsson proved to be a disappointment. We were supposed to be working together and he was to get Harry out of the way when you were staying at the inn, but he didn't have the stomach to go through with the plan.'

'And what was your plan?' asked Bridget, hoping she could keep Ingrid talking until Harry arrived and rescued her.

'To abduct you and hold you to ransom. Then I would have killed you anyway.'

Bridget could believe that of Ingrid—it seemed she'd totally lost her senses. 'Harry is not such a fool as to hand over money to the likes of you without some evidence that I was still alive.'

'You really do have a nasty habit of pointing out the errors in my plans,' said Ingrid crossly. 'You always were quick-witted, but not as much as I am.'

Suddenly she withdraw a cudgel from beneath her habit and came at Bridget, but Bridget seized hold of the other woman's wrist. The two women struggled and then they overbalanced and went tumbling down the stairs. Bridget made a grab for the rope that acted as a rail, but Ingrid continued to tumble and hit a bend in the wall and then disappeared.

Bridget continued to slither down the stone steps with the rope burning her hands. Then unexpectedly the rope came away from the metal rings that held it and she screamed as she felt herself falling. Suddenly there were arms there to catch her and she was being held tightly against Harry's chest. She could do no more than cling to him.

'It is all right, sweeting. You are safe,' he reassured her.

He had called her sweeting and for that and saving her from hitting the ground he deserved not just one kiss, not two, but many kisses, she thought, and proceeded to pepper his face with them.

'Am I to believe from this behaviour that I am forgiven for my many failings and that you love me?' asked Harry humbly.

'I deem you can take that for granted,' replied Bridget, 'but you do have some explaining to do.'

'Agreed,' said Harry.

At that moment there was the sound of voices outside. Reluctantly, Harry put her down, but he held her hand firmly and led her down the rest of the stairs. There at their foot lay Ingrid, and bending over her were Joe and Joshua. 'Is she dead?' asked Bridget.

'No, but she's unconscious,' said Joshua.

But Bridget scarcely heard his answer because she had caught sight of the stocky figure of a middle-aged man with greying red hair. She could only stare at him, stupefied.

'So Harry was right, and there ye are, lass,' said Callum.

'Father!' she whispered, scarcely able to believe it was really him. He had aged since last she had seen him, and all the anger and hurt she had felt towards him evaporated. She felt Harry release her hand and she went forwards and into her father's arms. She loved him despite his being an old pirate and reprobate and having put her and Harry through so much trouble. She was vaguely aware that Joe and Joshua were lifting Ingrid and carrying her outside, but all that mattered at that moment was that she had the two men that she loved most dearly here with her.

After she and her father had both shed a few tears, she

drew back from him. 'How could you steal Harry's ship and consider revenging yourself on Patrick O'Malley more important than reassuring yourself of my safety and letting me know you were safe?' she demanded in one breath.

'I did it for ye, lass,' he said, his hands splayed on his thighs. 'I had to get my hoard back to provide you with a dowry. Never did I think my brother would turn out to be such a black-hearted villain, and not for one moment did I imagine you would go off in search of me and Black Harry, here. I never thought you'd be captured by pirates and then taken by a slave trader. I'd go down on me bended knee to ye, if I could get down there and beg yer forgiveness. But I'm getting old and ma joints are stiffening up. I can only ask for yer forgiveness.'

'I don't know if I should forgive you, Father, although I deem some good has come out of what you've done,' said Bridget, her face softening.

'Aye,' said Callum, perking up. 'Yer've married a good man. If only I'd known years ago that Harry was heir to a manor and a business I'd have sought him out after he'd escaped the pirate ship and have arranged a betrothal between the two of you.'

'If only I'd known that as well and had Bridget been a little older, then I might have agreed to it,' said Harry, winking at his wife.

'But it is not too late for my father to pay over my dowry to you, Harry,' she said.

Harry was about to say he had no need of it, but recognised that this was important to her. 'You are worth more to me than your father can ever give me,' he whispered, bringing his head close to hers, 'but I'm certain I'll find plenty of ways to use the money. If naught else we can put it in a trust for our children.' Bridget blushed and murmured that she could not think of anything better. 'Then let us go and break the news to Rosamund and Alex that your father has returned and all is well,' said Harry.

It took some time for Callum's tale to be told and it kept all their attention. Bridget smiled when she heard him say that he had met Juanita in Lisbon down at the quayside. Apparently she had foreseen his coming and was waiting for him. Bridget could easily imagine the old woman speaking those words and felt again that mixture of doubt and willingness to believe in the supernatural. She wondered if she would ever see her again. She also heard how Callum had recognised the *St Bridget* in Dover harbour and after speaking to Hans had set sail in *Odin's Maiden* for the Lancashire coast. His nephew he had sent north to Scotland in his own vessel. Fate had led Joshua to Liverpool in Master Larsson's wake after he had parted from Ingrid. There Joshua had spotted *Odin's Maiden* and the *St Bridget* anchored off Liverpool for some essential repairs. He was swift to carry the news to Harry, who had wanted to see for himself that Callum was alive—and if so to bring him to Appleby and surprise Bridget.

'It certainly surprised me,' she said, when at last they were alone together in their bedchamber.

'Aye,' said Harry, frowning, 'but I should have stayed here at your side and kept you safe.'

'You cannot blame yourself for Ingrid's actions,' said

Bridget. 'Now can we forget her and everyone else but us right now?'

'I'd like nothing more,' said Harry. 'I am debating whether it is time we began to start building our family again.'

Her eyes twinkled. 'I am in favour of doing so,' she said boldly.

'You don't mind my scar, then?' he asked tentatively, touching it.

She reached up and kissed the puckered skin tenderly. 'Is that a good enough answer?'

He sat with her on the bed and ran his fingers through her glorious hair and brought her face close to his and brushed her lips with his back and forth until she desperately wanted him to kiss her deeply, madly, passionately.

She took hold of his jaw and said, 'Be still,' and kissed him hungrily.

She had no notion of how long that kiss lasted, but her lips parted beneath his and his tongue dallied with hers in a spine-tingling fashion. Then he drew her up so that they both knelt on the bed and he stripped her to the waist and bent his head and captured the tip of a breast between his lips. She gasped as a shaft of pleasure darted through her to form a curl of heat between her legs as he continued to caress her breasts.

Trembling, she wanted to feel his naked skin next to hers and began to unfasten his shirt and explore the chest beneath. She was aware of the amulet on a chain about his neck and brushed it aside. Her heart was beating rapidly and she was aware of the long line of his thigh against hers. He pushed her gently backwards on the bed. She helped him remove her gown by kicking it off when it bunched around her ankles.

He left her only for a moment, but before her skin could cool, he was beside her once more, caressing her all over with fingers and lips until she was aflame with desire. Then they became one and she could feel the pleasure building up inside her. It unfolded inside her like the petals of a flower as he drove deeper inside her. She was breathless with pleasure and all her senses were sending urgent messages coursing through her body. Her pleasure grew and intensified until it finally erupted. As he reached his own climax, a secondary wave of bliss washed over her and she knew that her husband was a man to keep his word and that she would conceive a child that night.

Epilogue

1505

'I believe I will buy your mother such a gown,' said Harry, gazing down at his daughter Aurora Bridget Jane. She was wearing the Appleby baptismal gown decorated with seed pearls.

Aurora gazed up at her father and waved a fist. She had come with the dawn, following on the heels of her twin, after an exhausting night in labour for Bridget. The children had been baptised straight after the birth in the house as was customary in such cases, but as Harry and Bridget had both wanted Alex and Rosamund to be the twins' godparents, a church service had been decided upon, just as soon as they were able to make the journey from Sweden. Now they were downstairs with Douglas and their baby daughter, Margaret Rose.

Bridget smiled into the face of her son, Henry James Callum, and lifted him from the cradle that had been intended for hers and Harry's first child. She rocked him in her arms and glanced up at Harry with a teasing expression in her eyes. 'You do not approve of the gown I am wearing?'

It was of saffron satin and decorated with amber gemstones that he had asked Alex and Rosamund to purchase for him in Sweden. It was a gift for Bridget on the anniversary of her nineteenth birthday.

'Of course,' said Harry, 'but I would like to see you in a cream satin gown decorated with large lustrous pearls.'

'They would cost a fortune, Harry,' said Bridget, kissing his cheek. 'And you spoil me quite enough.'

'But your neck is bare,' he said, looking around for Dorcas, who was proving to be an excellent nurse-maid.

The girl hurried forwards and took Aurora from him and nestled her in the crook of one arm. Bridget stepped forwards and placed Henry in her other arm. Singing softly to the babies, Dorcas left the bedchamber. Bridget remembered how happy the girl had been a year ago when Joe had returned safely from Liverpool, so much so that she had kissed the youth enthusiastically. Joe had blushed to his ears, but he had kissed her right back. As for Joshua, he had visited the lass he had loved as a boy and discovered she was a widow. They had been married forthwith and they were blissfully happy.

Ingrid, on the other hand, was still confused. The bang on the head she'd received when she had fallen down the stairs had scattered her remaining wits and so she had been transported to the nearest convent and placed in the care of the nuns.

Harry closed the door and unfastened the silver

amulet from about his neck. He turned Bridget round and then, lifting her lustrous auburn hair, he fastened the clasp before kissing the nape of her neck.

She faced him with a smile. 'Thank you. I deem this is precious to you, so it will also be to me.'

'It betrayed me, though, did it not?'

Bridget remembered that moment of recognition and smiled. Then she closed her eyes and dreamily began to undo a fastening on his doublet. She poked a couple of fingers through the opening and managed to touch his skin. Reluctantly Harry stayed her hand and then raised it to his lips. 'There is naught I would like more than to toss you on the bed and make love to you, but we have our children's baptism to attend.'

'Our children,' she whispered and her eyes were suddenly bright with tears. 'But we will never forget the one we lost, will we, Harry?'

'Never,' he said.

'I will always be grateful that you found me on that beach in Madeira, my dearest Harry.'

'No more than I, sweetheart,' he said, gathering her into his arms for one last kiss before joining their children and the family that was so dear to them.

* * * * *

The Regency Ballroom Collection

Discover more romance at

www.millsandboon.co.uk

- ❤ WIN great prizes in our exclusive competitions
- ❤ BUY new titles before they hit the shops
- ❤ BROWSE new books and REVIEW your favourites
- ❤ SAVE on new books with the Mills & Boon® Bookclub™
- ❤ DISCOVER new authors

PLUS, to chat about your favourite reads, get the latest news and find special offers:

- 🟦 Find us on facebook.com/millsandboon
- 🐦 Follow us on twitter.com/millsandboonuk
- ❤ Sign up to our newsletter at millsandboon.co.uk

The World of Mills & Boon®

There's a Mills & Boon® series that's perfect for you. We publish ten series and, with new titles every month, you never have to wait long for your favourite to come along.

By Request

Relive the romance with the best of the best
12 stories every month

Cherish™

Experience the ultimate rush of falling in love
12 new stories every month

Desire™

Passionate and dramatic love stories
6 new stories every month

nocturne™

An exhilarating underworld of dark desires
Up to 3 new stories every month